MW01624768

"Seth ar
are well
levels. A
you have
Lisa Marie

—*Library Journal* on *The Stranger*

"This was a fabulous fast-paced read, simply addictive. Sexy, with a touch of darkness, and humor to boot! But the best are the strong, sympathetic, multi-dimensional protagonists and the way their love evolves. If you haven't discovered Anna del Mar's books yet, you're missing something."

—*Midwest Book Review* on *The Stranger*

"I was totally taken in by this one. Del Mar has a very vivid way of story-telling, with well-developed and often complex characters. The supporting characters always leave a mark, which is the perfect setup for the next in any series."

—*Happy Ever After Romance Book Reviews* on *The Stranger*

"The unexpected twists to this exciting story kept me enthralled until the last fascinating word... A wonderful start to the series and I can only hope that future stories continue to showcase such compelling characters in equally exciting and mesmerizing situations."

—*Night Owl Reviews*, 5 stars and top pick, on *The Asset*

"*The Asset* by Anna del Mar will take our heroine on a dark, emotional rollercoaster in order to get her happily ever after...but she will get it! This is the debut novel for the Wounded Warrior series and I for one can't wait for the next book in the series. This author has captured my attention with her well-written words, strong characters, and vivid storyline."

—*Harlequin Junkie*

"Whether you are a character driven reader or a plot driven reader, *The Asset* will appeal to you. This is a kick butt book with a strong romance, strong characters and action galore"

—*Book Briefs*

Also from Anna del Mar
and Carina Press

The Wounded Warrior Novels

Romantic Suspense

The Asset
The Stranger

The At the Brink Novels

Erotic Romance

At the Brink
To the Edge

ANNA DEL MAR

THE STRANGER

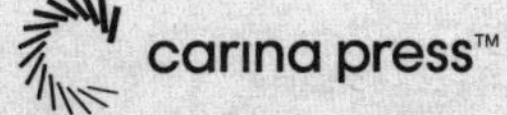

If you purchased this book without a cover you should be aware that this book is stolen property. It was reported as "unsold and destroyed" to the publisher, and neither the author nor the publisher has received any payment for this "stripped book."

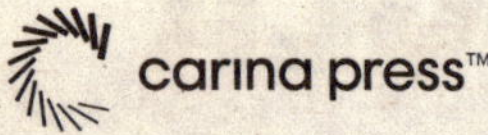

Recycling programs for this product may not exist in your area.

ISBN-13: 978-1-335-47379-0

The Stranger

Copyright © 2016 by Anna del Mar

All rights reserved. Except for use in any review, the reproduction or utilization of this work in whole or in part in any form by any electronic, mechanical or other means, now known or hereinafter invented, including xerography, photocopying and recording, or in any information storage or retrieval system, is forbidden without the written permission of the publisher, Harlequin Enterprises Limited, 225 Duncan Mill Road, Don Mills, Ontario M3B 3K9, Canada.

This is a work of fiction. Names, characters, places and incidents are either the product of the author's imagination or are used fictitiously, and any resemblance to actual persons, living or dead, business establishments, events or locales is entirely coincidental.

This edition published by arrangement with Harlequin Books S.A.

® and TM are trademarks of the publisher. Trademarks indicated with ® are registered in the United States Patent and Trademark Office, the Canadian Intellectual Property Office and in other countries.

www.CarinaPress.com

Printed in U.S.A.

Dear Reader,

Thank you for choosing to read *The Stranger*. A few years ago, my kids dragged me out of my writing studio for a family trip and I fell hard for magnificent, spectacular Alaska. Since then, I've been back every chance I get. This novel was born out of my love and admiration for Alaska and the extraordinary people who make it their home.

If you liked *The Asset*, you're going to love *The Stranger*. *The Stranger* is the second novel in my Wounded Warrior series, a collection of hot, smart romances about strong heroines and the brave heroes who'll protect them with all they've got. Cool fact: you don't have to read the series in any particular order. In all of my books, brawn + brains + heart = sizzling-hot heroes.

About the twist at the beginning of *The Stranger*. It happens. I should know. Dream chasers are common in my family line. So be prepared to suspend your disbelief. You'll see what I mean.

I had a blast writing *The Stranger*. I hope you have a blast reading it.

Enjoy,

AdM

To my kids, who dragged me out to a distant wilderness where I fell madly in love with the beauty, the people and the spirit of Alaska.

THE STRANGER

ONE

TROUBLE WELCOMED ME to Alaska. It ambushed me in the guise of an invisible patch of black ice that launched my car spinning into a triple Lutz. I pumped my brakes. Nothing. My rental careened over the ditch and bounced down the steep ravine. The rocks pummeling the undercarriage rattled my brain. I was distantly aware that the shriek piercing my eardrums came from my throat. My headlights illuminated the spruce that materialized before me, down to the huge, corrugated trunk that collided with the hood, bringing my involuntary detour to a jarring stop.

Silence. Only the sound of my ragged breath and my pulse, pounding in my temples, interrupted the atmospheric quiet. I pried my fingers from the wheel and stared at my shaking hands. They flickered in and out of focus until I managed to even out my breaths.

The good news? I was alive and, although the wreck had probably relocated some of my internal organs, nothing seemed broken. The bad news? The air bag hadn't gone off and pain throbbed in my thigh and somewhere behind my ear. Crap. I'd come to Alaska to find my wayward sister, but my search had hit a major snag. Time to figure out how bad of a snag it was.

My hand was still quaking as I reached into my purse and found my cell. Zero bars. I groaned. What was the point of technology if it never worked when you needed it most? I snatched my purse and pulled on the door handle. The door refused to open. I scooted across to the other seat and opened the passenger side door, grateful to crawl out in one piece.

The cold hit me like a slap to the face. My nostrils flared and my lungs ached with the arctic wallop. To a tropical gal like me, the air smelled as though someone had stuffed a live Christmas tree in the freezer. Delicate snowflakes floated in the air like tiny speckles of silver. This was the first time I'd seen snow in real life. It was pretty, kind of magical really, but the cold crawled under my skin, stiffened my muscles and clung to my bones. I pulled my hood over my head. Had it been this cold when my plane landed in Anchorage?

My wrecked rental was wedged between the slope and the spruce like a deflated accordion. I had no prayer of backing it up the hill. I tackled the ravine, scrambling on all fours, and followed the wheel ruts up the slippery incline. It wasn't easy. I wore a narrow pencil skirt under my Burberry trench coat, and a pair of four-inch heels I now wished I'd never bought.

It served me right for allowing my stepmother to choose my outfit for the Darius project presentation. Louise was a sucker for shoes—the taller, the better. Note to self: never again relinquish your feet to someone else's sense of fashion when it's you—and you alone—who has to suffer the resulting torture.

I'm not sure how long it took me to climb back to the road, but by the time I reached the top, my toes had gone numb, my hands ached and my fingertips had turned white. The road I'd been driving on looked totally benign, not like the camouflaged skating rink that had hurled my vehicle into the ravine.

I clapped my hands together to warm them up. The sound echoed for miles around me. Stuck in the Alaskan wilderness. Unreal. It was an unlikely predicament for a gal who'd much rather be at the beach. Shark attack? Sure, it wouldn't surprise me if that ended up being part of my obituary. But frozen alive? Only if it involved a freak accident in Publix's frozen food section.

"Summer Silva, get your act together," I said out loud to break the eerie silence. My father hadn't clung to a capsized raft for three days in the Florida Straits in order for me to die on my first day in Alaska.

I straightened my coat, shoved my hands into my pockets, and began to walk. A layer of slush-covered ice crackled beneath my heels. Crap. My feet slid every which way and my legs wobbled. *Steady, Silva.* I could handle the unwieldy shoes…on firm, unfrozen ground. The only ice I'd ever dealt with came out in little cubes from the automated dispenser in the freezer door.

Five minutes later, the cold skewered me and not a single car had made an appearance. I leaned into the bitter wind. I wasn't made of sugar and spice. I was tough, and I meant to get out of this one, but I was majorly pissed. I was so going to give Tammy a piece of my mind when I found her.

I envisioned my sister lying on a white pelt in front of a roaring fireplace. I mouthed off into the deepening darkness. I was the levelheaded one. I was the one who always followed the rules, cleaned up the messes, did the responsible thing. And yet, right now, I was the one freezing my ass off on a desolate Alaskan road.

The headlights caught me by surprise. They sprang out from behind the curve and pierced the dusk. I waved my hands to flag down the speeding vehicle. As it got closer, I made out a Ford F-450 Super Duty, black as night, the type that would've made my truck-obsessed sister drool with envy. The truck drove right by me before the taillights lit up and it skidded to a stop, then accelerated in reverse.

The window whirred down to reveal the warmth and comfort of the softly illuminated cab. The leather-scented, heated air wafted from the window and teased my frozen senses. A man sat at the wheel, enveloped in a black thermal jacket that I would've gladly traded a thousand bucks for, on the spot. His face might have been handsome, if it hadn't been distorted by the scowl that wilted my poor attempt at a smile.

He more or less growled. "Who the hell put you up to this?"

"Excuse me?" I clutched my hood against a sudden burst of wind.

"You better come clean right now," he bit out in a tone that matched the frosty temperature. "A name. I want to know who the hell hired you and what you were expected to do."

"Hired me?"

"Don't play dumb with me." He eyed me like a wolf eyed a meal. "Who was it? Was it someone related to me? I swear, if you don't tell me this goddamn minute, you're going to be sorry."

I stared at the man in the cab, unable to comprehend his rage. What on earth was he talking about? The fury blazing in his striking amber eyes frightened me. As it was, I was so cold I couldn't think, let alone make sense of what he was saying. I rubbed the sore spot behind my ear. Maybe I'd hit my head harder than I thought. Maybe this was a dream or a nightmare. Oh,

God. My stomach clenched. I really hoped I was awake. I shoved my hand up my sleeve and pinched my arm. It hurt. In fact, a lot of me was either throbbing or aching. A good sign, yes?

"Well?" he said. "Are you going to speak up or are you dumb, deaf, and mute?"

"Um, no." I rubbed my arms. "I usually have a lot to say. It's just that…well…I'm cold and you—I'm really sorry to have to tell you—but you sound like a crazy person."

He launched another blistering glower in my direction. "For the last time," he said, his tone intractable, "who the hell put you up to this?"

"Nobody," I said. "I don't know what you're talking about. My car skidded off the road and I've got no cell reception."

"Your car?" He looked up and down the road. "I don't see a car. Where is it?"

"Back there somewhere."

I'm not sure whether my treacherous heels slid on the ice or if fatigue did me in, but my feet went out from under me and, though I clung to the window, I landed on my knees.

"Ow," I might have said aloud.

"What the hell?"

I let go of the window and my dignity at the same time. I surrendered to the elements and settled precariously on the frosty ground. The cold iced my shins, traveled up to my core, and chilled my spine. I was about to pass out from exhaustion. I'd been up for over seventy-two hours. On top of that, I was suffering from a bad case of jet lag. If all of that wasn't enough, the wreck had jarred my senses. I wasn't in good shape and I knew it.

But I couldn't allow myself to go unconscious. No, sir, no way in hell. I knew the risks of passing out in front of a stranger too well. I just needed a moment to gather my strength, defrost myself and get my act together. I leaned my forehead on the door and, basking in the warmth radiating from the undercarriage, forced myself to stay alert. Surely, I could get some help, the crazy man would go on his merry way, and I could move on to finish what I'd come to do.

The engine quit. The truck quaked with the slam of a door. Angry steps crunched on the road. A pair of hiking boots parked by my side. I looked up and cringed. The man's scowl pummeled me. From my perspective on the ground, he soared above me, tall and imposing, a giant really. His knees cracked when he crouched next to me.

"Did Alex hire you?" he said. "Alex Erickson?"

"Who?"

"Are you telling me you don't know who Alex Erickson is?"

"I don't."

His breath came out in angry puffs that condensed in the air. "Do you know who I am?"

"No clue," I said. "Am I supposed to know?"

"You tell me." He looked like he was about to spit fire. "If no one put you up to this, then what the hell are you doing out here in the middle of nowhere?"

"Not taking a walk in the park, that's for sure."

My throat made this weird noise, a cross between a sob and a giggle, a sound that combined confusion with hilarity, fear with absurdity. But I wasn't going to cry.

No freaking way. I wasn't going to panic either. The part of me that felt utterly ridiculous kneeling on the frozen pavement in the middle of nowhere won out. I pressed my hand over my mouth, but the quiet giggles leaked out anyway.

The man rubbed the back of his neck and frowned, a dip of full eyebrows that screamed vexation. "Do you think this is funny?"

"Funny?" I couldn't stop giggling. "No, not funny, more like hilarious."

"Jesus Christ." He raked his fingers through his longish hair, leaving a bunch of straight, flaxen strands in disarray. He didn't know what to make of me, but he sure knew how to scowl.

The shivering, combined with his radioactive glower, stifled my giggle attack. I forced myself to pay attention. Determination whetted the man's features and set the line of his jaw into a straight angle. A shade of stubble covered the lower half of his face, imbuing him with a golden glow that echoed the gleam in his eye, but there was nothing soft in his stare, not a hint of humor or friendliness.

At least he looked clean and groomed, unlike the rugged, hygiene-challenged bunch I'd met in the back-to-back episodes of *Alaska's Bush Men* I'd binge-watched on the plane. Alaska had never been on my long list of places I wanted to visit, and after watching the show, I'd questioned my sister's sanity along with that of people who lived away from even the most basic human comforts. Now I wondered about this surly stranger too, the first off-the-grid Alaskan I'd met.

"Is your cell working?" I said. "Could you please call the police?"

"There's no reception on this stretch of road." The copper-hued eyes probed my face. "If you really need help, I'm all you've got."

Great. Just great. The world whirled around me. I steadied myself against the truck. Three days ago, I'd been in the middle of the most important presentation of my professional life when Louise had called to tell me about my stepsister, Tammy. I'd already been short of sleep and high on stress, but since then, I'd been on the go, trying to get to Alaska.

The earth beneath my knees shifted again. I tightened my grip on the truck and took a deep breath. I wasn't one to fall apart so easily. *To bad weather, a brave face,* my father used to say, quoting an old Spanish proverb. I might be out of my comfort zone, but I hadn't given up on my pride just yet. I straightened my coat and, balancing carefully on one knee, planted one foot first, then the other. I rose slowly from the iffy crouch.

"Oops!" My heels skidded in opposite directions. I fell, bounced on my butt, and ended up sprawled on the ground all over again, rear smarting from the impact. I cursed under my breath.

"Dammit." The man hooked his hands under my arms, lifted me up, and set me upright. "There. Do you think you can stand on your own?"

"Maybe," I mumbled, rubbing my ass. My legs buckled, but I steadied myself on the truck and willed my feet to stick to the ground.

"You're shivering." He opened the car door. "Get in."

"No, thank you." Even if I was freezing, there were rules about cars and strangers. "Can you please call for Roadside Assistance?"

The man actually scoffed. "No reception, remember?" He eyed me impatiently. "Lady, you do know that there's a storm barreling down on south central Alaska, right?"

"The clerk at the airport did mention that."

"But did he mention that anytime now, a Bering Sea superstorm is expected to bring blizzard conditions with winds in excess of sixty miles an hour?"

"Yeah, no." I swallowed a dry gulp. "He didn't put it quite as bad as that."

"It's going to get a hell of a lot colder," the man said. "Emergency services went on lockdown about fifteen minutes ago."

Fabulous, just fabulous.

"What I'm trying to tell you," he explained in a strained tone obviously intended for the dimwits among us, "is that—assuming you're not a trap—I'm your only option at the moment. So get in the damn truck, before you freeze your ass off."

Dressed in his black jacket and blue jeans, glinting with all that gold in his eyes and hair, he looked perfectly normal. Minus the scowl, he might have even been good looking. But his bad temper and my flash-frozen brain made for a bad combination. Plus, there was a good chance he was more than paranoid and grouchy. Maybe he was off the grid in more ways than one.

"Look," he said. "I've had a long day and I'm in a shitty mood."

I rolled my eyes. "No kidding."

"I wasn't expecting this. You. Whatever."

I perched my fist on my hip. "Do you think I was expecting you?"

"Just get in, okay?" He gestured to the cab. "I want to get indoors before the storm hits."

"Oh, I don't know." I considered both, the brawny guy and his burly truck. "Where I come from, hitchhiking is dangerous."

"Too bad," he said. "In Alaska hitchhiking is a common form of transportation."

"As far as I know, you could be a serial killer."

"So could you." He held the door open for me. "And my risk is higher than yours since, according to the Discovery Channel, female serial killers have been proven to be more dangerous than male serial killers."

I'd either met my match or found the only other person in the world who watched as much Discovery Channel as I did.

"Get the hell in," he said impatiently. "We're running out of time."

The weather was getting colder. The wind had picked up and the snow fell in bigger, wetter chunks. I was shivering violently, but still, I hesitated.

"Can you please take me to the nearest gas station or hotel?" I said, trying to keep my voice from quavering.

"The nearest gas station is sixty-five miles that way." He stuck out his thumb and pointed behind him. "The nearest motel is seventy-eight miles in the opposite direction. There's no time to get there. My cabin is close by and I have the full intention of being there by the time the storm hits in…" he paused to look at his watch, "…anytime now."

The mention of the word "cabin" did nothing to appease my fears. I'd seen plenty of "cabins" in my reality show marathon. I didn't want to spend a moment—let alone hours—chewing on squirrel parts in a rustic shelter without heat, electricity, or plumbing, especially in the company of a pissed-off guy whose actions so far put the *strange* in stranger.

"What is it going to be?" he said. "I'm willing to play the female killer odds if you decide you don't want to turn into an icicle. It's your choice, but I'm hauling ass right now."

What's the use of choices when one has none?

I said a little prayer, shuffled on the ice and, balancing carefully on my unwieldy heels, climbed into the front seat. He helped me up, shut the door, and walked around the truck. My head began to hurt, pangs of pain stabbing behind my eyes. Not good.

The man climbed in next to me in the cab. "Strap in."

He switched on the ignition, pressed on the pedal and accelerated down the icy track as if truck skating was an X Games signature event and he was going for the gold. My knuckles tightened around the door handle. I bit down on my lips, but the backseat driver in me was out of control. Whether he was a serial killer or not was irrelevant. We were both going to die today.

He glanced in my direction. "You got a name?"

"Yes." I pressed my frozen fingertips against the heating vent, reveling in the blessed heat.

"Well?" he said in that demanding tone of his.

I stared at him, mystified by his persistent state of grouchiness. "Well what?"

"Are you going to tell me what your name is or what?"

"Oh." I was close to frozen stupid. "My name is Summer, Summer Silva."

"Summer in Alaska?" He stared at me for an instant,

then burst out into quiet laughter. "You're a little late. Summer arrived in Alaska just in time to meet winter."

Maybe it had something to do with the fact that I hadn't slept in a while, but yeah, no. He wasn't going to laugh at my expense. I narrowed my eyes on him.

"That's quite the glare." He suppressed another round of laughter. "I didn't mean to be rude."

"Well, you are rude, a lot rude in fact, accusing me of God knows what and acting like a total jerk."

"Sorry," he said. "It's just that... Summer in Alaska." His lips twitched. "You've got to admit. It's pretty damn good."

"Are you drunk?" I said. "Because if you are, maybe *I* should be doing the driving. I imagine they've got laws in Alaska, including some about drinking and driving?"

"You're turning out to be a piece of work," he said, smirking. "Bossy too, for someone riding in *my* goddamn truck. Here I am, doing you a favor, not letting you freeze off your pretty little stuck-up ass and yet you're being a smartass and giving me attitude."

"Are you for real?" He had a lot of nerve calling me a smartass. "You're not exactly attitude free yourself."

"And yes," he added, ignoring my comment, "we do have some laws here in Alaska, although not nearly as many as they've got in the lower forty-eight. As to your question, nope, I'm not drunk, haven't had a drop all day. Should've, but didn't."

"What's that supposed to mean?"

"I mean that if there was ever a good day for drinking, today was it." He stomped on the clutch and shifted gears. "But no, unfortunately, I'm not drunk. That and the shitty day probably explain why you're getting a double dose of sarcasm."

"Sorry about your shitty day," I said. "But you need to mellow out. Do you always go around trying to bully people into doing whatever you want?"

"Pretty much." He flashed what could've been a semi-contrite glance in my direction. "Look, I apologize for my lack of manners." He offered his hand. "My name is Seth, Seth Erickson."

I shook his hand, mostly because, sarcasm aside, he was making an effort to be civil. Plus, he was a fellow Discovery Channel watcher. His hold was firm, hot, and supremely comforting to my fingers. My entire body wanted to shrink into his grip if only to bask in his radiant heat. My fingertips tripped against the unusual texture at the bottom of his hand. I spotted a patch of mangled skin scarring his palm, crawling up his wrist and disappearing into his sleeve. He caught me looking and covered most of the scar with a self-conscious tug of his sleeve.

"You've got some icy fingers there." He tapped on the console's screen and punched up the temperature of my heated seat. "Tuck them under your thigh. Trust me. It's the quickest way to warm up those puppies."

He was right. Trapped between the heat of my body and the seat, my fingers began to thaw.

"Where the hell are you from?" he asked.

"Miami."

"Ah." He smirked. "That explains it."

"Explains what?"

"Your inability to cope with ice. And the outfit."

I looked down at myself. "What's wrong with my outfit?"

"No gloves, hat, boots, or a proper coat," he said.

"When I first saw you I thought you were either crazy or—well—you know."

"No, I don't know."

"I thought maybe you were a plant, someone looking for attention, or more specifically, *my* attention."

I stared at him for a full thirty seconds, unable to figure out what he meant. "What are you talking about?"

"Nobody in their right mind out here wears skirts and high heels on the roads, except the occasional call girl, playing a pre-ordered role or meeting a very specific customer…"

"Oh no you didn't." What was wrong with this man? "You thought I was a whore?"

"I couldn't see beneath the coat…"

"Are you like…freaking insane?"

He cleared his throat. "It was probably the heels that gave me the wrong impression…"

"You're out of your mind, you know that?" I snapped. "First you think your family is out to get you. Then you think I'm…what? A prostitute? Which implies that you think someone in your family was going to set you up with a…Jesus!" I rubbed my temples, wishing that I'd never come to Alaska and also that I'd ditched those damn shoes. "I really want to go home."

"Don't get upset." His eyes betrayed a hint of concern. "I would've bought the look if I'd seen you down in, say, Ketchikan getting down from one of them fancy cruises. For future reference, Alaska 101: dress warm, keep dry, stay warm. That coat might look fine for a fall afternoon on Fifth Avenue, but in Alaska? It'll kill you faster than a dip in the Bering Sea."

Great. Advice from Mr. Sunshine himself. His condescending tone annoyed the hell out of me. "Okay, fine, maybe I'm not properly dressed for the weather, but that's only because I had no time to plan for this trip. I'm not as stupid as you're making me out to be."

"No offense," he said, "but all the tourists are gone. What the hell is someone like you doing all the way out here at the end of September?"

"It's kind of a long story."

"I don't know why," he muttered, "but I'm itching to hear it."

"If you must know," I said, "my sister ran away with a guy she met on the internet. He's from Alaska and I came to find her."

He flashed me a skeptical look. "Is your sister stupid?"

"No," I said, but at times like these, I wondered. "Tammy is just…impulsive."

"Has she done stuff like this before?"

"Well, yeah, but it's not really her fault."

"What do you mean it's not her fault?"

"She struggles with bipolar disorder."

"Hey, lady, Summer—right?" he said. "There's no excuse for stupidity. I've met people with all kinds of injuries and disorders who know better than to run away with a stranger they met on the internet."

"I know, but Tammy is…"

My cell rang to the tune of chirping birds. Reception. I had reception! I groped through my purse until I found the phone.

"You might get a minute or two if you're lucky," Seth cautioned. "After that, nothing for a while."

My tepid fingers fumbled over the keypad, accidentally hitting the speaker in the process. "Hello?"

"Did you find Tammy?" Louise's voice blared in her

best Brooklyn accent, shrill, loud, and capable of busting an eardrum or two. “Where is she? Is she okay?”

“Calm down.” I tried to turn off the speaker but my stiff fingers succeeded only at increasing the volume. “I’m on my way to find her now. There might be an itsy-bitsy delay. The weather is not cooperating, but don’t worry, I’ll find her.”

“Are you locked in a fancy hotel room?” Louise demanded. “You won’t find Tammy from behind a bolted door.”

“Of course not.” Louise could be such a witch when she was anxious. “I promised you I’d find Tammy and I will.”

“I sure hope you’re not enjoying room service while your sister is gone and I’m here, suffering, imagining all the terrible things she could be going through…”

“Please, don’t be a drama queen,” I said. “We don’t have any evidence to suggest that Tammy is in immediate danger.”

“Find your sister!” Louise’s voice flickered in and out of range. “Find her! I don’t care what you have to do, just do it…”

The phone lost all its bars again and the call dropped. The narrow reception zone had ended. Part of me was grateful for the reprieve. The other part knew I was cut off again. The headache throbbing behind my eye intensified. The sights blurred before me.

“Hey,” Seth said. “You okay?”

“Fine.” I dropped my cell in my purse and straightened my back, fighting the exhaustion.

“Who was that very loud woman?”

“My stepmother.”

“Is she right in the head?”

"She's just worried about Tammy."

"Something's not adding up here." He rubbed his wide back against the seat like a great big bison scratching against a tree. "Your sister's an idiot. Your stepmother demands that you drop everything and go chase her. Your family? Sounds like a major clusterfuck."

"Look who's talking." I sniffed. "My family may be a little different, but we love each other. We don't hire people to try to set each other up. Sure, we can be loud and a tad dramatic on occasion, but honestly? Your family sounds a million times more screwed up than mine."

His mouth twisted into the sarcastic smirk he favored. "You might have a point there."

"Yeah, you bet I do." I leaned back on the headrest. After a two-day journey, a three-hour drive, and a car wreck, I felt as if someone had taken a bat to me.

"You're looking very sleepy there," he said. "Talk to me. Are you all right?"

"I'll live," I mumbled, rubbing the knot behind my ear.

"Are you hurt?" He turned on the cabin lights and leaned over to inspect my head as he continued to drive. "Is that a bruise behind your ear? Hell, I didn't notice before." The truck swerved in the road. "Did you hit your head when your car went off the road? Are you sure you're all right?"

"Just concentrate on driving straight, please." I inched away from his touch and switched the cabin lights off. "I'm a little tired, that's all. I haven't slept for a few days."

"A few days? That's not good." He groped behind the seat, opened the top of a small cooler and, after grabbing a bottle, handed it over to me. "Here you go."

"No, thanks." I wasn't about add alcohol to my troubles.

"It's not for drinking." He pressed the cold bottle to the side of my head. "It's to keep the swelling down."

"Oh." I took the bottle from him and held it against the lump.

"Hang on tight," he said. "That's a real nice handcrafted lager. I wouldn't want it to go to waste."

"Got it," I said. "Hanging on to the brew over here."

He smiled, a genuine, eye-lightening grin that eased the angles on his face and radiated charm and warmth. Could a guy who smiled like that really be a jerk or a serial killer?

The world around us turned into a white maelstrom. The wind wrestled with the truck. The road became invisible under a new layer of snow. Seth geared down and kept his eyes on the road as we negotiated some hairy turns and the road's deteriorating conditions. In all my twenty-nine years of life, I'd never seen weather like this.

"We're not beating the storm, are we?"

"This is just the beginning." He tilted his head and surveyed the sky. "It's going to get bad soon, thirteen hours of very nasty wind, snow, and ice."

My timing sucked. "And I thought this was bad."

"This is nothing." He slowed down to maneuver over a bridge. "I don't suppose you get blizzards in Miami. But don't worry, we're almost there."

"Goody," I mumbled.

I knew my chances of getting to a hotel tonight were nil, but I needed to keep it together, at least until we got to the cabin. With a little luck, it might be a two-room cabin, with a door and a lock between me and the rest of the place. A door chain would be nice, but I could always improvise.

I eyed the man riding next to me. Maybe under all that hubris, he'd turn out to be a decent human being. After all, he had stopped to help me. I toyed with the idea of giving him a quick rundown of my condition, but my hackles went up. No way. He was a stranger and a guy and maybe even a little off, with all that paranoia. I knew from experience what would happen if I warned him. No need to add premeditation to humiliation.

All of a sudden, my vision narrowed. My thoughts slowed down to a crawl. My body slacked and my eyelids slammed over my eyes like hurricane shutters. I ran out of time and energy at the same moment. Oh, crap. I knew exactly what was happening to me.

"Hey, Summer." Seth's voice came from far away. "We're almost there." He shook me softly. "Wake up. Stick with me, girl."

I had no time to explain.

"Make sure you lock the door," I mumbled, before I conked out.

TWO

SOME DAYS, LIFE was a cross-eyed bitch. It screwed with you so bad that you wanted to kick it in the ass and send it to hell. It slammed you like a goddamn RPG and then crushed you beneath metric tons of crap. As I parked in the garage and carried Summer out of the truck, I was sure today was one of those days.

She wasn't very heavy, but she was tall and long-limbed, and totally limp in my arms. I was glad for the elevator that took us up from the garage. Considering I'd been in a wheelchair when I first moved into the cabin, the elevator had never been a luxury. It came in handy again tonight.

I took Summer to my room and laid her down on my bed. My military emergency medical training kicked in. I grabbed the flashlight from my drawer, lifted her eyelids, and shone the light in her eyes. Her pupils contracted into smaller dots. Good. I let out my breath. She hadn't suffered head trauma or cranial bleeding.

I checked her vital signs. Her pulse was strong and her breathing regular. She felt a little cold to my touch, but she wasn't hypothermic. I took off her useless coat. Sure enough, her skirt felt damp to my touch and the insides of her shoes sagged with melted snow. Such was the fate of fashionistas in off-grid Alaska. With the flip of a switch, I turned on the fireplace then got to work stripping the rest of her clothes.

I was still having trouble believing that she wasn't one of Alex's schemes. He'd like nothing better than to find a way to screw me publicly before the upcoming board meeting. Yeah, the motherfucker had tried worse before. That's why I'd been so sure that the high-heeled, long-legged mirage strutting her stuff down the deserted road had been a setup when I first spotted her. Given the circumstances, what the hell was I supposed to think?

But thirty seconds after meeting her, my gut told me Summer couldn't be part of a scam. I trusted my gut. It'd navigated me through war and peace and it usually gave me reliable readings. Summer felt earnest to me, sincere, fiery and opinionated, but not fake.

No, I didn't think she was lying. The bruise that blotched her thigh confirmed her story, and so did the bump on her head and the smaller bruises on her legs. Her car hadn't just skidded off the road. This girl had been in a wreck.

I found no broken bones, open wounds, or signs of internal injuries. It was all very good news, because the chances of me getting her to a hospital tonight were exactly zero, given the storm raging outside. She had admitted that she hadn't slept for days. She was probably suffering from exhaustion. Her lights might be out, but she wasn't going to die on me.

I felt like a goddamn scumbag. My stomach churned when I remembered my reaction on the road. The shock in her green eyes at my attitude was probably authentic. I'd been such a jackass, accusing her of collusion, neglecting to notice her distress. Part of it had been her fault. She hadn't told me she was hurt and, slipping and sliding aside, she carried herself with poise, as if nothing was wrong with her. The rest of this clusterfuck rested squarely on my shoulders. The shitty day and the ongoing feud had gotten to me. Way to go, jerk.

My eyes wandered as I finished undressing her. I couldn't help but notice her body's fine curves. I hadn't taken off a woman's clothes in a while. These days, I ran high on stress and short on joy. I trailed the long line of her back, appreciating the smooth stretch of tanned olive skin, soft and even beneath my fingertips.

Dammit. This woman just seemed to call out to the idiot in me. I covered her with the down duvet. She'd be warm for sure. I fetched a glass of water and some ibuprofen, lifted her up on the bed and braced her head against my chest, inhaling a lungful of her scent in the process.

"Hey, Summer." I shook her gently. "Wake up, just for a sec. I've got something that'll help you feel better. After that, you can get back to sleep."

She stirred in my arms. For a moment, her eyes opened into narrow slits. I put the pills in her mouth and pressed the glass to her lips.

"Drink up," I said. "Now swallow. Good. Are you warm enough?"

"Tired," she mumbled before her lids fell back into place, shutting out the light.

I laid her back on the pillows. She was out cold. For a guy who hardly ever slept more than three hours in a row, I envied her capacity to disconnect from the world. She looked peaceful.

I studied her face, where a set of well-constructed lips presided over her features. A pair of dark, hard-angled eyebrows broadcasted her emotions, live-tweeting her thoughts without censorship when she was awake. Cut straight to just above the shoulder, the blunt lines of her thick black hair added a sense of competence to her features. She had this kind of hard, precise, unconventional beauty, and perhaps because there was so much definition built into her face, the engineer in me found the construction fascinating.

I ran two fingers over a crescent-shaped mark on her neck. It felt smooth to my fingertips. Parked slightly below her ear, it looked like a moon sliver, a waning moon, to be precise. I wondered if it was a birthmark or a tiny burn, something she'd acquired along the way, a miniature version of my not-so-delicate scars.

Enough speculation already. I barely knew the woman. The odds were low that she was part of a conspiracy, but I couldn't afford to take the chance. I looked through her purse and found her wallet. Summer Silva, age twenty-nine, resident of Key Biscayne. According to her business card, she was an associate architect with Carrera and Associates.

I scrolled through her cell and looked through her contacts, recent calls, emails, and messages. The stepmother texted like a certifiable maniac and emails from work crammed her inbox, but I found nothing that could link her to Alex or anyone in my family. Still, I had to be cautious.

I changed into my sweats and a T-shirt and, punching the keys on my tablet, checked the cabin's overall status. The solar panels had retracted properly. The generator had kicked in. I punched a few buttons to secure the doors and engage the storm-protection systems. Purring softly, the translucent shutters lowered in sequence, securing the house against the wind. All systems were go.

I put Summer's wet clothes in the dryer on my way to the office. I sat down on my chair and rubbed my back against the leather. The old injuries were acting up tonight. The satellite connection was out of commission, but I activated my backup communication system and made a quick call to Jer to ask for his help tomorrow.

It was close to ten o'clock when I finished talking to my brother, which meant that it was around six o'clock at corporate headquarters in New York, an hour after regular office hours. No problem. My chief of cyber security was a workaholic who insisted on being on call 24/7. Sure enough, John Spider's face showed up on my screen at the first ring.

"Hey," Spider said, sharp features pixelated but recognizable. "I guess the new backup communication system is working."

"So far, so good," I said.

Spider was a bit of a singularity, a middle-aged west coast surfer with a killer IQ living on the east coast. He was a legend in cyber security, which meant he was also a legendary hacker. He'd been my professor and mentor at MIT. He was also my friend.

"I'm tracking that monster storm in your neighborhood," Spider said. "The satellite pics are cool, man. But I can't imagine you called me to chitchat about the weather."

"You're right," I said. "I need you to look into something, quick turnaround."

"Sure thing," Spider said. "Whatever you need."

I held the driver's license up to the camera. "Summer Silva."

"Oh, a dudette?" Spider flashed his crowded teeth

and took a screenshot. "Good going, man, is the old Seth back?"

No, the old Seth was dead. He wasn't coming back, but I refrained from stating the obvious because, even though Spider was nosy as hell, he didn't deserve my rage.

"Can you do the job or not?"

"Of course I can." Spider's awful grin widened. "She looks hot."

"Shut the hell up."

"I mean it," Spider said. "You got your eye on her?"

"Sudden visitor," I said. "Satisfied? Can you zip it now?"

"Got it." He plaited his fingers together and cracked his knuckles. "Call you right back."

I returned the driver's license to Summer's wallet and stuck my head in the bedroom. Rolled up in the duvet, she was out like a marmot in a winter burrow. I went back to my office and caught up with the workload. Today's emergency had really screwed up my schedule. I answered my emails then turned my attention to the financial reports piling in my inbox. The board meeting was coming up in less than a month and I was on the hunt.

I studied the financials closely. Alex had to be siphoning money out of the company, but how and from where? I dove into that. The best byproduct of a solid work addiction was that it made time pass faster. Somewhere around midnight, my screen beeped and Spider came back online.

"Hiya," he said. "Summer Silva, daughter of Cuban-American architect Miguel Silva, an immigrant who arrived during the Mariel boatlift in 1980. He's credited with the design of some of Miami's most innovative buildings, including the iconic Fountain Way, a high-rise residential complex taught in architecture schools all over the world."

"What's his personal history?"

"Married, then widowed. Dudette's mother drowned in an accident when she was a kid. Father remarried after that. He took a huge financial hit during the recession, got sick and died five years ago."

Images flashed on the screen as Spider spoke, pictures of the Mariel boatlift and a newspaper interview with Miguel Silva himself, describing a harrowing ordeal when his boat capsized in the Florida Straits. Obituaries, marriage, birth, and baptismal certificates paraded before my eyes, as did Summer's school records all the way to her university transcripts.

"She's an architect," Spider said. "Graduated with high honors. Works for—"

"Carrera and Associates," I said. "Get to the main point."

"I found no contact between her and Alex Erickson and no connection between her and anyone in your family."

Best news so far.

"Perfect credit report." Spider punched the keys as he talked. "Makes her student loan payments every month, rent, utilities, blah, blah, blah. Uses her iPhone to pay for her café-con-leche every morning. Loves the beach. Posts architectural pics on Instagram and FB, but that's it for social media. She's got a passport, but she hasn't been out of the country as far I can tell."

"Talk to me about money," I said. "Sudden fluxes?"

"None traceable." Spider sent more documents to my

screen. "Bank accounts check, phone records check, medical records show a clean bill of health on her last physical. Prescriptions are limited to birth control and sleeping pills."

Jesus. "How the hell did you get into her medical records?"

"I'm good."

"Or really bad, depending on whose perspective."

Spider's grin widened to show his longish fangs. Maybe it was because of his last name, but whenever he smirked like that, I thought of a tarantula rearing to attack.

"Here's some interesting shit." Spider's fingers clicked on his keyboard at top velocity. "An early marriage. She was nineteen. He was older, twenty-five. Sergio De Havilland, trust fund baby, jet-setter and prominent socialite. They met first year in college. The marriage lasted less than a year. That's as much dirt as I got. Since then, she's been a disgrace to decadent living. No arrests, not even a parking ticket. Don't know what to tell you. She's spic-and-span."

"Roger that." Why the hell did I feel so relieved? "Anything new on the Alex project?"

"I've got the team looking," Spider said, "but so far, the field is an open crapshoot."

"The board meeting is coming up."

"On it." Spider waved. "Later, dude. Stay warm."

I worked for another hour or two, listening as the storm buffeted the cabin with furious blows. At some point, I heated some chicken soup on the stove and wolfed some of it down at the kitchen counter. I left the pot on the stove, in case Summer woke up.

Giving up my bed was a major concession, but I'd

been brought up right, so I set myself up on the couch. I lay there for a long while, but I couldn't sleep. The cushions poked at my sore spots and every time I closed my eyes, I saw Danny, dead in his wheelchair.

My day had started very early with *the call*. Death was no stranger to me, but after trying to help Danny recapture his life, his death felt a hell of a lot like defeat. Maybe if I had known how depressed Danny was, things might have turned out differently.

Danny's death got me thinking of Shawn, my copilot, and Jonesy, my flight engineer. Maybe they'd be alive today if they'd gotten into some other Pave Hawk with some other pilot. Maybe they'd have survived the attack if they hadn't been flying with me. Maybe if I'd banked sooner, the RPG would've missed us.

Hell, I hated maybes.

The men's faces echoed in my mind. Friends gone. Lives ended. The list was getting longer. My back was killing me. My breaths came out shallow and rattling. Memories of the flames taunted my skin. Too much heat. Too much grief. Too much nothingness. *Shut it out, shut it all the hell out.*

I got up from the couch, went back to my office and marched out of the side door. The cold startled my lungs. The snow blew horizontally over the house, but the structure itself shielded the side porch from the wind. On this spot, the snow fell almost gently from the roof, piling into a two-foot crust that blanketed the deck. The snow crunched under my bare feet, but the contact failed to cool me down. I stripped off my clothes, knelt down and, stretching my arms, lay on my back. I fathomed a wave of hissing steam rose in the air when my body hit the snow.

The surviving nerves in my back's mangled skin screamed. My skin burned, not with the flames I remembered, but with purifying cold. The chill flared. I pressed my body harder against the snow and held fast, until my entire back went numb.

Relief at last.

I rolled in the snow like a polar bear, rubbing my head against the white fluff, turning back and forth from my belly to my back. I inhaled the scent of frost deep into my lungs, banishing the stench of ashes and burning flesh. I bit down on a mouthful of snow and tasted ice's purest flavor. It traveled down my gullet to my stomach in a cooling path.

I lay there until the lethal heat in me was obliterated, until every part of me had chilled and my body began to shiver. Even then, I stayed for another minute or two, relishing a moment's peace from the heat, listening to the wind's eerie song, watching the flakes swirling in the wind, numb, inside and out.

Weird? What the hell. This was why I lived alone. A guy tested by death and tried by fire had to do whatever he could to survive.

By the time I stumbled back into the house, my skin tingled with fresh blood, flushing my body and pumping vigorously through my system. The heat was gone, replaced by cool, calm, and hopefully lasting numbness.

I locked the side door, dried off with my T-shirt, and donned my sweats. I heard a noise, so I padded out to the hallway with the wet T-shirt in tow. The bedroom door was open. I'd closed it before. I peeked in. The bed covers were thrown aside and the bed was empty.

I walked out to the great room and called out, "Summer?"

She didn't reply, but a rattle on the other side of the house caught my attention. I set out toward the noise. I scanned the kitchen in passing and saw that the lid was off the pot. The soup was all gone. I turned the corner into the dining room and stopped dead in my tracks.

Outside, the storm was in full swing. The wind howled and swirls of snow gave the night a spectral glow that seeped through the shuttered glass doors. Inside, a configuration of feminine curves comprised Summer's dark outline against the storm's tenuous light.

I took in the proportionate build of her shoulders, the contour of her torso as it tapered at the waist and flared out at the hips, and the long line of her legs. She stood there, with her hand on the handle and her nose pressed against the glass, stark naked.

"Summer?" I said tentatively. "What are you doing?"

"I need to go." She fiddled with the lock. "I've got to find her."

"Who?" I said. "Your sister?"

"I need to find her."

"You can't go out there," I said, not a little alarmed. "It's freezing. You'll die."

"But I have to go."

What the hell was she thinking? "There's a storm, remember? A bad one."

She either ignored me or didn't care what I had to say. I had an urge to throw her over my shoulder and take her back to bed, but seeing as she was butt naked, I refrained from approaching her.

"Listen to me," I said instead. "You're naked. Summer, stop. Turn around. Look at me."

This time, she listened. She turned around. The beam of a security lamp outside pierced through a high window and illuminated her face, framing her eyes in a rectangle of soft light. Her gaze fell on me. Her green irises looked almost translucent in the eerie light, glowing silver like a pair of light reflectors. Holy shit. For a moment there, she scared the crap out me. I stumbled back before I got it together and realized it was a trick of the lights.

And yet the intensity in her eyes unsettled me. Her stare flowed free and brazen over my body, taking me in without hesitation. She made zero effort to avert her eyes or disguise her curiosity. I remembered I wasn't wearing my shirt. Dammit.

My stomach burned with a flush of acid reflux. I felt completely exposed, baring my scars for her perusal as if I were a circus freak. But if she found the sight of my burns repugnant, her face didn't betray her revulsion.

I twisted the wet T-shirt in my hands. Anger burned through me. If she could look at me like that, then I could do the same. I raked my gaze over her body, equally brazen and bold. My stare tripped on her tan's crisp outline. Pale triangles highlighted a pair of high breasts, contrasting against the rest of her bronzed skin. Inside the white triangles, the dark circles of her oversize areolas emphasized her body's striking geometry. The visuals had me reeling.

She shielded her eyes with her hand and squinted at me. "You are...extraordinary."

"Pardon me?"

"You're amazing." She reached out and, shattering the invisible boundary between us, traced her fingers over my jaw, pads rustling quietly against my stubble. "You're like a solar flare."

The contact zapped me with a burst of connectivity, setting abuzz every nerve in my body. Her fingertips brushed over my skin like the softest cotton, but her touch was also sharp and intense. My body coiled, my hands fisted, my jaw clamped down. I'd been cool and numb a moment ago. Now I was beyond hot, on fire all over again.

I bit out the words. "What the hell are you talking about?"

"Your aura." Her fingers traveled down my neck, over my shoulder, and then detoured to settle over my heart. "Your life force. It's very strong, impressive really."

"Jesus." Was she one of those new age hippies who embraced weird ideas like auras and nudism, at least after working hours? "Don't tell me you believe in that junk."

"You don't see it?"

"No!"

I don't know why, but my heart raced and the room felt off-kilter to my spinning head. Those eyes. When she looked at me like that, my brain shut down. My gaze wandered and ended up roving over her breasts again. I forced myself to focus on her face.

Maybe it had something to do with the fact that I'd brought a strange woman to my house and she stood before me, naked, talking about auras and shit. Maybe the fact that she seemed to feel perfectly comfortable in her skin rubbed me the wrong way, since I felt the exact opposite. She didn't fear or shun me. She seemed completely undaunted by my scars and at ease, whereas I was having more than a little trouble concentrating.

Maybe I also felt rotten because I'd had the day from hell. Danny's death had shaken me much more than I first realized. Life didn't seem to amount to much lately. Hell, I couldn't even trust members of my own damn family. What was the purpose of living like this?

"I'm really sorry," Summer said, with alarming kindness.

"For what?"

"For your pain," she said. "For your sadness."

How the hell could she know?

"The tendrils in your aura." Her eyes explored the space around me. "They're beautiful, but those dazzling explosions must hurt inside."

I gritted my teeth. "That's a load of bullshit, you know that? Can you stop talking crap and acting weird?"

She shrugged and that's when I noticed a trickle of soup smearing the side of her mouth.

I wiggled a finger by my lip. "You've got something there."

She wiped her mouth with the back of her hand.

"You didn't get it." I grabbed a towel from the kitchen counter and wiped it off myself. "Now it's gone."

"I was hungry," she said as if apologizing. "It was good."

"No problem," I said. "I left it out for you. Is that a dribble of soup on your chest?"

"Oh?" She looked down at herself.

On impulse, I reached out and wiped the drops off her breast. The impressive span of her areolas wrinkled. Her nipples puckered in unison. They weren't the only body parts hardening in the room. For the first time since my Pave Hawk went down in Afghanistan, my body coiled with urgency and my cock swelled with a rush of blood that squeezed the breath out of my lungs.

Jesus fucking Christ. After all this time, I was horny as hell.

Get it together, Erickson. I tried to disguise my body's reaction. "We ought to get you back to bed," I said. "That bruise on your leg is probably hurting just about now."

"I don't feel any pain." Her translucent eyes widened into immense saucers. "But you did. You still do."

Her fingers traced the scar that ran from the heel of my hand, behind my arm and over my shoulder. My skin reacted to her touch. Not with pain or discomfort, but rather with a prickle of...anticipation?

She examined the long scar then circled behind me to trail its path on my back. Her touch was light over the raised divide where healthy skin met healed flesh. A pleasurable tingle traveled through my spine. It resonated through my body as if amplified by a loudspeaker. It reminded me that most of my burns had healed and contact could feel good.

I closed my eyes, enjoying her light, feathering strokes, astonished at my new skin's ability to feel pleasure. Her touch sent tingles all over my body, like fine snow cascading over my shoulders. Her fingers were gentle and yet the contact rattled me. Other than the doctors and nurses, I hadn't allowed anyone else to see or touch my scars. Until now.

"What happened to you?" she asked.

"I burned, isn't it obvious?" I lashed out like a goddamn adolescent.

Her hands traveled the scar's arbitrary path down my back. "You healed well."

"I guess I was one of the lucky ones."

I'd sustained burns over twenty percent of my body.

Half of those, about ten percent, had been third-degree burns, mostly on my torso and back. Top-of-the-line, grueling medical treatment, skin grafts, surgery, and therapy had reduced scarring and minimized loss of skin elasticity and function. But some of my skin still had a raw, mangled, leathery look and there were days when my nerves misfired loads of phantom pain.

Summer's touch burned too, but in a completely different way.

She came around and faced me. With a single finger, she traced the scar down my chest. My body flooded with waves of euphoric tingles. Her hand tripped on my waistband. I caught her wrist and stilled her hand. What the hell did she want from me?

"I can help," she whispered, barely audible.

"I don't think that's such a good idea."

"Why not?" She tilted up her face, daring me with her lips.

Why was she looking at me like that? Was she teasing me? Mocking me? Provoking me?

I kissed her.

Her lips were soft beneath my mouth and her tongue replied with urgency that matched mine. Ignition. My motor roared to life and my rotors engaged. The longer my lips lingered on her mouth, the more intense my need got. She tasted like my favorite meal, warm soup, enhanced by her tongue's sweet addition. My hands craved the feel of her healthy skin. Should I allow myself to touch her?

Christ. I was caught in a wind shear and heading straight for a high-voltage wire. It took every ounce of my willpower to break off the kiss. When I finally did, she let out a little moan of protest. I rested my forehead on hers and struggled to regain my breath. I didn't know her and she didn't know a goddamn thing about me. I didn't want to harm her, physically or otherwise. For God's sake, just yesterday she'd been in a car wreck.

There were also other considerations. She could still be a trap, was certainly acting as one, despite my gut feeling and even though Spider had found no evidence to that effect. Hell, I couldn't afford mistakes right now. The attraction felt strong, too powerful for my own good. I was used to being in control, even if this moment felt a lot like a burst of turbulence.

My mind radioed a warning signal. *Walk away, Erickson.* Then my brain short-circuited and went out of commission. Fool. I wanted to clobber me silly. After all this time living on automatic, going through the motions and feeling nothing but anger, loss and regret, she'd shown up and, suddenly, I was up and going at last. Hell, I even knew from Spider's hack that she was healthy and on birth control, so I had an all clear. How long was I going to keep delaying life? Until I was old, bitter, and alone? Until I turned into a rusted wreck of myself? Until I gave up, like Danny had done today, and put a bullet through my head?

No, I wasn't going to end up like that. Seize the moment and forget the rest. It wasn't often that life offered a truce, a gift, whatever the hell you wanted to call this. What was wrong with accepting it?

Ultimately, the choice wasn't mine. It was hers and she made it, showing none of the trepidations that paralyzed me. She cased my face with her hands, rose up on the tips of her toes and kissed me. Jesus. The sweetness of that kiss. I was caught for good and committed to her flight path.

She trailed a line of kisses down my neck, sliding her lips over my nipples, running her hands over my body, tasting old and new skin with the tip of her tongue. I couldn't have moved away from her even if I'd wanted to. She made me feel healthy, as if there was nothing wrong with my body; free as if there was nothing wrong with me.

The moment felt a lot like a dream, like a young man's fantasy, fashioned in a hospital bed in between operations and debriding sessions. But the moment also felt more real than anything I'd experienced since my helicopter went down. I gasped when she eased herself onto her knees and kissed my belly and my groin, sliding my sweats down my legs until they crumpled at my feet.

She didn't hesitate. She took my erection in her hands and ran her lips up one side and down the other, planting little kisses along the way. All my blood surged toward her lips. I clenched my jaw as she swallowed me whole. The world spun. Her mouth was hot and wet, swirling with the currents of her rippling tongue. Months of pent-up need clobbered me like an RPG. My legs wavered.

I leaned on the kitchen counter and clutched the granite until my fingers hurt. Her mouth felt…incredible. I wanted to explode every single time she swallowed me. It was as if I were the most succulent treat she'd ever tasted, as if she was famished too, and her hunger just added to my starvation.

The hell with the world.

Some days, life was a lift from an inaccessible mountain ridge; a dump from a high hoist on the smoldering flames of someone's existence; a stranger with the lips of an angel kneeling at my feet. I had no defense to fight this, no will to evade whatever the hell this was. My hips conformed to the rhythm of her mouth, pumping obediently into her throat. My fingers entwined with her hair, attempting to steer her head and mouth, which needed absolutely no guiding.

"Christ." I swore under my breath. "For your sake, you better stop."

She mumbled something impossible to understand.

"I mean it," I rasped. "You ought to stop now."

She paused and looked up, lips glimmering in the light, eyes luminous, fist pumping me softly. "Do you really want me to stop?"

I gulped. "I'm thinking about you."

"Aw, you're very kind." She offered me a small, smug smile that made my dick jerk in her hand. "I can see that about you. You worry. But you need me and I need to please you. Do you want to come?"

Hell, I could've come just from the sight of her.

She kissed the tip of my cock, released me and got to her feet. Her eyes never left my face. She took a couple of steps backward and leaned back against the dining room table. "I don't think you realize how beautiful you are."

"Me?" I scoffed. Had she not noticed my scars?

"Your light dazzles." She scooted onto the table. "But you're also very sad. I don't want you to be sad."

My mouth must have been hanging open. Objections clogged my throat. I knew better, of course I knew better. I was a thirty-four-year-old man with plenty of experience in the female department—albeit all pre-crash. I was used to power and the games people played and had an excellent grasp of the mechanics of consequences. But at that moment, nothing much mattered, except that *she* wanted *me.*

I approached her with trepidation. Despite the warnings blaring in the back of my mind, there was nothing in that moment I wanted more than her. It was as if I were anchored to her by a bungee cord. The more I contemplated moving away from her, the more she pulled me in her direction.

It was an irresistible pull. How could it not be? Bracing on her elbows, she reclined on my table, enriching the wood's blond hues with the shades of her skin, enhancing my views with her body's original beauty.

"Don't be afraid." She separated her knees and displayed herself, giving me a new perspective of her tan, where a pale rectangle highlighted her closely cropped mound and offered a full, stunning view that left nothing to the imagination.

My erection hardened with a new, excruciating rush of blood. My cock ached from the need. *Hold back*, my head cautioned. *Full ahead*, my body urged.

"I've been waiting for you for a long time," she said. "You need me, and I? I really need you."

My head spun. My chest expanded and contracted with ragged breaths. My dick ditched all my objections, went rogue and took command of the mission. I was on her in three steps. Cradling her head in my hand, I lifted her face to my mouth and consumed her lips, querying her mouth with my tongue, inhaling her heady scent, sun-warmed sand, tropical sea breeze and coconut milk.

Her mouth responded with mind-boggling generosity. Her body flushed beneath my hands. I laid her carefully on the table and allowed my eyes to roam over her face before I settled on her eyes.

"Are you sure?" I said. "Stop me now, because I don't know what will happen if I get a taste of you."

"I know." She smiled, a warm, caring, trusting smile. "I want you in me right now."

How the hell could I walk away from that?

I scooted her to the edge of the table and fitted myself between her legs. I rubbed myself against her and found her ready. The discovery had me shivering with need. Every cell in my body reared up, primed and ready to go. I was suddenly bursting at the seams.

I pressed my cock against her opening and, meeting her gaze, asked for her permission one more time, this time without words, because I doubted she could hear my voice over my heart's frantic roar. She nodded and I slid into her body. It opened up to me like a brand-new world.

The pleasure. I wanted to cry from the pleasure. I wanted to thank her for bringing back the memories of physical joy that my body had forgotten. I closed my eyes. In one slow stroke, I went to the bottom of her. I was suddenly afraid that she'd change her mind; that this would be the only dip I'd take in her sea; that this single moment of bliss was all there was left for me.

But when I opened my eyes again, there was no reluctance in her gaze, no regrets, no hesitation. Her eyes widened, her mouth pursed and her eyebrows lifted in appreciation that lent confidence to my strokes. Her body was lean, fit, and greedy for me. Her breasts fitted perfectly in my hands, as if they'd been custom-tailored to my hold. Her nipples stiffened against my palm, transmitting the same type of desperate message that drove my cock. I bent low over her and brought one of her breasts to my mouth and, after circling her areola with my tongue, closed my lips around her nipple and suckled.

Her quiet moan revved up my need. The pleasure of savoring this woman's body walloped me, the thrill of connecting with another human being, sharing flesh and trading joy. I found myself working for her pleasure sounds, plowing her for the sake of hearing her music, listening for it with all my senses.

Her breaths quickened and her back arched like a bridge to some promised land I'd forsaken long ago. She started to come, right there and then, without pretense or notice, without warning or restraint. Her body convulsed beneath mine. Her face flushed and a small vein swelled on her neck. Her voice rumbled low and quiet behind pressed lips as she surrendered to the pleasure rattling her body and squeezing my cock.

I was shocked and pleased all at the same time. My cock reacted to her pleasure with the unbearable throbbing that forecasted an imminent explosion. I toyed with the idea of holding back and making her come again, but it was wishful thinking on my part. After all this time, I couldn't hold back. Her body compressed around me with astonishing strength, persuading me to come along for the ride. Once again, I had no choice.

I came with her. I came so hard and for so long that my heart about gave out. The extraordinary event that dazzled my body wiped me out. Gone. I was gone from my senses, for how long, I couldn't tell. Burrowed in her body, I was free of mine, no pain, no burning, no thoughts, on a journey that included only the bliss of her.

I fought for breath. Even after I returned, when my consciousness slammed me back into my body's frame, I couldn't move. My legs refused to hold me. I just lay there, leaning on my elbows, trying to draw in some oxygen, holding on to her as if she were my only way back to the real world, as if in her body I'd discovered a tunnel back to life and her breath was essential to mine.

She held on to me too, fingers trailing over my back's patched skin, soothing me with a soft touch that didn't discriminate against my scars, imbuing my lungs with her tropical scents, absorbing every ounce of me. Wrapped in her arms, I was also enveloped in her affection, as if we were old friends and practiced lovers, as if I had always been meant for her and she had always belonged with me.

I'd had plenty of sex in my life, but sex like this?

When my legs finally regained some semblance of strength, I gathered her in my arms and carried her to my bed, where we made love again and many times after that. All night long, the house shook and the storm blew fierce and dangerous around us, but I didn't care. I had my own storm going and it wasn't abating. And she? She was the superstorm of a lifetime.

THREE

I WOKE UP rested and relaxed, with my head propped up on a comfortable surface that rose and fell in an even cadence and a steady beat drumming against my ear. The neutral scent of baked oats and shea butter filled my lungs, spiced by a distant medicinal note I couldn't place, sharp, but not unpleasant. I was warm and comfortable and for a long moment, I felt as if I lay on the sand basking in the sun and listening to the surf. Then I remembered something odd. Last I knew, I'd been in Alaska, far away from my favorite Florida beaches, searching for Tammy and on my way to a rustic cabin.

I sat straight up and took in the place. The ultramodern king-size bed, the sleek furnishings, and the abstract paintings hanging on the walls made for a luxurious bedroom that couldn't possibly belong in a wilderness hut.

I tried to shake off the confusion, but it only got worse when my gaze fell on the man lying next to me. My heart flopped.

I recognized the amber-eyed stranger who'd picked me up on the highway. Seth. He was also the one who had the potential to be a serial killer. *Don't freak out, Summer, not yet.* I repressed a rush of emotion and forced myself to think this through.

This had to be *his* house. I was in *his* bed. Holy crap. Why then wasn't I scared stiff of him?

Because of my dream, the only thing I remembered from last night. *Safe*, a familiar voice echoed in the back of my mind. *You are safe.*

Then why the hell was I in Seth's bed?

His eyes were closed, but the sides of his mouth were turned up, as if he was having a good dream. Then I noticed he was naked. *I* was naked. If that wasn't alarming enough, his dick was swollen to shocking proportions.

Feel free to freak out anytime now, girlfriend. I dove out the bed like a marlin in full fight. A bloodcurdling scream burst out of my throat and pierced my ears. The man rolled off the bed and landed at a crouch, yellow eyes instantly alert. "What the hell?" He straightened, scanning the room for some unknown danger.

I ripped the sheet off the bed and covered myself, but I got a full frontal of him. He stood across the bed, revealing impossibly broad shoulders drawn tight at attention, a flat stomach, and sleek limbs with a hint of discreet but efficient muscle that even a guy-averse coward like me could admire. Most shocking were the red patches of mangled skin that blotched his body like malevolent tentacles, and—oh my freaking God—that stubborn erection.

"Get away from me!" I threw the pillow at him.

"What the hell?" He caught it in midair and blinked the sleep out of his eyes. "What's your problem?"

"You're naked!"

"You're naked too." He dropped the pillow on the bed. "And it didn't seem to bother you at all last night, when you were walking around my house like Lady Godiva, strutting your stuff, telling me that you wanted it as much as I did…"

"What do you mean?" A bunch of bricks tumbled in my stomach.

"Last night?" His eyes widened and his fair eyebrows climbed on his forehead. "Don't you remember?"

"Remember what?"

"You and me?"

I shook my head, heart pounding, mind spinning, trying to remember something, anything… "I…" I gulped dryly. "I've got nothing."

"Are you trying to tell me you don't remember?"

It took everything I had to ask. "Remember what, exactly?"

"Jesus Christ." He ran his hands over his face, shaking his head. His mouth tightened into a straight white line as anger replaced the confusion distorting his features. "Allow me to refresh your memory," he said and not kindly. "Last night, you were a fine piece of ass if there ever was one. And just in case you're scheming, my memory is clear: I didn't seduce you. I tried to persuade you that it wasn't a good idea. But you insisted. *You* came on to *me*."

No, no, no. Holy shit. *I* had seduced *him*? Oh my freaking God and all the saints, please, don't let it be true. I felt the tilt as I started to slide down a very steep cliff. Not again. My thoughts sputtered. Maybe it was all a lie. Proof, I needed proof. Beneath the sheet, my hand shot to the space between my legs. My fingers found the evidence. The bottom dropped out from under my world and my stomach led the plunge as I fell into the void.

"Is it true?" I couldn't breathe. "Did you—? Did we—?"

"Hell, yeah," he said. "We did and you were really up for it."

Run. It was the only thing I could think to do. *Escape.* The pressure building in me propelled me toward the door. Out, I needed a way out, out of this room, out of this house. I bolted blindly from the bedroom, into a hallway, past a huge bathroom and through a set of doors that dead-ended in an enormous walk-in closet. I slammed the door behind me and dove to the back of the closet, where I wedged myself in the corner between rows of fine jackets and hugged my knees to my chest.

My heart pummeled my breastbone. My belly churned. I really, really wanted to throw up. I was beyond shocked, mortified. My impulse was to hide, from him, from the world. I banged the back of my head against the wall. It had happened. Despite my best efforts and after years of precautions, my worst nightmare had been realized.

I wanted the earth to swallow me. I wanted to disappear from this place. Instead, there was a knock and Seth slipped in through the door, fully dressed in his sweats and a T-shirt, thank God. I snatched one of the jackets from the rack and draped it over my naked self. The grim expression on his face chilled my gut.

"So," he said. "You *are* Alex's tool."

"I'm nobody's tool!"

"If you think you can take me for a fool, you're wrong," he spat in his exacting tone. "I'm going to beat you at your game."

"I'm not working for anyone!" And I didn't need his paranoia on top of everything else.

"Don't you dare play victim with me." He poked an accusatory finger in the air. "You were a willing fuck last night. You're in for a huge surprise if you think you can con me, or sue me, or worse—"

"Stop it!" The tears burned in my eyes. "I'm not going to do any of that."

His eyes narrowed. "What did you say?"

I blinked through the sting and took a deep, rattling breath. "I'm not going to sue you, or accuse you of anything. I'm not that kind of person."

The furrows deepening on his forehead betrayed his confusion. "So you're not in this for the money?"

"What money?" I clenched my teeth and found my backbone. "And who the hell are you anyway?"

"You swear you don't know?"

"Give me a break," I muttered. "I thought you were an Alaskan mountain man living in a wilderness shack somewhere. But look at this house, this closet." I gestured around me. "Unless you hunt in Italian silk, you're no frigging mountain man."

"I run my family's company."

"Great, wonderful, good for you," I said. "By the look of all this, it must be quite the company. But I don't give a crap about your money."

That shut him up, but only for a moment.

"So you remember, right?" he said. "You remembered what happened last night?"

"No." A bunch of fat tears escaped my eyes and trickled down my cheeks.

"You have no recollections whatsoever of anything that happened?"

"None." I swallowed the sob stuck in my throat. "Give me thirty seconds to get my head on straight and I'll get the hell out of here."

"You're leaving?" His frown was now permanently stamped on his face. "Just like that?"

"Of course I'm leaving!" I sniffled. "I just need a moment."

The spot between his brows wrinkled into an inverted V. His yellow eyes fixed on me. "Can you please stop crying? It's very unsettling to have a woman sobbing in my closet."

"I'm trying." I wiped my tears but dammit, more kept coming.

"Let me see if I understand this clusterfuck." He crossed his arms and leaned against the door. "You don't remember a thing about last night, but you're willing to believe that things happened exactly as I say?"

I nodded.

The V deepened between his eyebrows. "Why?"

It was an excellent question, but there was no way I was ever going to tell him about my past, or about my dream, the only thing I remembered about last night. It replayed in my mind now, fresh and vivid.

In my dream, Seth had been lying on the snow, rolling on it, relishing it like a child playing in the sand. And suddenly the snow had turned to sand and the sand had turned into a beach where the waves drew a ruffled pattern before retreating into the vast ocean that stretched out to the horizon. From the sea's emerald waters, my mother emerged, black hair streaming with kelp wreaths, face gleaming with shimmering trickles of water.

"Trust him," she said in her quiet way. "Loneliness is a sorry state of the soul. You needed him and he needed you. You offered, he accepted. Don't be afraid. You are safe. He will not harm you."

My mother disappeared beneath the ocean. The ocean retreated into the wave, and the wave became the sand, which turned back into the snow where Seth swam in the confines of his frozen sea. Maybe I was nuts, but I knew that the man before me hadn't hurt me, because my mother only came to me when I was in need and she never lied in my dreams.

Of course I couldn't tell any of that to Seth. He'd think for sure I was a lunatic if I did.

"Well?" he demanded. "Why the hell would you believe me if what you say is true and you can't remember squat about last night?"

"I…um…I have a hunch you're a straight shooter."

He tilted his head, his face openly skeptical. "You hardly know me."

"I've got a sense for people," I mumbled. "Um… never mind."

"No, please." He rolled a hand in the air. "By all means, explain."

He didn't look nearly as furious as before, although his eyes bore into me like golden blades.

"I can't really explain," I said. "I just…know. Besides…"

"What?"

"I know the risks."

His frown deepened. "What the hell is that supposed to mean?"

"It doesn't matter." Damn the tears flooding my eyes again. "I'm sorry about what happened. I'm sure it was really weird last night."

"I didn't say that."

"I get it, okay?" I gritted my teeth. "I already apologized, so let's just forget about it."

"You want me to forget what happened between us?"

"Yeah, I think it would be best." I took a deep breath

and steadied my voice. "I'm going to get dressed. I'll call Roadside Assistance and then I'll leave. You'll never hear from me again. End of story."

"I don't get it," he said. "Why can't you remember what happened last night?"

I groaned. "Can we please be done with this conversation? The only thing I ask of you is that we keep this between us. Promise me you won't tell anyone?"

He clenched and unclenched his fists. "So now you think I'm some sort of a creep who goes around talking up his sexual exploits or something?"

"No, but—"

"Forgive me if I'm being pushy, but I've got a naked woman crying buckets in my house who says she doesn't remember anything about a very intimate encounter that I recall to the last vivid detail."

I blushed, wishing fervently that I could click my heels and disappear from the closet.

"So," he said, "I think I should get some answers."

"You won't believe me." A new flood of tears distorted his image. "And even if you did, you won't like my answer."

"Thanks for the heads-up," he said. "Now, can you please answer the question?"

"Will you leave me alone if I do?"

"Maybe," he said, "*if* you tell me the truth."

The stubborn set of his mouth announced his resolve. This man was no fool. He wasn't a pushover either. I needed to get away. But I also recalled his concerns about someone in his family who wanted to set him up. I didn't understand any of that, but I figured he wasn't going to let me walk away unless I answered his questions and cleared his suspicions.

I more or less mumbled, "I wasn't awake."

His eyes narrowed. "What did you say?"

"I said I wasn't awake, last night, when we did it."

His eyebrows clashed over his nose in the sort of blood-curdling frown I'd never forget. "Are you telling me that you were asleep when we had sex?"

Of course it would sound crazy to him. I wiped the tears from my cheeks and stuck out my chin. "Yes, that's exactly what I'm telling you. I was sleepwalking."

I watched Seth process what I had just said. Disgust? Loathing? Disbelief? My stomach clenched. His gaze fastened on my face with such intensity I had to look away.

"You walk in your sleep," he said flatly. "And you don't remember anything that happens when you're sleepwalking."

"That's the short of it."

"Pardon my French," he said. "But are you shitting me?"

"See?" I threw my hands up in the air. "I knew you wouldn't believe me."

He paced the span of the walk-in closet. "I've heard some morning-after stories, but yours? Man, yours trumps them all."

"It's not a story."

"Maybe I could believe you if I hadn't been there." He stomped back and forth, big bare feet pounding on the carpet. "But you were awake, very awake."

"I told you the truth," I said. "Now leave me alone. What does it matter to you anyway?"

"Oh, it matters to me all right." He halted midstride, planted his feet apart and faced me. "This is all wrong on so many levels. First off, I don't like the idea that you think I'm such a creep I'd want to have sex with someone in their sleep. I'm not oblivious. I would've noticed if you'd been asleep."

"It's not always so easy to tell."

"Explain."

"I'd rather not."

"Explain." He insisted. "I was there last night. I've got a right to know."

God, I really wanted to end this conversation. But he was determined. I wouldn't be able to leave until he made sense of this mess and the stupid tears kept coming, making it hard for me to think clearly. How I hated crying. It was such a wasteful, useless thing to do. I was strong. I could do this.

I took a deep breath and spoke tentatively, trying to keep the quiver from my voice. "I suffer from a sleep disorder that's triggered by certain conditions."

He rumbled. "Go on."

"I'm not crazy or anything like that."

If you say so, his eyes said, but he just nodded. "Okay."

"Fatigue, illness, and stress are all factors that trigger the disorder," I offered cautiously. "I was suffering from some of those last night, plus jet lag."

"How does this…'disorder' work?"

"First, I'm overwhelmed by a sense of exhaustion," I said. "Then I get this headache, right behind my eyes. Sometimes, without warning, I just fall asleep. I go into slow-wave NREM sleep stage and I wander. That's what happened last night."

"But…" He grappled for words. "I saw you. I swear. You were not asleep."

"I might have seemed awake to you," I said. "But believe me, I was asleep and that's why I can't remember."

"Why didn't you warn me?"

Because warnings were dangerous. "I told you to lock the door."

"Bullshit," he said. "If what you're saying is true, you should've warned me."

He was right but he was also very wrong. The last time I'd warned someone about my condition, things hadn't gone very well for me. I gave a little shrug. There was nothing I could say in my defense.

"Fucking unbelievable." He raked his hand through his hair. "I don't even know where to start unraveling this mess."

"There's nothing to unravel," I said. "I'm sorry and I'm leaving. That's the end of it."

He considered me for a long moment, then grabbed a flannel robe hanging from the back of the door and handed it to me.

"I need to think about this," he said. "Take a shower, get dressed. We'll regroup when you're done." He gave me a last probing look and left the closet, closing the door behind him with a quiet *click*.

I buried my face in my hand and let out a torrent of tears. I'd done this to myself. I knew better than to push my limits. But Louise had been so upset, and I'd had to find Tammy…

Get up, Silva.

Get going. I uncoiled from my place in the corner and got to my feet. My joints screeched like rusty hinges. *Ooof.* I felt like an old woman. It was going to be a long day. I hung up the jacket, wedged my arms into the robe's sleeves and knotted the belt at the waist. The robe trailed on the floor behind me as I shuffled to the mirror.

The mirror confirmed that I looked exactly as I felt. My nose glowed like Rudolph the Red Nose Reindeer's. My eyes were bloodshot and my hair stuck up every which way. A bruise blotched my thigh. What a mess. I was ashamed of myself. I didn't know what bothered me the most, that I'd offered my body to a perfect stranger, that he'd taken me up on the offer, or that I didn't remember a thing. All three, I supposed.

I dried my face on the robe's sleeve. It would've been easy to blame Seth for my troubles. Of course, he could've refused me. But I knew better. Louise and Tammy said I looked completely awake when I sleepwalked and he'd had no way of knowing that. Rationally speaking, he was only one of the many elements that came together to precipitate last night's episode. The stress of Tammy's disappearance and the Darius project presentation hadn't helped. Sleep deprivation, jet lag, and the wreck had pushed me over the top. I'd put myself on a deserted Alaska road in those conditions. I'd done this to myself.

I gathered my courage and padded out of the closet into a massive, spa-like bathroom. A pile of fine towels was set out on the counter, along with a brand-new toothbrush, a bottle of over-the-counter painkillers, and a box of Kleenex. Seth was thoughtful, or perhaps he meant to be practical in order to rush me out of his life. Yeah, that had to be it. Get the psycho out of here. I couldn't blame him.

I stepped into the huge shower and turned on the levers. Several different types of showerheads produced luxuriant flows of water. I settled beneath the enormous faucet jutting out from the wall and allowed my tears to flow. Wasting all that water went against my grain, but I was having trouble sorting out my feelings.

I didn't feel violated, exploited, or abused. Except for my dignity, I wasn't harmed, and thank God—and my dermatologist, who'd prescribed birth control to keep my skin clear—I'd been protected. I did feel helpless and vulnerable, humiliated and defeated. I was a failure, an out-of-control freak. I was destined to spend the rest of my life sleeping alone in my locked bedroom, unable to trust anyone or venture beyond my little condo, for fear of being taken advantage of. I was doomed like my mother.

Snap out of it, girl. I couldn't afford to wallow in self-pity. I didn't want to add pathetic to the long list of insults I'd crafted for myself. Forward, I had to move forward. I had to find Tammy, get back to Miami and reclaim my life.

The long shower revived me. The painkillers helped. I wrapped myself in the big, soft towel. I combed my hair, brushed my teeth, and made my way out to the bedroom. The door was closed. The blinds were drawn. The bed was neatly made. My skirt, blouse, and underwear were laid out on the bed. Next to them, I spotted my overnight bag and my laptop.

I almost squealed with relief. The bag meant that my car must be nearby and drivable. I could make a quick escape and never have to meet Seth Erickson's toxic glare again. I looked through my bag. In the absence of time, Louise had packed it for me. My toiletries would come in handy, but the rest? It was all cute and Florida fashionable, but not exactly suitable for Alaska.

My eyes shifted to the small pile of neatly folded garments next to the bag. Socks, silk thermals, a pair of black leggings, and a plaid flannel shirt. They looked a lot better suited to the weather, and warm and comfortable to boot. There was even a pair of hiking shoes on the floor next to the shriveled husks that had once been my high heels. I didn't know where he'd gotten all this from, but he'd thought of everything.

I got dressed. The leggings were a little loose on me but, much to my amazement, everything else fit, including the shoes. I found my cell on top of my purse and scrolled through the texts and emails on my screen. Crap, between my boss and Louise, there must have been two hundred messages waiting for me.

Time to get out of this mess. I gathered my stuff, padded out of the bedroom and turned right at the foyer. Judging from the bedroom suite, I already knew this place was no primitive hut, but my expectations were blown out of the water as the hallway opened into a grand room, an astonishing space that the architect in me relished on the spot.

High beams supported the tall ceiling that gave the room extensive proportions. To my left was a fully stocked, top-of-the-line, modern kitchen designed with a keen eye for beauty and functionality. To my right was a sitting room centered on a sleek, granite fireplace. Ahead of me was a grand living room, flanked on all sides by banks of windows ascending to the ceiling, revealing the huge deck beyond and the most stunning view I'd ever seen.

I stood before the windows, gaping. The storm had passed. The sun illuminated a shimmering landscape of pristine snow and crystalline ice melting into puddles and rivulets. The house perched on a cliff overlooking a pebbled beach, a deep sound, and a massive mountain range. On the south side, the mouth of a river opened up to the bay.

"Beautiful, isn't it?" a voice said from behind me.

I turned around and faced a hunk of a man, a Nordic god, all flaxen and gold, *the* definition of beauty in the flesh. He was the most handsome male specimen I'd ever seen and when he shined his smile on me, it warmed me like the Florida sun.

"Seth always knows how to pick them," he said. "He chose the right spot for this place."

My tongue weighed a ton. Those blue eyes. I couldn't tear my gaze away from his face or muster a single intelligent word out of my mouth.

A door slammed, breaking the trance. Seth turned the corner and stopped to stare at me. His face dropped to the severe scowl he seemed to favor, at least when I was around. He clutched his cell in one hand and seemed to be in a worse mood than before.

"I see you've met my little brother, Jeremy," he said in his acerbic tone. "Go ahead, take your time, gawk some more if you'd like. The entire female race fawns when Jer is near."

I made a point to close my mouth. Nothing much I could do about the blush on my face.

"Kindly ignore my brother, the caveman." Jeremy offered his hand. "He has a tendency to devolve when he's annoyed. You didn't tell me your hitchhiker was a looker, bro."

"Hi." I shook his hand, trying to jump-start my thought process. "I'm Summer."

"Summer in Alaska?" Jeremy's laughter reminded me of Seth's. "You're late!"

"Lay off." Seth busied himself in the kitchen. "She's heard that one before."

He was dressed in a pair of blue jeans and a black, long-sleeve shirt that showcased his broad shoulders and his tapered waist. Beneath the jersey, the muscles in his arms flexed nicely as he operated a fancy espresso machine. He moved about the kitchen with purpose, but he glanced at me every so often, aiming his reproving glare in my direction. Crap. When he looked at me like that, I wanted out of here.

Both brothers were tall, a few inches above six feet, with long legs and strong builds, mountain men, but of the clean-cut kind. Their coloring and shapes were almost identical, but Jeremy's hair fell in curlier waves and his features were softer and refined. In contrast, Seth's hair was straight, his nose was a tad too long, and his features were blunt and defined—kind of like his personality.

Seth slammed a mug on the kitchen counter.

I looked at Jeremy. "Was your brother born a grouch or did a bug crawl up his ass recently?"

Jeremy burst into laughter. "I like her, Seth. You won't be able to bulldoze over her."

"She's no pushover, that's for sure." Seth offered me a steaming mug. "Peace offering?"

I hadn't realized we were at war until that moment. Hell, according to him, we'd gotten along fine last night. I suppressed the twinge of desire that stirred between my legs. My body must've remembered something, because I was suddenly flushing all over and my nipples were poking through my bra with a ferocity that left me breathless. I tried to hide my fluster by plucking the cup out of his hands and taking a long sip.

The robust espresso hit my taste buds, along with the silky flow of scalded milk and lots of sugar, my definition of morning glory. Oh, my God. Had I died and gone to heaven?

"This is pure deliciousness." I savored another gulp of liquid sweetness, relishing the heat. "How did you know that I was a café-con-leche kind of girl?"

"Lucky guess?" he mumbled, but he looked totally guilty of something.

He gestured to a padded chair.

"Oh, no, can't stay, no way," I stuttered. "Sun's out, storm's done, got to find Tammy."

"Sit," he commanded, all traces of courtesy gone.

My temper flared. "I'm not a dog, you know."

"Summer?" Jeremy patted the couch next to him. "Why don't you please sit down and finish your coffee? Seth's manners leave a lot to be desired when he's in a mood, but he wants to have a little chat with you."

My fingers tightened around the mug. God help me. Seth wouldn't be so crude as to bring up last night in front of his brother, would he?

"But…"

"It's about the car," Seth said.

A wave of relief washed over me. I settled down on the couch. "Okay, but let's be quick."

Seth sat on a chair across from me. His long, strong legs folded at either side of him in a swift, efficient motion that stretched his jeans over a pair of impressively defined thighs. My gaze drifted to the space between his legs. I caught myself trying to remember what the bulk trapped there looked and felt like. *Jesus, Silva, eyes up.* Bad move. When I snapped my head up, his stare met mine with an almost magical intensity. An intimate, pervasive frisson swept up my spine, prickled the hairs on my limbs, and warmed my lower belly.

Rats. What was happening here?

Like the moisture dampening my panties, the words just trickled out of my lips. "I really do need to get going." Fast. The fastest, the better.

"And how exactly do you propose to get going without a car?" Seth said.

I frowned. "I thought the car was here."

"Well, you were wrong. It isn't."

"Jesus, Seth," Jeremy said. "How come you sound like the big bad wolf all the time?"

"The big bad wolf?" I started to laugh, because the mental image fit exactly, but my giggles wilted under the heat of Seth's terrible glare. "You have to admit, your brother might be right, you do bark a lot, at least half of the time…"

"Let's get this over with." Seth jerked his chin at his brother.

"What Seth meant to say," Jeremy clarified, "is that your car is too badly damaged for you to drive. That was quite a wreck you got into. It's a wonder you didn't break something."

"You went out there?" I said. "You found the car in the ravine?"

"Seth called me last night and asked me to go first thing in the morning," Jeremy explained. "So once the storm was over, I drove out there, got your stuff, called the rental company and had the car towed."

"Oh, wow." I was used to fixing other people's problems, not the other way around. "I really appreciate you doing all of that for me. I'll need to rent another car. Is there any chance you could give me a ride to the nearest town?"

Seth grumbled. "I don't think anyone around here will want to rent you another car for a while."

"Why not?"

"You've got no business driving on ice," he said. "Plus, you've got another, more serious problem."

"Which is?"

"You didn't end up in a ravine by accident."

"What?" I looked from one man to the other. "I don't understand."

"What Seth is trying to say," Jeremy said, "is that mechanical reasons caused the wreck."

"Really?" I set my mug down on the coffee table. "What kind of mechanical reasons?"

"Let's see." Jeremy tapped his fingers on his thigh. "What's the best way to explain this to you?"

"Oh, for Christ's fucking sake," Seth snapped. "Stop tiptoeing around her. She can take it." He clobbered me with his eyes. "Somebody fucked with your brakes."

I stared at him, unable to understand. "What did you say?"

"Somebody tried to make a colander out of your brake lines," he said. "The same son of a bitch who tried to kill you."

FOUR

I COULDN'T PEEL my eyes away from Seth. My taut nerves strained like rubber bands about to snap. He looked totally serious. Not a hint of humor in his gaze. Still, I had to ask.

"Are you guys messing with me?"

Jeremy shook his head.

"It's no joke," Seth said, his face set on grim. "Somebody tried to kill you."

"No way," I said. "That's absurd. Maybe it was an accident. Brakes fail all the time. Maybe the lines were old?"

"Nope." Seth leaned over and showed me the screen on his cell. "Take a look. The rental company said the car was almost new and the lines show small, clear punctures evenly spaced, made with a sharp object."

I looked at the pictures of my rental's brake lines. He was right. Those holes were man-made, even I could tell. My belly went cold.

"I don't get it," I said. "Why would somebody want to kill me?"

"You tell us," Seth said. "Is there anyone in your life that would benefit from you dying in a car accident?"

"No," I said. "Nobody."

"Think about it," Jeremy said. "Do you have a life insurance policy? Is there an inheritance? A large bank account? A property that someone else wants?"

"That's a 'no' four times in a row," I said. "The only thing I own is a lot of student debt."

"How about a grudge?" Seth said. "Have you had problems with anyone? Has anyone threatened you or tried to harm you, maybe your ex?"

I narrowed my eyes on him. "How do you know I have an ex?"

"I made an assumption."

"I get along with people fine," I said. "And if you absolutely have to know, I haven't talked to my ex in a long time. He lives overseas and wouldn't dare mess with me. I made sure of that."

"Okay," Seth said skeptically. "What about your stepmother or your sister? Do they have any reason to want you dead?"

"Of course not!" I dug my nails in my palms. "We're family. Get it? FA-MI-LY. We love each other. We help each other. How could you even suggest such a horrible thing?"

"Sometimes families don't get along."

"Just because your family sucks doesn't mean that mine does."

"She may have a point there," Jeremy put in.

"This is not about me or my family," Seth said in a strained tone. "You need to set your emotions aside."

I shot him an icy glare. "Sure, I'll do that, as soon as you stop being a condescending prick."

"Jesus, woman." He swore under his breath. "I'm trying here."

"Then try harder," I said. "I don't do well with people who talk down to me."

Seth's face flooded with crimson. "I wasn't—"

"Hey, kids?" Jeremy interrupted. "Let's keep it cool.

Okay? Summer, Seth just wants you to look at the situation objectively."

"I am looking at the situation objectively!" I said. "Louise and Tammy would never harm me. Never. Period. End of story."

"If you say so," Seth muttered.

"I do say so!"

"Easy now," Jeremy said. "No need to get upset."

I took in a calming breath. Seth had a nasty way of making my temper flare. Not that it was so difficult to make me mad. I blamed my Latin blood for my bluster. But that man…he was an agitator to my emotions. He brought out the worst in me. The most difficult part? I couldn't really think straight around him.

I was pretty sure he emitted some kind of electrical signal that disrupted my thoughts. I hated to admit it, but I liked the way he systematically looked at a problem, like an engineer. Or an architect. Unfortunately, the problem at hand was me.

To top it all, the spectrum of what had happened between us last night taunted me in a very physical way. I couldn't help but wonder: How had his nice, firm, sexy body felt between my arms? Had I liked him? Had he liked me?

Get a hold of yourself. I pressed my legs together. I couldn't believe it. Me, Summer Silva, daydreaming in the middle of a nightmare, salivating after a total stranger while sitting in his living room having a discussion about…what else? Murder, possibly mine.

I pressed the delete button in my mind. I wasn't going to let my thoughts wander again. Whatever happened last night, it was over, done, *finito.* And no matter how hard he tried, he wasn't going to convince me that my family was a danger to me. No freaking way.

"I can guarantee that this is not about me," I said. "For sure. You've got to believe me."

"Maybe it was a crime of opportunity," Jeremy said.

"Stealing a purse in the street is a crime of opportunity," Seth said. "Puncturing someone's brake lines? That's premeditated murder." He considered me closely. "It took you what? Three hours to drive up here from Anchorage? So, the lines were cut after you left the rental lot. Otherwise, you would've lost your brakes sooner. When was the last time you stopped and lost sight of the car?"

I had to think about that. "I used the restroom at a rest stop before I turned off the interstate."

"Then that's where it happened," Seth said. "That's where the investigation begins."

"Wait," I said. "What investigation?"

"The police are investigating," Seth said, "and I've asked our security people to take a look as well."

"You have security people?" God almighty. "Of course you would. No, hey, no." I lifted a hand in the air. "Don't even try to explain. Your family's mega business, right? Never mind. This is all ridiculous. Sorry, guys, but this has to be some sort of a mix-up. Maybe someone confused my car for someone else's?"

"It's a possibility," Jeremy said. "Gangs? Mistaken identity? Drug trafficker spat?"

"Like it or not, the police want to talk to you," Seth said.

"Fine, I'll talk to the police," I said. "But I'm telling you right now that this is much to-do about nothing. Right now, I'm going to go find my sister, before my stepmother goes nuclear. I have twenty-nine missed calls and seventy-two texts from her just in the last hour."

"Jesus," Jeremy said. "Seth did say your family was a little off."

I shot Seth a cutting glance. "Sounds like the pot calling the kettle black."

Jeremy laughed. "Feisty."

Seth rolled his eyes. "No kidding."

"Hey," I said. "I'm sitting right here."

"You call it like you see it, every time," Seth said. "Annoying, maybe, but nothing too terribly wrong with that. Don't look at me like that. I just gave you a compliment."

"Has anyone told you that you suck at giving compliments?"

Jeremy grinned. "That's so true."

"Who the hell made you judge and executioner?" Seth took a deep breath and aimed his yellow glower in my direction. "Where's this sister of yours, anyway?"

I flipped my hair and stuck out my chin. "What is it to you?"

His ears flushed so red I feared the top of his head might blow up. "Just tell me, please?"

"Maybe we can help," Jeremy suggested.

Well, I supposed that at this stage in the game, a little help couldn't hurt.

"Let's see." I scrolled through my messages and found the information I'd copied from Tammy's computer. "I went to the police first, but they said that Tammy didn't meet their criteria as a missing person. So, I went to this guy's address in Anchorage next, but the neighbors told me he was at his family's cabin somewhere up here. His name is…Nikolai Golov."

"Golov?" Seth's eyebrows knotted over his nose. "We know the Golovs quite well."

"Really?" Awesome news.

"I went to school with Nikolai," Jeremy said. "He's worked for us out on the Dalton. He's a jack-of-all-trades, decent sort of fellow. Didn't make him for an internet stalker."

"Do you know where his family lives?"

"The roads are a mess," Jeremy said, "but I'll be happy to drive you out there."

"No need," Seth cut in. "I'll take her."

Jeremy's eyes widened in surprise. "Are you sure?"

"Sure as shit," Seth said. "Don't you have some construction projects to manage or something?"

"Don't you have to negotiate a contract with the governor *and* a board meeting coming up?" Jeremy countered. "I thought you couldn't afford to waste your time babysitting."

I glared from one man to the other. "I don't need a babysitter."

"I said I'd drive her and I will." Seth's tone forbade further discussion.

"Okay, bro," Jeremy said, "but don't underestimate Alex."

"I won't." Seth snatched his keys from the counter. "Want to help me load the truck?"

"Sure." Jeremy got up.

"Can I help?" I said.

"You'd be no help at all, so stand down," Seth said. "Eat something. There's food in the pantry. Come down in twenty."

I thanked Jeremy for his help and watched the brothers go. Talk about contrasting personalities, Mr. Charm and Mr. Grouch. My stomach grumbled, so I checked out the refrigerator. Other than a jug of milk and a carton of orange juice, it was empty. A quick look at the freezer revealed more desolation. I closed the freezer door and opted for the box of high-protein cereal I found in the bleak pantry. It tasted like dirt, but it was food.

I tackled my messages on the cell. My boss, Hector Carrera, answered as soon as I replied to his frantic texts.

Where are you?

AK, I wrote back. Searching.

Tammy?

Nothing yet.

Need you back ASAP, he texted. Need third floor redesign for Darius.

Email new specs, I wrote. Will email redesign by tonight. You won't even know I'm gone. GTG.

I ended the text exchange before we got testy with each other. Hector had given me such a hard time about leaving for Alaska. I couldn't understand why he was so upset about me taking a few days off. First off, he knew I was a hard worker. The project was going to get done and on time. My work record spoke for itself. Nobody worked as hard as I did. Nobody.

Second, I had the time off on the books. I should be able to take it if I needed to. I'd kind of told him that.

He hadn't liked it at all. Third, Hector had been my dad's business partner. He knew Tammy and Louise really well. He knew all about our family and that I took care of them.

On the other hand, I couldn't take my job for granted. I needed it to make ends meet and help Louise and Tammy with their bills. Plus, deep down, I hated to disappoint Hector. He'd always been there for my dad and, after his death, he'd been there for my family as well. He'd given me a job when I graduated in the middle of a recession and no one was hiring. I owed him my hard work and tons of gratitude. I decided on the spot to work late tonight and blow his mind with a kickass redesign. Meanwhile, I had to find Tammy and get the hell out of Alaska.

My mind drifted back to Seth Erickson. Yes, I was leaving, but still, I was really curious about him. *Don't do it, Silva.*

Don't bother. I considered the cell in my hand. Oh, what the hell. I googled him. Everybody did it these days. Right?

His business bio came up. CEO of Erickson & Erickson Enterprises, the largest family conglomerate in Alaska. The company was valued in…the billions? I had to close my mouth. Lots of pictures of him with presidents, governors, senators, rig workers, construction workers. Impressive.

I did a little bit more internet sleuthing. Not an iota of personal information, no social media presence, nothing. Either he had no personal life, a possibility considering his sustained level of irritability, or he'd devoted some serious resources to protecting his privacy. A cleanup job, maybe?

Oh, well. What did I care anyway? I was out of his life today. I drank the milk out of the cereal bowl, tucked the dish and spoon in the dishwasher, grabbed my purse, bag, and laptop, and made my way down the stairs. Good-bye high-tech cabin. Farewell amazing views. Sayonara hunky stranger and associated, assorted complications. First order of business: find Tammy. Get her to Anchorage. Go back home. Second order of business: keep my job. Finish the Darius project. Forget that Alaska had ever happened to me.

That was the plan and I intended to stick to it because Seth was way out of bounds and I was not on the market. Besides, I couldn't bear the thought of spending one more second than was absolutely necessary exposed to his radioactive glare.

FIVE

By the time I heard the door open upstairs, Jer had left, the snow machine was loaded on the truck, and I'd talked to my assistant and rescheduled all of my video-conferences for later in the day. I was stuck in a piss-poor mood. In the last forty-eight hours, I'd gone from the low of Danny's death, to the highpoint of my extraordinary night with Summer, to the pits of the worst morning-after that two people could have.

It served me right for giving in to an impulse, for detouring from logic and reality. Wishful thinking was for idiots. Who the hell would want to be with me anyways? It wasn't only the scars. It was the shit going on in my head. Last night I had stepped into an alternative reality. Now I was back and ready to deploy my brain instead of my dick.

I cinched the truck bed's straps and took a deep breath, trying to calm the acid roiling in my stomach. I thought about the security camera footage I'd reviewed this morning. It showed a grainy, black-and-white rendition of the stunning woman lying on my dining table and the balance of our encounter. I looked for clues, but other than that ethereal, translucent look in her eyes, I couldn't find anything that should have suggested to me that she'd been sleepwalking.

The footage was proof of consent, but it also showed that I wasn't completely clueless. Summer had wanted me as much as I had wanted her. My imagination hadn't manufactured last night and, whether she remembered it or not, something had happened between us. Something in addition to the sex.

She wasn't part of Alex's plan. She couldn't be. Her attitude wasn't consistent with deception. The additional call I'd placed this morning backed up my gut feeling with facts. I hadn't met too many women in my life who'd pass up the opportunity to exploit a situation like this one. Not Summer. So far, she didn't seem to be about the money, or about power or control.

Then there was the murder attempt. In my fucking backyard, no less. The state troopers and Spider were on the trail, but there was nothing in her background that suggested this kind of trouble. Maybe she was right and it was a mistake or a random act of violence. Who the hell would want to kill Summer?

Well, it wasn't going to happen, not while I was around. As to the rest, my mind was a one-way street. Summer might not remember what happened last night, but I did. How a single night with a stranger had turned me into the horniest son of a bitch in Alaska, I couldn't begin to explain. But I had to face the music. My body buzzed when she was near. Hell, I was getting hard just thinking about her.

I cranked up the winch one last time, visualizing a plunge in a glacial lake, willing my blood to flow elsewhere. I wondered if this is how moose bulls felt during the rut. I wanted more of what I'd had last night, more of her. If she remembered, she'd want more too. I made up my mind. If I had to go to extremes to flush out the truth—and jostle her memories—then I would.

"Helloooo?" Summer's voice came from the top of the stairs.

Showtime.

"Ahoy, down there." She inched down the steps. "Please don't shoot. I come in peace. If I had a white flag I'd wave it, but I didn't pack one and I bet hell would have to freeze over before you ever owned one of those. Permission to come below?"

My lips twitched. I waved her down. "Permission granted."

She stepped down the last of the stairs, taking in my garage as if she'd never seen one like it, which was probably true, considering that I'd designed the house around the garage and I was damn proud of it. She checked out the bikes, ATVs and motorcycles parked on the heated concrete floors.

"Do you play every sport known to man?" She studied the gear organized on the shelves, equipment for kayaking, fishing, hiking, ice climbing, skiing, you name it—it was there. "Are there any toys missing from your collection?"

"Since you asked," I said, "the planes and the helicopters, we keep at the hangars."

"The hangars, eh?" She giggled under her breath—*do-re-mi-fa*—a delicate, distinctive singsong laugh that ended on a suspended note, the kind of sound a guy could get used to having around. "You talk as if everyone owns hangars in Alaska."

"Many do. Alaska is a big state and we don't have that many roads." I took the bags from her hand. "Why are you bringing these?"

"I'm hoping to go home today."

Not if I had anything to do with it.

"You're in a big rush," I said, stowing her bags in the backseat. "Do you hate Alaska that much?"

"It's not my natural habitat, that's for sure." She rubbed the back of her thigh, where I had intimate knowledge of the bruise that marred her superbly constructed body. "Ice and gravity make for a brutal combination. But truth be known, I don't want to get fired. Some of us have to work for our tiny, puny, human garages."

I found myself laughing, something I didn't do very often these days. Her mouth turned up in a crooked smile. Considering her earlier tears, the smile felt like a huge accomplishment.

"Wow." She studied the garage, taking in the ceiling beams, the massive hydraulic columns, and the springs-with-dampers base isolators. "This is a seismic support system on steroids. Who designed this incredible house?"

My chest may have puffed a little. "I did."

"I thought you were some sort of a businessperson."

"Me? No," I said. "I spend a lot more time with financial reports these days, but I'm an engineer by training and I like to tinker. This is my version of an experiment."

Her eyes followed the beams. "Clever, innovative, and probably very pricey." Her hands caressed the pylons with an appreciation that made me jealous. "Do you think it'll work?"

"We'll see when the big one hits."

She flashed me another smile and, judging by the way my dick yanked on my groin, I had to wonder if the big one hadn't already hit.

I opened the door of the truck for her. "Let's get going."

She stopped before she climbed on the cab and met my eyes. "Why are you doing this?"

"What?"

"Driving me out there," she said. "Helping me find my sister."

I had a long list of reasons and the need to anticipate Alex was still at the top. Other reasons were plain and selfish. But sex wasn't the only answer and some of my other reasons were not easy to explain. In fact, I wasn't even sure I understood them exactly. Maybe I wanted to make it up to her, just in case she wasn't a plant, for being clueless, for being a jerk. Perhaps, I wanted to show her Alaska, to share with her the beauty of the wild land where I made my home. For sure, I needed her trust to achieve my objectives. But maybe, just maybe, I wanted to help her because I liked what I'd seen from Summer Silva so far and I wanted to know more about her.

"I don't mind helping out every once in a while," I said instead. "Now get in. There's weather coming in later today, and I've got to get back to work as soon as possible."

I'd already installed the front snowplow on the truck so, as I drove out of the garage, I scraped the way along the driveway, through the automated gates and across the bridge.

Summer craned her neck and looked back. "Do you live on an island?"

"The property is surrounded by the sound and the river, that's true."

"Looks like a pretty big island." She glanced at me. "You live alone there?"

"I like my privacy."

Those eyes. They were analyzing me, drawing conclusions about me, knocking at my door in a way that fired my blood. I was usually the one doing the analyzing, but if I had to put up with her curiosity to satisfy mine, then I was game.

The roads were a mess of mud, snow, and ice, but the F-450 plowed through the stuff like an elephant stomping on ants. Summer looked nervous riding next to me, fingers tight around the door handle, feet pressing on imaginary pedals. I had to suppress a smile. She was the original backseat driver.

"Why did you become an engineer?" she asked as I drove.

It was a pretty neutral question, one I could answer.

"Engineering is the science of problem-solving," I said. "My father wanted problem solvers, not spoiled brats. I went to MIT, Jer graduated from Caltech and Ally went to Stanford."

"Who's Ally?"

"Ally's my little sister," I said. "She just got married last year. She lives in Anchorage. You're wearing her clothes."

"Oh." She looked down on herself. "I'll have to send her a thank you note or something. I'm lucky she's got good taste. So your family owns a construction firm?"

She was fishing for additional information. I wasn't much of a talker, but I was a damn good fisherman. I knew to let the reel out before bringing in the catch.

"My family owned a construction firm back in the seventies when my dad and his brother first founded the company," I said. "Now we're a highly diversified conglomerate: energy, fisheries, forestry, mining, infrastructure. But enough of the boring stuff. Let's talk about you."

"What about me?"

"Sleepwalking?"

"Oh." Her shoulders slumped. "Do we have to talk about that?"

"I'd like to."

"Maybe we could pretend it didn't happen at all?"

"I don't want to forget or pretend."

"Ooof." She sounded like a deflating balloon. "Look, I take full responsibility. I don't mean to make excuses for myself, but I didn't choose the disorder. It chose me."

"I understand that somnambulism runs in families." I ventured out into the open. "Something about genetic predisposition?"

"How do you know?" She glanced at me then returned her eyes to the road. "Most people don't know anything about it."

"I looked it up."

Her green eyes lit up on me. "Just now?"

"Yep," I said. "This morning, after you told me about it."

"You're fast."

"I'm a problem solver," I said. "I needed to know."

"Why?" she asked.

"You're a nosy little witch."

She rolled her eyes at me. "Says the problem solver who needs to know."

"Look," I said. "I might be oblivious sometimes, but stuff does matter to me. The idea that I couldn't tell you weren't awake last night bothers the hell out of me."

"Interesting," she said. "Maybe there's a decent human being beneath all that bluster."

For the third time in a row, she smiled at me. I'd hit a lucky streak. Her eyes sparkled like landing lights. Her expression reminded me of the way she'd looked at me after we'd both come last night. I glanced at my lap. *Down boy.* Pity her approval wasn't going to last.

"Hang on to the concept of me being a decent human being if you will." I turned right at the crossroads. "You're going to need it, because I looked you up real good."

"You looked me up how?" She opened her mouth and closed it. "Wait. You thought I was a trap. You said you had security people. You knew about my ex. You even knew I liked café-con-leche in the mornings. Oh, my God." She figured it out all on her own. "You had me investigated?"

I lifted a noncommittal shoulder.

"But…" She grappled with the notion. "Why?"

"I needed to know who you really were." I monitored her reaction. "Don't look so goddamn sanctimonious. I bet you looked me up too. Come on, at the very least, you googled my name."

Capillary meltdown. Instant confession. She flushed so red I feared her face might ignite. Lying? Not possible for Summer. She just wasn't wired for it.

"Look, I don't blame you," I said. "In fact, I think snooping is a sign of brainpower."

"I bet." She eyed me sullenly. "You probably think you're a genius, especially given that you know intimate details about my life, whereas googling you gave me the company line and squat about who you truly are."

"A man in my position…"

She groaned. "Stop it, will you? I don't want anything from you, so spare me the paranoia."

"I'm just trying to understand your sleeping disorder."

"Very grand of you," she said. "Leave it alone."

"I don't want to leave it alone, which may explain why I called Dr. Sanchez and asked her about it."

Her hands fisted on her lap. "You called Dr. Sanchez? *My* Dr. Sanchez?"

I felt like a fucking scumbag, but what else could I do?

She grappled for words. "I… You… How did you even know about Dr. Sanchez?"

"I looked through your cell," I said. "I found her name in your contacts along with the number for the Coral Gables Sleep Disorder Center."

She was speechless, blown out of the water and not in a good way. If she couldn't get past this part, what were my chances she'd get over the rest?

"You looked through my cell?" She gaped. "You called *my* doctor without asking me?"

"Hear me out, before you bite my head off," I said. "I needed to know that everything you said was true. You must admit, your story wasn't exactly probable. I also needed to know that you were going to be okay."

Her brows clashed above her nose. She tossed the hair away from her face with an angry flick and stuck out her chin. "Sure, now you're all about my well-being. What about your crazy accusations about me working for someone else? Did those have anything to do with your 'investigation'?"

She was sharp, mad, and right on, so I opted for the fifth.

"What about my privacy?" she said. "What about patient-doctor confidentiality?"

True to myself, it was truth over manners. "When it comes to your privacy, last night pretty much took care of it. I've seen parts of you, you'll never get to see."

"Stop!" She slapped her hands over her ears. "Too much information."

"As to Dr. Sanchez," I continued, "she didn't confirm or deny that you're her patient. Once I set up my telephone consultation, your name never came up again. She simply listened to what I had to say and answered my questions strictly from a theoretical point of view."

"Theoretical my ass!" she snapped. "I might have a rare sleep disorder, but you suffer from a severe personality disorder."

"Try not to get upset."

"How on earth could I not be upset?" Her green eyes blazed. "You think I'm out to get you somehow. You called my doctor without asking me. And before that, you had sex with me while I slept!"

"Fuck." That last point really bothered me. "Now, see, that's why I had to call the good doctor, because you didn't look like you were sleepwalking. You were totally present during our…err…activities."

"Activities?" She gasped. "You mean we did it more than one time?"

"We did," I said. "Several times."

"Holy shit." She buried her face in her hands.

I should've kept that detail to myself.

"I wonder," I said tentatively. "Would it help you remember if I tell you what happened?"

"No!"

"The doctor said that, sometimes, people who are exposed to footage of their sleepwalking activities remember things."

"Pictures?" She stared at me, horrified. "You didn't, did you?"

"Of course not." The security footage didn't count as a sex tape; did it?

"Okay, good." She settled her hand on her chest and forced herself to take in little breaths.

"But I still need you to remember."

"Why?"

"Because…" It bothered the hell out of me that I'd had the most spectacular night of my life and she didn't even know about it. "You need to understand. You acted lucid. You wandered all over the house. You drank a pot of soup."

"Really?" she said. "I don't think I've done that before."

"The doctor told me that each sleepwalking episode is different," I said. "She also said that in some cases, the sleepwalking behavior evolves into more complex activities, working, traveling, and doing all kinds of stuff while sleepwalking. Last night, you told me you were hungry."

"I talked?"

"Of course you talked," I said. "You carried on entire conversations."

Her forehead wrinkled in thought. She gnawed on her lips. The gesture reminded me of her mouth on my dick. My body remembered every detail even if she didn't. I got hard on the spot. Dammit.

"I don't think I've ever talked in my sleep before,"

she said. "Tammy and Louise say I'm quiet as the dead. It freaks them out."

"You were a regular chatterbox when you were with me."

"What did I say?"

"Lots of things." I took the ramp off the highway and turned onto a country road. "You talked about my aura."

"Your aura?" She scoffed. "I don't believe in that nonsense."

"Apparently you do, at least when you're asleep."

"No way."

"Yes way," I said. "You said my aura was a good one."

"I did?"

"Something about a solar flare?"

She shrugged and shook her head. "Zero, nada."

I was getting nowhere fast. "The doctor also said that some people show signs of enhanced sensorial perception during sleepwalking episodes. You were very—what's the word the doctor used?—empathic. It was as if you were plugged directly into my emotions."

She gave me a ribbing glance. "So you've got other emotions besides paranoia, perpetual wrath, and inappropriate curiosity?"

"Ha," I said. "Very funny."

"Good to know." She allowed herself a crooked little smile then sobered up. "How was I plugged into your emotions?"

I didn't really want to talk about my shit. But Summer, something about her, she made me feel like maybe I could. Besides, I needed to establish a baseline with her. I had to give something—or at least make an effort—to get something in return.

"First off," I said, "you didn't mind my scars."

"Why should I've minded your scars?"

"People don't like to look at stuff like that."

"Scars are just that, scars," Summer said. "My dad had several scars from his fight with cancer. I didn't think they were ugly. They were just part of his body's history."

Now there was a novel concept I could dig.

"Your scars show that you have amazing healing abilities," she said. "I mean, don't get me wrong, it's hard to think about what you went through when you got those, but you survived and you're a good-looking guy any day, with or without scars."

Her heightened sense of empathy extended to her waking hours. Plus, she thought I was good looking. Or was she playing me like a goddamn fiddle? I spotted nothing but sincerity in her eyes.

The road came to an end. The pavement turned into a gravel road covered with snow, mud, and potholes the size of lunar craters. I slowed down and, edging the worst of them, drove forward.

"What else did I say last night?" she asked.

"You said something along the lines of me being sad."

"Oh." She took that in. "And were you?"

"You ask a lot of questions."

"Look who's talking."

It took all I had to push the words out. "I lost a good friend of mine yesterday. His name was Danny. He shot himself."

"I'm sorry." She reached over and gave my arm a little squeeze. "Are you okay?"

"Fine," I said. "He was the one who died."

Her touch zapped through my arm and jolted me to the core. Up and down, my cock was beginning to feel like a busy drawbridge. I found myself regretting that her touch had been so brief. The sympathy in her eyes fucked with my head. I swallowed a dry gulp.

"Were you guys close?" she asked.

"We flew many missions together."

She cocked her eyebrows. "Flew?"

"Helicopters," I said. "Alaska Air National Guard."

"Oh, so on top of everything else, you're a pilot for the National Guard?"

"I was."

"You don't fly anymore?"

"Of course I do, fly, helicopters, I mean." Damn those probing eyes. "I'm just not actively flying for the Guard at the moment."

"Is that how you got hurt?" she said. "In a helicopter crash?"

"We're getting off topic here," I said. "The point I was trying to make was that last night you were fully interactive. There was a connection there."

"A connection?"

Time to swing the bat.

"The thing is, Summer, you intrigue me."

Her nose wrinkled. "Intrigue you?"

"I'd like to get to know you better."

"What?" Her eyes widened and, for a full ten seconds, she stared at me, incredulity written all over her face. Then her expression transformed. Gone was the shock, in was a straight-lipped glare, a gesture of pure and absolute defiance. "No, uh-uh." She poked her finger in the air. "You need to know: Regardless of what happened last night, I don't sleep with strangers, awake or asleep."

"Okay, fine," I said. "I promise I won't ask you to sleep with me. Instead, I'll wait until you ask me."

The blistering look she gave me was strike one. "I would never ask you!"

She had a way of daring me without even knowing it. "Never say never."

"Seth Erickson, you better wipe the smirk off your face right now." She huffed. "What happened last night was an accident, nothing else. Just because you own half of Alaska, doesn't mean I'm going to do what you want. I don't care if you think you're God's gift to women."

I counted her strong reaction as strike two. I don't know why, but her calling last night an "accident" raised my hackles.

"It's not all in my head." I charged full steam ahead. "There was an attraction last night, and lots of chemistry. I don't think we were done."

"Not done?" She gawked. "Are you always this blunt?"

"Yep."

The green eyes scoured my face. "Why would a guy like you ever want to hang out with someone like me?"

I shrugged. "Maybe I find you interesting."

"Or easy."

This was not going well. "Look, could we maybe just start again from scratch?"

"Start what?" she said.

"This." I motioned between us. "You and I. We."

"We?" If looks could pierce, I'd be full of holes. "I don't get you. Is this your idea of…what? Asking me out or something?"

"I'm good with that, if that's how you'd like to call it."

"Are you off your freaking rocker?" She stared at me.

"Is it such a bad idea?"

"It's a terrible idea and you know it!"

"Why?"

"I'm from the other side of the world," she said. "I'm tropical, you're arctic. I'm a surly witch and you're grouchy as hell. I suffer from a very inconvenient disorder that makes dating very hard. In fact, I'm not interested in dating at all. The only thing that stands between me and disaster every night is a sturdy door chain."

"Is that what you do at home?"

"Yeah, but that's neither here nor there," she said. "You and I? We've got nothing in common."

"Except a really great first night together."

"Which I don't remember," she said pointedly. "Forget it. This discussion is over. Besides, I don't date men with prickly beards."

I knuckled my stubble. "Technically, this is more like benign neglect than a beard."

"I don't date men with facial hair or whatever you want to call that stuff on your face."

"You're making this up."

"I don't date trust fund babies either," she said. "No, sir. I'm real firm on that rule. I'm pretty sure you're one of them."

"One of who?"

"Boys with trust funds," she said. "Men with tons of money who think they can buy women. Nobody owns me, that's for sure."

Ah. She was talking from experience. I remembered what Spider had said about her early marriage to a wealthy Miami socialite. It had lasted less than a year. I suspected things had gone really wrong for her in that relationship. Had it tainted her views on all men?

"Do you want to talk about him?" I said.

"Him?"

"Sergio De Havilland," I said. "Your ex?"

She glared at me. "How do you know his name?"

"I looked you up. Remember? I looked him up too."

"Back off," she said. "You are really testing my boundaries here."

"Was marriage that bad?"

"I'll never, ever make that mistake again," she said. "But I don't want to talk about him. You will not mention that name in my presence ever again, understood?"

"Yes, ma'am." I saluted, half-heartedly. How was that for a strong reaction? "No more mention of the son of a bitch. Just out of curiosity, how many guys have you dated since your ex?"

"None of your business!"

"I'm going to go out on a limb and say the number is close to zero."

"Excuse me?"

"Why, with all those rules," I said, "the statistical probabilities severely restrict the number of likely candidates."

"What are you talking about?"

"Mathematics," I said. "Given all your rules, the odds of you finding an agreeable candidate are very low, which is why I can guess—with a respectable margin of error—that you haven't been dating much."

She huffed prettily. "Seth Erickson, you're way out of line. Who gave you the authority to commentate on my life?"

"The way I see it, I'm already involved in your life," I said. "We've slept together. I'm in."

"Stop." She lifted a finger in the air. "As soon as I find my sister, I'm going back to Miami and that's that."

She was stubborn all right, but I was fascinated with her and more motivated than ever to stick to my plan. Challenges didn't faze me—on the contrary, they energized me—and Summer was a challenge in every sense of the word. It was a done deal in my mind. Before this was all over, I was going to seduce her all the way back to my bed.

I made a turn at the next crossroads. The road was barely visible under a layer of snow. The forest shaded the road and the snow hadn't melted much. I lowered the snowplow and worked my way up the hill. The truck could only take us so far in these remote parts.

I spotted the question on her face before she gathered the courage to ask it. "Go ahead, ask." I changed gears and tackled the steeper terrain. "I'll be honest."

She gave me a crooked little smile. "No offense, but that's what I'm afraid of."

I laughed. The more we talked, the more I liked her. "I admit that in my case, honesty is more of a vice than a virtue. What is it you want to know?"

The little line that wrinkled her forehead announced her inner struggle. She wasn't sure she wanted to trust me with anything, including the question clearly boggling her mind. She stole another look at me, took a deep breath, and lowered her voice. "Did I like it?"

The question got my heart pumping. "You gave every indication you did."

She let out a sigh and then cautiously forced the words out. "Did *you* like it?"

My pride and my sense of self-preservation reared up. So did my dick. Putting all my eggs into this basket sounded like the most dangerous proposition yet since coming back from Afghanistan. A sleepwalker. Hell. It was odd as hell. A possible plant with all the dangers that entailed. But those eyes. They were capable of wrecking even the most thorough risk assessment matrix.

"I did like it," I said. "I liked *you* very much indeed."

The breath caught in her throat. Her face flushed and her eyes darted away from mine, but not before I caught a gleam of what…satisfaction? The emotions I spotted in her eyes brought back memories she would've found completely inappropriate.

The top of the hill confirmed that it would be impossible to tackle the last part of the way in the truck. I cleared a spot on the side of the road and parked. I turned off the ignition, reached to the backseat and handed her snow pants, a jacket, a beanie, and a pair of gloves.

"You'll need these."

I reached for my snow pants and, unzipping the ends, maneuvered around the wheel, pulled them over my boots, lifted my hips off the seat and buckled them on. "When did you start sleepwalking?"

"When my mom died." She zipped up her coat. "She walked to the ocean in her sleep and drowned. I was twelve."

Tough break. "Do you remember the first time it happened to you?"

"How could I not?"

"Well?"

She hesitated. She really did have a trust issue going

on, but hey, so did I, so I couldn't blame her. The struggle on her expressive face was easy to read. I could almost hear her mind working, trying to figure out if she wanted to tell me and how much.

"I woke up eighteen miles away from home," she said, "at the cemetery, on my mom's tomb, drenched from the rain, with my bare feet all cut up. I had no memories of how I'd gotten there."

Jesus.

She squeezed the bridge of her nose. "I have no idea why I just told you that."

"Because I asked you." No way but forward. "What about sex? Had you ever had sex in your sleep before?"

I could see the blood flushing through her face's capillaries.

"That's a rude question."

"In that case, you don't have to answer it." I'd just hit her wall.

I opened the door, but before I could climb out of the cab, she reached over and put her hand on mine, a touch that rattled my body and rerouted my circulation.

"It's okay." I laid my hand over hers and willed my heart to slow down. "You can tell me."

"Once." She swallowed with an audible gulp. "It happened once before, only once."

That's why she'd been so upset. That's why she'd warned me to lock the door before she passed out in the truck. That's why she hadn't told me about her condition, because something similar had happened to her while she sleepwalked way before we met and her experience had marked her.

I knew exactly when it happened. When she was nineteen, when she married the son of a bitch. The sadness I spotted in her green eyes sparked my protective instincts. Had she been hurt?

Nobody was ever going to hurt Summer again, not while I was around. Nobody. The short marriage had puzzled me from the beginning, but with her admission, her character came through loud and clear. The last time she'd had sex while walking in her sleep, she'd married the guy.

"Thank you," I said.

Her eyebrows rose on her forehead. "For what?"

"For telling me the truth." I kissed her gloved knuckles. "And by the way, so that you know? The next time I make love to you, I promise, you'll be wide awake."

SIX

THE PRISTINE LANDSCAPE flew by as we ripped through a sea of white, trailing a wake of shimmering snow. Our tracks were the only marks on an immaculate geography. The snow machine roared between my thighs like a powerful beast. I clung to Seth, enjoying his heat. The ride was almost as thrilling as the feel of his body in my arms and, I swear, even though I couldn't recall squat about last night, my body remembered everything.

Oh, lord. Why was this happening to me? Not content with the sleepwalking episode, I now floundered while awake. The conversation we'd had in the truck echoed in my ears. He wanted to get to know me. He'd said so. He wasn't freaked out. He liked me. Me.

Could I really believe him?

I was in deep trouble and I knew it. I couldn't trust him, I couldn't trust anyone outside my family. If nothing else, life had taught me that. But every time he looked at me, something inside of me reacted with visceral longing. He was right. There was a connection between us. And his touch—it had the potential to blister me on contact. The promise he made, right there at the end, before we got on the snow machine repeated in my head. What was I supposed to think about that?

It was as if he knew something I didn't, as if ending up in his bed again was a foregone conclusion. The gall of the man, thinking *I* was going to ask *him* to sleep with me. I wasn't that desperate…was I? I wasn't reckless either. It made me crazy that he'd think I'd simply fall into his lap like some stupid broad without an ounce of self-respect. But it drove me even crazier that a part of me wanted to do just that, not fall but rather land on his lap with perfect accuracy to rediscover the pleasures he'd hinted at.

This was not like me at all. I had to get out of Alaska now. I had to get away from him, before I fell into the same trap that had almost destroyed my life before.

The snow machine slowed down from a roar to a purr. A cabin appeared at the turn, a weathered, rambling, A-frame log construction, bigger than I'd imagined but consistent with my reality show-shaped expectations, including a pair of enormous moose antlers hanging above the door.

Seth yelled over the noise. "The Golov homestead."

He brought the snow machine to a stop, dismounted, and, taking off his helmet, climbed the stairs and pounded on the door. I took off my helmet and looked around. A collection of sheds, an old truck raised on blocks, and piles of rusting scrap surrounded the cabin, all covered in a fine layer of snow.

"Nobody's home." Seth studied the tracks on the snow, which headed toward a narrow trail through the woods. "Maybe the Golovs are down by the lake. I'll go check. Wait here."

With brisk, purposeful strides, he disappeared into the forest. I sat on the stairs, listening to the eerie silence around me, interrupted only by the cry of an eagle, flying high above. At least I thought it was an eagle.

Cack.

Cack.

Cack. The noise got my attention. It came from the back, so I circled around the house. I spotted a rickety awning by the lake, but the clothesline caught my attention. My heartbeat tripped. A familiar blanket printed with colorful trucks rippled in the breeze. I marched up to the line and snatched the blanket off the line. The fabric was soft between my fingers. It was Tammy's blankie all right. Tammy was here! She may be twenty-seven and she'd kill me if I told anyone, but she never went anywhere without her blankie.

The crack of a shot rang in the air. A bullet whizzed by me and plinked against the nearest rust pile. I dove to the ground and elbowed myself behind the pile in time to see a rotund little woman wearing rubber boots and a bloody apron, wielding a gun almost as tall as she was wide.

"You thief!" The wild woman fired again. "Drop it!"

Seth came galloping out of the woods. "Anya, stop!"

The woman's weapon shifted in Seth's direction.

"She's got a gun," I yelled.

The gun jerked back toward me and loosened another shot.

"Wait, Anya!" Seth shouted, waving his hands in the air. "It's me, Seth Erickson!"

"Is that you, Seth?" The woman kept the gun on me but squinted in Seth's direction, motioning for him to step closer. "Why, speak up! Why didn't you say so?"

"I did say so." Seth approached the woman, arms up, palms bared in the air.

"Yeah, it's you all right," she blared. "Your timing's good. I've got a thief pinned over there—one I'm gonna shoot full of holes."

"You're not shooting anybody." Seth wrapped his

fingers around the rifle and gently wrestled it off her hands.

"What?" the woman yelled. "Do you want to do the shooting?"

"That's my friend over there," Seth said.

"Who?"

"The thief," Seth shouted.

"Speak up." The woman cupped her ear. "There's no use in you chirping like a squirrel."

"Where's your hearing aid?" Seth yelled at the top of his lungs.

"What?"

"Your hearing aid!" Seth tapped his ear. "I know the boys bought you a hearing aid, a nice one."

"Wait." The woman grappled through her pockets. "Maybe I should put in my hearing aid."

"Good idea." Seth called out to me. "Are you all right?"

"I'm alive." I came to my feet slowly, keeping my eyes on the woman as I dusted the snow off my coat, ready to dive for safety, should she suddenly reclaim her gun.

The wild woman found the hearing aid and inserted it in her ear. "Ah, yes, much better," she said. "That little thief over there tried to steal a blanket off my line." She turned in my direction and lifted a fist in the air. "You've got no business messing with other people's clotheslines."

Seth motioned for me to join him. "Do you want to explain?"

"It's Tammy's blankie," I said, approaching with care.

"You know Tammy?"

I nodded, studying the woman before me. A wiry puff of gray hair sprang from beneath her knit hat like a tangled nest, framing a wide face with heavy jowls and brown skin webbed with wrinkles that deepened around her tiny brown eyes.

"Sweet girl, Tammy," Anya said. "Why didn't you say you knew her before now?"

"Because I was busy ducking your bullets?"

Seth shook his head and peeled his eyes, but his warning came a little too late.

"Why, you're a damn hothead, aren't you?" Anya glared. "Do you think you can strut into someone's property and get something other than bullets?"

This time, I heeded Seth's warning and held my tongue. No sense in getting shot for nothing.

"Summer is Tammy's sister," Seth put in.

"You are?" Anya's tiny eyes bore into my face. "But she's so…blonde and you're so…not blonde."

It was a reaction I got often. "She's my stepsister."

"Ah." Anya's smile pressed her eyes into slits and added a new layer of wrinkles to her face. "That Tammy. She belongs to the air. You, on the other hand, you belong to the fire."

I looked to Seth. What was she talking about?

"Anya's one-fourth Athabaskan, a little Russian, and a hundred percent Alaskan," he explained. "She's got her own set of beliefs going."

"Come on, I've got chores to do." The woman waddled toward the awning. "Where have you been, kiddo? Since my Vik moved to Barrow, you haven't been by to see me."

"Sorry." Seth motioned for me to follow them. "I've been really busy."

“Busy, that’s all I hear from you boys.” Anya turned to me. “Vik and Seth ran around together in high school. Seth could put down pounds of my *pelmeni*.”

“Best dumplings in Alaska.” Seth smiled briefly then got serious again. “Summer here is looking for her sister. Where’s Tammy?”

“She and Nikolai arrived a few days ago,” Anya said.

I was ecstatic. Tammy was here, very near. I’d persuade her to go home with me. We’d be gone from Alaska and all my troubles would be over.

The awning turned out to be a fish-cleaning station, complete with an outdoor counter, currently smeared with fish guts and an impressive knife collection, including the most intimidating cleaver I’d seen in my life.

Large glass jars lined the shelf. Some looked like they were filled with the remains of gruesome experiments. Others held only a whitish liquid. The sharp scent of brine struck my nose, white vinegar, mixed with salt and something else, onions maybe?

“What’s the matter, *cheechako*?” The woman grabbed a huge pike by the tail and dropped it on her counter. “You’re too good for pickled fish?”

“Oh, no,” I said. “It’s just that I’d never seen it done, you know, the pickling thing.”

“You’ll be glad for pickled fish when the snow is high and the weather sucks,” Anya said. “So keep your wrinkled nose to yourself and learn.”

Her cleaver fell with a sudden *clack*. I jerked. The pike’s head fell off the chopping block as if struck by a French guillotine. The fish’s tail came off next, before the woman traded the cleaver for a smaller knife and gutted the fish. The gore. My stomach pitched. I put my hand over my mouth and tried very hard not to retch.

The woman flashed me another look. I smiled weakly. She wasn't buying it.

"This is a lot of fish for one woman." Seth bent down to examine Anya's basket. "Where did you get all of these?"

"I got lucky," Anya said, filleting the fish like an automated machine.

I cleared my throat. "I'd like to see Tammy. Is she in the house?"

"Impatient, too." Anya cut the fillets into smaller pieces and dropped them into the brine. "You don't got many virtues, do you? Tammy now, she's soft like a baby seal's fur. But you? You're stubborn, dark and stormy. Bossy too, if I judge you right."

Eyes sparkling, Seth coughed into his fist in a blatant attempt to hide his laughter. So what if I had a bit of a temper. He wasn't exactly cold-blooded. The smartass was having fun at my expense.

"My Nikolai is a bright boy," Anya said. "Airy too, like the girl."

"I wouldn't mind meeting Nikolai…" to give him a piece of my mind. The sly Don Juan had stalked my sister across the internet and bamboozled her into coming out here.

"You leave my Nikolai alone." Anya pointed the bloody tip of her knife at me. "He's a good boy, maybe a bit rash sometimes, but a nice boy he is."

A bit rash? Talk about the understatement of the year. He'd lured my sister to Alaska!

"Where's Tammy?" I was done tiptoeing around. "I want to see her right now."

"They arrived here earlier this week," Anya said. "But they're not here anymore."

"What?" I glared. "Why didn't you say so?"

Anya traded a suffering look with Seth. "This one doesn't have an ounce of patience."

"Not even a gram," Seth agreed wholeheartedly.

"Are you sure they're not around?" I said, suspecting the woman of aiding and abetting in the pair's escape.

"Of course I'm sure." The woman eyed me crossly. "I might look decrepit to you, but I can count heads in my own house and there aren't any asses parked next to my fire."

"I didn't mean to—"

"I know what you meant, so be quiet!"

"Summer's just worried about—"

"Hush, Seth, you too," she said. "You might be the great Seth Erickson around these parts, but since you're reeking like a musk ox at the rut, your messed-up mind might have forgotten that I'm not an idiot. I don't need an interpreter to talk to outsiders. I didn't raise seven boys on my own without my faculties."

With a tilt of the head, Seth urged me to apologize.

"I'm sorry if I came across wrong," I said. "I'm a bit blustery sometimes."

"Blustery like wildfire," Anya agreed, "and crossed like a moose with a toothache."

"Tammy's my baby sister and her mother is very worried." I held up the colorful blanket. "Tammy wouldn't forget this. She wouldn't go anywhere without it."

"Well, now, see, she did," Anya said. "Go figure."

"Do you have any idea where Nikolai and Tammy went?" Seth asked.

"South, maybe." Anya scooped a handful of fish guts off her cutting board. "Or maybe they mentioned Denali and Fairbanks, I can't remember for sure. Nikolai wanted to show Tammy Alaska. But I'm sure he said Kenai first. Or was it Katmai?"

I suppressed a groan.

"Alaska is a very big place." Seth's eyes met mine. "Without knowing which way they went, they'll be difficult to find."

"But I have to find Tammy."

"Now, child," Anya said. "Why would you try to trap the wind in your fist?"

Trapping the wind in my fist? Is that what I was trying to do?

No way. Anya didn't know Tammy. She didn't know that Tammy suffered from bipolar disorder and that she often needed help to snap out of it. She didn't know how to soothe her manic moods. She hadn't wiped my sister's tears when depression gripped her, and she didn't know that, sometimes, Tammy forgot to take her meds.

Oh, my God. What would happen if Tammy forgot to take her meds? Nikolai wouldn't know what to do. I felt sick to my stomach. I had to find Tammy, before it was too late.

"Don't worry." Seth squeezed my arm. "We'll find her."

"Stop worrying about others and pay attention to yourself," Anya said. "You dream chasers are all the same."

I frowned. "What did you just call me?"

"Dream chaser," Anya said. "What? Do you think I'm blind? Well, I'm not blind. I see the mark on your neck."

"This mark?" I fingered the crescent birthmark below my ear.

Seth eyed the mark. "What about it?"

"It's the mark of a dream chaser," Anya said. "What is it that they call it in the lower forty-eight? Sleepwalkers?"

"But..." I grappled for words. "How could you know?"

"I know a dream chaser when I see one," she said. "I would've known you even if I hadn't spotted the mark on you. It's the eyes, you know. They've got a tendency to glaze over when the person's tired, upset, or thinking."

"Really?" Seth leaned in to examine my eyes.

His nearness sent my cells into a tizzy. "Stop that." I shrunk from him.

"My grandmother was a dream chaser," Anya said. "She wandered the forest at night and we'd have to go after her so the wolves wouldn't get her. Back then, wolves were plentiful, a real nuisance. If you ask me, that's the problem with dream chasers. They chase dreams while you chase them."

I was stunned. Was there really such a creature as a dream chaser?

"What do you know about dream chasers?" Seth said.

"The Athabaskans talk about them in their stories," Anya said. "Dream chasers, walking barefoot in the snow without feeling cold or pain. In the winter, they'd freeze sometimes. In the summer, the tribes would follow them to the herds or to the best fishing spots. They've got remarkable instincts when they walk. They have to chase. It's a blessing and a curse."

"Chase after what?" Seth said.

"A dream, of course, but only they know which one. The dream is deep inside of them, which is why they can only chase while they sleep. What?" Anya said. "The elders in your family never explained it to you?"

"My mother died when I was young," I said. "The doctors said..."

"Don't get me started on doctors." Anya waved a dirty hand in the air. "Those quacks don't know squat about the human spirit. The Athabaskans, they knew. Just as they understood that the wind must blow and the fire must burn and the earth must quake and the water must flow, they knew that the chasers must chase."

Dream chaser. The name sounded intriguing, a lot more palatable than sleepwalker, somnambulist or parasomniac, and better than any of the dread-inducing sleep disorder labels that implied I was inadequate, nuts, or irreparably sick and headed to an early grave. Did I have a dream I chased?

"Hey." Seth squeezed my hand. "Are you all right?"

"Fine." I fought an urge to cling to his hand. "I've never heard it explained like that, that's all."

"Ah, see, my sharp tongue struck bull's-eye." Anya set her knife down, wiped her hands on her apron, and untied it from behind her neck. "After raising my boys, I forget what it's like to talk to girls. You've got to strike hard and fast to get through a male's thick skull. Not so with girls. She might be stubborn, Seth, but she listens. Listening is a sign of intelligence. Come on, girl, you need a drink."

"Oh, no, thank you, I don't drink."

"Rubbish." Anya started toward the house. "We all drink. I'll make you some hot chocolate if you'd like. Nothing pickled, I promise."

I SAT ON Anya's ancient checkered couch sipping my hot chocolate, absorbing the heat from the fireplace. The thermometer on Anya's deck indicated that it was forty degrees outside. Anya praised the sunny day and Seth seemed to think it was warm outside. Poor people. They didn't know any better. Warm was eighty degrees and up.

Anya set a steaming mug in front of Seth. "I heard something about Alex, that he was going for it again."

"He's welcome to try." Seth pursed his lips and blew on his mug. "Hell, some days I think he deserves the whole damn mess."

"You don't mean that foolishness," Anya said.

She took a seat next to Seth and sipped from a fine English teacup as if she'd suddenly transformed into a Russian czarina. There was more to her than meets the eye. I felt a bit like an interloper, but I listened to Anya and Seth's conversation anyway.

I didn't really know what they were talking about, but I did recognize the name Alex. Seth had mentioned it the first time we'd met on that desolate Alaskan road. He had thought this Alex person had hired me to trick him. Seriously, what kind of messed-up family were the Ericksons?

"Alex's got the boys at the mill riled up," Anya was saying. "He's promised them all sorts of goodies if they stick with him."

"It's Alex we're talking about." Seth sipped on his drink. "If the boys at the mill believe him, then they're idiots."

"The thing is," Anya said, "you've promised them nothing."

"I've promised them the jobs they've got," Seth said

testily. "And I'm trying to live by that promise, despite Alex's best effort to break up the company."

"Word is he's gotten friendly with some high-up people. Talks an awful lot about Washington and them on the outside. He did a lot of politicking when you were gone, and after, when you were down."

When he was down. I glanced at Seth. He'd been very sick and for a long while. But these days, his body gave no sick vibes at all. He looked quite healthy to me, which might explain why every time his eyes settled on me, my nipples stiffened and my rebellious pussy clenched. My body's messages were clearly intended for his, although I did my best to suppress all the chatter by sinking into my chair and slumping.

Seth's attention shifted back to Anya. "How is it you know all this when you hardly ever step out of the homestead?"

"I watch out for my boys." Anya patted Seth on the cheek. "Be careful. Will you?"

"Always am." Seth squeezed her hand.

"I've got something for you." Anya padded over to a drawer and pulled out a small package, which she unwrapped for Seth. "I got you what you wanted."

Seth stole a look. I couldn't see what was in the package, but his eyes lit up. He flashed Anya a smile capable of smelting bone and steel. "How did you manage?"

"I went to see the old man a few weeks back," Anya said. "He was kind to us. I think she'll like it very much."

"Hell, yeah," Seth said. "She's going to love it. Will you be there?"

Anya scoffed. "You know how I feel about brown-nosing brownnosers."

"I feel the same way," Seth said, "but I bet she'd be thrilled if you came."

She? I wondered who they were talking about. Maybe Seth had a girlfriend. Maybe he was playing with me after all. Whoever she was, I found myself resenting her on the spot. I didn't want to stick around to hear about this mystery woman. Besides, I couldn't ignore nature's call anymore.

"Excuse me?" I said. "May I use your restroom?"

"Out the door to the left," Anya said. "Follow the red rope."

"The red rope?"

"So no one loses their way at night," she explained. "So you can find the outhouse in the winter among the snow drifts."

An outhouse. Of course. A hole in the ground.

I followed the red rope to the outhouse. It was a good ways from the house. The thought of trudging through the snow in the dark gave me the shivers, but at least it was daylight now. Once I got there, it was nicer than I expected. It even had a Styrofoam seat to pamper the backside and a generous supply of toilet paper.

With my business done, I stepped out of the outhouse and headed for the cabin. My boot splashed in a recent puddle on the trail. A sharp odor tainted the air. Three steps later, I heard a strange sound, a gruff *huff* coming from the bushes along the path. I slowed down, peered into the bushes and saw…

A bear.

My stomach dropped to my feet. My brain cut out. For a moment, I couldn't believe my eyes. Oh, no. It couldn't be. A bear couldn't happen to me. Then the bear puffed and charged out of the bushes. I turned around and, screeching like a freaked out banshee, ran for the cabin.

My bloodcurdling shrieks echoed through the forest and beyond the lake. People in Miami could hear me screaming. Branches crashed behind me, but I didn't look back. My legs pumped on automatic. My heart battered my chest from the inside out. Ahead of me, the cabin's back door opened and Seth stepped onto the deck.

"Don't run!" he shouted as he grabbed Anya's rifle, vaulted over the railing and advanced toward me. "Stop, Summer. Stop running!"

My legs kept going even after he caught me by the waist and dropped me behind him. Was he insane? I didn't want to die. The bear was right on my tail!

"Keep still." He planted his feet apart, cocked the rifle and aimed it at the bear.

The beast halted at the edge of the yard. It was dark and enormous to my eyes. It huffed and puffed, making this odd sound, popping its teeth.

"No, bear, no," Seth yelled, as if he faced a dog and not a seven hundred-pound behemoth. "Fuck off bear, get the hell out here. Go away you fucking dumbass!"

I stared from the bear to the man. The bear was hard enough to process and terrifying in its own right. But Seth's actions were even harder to accept, because this stranger—this person who wasn't part of my family and who had no reason whatsoever to give a hoot about me—stood between me and a freaking grizzly as if he cared, as if I was worth the risk of a mauling and he had a stake in my future.

Seth shot a bullet into the ground. The bear startled

and took off. I watched in awe as the powerful creature galloped into the woods like a hulking Clydesdale.

Seth stalked to the edge of the clearing, peered into the forest and made sure that the bear was gone for good, before he came back and peeled me off the ground. "Are you okay?"

"Fine," I said, pretending I was cool as ice, even though my legs wobbled dangerously beneath me. Crap, I could barely stand. This place brought out the idiot in me. I pushed Seth away, took a step and faltered. I ended up on the cold Alaskan ground again, where I seemed to belong lately.

Seth sighed and hooked the rifle over his shoulder. "Come on." He pulled me up and, bracing me with his arm around my waist, cradled me against his chest, lending me the strength to stand. "Lock them knees. Yep, that's good. Anya has to be feeding them again. It's the only reason why that old bear was hanging around here."

"Feeding bears?" I clung to him as if he was the pillar of my world. "Isn't that illegal?"

"Sure it is," Seth said. "Try telling Anya that. She's a scientist by training and a shaman by vocation who thinks the bears are her friends. And no one has the right to tell her how to treat her friends."

"She's crazy," I said. "That bear was going to eat me whole."

"That bear was probably as surprised to see you as you were to see him," Seth said. "It knows Anya's scent, but it doesn't know yours. Never run from a bear. Food runs."

"Oh, my God." My voice quavered. "A bear. A bear!"

For pity's sake, in what bizarre alternative universe would I find myself fleeing from a freaking bear?

I crumpled in Seth's arms, closed my eyes and tucked my head beneath his neck, inhaling his soothing scent—baked bread and steaming oatmeal. The fear receded to the back of my mind. My body warmed to his touch. My pussy squeezed at the feel of his strong muscles flexing under my palms. For an amazing, indulgent moment, every cell in my body vibrated with desire and I wished I never had to leave his arms' refuge. Had he been willing to take a shredding of fangs and claws for my sake?

I mumbled, "You stood between me and the bear."

"No big deal," he said, pretty much holding me up.

"No big deal?"

He didn't know what I knew about the nature of the human species, males in particular. He didn't know about the predators out there. He didn't know that strong, competent, independent women like me took care of other people, not the other way around. Strong and competent I might be, but I hadn't felt safe since my sense of self-worth had been gutted like one of Anya's fish during my terrible marriage. Until today, when Seth had stood between me and the bear, and right now, as he sheltered me in his arms.

Oh, my God. Was it really me making these strange connections? I'd sworn off trust altogether. I didn't trust people, never believed what they said. But Seth? He spoke loads with his actions and part of me believed everything he said.

I kept going back to the part about the bear. A bear. An incongruous sound bubbled at the back my throat and I couldn't stop it.

"I need to get out of here." I giggled like a madwoman. "There are no bears in Miami. I need to go home."

"You're okay." He hugged me against his chest, stroking my hair, tilting up my chin until my eyes met his. "Listen to me. The bear's gone. You are all right."

"This place?" I said with tears in my eyes. "It's going to kill me."

"No way." His lips came down on mine and brushed ever so softly against my mouth, leaving me wondering if I'd imagined the extraordinary heat that singed the breath out of my lungs and melted my leg bones. Whoa. I wanted more of that.

"Summer Silva," he murmured, his thumb idling over the corner of my mouth. "I've got your back. Nothing bad will happen to you under my watch. And always remember: you're way too stubborn to let Alaska kill you."

SEVEN

THE RIDE HOME was a lot quieter than I liked. Summer stared out the window and I was worried about some of the things I'd learned at Anya's. I was running late for my meetings and the weather had changed again. Leaden clouds spat sleet at the windshield.

Alaska wasn't helping out much with my objectives. The woman attracted trouble, no doubt about it. Since her arrival, Summer had experienced a wreck, a superstorm, an assassination attempt, and a sleepwalking episode that she deeply regretted. Just today, she'd been shot at, sickened by fish guts, and charged by a bear. And then I'd succumbed to the temptation and kissed her. Okay, barely kissed her, but without her permission.

No wonder she hated Alaska.

Her cell rang as soon as we got back on the highway. She looked at it but didn't answer.

I guessed. "Tammy's mother?"

"The one and only." She sighed. "What am I going to tell her?"

"That, unlike you, her daughter's having a grand old time in Alaska?"

"We don't know that."

"But we suspect it," I said. "Otherwise, she would've been back home by now, don't you think?"

Her shoulders slumped. "I don't know what to think."

Her phone rang again.

"Crap." She let out a little groan. "It's Hector Carrera, my boss. He's probably going to ream my ass."

She accepted the call and put the cell to her ear. I could hear the man yelling at her even though the phone wasn't on speaker. The son of a bitch didn't hold back.

"Hector, I swear," Summer was saying. "You'll have it by tonight. Yes, I'll be back as soon as I find Tammy." She paused and listened. "Yes, yes, I'll get on a plane as soon as I can. No, I don't know when yet. Look, I'll work all night if necessary and I'll get those changes to you stat."

She looked miserable when she hung up.

"I don't know what to do," she said. "If I stay too long, Hector is going to fire me and I won't be able to help Louise and Tammy with their bills. But if I leave without my sister, Louise is going to have a meltdown and God knows what will become of Tammy."

"You can work remote," I said.

"Yeah, thank God for small favors." She sighed. "As long as I have Wi-Fi capable of dealing with large files, I should be able to keep up. Can you drop me off at a hotel on the way? Any hotel with Wi-Fi should do."

No way was I going to let her stay alone at a hotel. Not when her safety was compromised and the son of a bitch who'd tampered with her brakes was out there, uncaught and perhaps even planning to hurt her again. The mere thought of it raised my hackles. And what would happen if she got out of her room while sleepwalking? Nope, it wasn't happening. There was only one place where Summer Silva would be safe in Alaska and it was with me.

"Wi-Fi is a relative term around these parts," I said. "Your average hotel doesn't have the kind of connection you need. You'll be old before your files go through. You can stay with me."

"Oh, no," she said, face flustered, head shaking with alarm. "I mean, um, thanks for the offer and everything, but I couldn't impose like that."

"It'd be no trouble," I said. "My house is possibly the only place around here that has the communication capabilities you need."

"The *only* place?" She seemed to consider the idea. "You're not expecting me to…um…you know…"

"No." Unless she absolutely wanted to, in which case, I'd be willing to be flexible. "Are you worried about another sleepwalking episode?"

"Maybe," she said and then softly, "yes."

Her fear tore into my guts.

"Look at it this way," I said. "I'm now officially educated on the subject of sleepwalking. I won't allow what happened last night to happen again."

She gave me an appraising look. "Do you really mean that?"

"I might be blunt, but I never say things I don't mean," I said. "Besides, I've got a sneaking suspicion you don't travel very often because you worry about sleeping in strange places."

"You're right about that one," she said. "Pretty pathetic, eh?"

"You're not pathetic," I said. "You're careful, that's all. Honestly? I don't blame you. A hotel isn't the safest place for you right now. What would happen if you managed to unlatch the door while sleepwalking?"

She gulped so loudly that I actually heard it. I felt like a goddamn terrorist, but I was on a mission. "Stay at the house."

"I don't want to take advantage of you."

"You wouldn't be."

"Maybe—if I decided to stay with you—could I pay for my stay?"

She was as proud and stubborn as they came. So was I.

"That's a negative," I said, "as in absolutely not necessary."

"I'm no freeloader," she said. "Maybe I can pay you some other way?"

She wouldn't appreciate the only kind of currency I craved.

"How about if I take over food duty while I'm here?" she said. "That refrigerator of yours is pretty sad. I could liven it up. My treat?"

"That might work." She wouldn't agree otherwise and she was correct, my refrigerator was a wasteland. "I'm all for food."

"We'll need to stop by the store."

"Here." I opened a text message and handed my cell over. "Type what you need and it'll be there when we get back."

She rolled her eyes. "You've got minions, I get it. It's impressive, but it defeats the purpose if you're paying for the groceries."

"Just type the damn list," I said. "Labor is the most expensive part of production and if it's that important to you, we'll figure it out later."

She hesitated, still wary. "Are you sure?"

"A hundred percent sure."

She took a deep breath, typed the list with nimble fingers then returned the cell to me. "There."

I let out the breath I'd been holding. Persuasion was

the better course of action and even though my plan was also self-serving, this was the only way I could think to keep Summer safe in Alaska. But it wasn't easy. If I really wanted her trust, I was going to have to try harder. I ignored the warnings about texting and driving and, thumbing the screen, added another item to the list before I pressed the send button and put the cell away.

"I have some ideas on how to look for Tammy," Summer said. "I compiled a list of hotels, motels, bed and breakfasts, and campgrounds in Alaska. I can start with Katmai and Kenai. Maybe someone, somewhere has seen Tammy and Nikolai."

Time-consuming. I liked it. "It's not a bad idea."

"It's better than sitting on my bum waiting for them to turn up."

"I might be able to help," I said. "We're well connected. I'll put out some feelers. Staying at the house, you'll be in place for a quick intercept."

"Thanks." She smiled. "You're turning out to be a real godsend."

Even though it was a little crooked, with a smile like that, she might as well have given me the Nobel Peace Prize. The thrill of seeing that smile superseded my guilty conscience. What the fuck. Being a godsend to anyone felt good enough. Being a godsend to her? Spectacular.

I smiled and headed home. Best I'd felt in years.

EIGHT

I SENT MY first hundred emails in a batch, along with a flyer that included Tammy's picture and my contact information. By God, I was going to find my sister and soon. I got up from the lounge chair and stretched my weary bones. After my excursion to Anya's, my interview with the state troopers, another long-distance scolding from my furious boss, and a quiet dinner with Seth that proved I was especially vulnerable to him, I was more determined than ever to get out of Alaska as fast as humanly possible.

A loud rattle startled me of my thoughts. The house echoed with a mechanical rumble. I followed the sound to the bedroom, where I found Seth, holding a fierce-looking drill as if it was an assault weapon. He was fully invested in attacking the doorframe.

"What are you doing?" With a tool belt hanging low on his waist and that long-sleeve T-shirt showing off his arms' defined shape, his handyman sex appeal rippled through me until every cell in my body was volunteering for a home-improvement project.

"Almost done," he mumbled, taking out the screw he held in his mouth and tucking it in his pocket before taking a step back to assess his work.

I recognized the implement he was installing as the most formidable door chain I'd ever seen. He was installing a door chain. For me? It was almost incomprehensible and perhaps because of that, I kept going back to the notion that he looked really hot tonight.

"Summer?" he said. "Are you listening to me?"

I forced myself to pay attention. "Sure, yes."

"What do you think?"

I examined the stationary bit on the wall and ran my fingers over the track attached to the door, an impressive metal device that clashed with the door's polished wood. "Looks…brawny?"

"Hell yeah, brawny is right." He drilled the last screw to secure the frame. "Commercial-grade parts, reinforced steel, extra-long screws, highest-rated commercial door chain available on the market. This baby isn't budging."

Wow. "Where did you get that thing?"

"I had it flown in from Anchorage along with your grocery list."

"You do know that I'm not The Hulk, right?" I said. "I don't rip out doors or crash through wood in my sleep. The only reason the door chain works is because I can't seem to muster the fine motor skills necessary to disengage the chain."

"That's why I stuck with a door chain." He closed the door and tested his newly installed contraption. "Otherwise, I might have selected a more efficient locking mechanism."

"You really don't have to do this. It'll spoil your nice door and…" Why did it pain me to admit the truth aloud? "I'm not staying for long."

The look he gave me curled my toes. How could he do that with his eyes? His stare challenged me to walk out of his house and his life right that minute. I should've taken the dare, but my feet wouldn't obey me.

"While you're here," he said, "I want you to feel safe."

Why was my heart racing like an off-beat drum? "Thanks, I guess."

His thoughtfulness contributed to the global warming taking place inside of me. I was beginning to see past the grouch I'd first met on that stretch of desolate road. It was hard not to. After all, he'd sheltered me from the storm, driven me to Anya's, inserted himself between me and a charging bear, and invited me to stay in his house so that I could look for my sister.

If all of that wasn't impressive, he was now installing a door chain for me. It was sweet, admittedly, in an odd and slightly creepy way. But yeah, that was me, odd and slightly creepy on account of my sleeping disorder and really turned on by a guy installing a door chain for me.

Get your act together, Silva.

A belated thought hit me. "If I'm sleeping in your bedroom, where will you sleep?"

"I'll be fine on the couch."

"I don't want to boot you out of your bed."

"Don't sweat it." Seth took his drill apart and tucked the parts away in the case's foam panels. "By the way, Spider, my chief of cyber security, had a hit on a security camera outside the rest station."

"Oh?" My belly flopped, even though I was sure this was all a mistake.

"Take a look and tell me if you recognize this guy."

He picked up his tablet from the dresser and clicked on a clip. It showed a black-clad figure wearing a hoodie, kneeling next to my rental and going at the brake lines. I shook my head. I'd never seen him before, but the bile rose to my throat. My mind simply couldn't accept what I was seeing.

"Hey, it's okay." Seth gave my shoulder a little squeeze. "You're safe and Spider forwarded the clip to the state troopers who interviewed you earlier today. If he's local, we'll know soon enough. Wait until I get my hands on that son of a bitch."

I don't know what shocked me most, what I saw on the clip or that Seth had gone to such great trouble to locate it and find the culprit.

He set the tablet aside. "Can I ask you a couple of questions?"

"Um..." The least I could do was answer his questions. "Sure."

"Do you know where your ex, Sergio De Havilland, is?"

My stomach churned at the name. "We don't talk about him." I modulated my voice, trying not to sound hysterical. "Remember?"

"What if he has something to do with what happened?"

"He doesn't." He wouldn't want to face the consequences if something happened to me.

"You seem so sure of that."

"I am," I said with as much equanimity as I could muster. "For all I care he's dead. Don't ever ask me about him again. Got that?"

"Okay," Seth said, but something about the glimmer in his eyes told me he wasn't ready to completely drop the subject. "Let's talk about Louise instead." He took off his tool belt, setting my cells abuzz in the process. "How did she end up married to your father?"

I didn't process a word he said because at the moment, all I could think about was what would happen if, after taking off the tool belt, Seth stripped off his pants too.

"Earth to Summer." His tawny eyes fixed on me. "Are you listening?"

"Huh?" Where had my mind gone? "Sorry. What were we talking about?"

"Your stepmother."

"Louise?" I tugged on my sweater's neck to let in some cool air. "Why do you want to know about her?"

"Just humor me, please?"

"Okay." I let out a resigned sigh—more likely a burst of steam, given the heat in me. Dammit, this wasn't like me at all. I hadn't had a crush on anyone in…years.

I fanned my face and made an effort to string the words together. "After my mom died, Dad became sick with cancer. He beat it the first time around, but he worried I was going to be alone if he died. So he met Louise, a widow with a daughter a couple of years younger than I was, who lived in our building. Louise fell head over heels in love with him. My dad liked her too, but I think he married her because he wanted me to have a family before he left this earth."

"Family isn't always a gift," he muttered.

"What did you say?"

"Nothing." He packed his remaining tools in an impressive-looking box. "How old were you when your dad and Louise got married?"

"Fourteen," I said. "Tammy had just turned eleven. Louise was good to me growing up. She was great to my dad."

"From afar, she seems a little…odd?"

"Odd?" I shrugged. "Louise has issues, don't we all?

But my dad picked her, so I take care of them now that he's gone, because that's what families do, take care of each other."

"That's what some families do," he mumbled, frowning distractedly as he organized the tools in his box. "Others bicker about money until the cows come home."

"It really bothers you, doesn't it?"

His head snapped up. "What?"

"The problems you're having with your family."

"We're getting off track." He closed the toolbox. "Back to your family. Are you sure there isn't an inheritance that might go to Louise if you're not around?"

"I've already told you: no inheritance. My father was practically ruined when he died. He lost all of his money on the Fountain Way project. His partner had to pay for his funeral. Why are you asking about Louise?"

"We need to look at everyone objectively."

"And she doesn't look very good to you." I crossed my arms and glared at him. "You found out about her spending problem. Her *private* spending problem. Am I right?"

"People do strange things because of money."

"I'm telling you, right now." I dug my nails into my palms. "Louise has her problems. She's loud, smokes like a chimney, drinks a little too much, and likes to play cards. But you've got to believe me: she loves me. She wouldn't wish me harm."

"I didn't mean to—"

"I don't like it when anyone meddles with the people I love," I spat out, unable to contain the fury flaring in me. "Back off. Leave Louise alone."

"Look, I admire your defense of your family, I really do but…"

"But what?"

"Blind faith is not going to help us find whoever tried to kill you."

"I already told you," I said. "That wasn't about me and it certainly wasn't about Louise or Tammy."

"But—"

"Stop it." I stomped to the door and held it open for him. "I'm tired. It's been a long day. I don't want to talk about this anymore. Can you leave it alone?"

"For now," he said with the kind of aplomb that drove me insane. He heaved the tool belt over his shoulder, grabbed the drill case and the toolbox, and made for the door. "Sleep tight, Summer. I'll be on the couch if you need me."

I WOKE UP GRADUALLY, like a swimmer emerging from the ocean, satisfied, refreshed, restored. The soft, thousand-thread count sheets caressed my skin and rustled quietly against my ear. Had I slept through the night?

I looked at the door. The door chain was in place. The room seemed undisturbed. I sat up and examined the floor. My God. There were no footprints on the talc I'd sprinkled on the carpet around the bed, which meant that, despite the stress of the last couple of days, I hadn't walked in my sleep last night. It was a happy, hopeful milestone for me, one that could only be explained by the realization that blew my mind: I felt safe here. Four thousand miles away from home with a guy sleeping on the couch just outside my door.

I splayed my hand over my thumping chest. Be still my little heart. My subconscious must have known things that my conscious mind didn't, because my mind urged me to get out of bed, find my sister and run.

I grabbed my laptop and checked my email to see if I had any news on Tammy's whereabouts. Nothing. I had no new replies to my inquiries. I'd follow up with phone calls today. I'd placed quite a few of those yesterday. Alaskans weren't particularly forthcoming with information. However, when I told them the whole story about my crazy sister who ran away with a guy she met on the internet, I usually got some sort of a reaction, even if it included sniggers and scoffs.

Time to face the day. And the guy outside. My pulse fluttered when I thought of him, but I marched myself to the bathroom and washed my face, resolved to put an end to my foolishness. I confronted my image in the mirror. No crushes allowed. So what if he was cute? So what if he was sexy, smart, and perhaps even insightful beyond the bluster?

I was no hormone-crazed adolescent. I was a grown woman with a good head on my shoulders. My attraction to him had to be a fluke or maybe a trick of my sex-starved body, unleashed by the accidental sexual encounter, a reaction to my self-imposed years of celibacy?

Yes, it made total sense. I brushed my teeth until my gums hurt. It was the sex muddling my mind. It didn't help that the architect in me found so many qualities about him intriguing. Like for example, the fact that he was always the master of his space. Outdoors, indoors, wherever he stood, his presence was commanding. I liked his vision, his point of view, the fresh perspective he applied to everything he did. The glimpses I'd gotten into his mind insinuated an intricate, tantalizing design. As to his body's blueprint, I found myself eager to inspect it in detail.

Oh, crap. There it was again. Those sudden surges of lust were getting exhausting. All I had to do was impose a little bodily discipline and I'd be fine. I let out a long breath. Easier said than done.

I put up my hair in a messy ponytail and marched out the door. Seth was busy in the kitchen, dressed in a pair of thermal jogging pants that highlighted the better parts of him. I couldn't help it. My heart drummed when he smiled at me, an honest grin that lit his eyes like a Miami dawn.

"Good morning." He held up a steaming mug. "I heard you moving in there."

"Is that…?"

"One café-con-leche for the lady." He delivered it directly into my hands.

I brought the mug to my lips and tasted heaven. "Hmm. You make the best café-con-leche in the world."

His grin widened. "A guy has to have some talents."

And a girl could get used to waking up to that smile every day.

He pointed to a little pile of clothes on the counter. "Time to get going."

"Going where?"

"Dr. Sanchez said that exercise is vital to curb stress." He finished the last of his coffee and put the mug in the dishwater. "So giddy up, dream chaser. We're going to chase all right. Nature is a healing agent and exercise is the best way to manage stress. We're going for a run."

"A run?" I glanced out the windows. "But…it's freezing out there!"

"It's not so bad," he said. "Come on. Let's go."

He wasn't going to take no for an answer, so I downed my coffee, got dressed, and donned a jacket. Seth, of course, was perfectly fine with only a thin running fleece. We stepped out into the brain-startling cold, trudging through the layers of fog blowing in from the ocean. The air smelled like frozen seaweed. It was already eight in the morning, but the sun was only now beginning to rise, imbuing the day with a weak promise of light.

Seth's running trail went around the island, enlivened with the occasional obstacle course. I traipsed after him at minimal jogging velocity, not so much because I wanted a high-impact workout, but rather running away from the cold chasing after my bones. My feet crunched on a frozen crust of dew, but with every step, my mind cleared. The day felt new to my senses. I smiled when I spotted a seal frolicking in the sound. Seth was right. The outdoors was good for the soul.

I was ecstatic when we came across the three-mile cairn, because the tip of my nose felt numb to my fingers and the stitches on my side had turned into all-out stabs.

"Turnaround time," I announced, completely out of breath.

"Wimp." Without missing a stride, Seth turned from the track. "This way."

"You know I can get back to the house on my own, right?"

"I'd rather you stick with me." His breath condensed into little clouds as he jogged next to me. "Knowing you, you'd run into some kind of trouble and then we'd have a mess on our hands."

"What kind of trouble can I get into around here?" I puffed my frozen breaths. "A bear?"

"A bear," he said, "a broken leg, a moose, the guy who punctured your brakes."

"Slow down." I gasped. "I told you that wasn't about me."

"It doesn't hurt to stay vigilant." His nostrils flared. "Especially since we didn't get any hits on facial recognition and we don't know squat about his motives."

"I'm not afraid of that guy," I said. "I'm not afraid of a moose either."

"You should be," he said. "They're the crankiest, meanest motherfuckers around. I'd take on a bear any day before I'd take on a moose."

"Really?" I said. "Hooves over teeth?"

"That's Alaska for you."

"House, door, safe." I rasped, bending over my knees.

"See you in a bit." He launched down the trail as if he were a turbo-charged Ferrari.

God almighty. He had commendable stamina, not to mention admirable glutes.

I took a quick shower, got dressed in yoga pants and a sweater, and laid out all the fixings for breakfast. Seth was holding his end of the bargain and so was I. I had just finished putting the biscuits in the oven when Jeremy strolled in, carrying a load under his arm.

"You're in time for breakfast." I added a setting to the table. "What's all this?"

"My biggest headache." He unloaded a bunch of folders and blueprints on the kitchen counter. "I thought maybe Seth could help me sort through it. This is the problem." He laid out a set of pictures before me.

"What am I looking at?" The pictures showed a number of rusted trailers and dingy metal rooms with furniture bolted down to the floor. "Abandoned prisons of Alaska?"

Jeremy laughed. "These are pictures from the only two hotels on the Dalton Highway."

"Hotel rooms?" I grimaced. "Someone would pay to stay in these?"

"These other pictures are from some of our exploration camps," Jeremy said. "This one shows housing units at one of the oil fields."

"Oh, my." I studied the pictures. "This is an architectural calamity."

"Yeah," Jeremy said. "My division has been commissioned to develop energy-efficient, sustainable, and environmentally friendly portable housing for research and exploration. It'd be nice if people enjoyed living in them as well, but that could be a reach."

"No kidding."

"The board wants to see a full proposal, but we're running behind," Jeremy said. "Our prototypes have failed to meet the standards."

"Hmm." I examined the blueprints. "I see that you've developed a platform system to keep the units elevated, but those pylons aren't going to cut it. Everything you put on the tundra melts and, if the tundra melts, then the platform will fail and the units will sink."

"Don't I know it." Jeremy braced his hands on the counter and shifted his gaze from the photos to me. "What would you do if you were in my shoes?"

"I'd find some other pylons that had a prayer of working."

"What about the housing units themselves?"

"I'd stick with the current specs for easy transport, but I'd make the units more livable. Small spaces can be efficient *and* comfortable." I clicked on my laptop and pulled up the architectural drawings for the Darius micro apartments project. "Like these."

"Wow. Impressive." A slow smile pulled on his lips. "I wonder..."

"Oh, no," I said. "No, no, no. I'm leaving, Jeremy. I'm not your girl."

He fluttered his spectacular eyelashes. "Seems to me, looking at these ultra-cool micro apartments, that you're exactly the right girl for this project."

"Nope, no can do."

"You'd be doing me a huge favor, and Seth too, mind you, he can use all the help he can get..."

I had no time for this, but even though Jeremy hadn't brought it up, he and Seth had both gone out of their way to help me out, and if I could help Seth even a little bit with the heavy burdens he carried...

The little twerp. "Are you trying to guilt me into doing this?"

Jeremy grinned. "Is it working?"

I groaned. "I know I'm going to regret this, but fine, okay, I can't say no to you," and especially, not to Seth. "I'll take a look and by that I mean a look, nothing else. But don't pin your hopes on me. I'm out of here as soon as I find my sister."

"Deal." Jeremy enveloped me in a big hug. "Thanks, Summer."

The sound of a throat clearing startled both of us. From his perch by the door, Seth beamed his radioactive glower.

"Good news," Jeremy said. "Summer's going to take a look at the lodging project."

"Awesome." Seth's voice lacked an ounce of enthusiasm. He whirled on his heel and stalked across the room, ripping off his knit cap along the way. A wave of steam rose from his head.

"Breakfast will be ready in five," I called after him, a tad too cheerfully.

"Not hungry." He made a straight line for the bedroom.

I startled when he slammed the door. What had just happened? And why did I feel as if I'd done something wrong?

"Damn." Jeremy stuffed the photographs back in the folder. "He's in a bad mood this morning. Maybe I should come back some other time."

I shrugged. "He was fine, earlier."

"He does that, sometimes, especially when he doesn't get any sleep."

My stomach soured. "What do you mean?"

Jeremy glanced at the pillows and blankets strewn over the couch. "He's got sore spots, you know, from the helicopter crash? His mattress is high-tech, gel-based, specially designed to avoid pressure points. If he doesn't sleep in it, he gets grumpy like an old man."

"Oh." He hadn't admitted to any of that when I brought it up last night, but now that Jeremy mentioned it, Seth's bed was especially comfortable. I felt like the most selfish bitch on the planet. "I had no idea."

"You wouldn't." Jeremy rolled up his plans. "Nobody would. He doesn't talk about it. Better to leave him alone when he gets into a mood. I'm going to go now."

"Why don't you come back tonight?" I felt totally guilty and somehow responsible for fixing whatever it was I'd broken. "I'll cook us a nice dinner and, if you leave those plans with me, I'll take a look and maybe the three of us can brainstorm some ideas."

Jeremy beamed his dazzling smile at me. "Sounds great, Summer. Thanks."

I walked Jeremy to the door and saw him off. The guilt in me wouldn't let off. I was trying to figure out what to do when my cell rang. "Hello?"

"How long is this vacation of yours going to last?" my boss said on the other side of the line. "When the hell are you coming back?"

"I'm sorry, Hector." My stomach churned. "It's just that I haven't found Tammy."

"I need you here," he said. "How much longer?"

"Um…I'm not sure…things aren't moving as fast as I want. Maybe a week?"

"A week?" I could hear the coronary he was having over the line. "An entire fucking week?"

"Sorry?"

"I need you here to work with the Darius people."

"I can deal with them from over here and they loved the changes I proposed yesterday."

"Yeah, sure," Hector said. "They liked the changes so much they want the fourth and fifth floor redesigned as well."

Oh, man.

"I can do that," I said, maneuvering the biscuits out of the oven one-handedly. "I promise, I'll take care of everything."

I wasn't sure I'd succeeded at appeasing Hector by the time I got off the phone, but hopefully, I'd bought myself some time. I called my assistant and gave him instructions on the materials for the redesign. By the time I hung up, the uneasiness in my gut had coalesced into a brick of worry.

I made my way to the bedroom. I knocked, but nobody answered. I let myself in. The door to the bathroom was open. Seth stood facing the mirror above the vanity. He looked as if he'd just stepped out of the shower, wearing only a towel around his waist as he smeared lotion on his scars' mottled skin. He didn't see me at first, so I had a moment to admire his body's proportionate build, his shoulders' strength and the narrowing path of his torso as it tapered to his hips. Then his eyes found me in the mirror and pierced through me like a pair of high-caliber bullets.

Yikes. I pretended I wore a Kevlar vest and squared my shoulders. "May I come in?"

"Not now." He whirled on his heels, stepped up, and tried to close the door on me.

"Please?" I caught the door. "Let me in?"

His fingers grappled with the door. "Can you at least wait until I get dressed?"

I stuck to my guns. "I'd like to talk to you now, if you don't mind."

"Fine." He let go of the door and padded over to the mirror, where he squeezed some lotion on his hand and twisted his arm at an awkward angle, trying to reach the scars on the middle of his back.

"That's a hard way to moisturize." I walked into the bathroom. "Why don't I do it?"

He refused to look at me. "I'm good."

"But—"

He snapped. "I said I'm good."

I flinched and I could tell by the look in his face that he regretted his reaction right away.

"Damn." He wiped his hand on the towel. "I didn't mean to yell at you."

"I get it," I said. "I can be a hothead sometimes."

"Yeah," he mumbled. "It happens."

I counted the brief exchange as apologies all around and put out my hand. "May I?"

With a resigned sigh, he handed me the bottle.

I squeezed a blob of cream on my palm. The smell of oats and shea butter wafted from the lotion, along with a clean, slightly medicinal note, the wholesome scents I associated with Seth. I moved to spread the cream on his back. He flinched when I touched him. His already stiff shoulders turned into a pair of iron lumps beneath my hands.

"Is this okay?" I spread the lotion over the crimson blotches that splattered the left side of his back like a bunch of wine stains.

He nodded but didn't meet my stare.

"Your skin is so cold." I reeled from the shock. "Did you shower with freezing water?"

"I like a cold shower."

He meant a glacial shower. He felt like an ice sculpture to my touch. I rubbed in the lotion, determined to bring some warmth to his body, working the cream into the long scar that snaked beneath his right shoulder, where the healed skin furrowed into a red, leathery surface.

I ached at the sight of the scars and yet I didn't feel repulsed by them. On the contrary. The scars reminded me of how strong Seth was, of his astounding capacity to heal. Beyond that, touching him activated the heat in me.

Sure, I'd seen him without his clothes once before, an image that powered my dreams last night. But this was different. I loved the way his body flowed under my touch, strong, vital, and handsome. Unpretentious layers of muscle rippled beneath my fingers, enticing my hands to further exploration. I traced the lines that formed quilt-like patterns of skin grafted onto his back. The healthy parts of his skin prickled with tiny bumps. My skin echoed the rippling, especially when I recalled that, beneath the towel, he was naked.

Shivers fringed my spine, tightened my sex, and moistened the space between my legs. I inhaled the scent that radiated from him, hot and male to the core, the intimate essence that had enveloped me all night as I slept on his bed. My body indulged in the memories my mind refused to acknowledge and I had a vision of me, entwined in his arms and clinging to him like an ivy.

I pressed my legs together and clenched until my teeth hurt. I was breaking my own rules again. When had I become such a wanton mess? If I had any sense, I should follow in Seth's footsteps and take a cold shower. But I'd trailed him to the bathroom for a good reason and nothing, not even a sudden lust attack, would prevent me from setting things right.

"Your brother's a good guy." I worked the lotion over his scars. "He's very smart."

"They don't graduate dummies at Caltech."

"I can tell he loves and admires you," I said. "He wanted your opinion on something today."

"Is there a point to this conversation?" Seth queried me with a frown. "If there is, just make it and move on. I'll be fine. You don't need to tiptoe around me."

God, he could be such a grouch sometimes! Oblivious too, for such a smart man. He had no idea of the effect he had on me and he didn't recognize the difference between wholesome admiration and desire. But I knew he and his brother were close. From watching them together, I could sense that Jeremy was one of the few people that tethered Seth to his world. I was afraid that by acknowledging one thing, I might end up admitting to something else, but I took a deep breath and called on my courage.

"I like Jeremy a lot," I said, "but not in *that* way."

The breath went out of Seth. I didn't know what else to say. Sometimes bluntness required bluntness. I worked the lotion into his skin, making sure that I covered the spot in the center of his back, where a patch of cracked skin oozed like a tiny volcano. He stood rigid as a beam, head down and eyes lidded, clutching the granite countertop.

"Am I hurting you?" I asked.

"No."

"Should I stop?"

"Keep going."

"You've got a troublesome spot here." I lingered around the lesion. "Does it hurt?"

"It's a stubborn SOB," he said. "It refuses to heal right."

"Maybe you should go to the doctor?"

"The doctor knows," he said. "He wants to do another graft."

"And?"

"I don't have time for a hospital stay right now."

"Perhaps you ought to make time," I said. "In the meanwhile, could we try something else?"

His head snapped up. *"We?"*

"Um…err…" I stammered like a total idiot. "I don't mind helping out while I'm around."

His eyes raked over me briefly then looked away. "The doctor gave me a medicated silicone patch for it, but I can't reach back there."

"Why don't I put it on?"

He hesitated. "Are you sure?"

I smirked. "Are you afraid I'm going to put it on upside down?"

He cracked a smile, but still, he wavered before he opened a drawer. It was crammed full of medicine bottles and ointments. I was shocked. Seth never let on that he was in pain or that he suffered chronic discomfort, never spoke about his injuries or complained. Fully dressed, he looked like the healthiest man in Alaska, and yet by the look of that drawer, he'd had to fight a steep uphill battle to get here.

He picked up a sterile pack and handed it to me. "I'm not sick anymore."

"I know."

He didn't want to be treated like a patient. He didn't want my pity either. I broke open the package, peeled off the sticker from the bottom of the patch, and pressed it over the lesion.

"I burned my arm once," I said, "taking a Pyrex out of the oven. It took weeks to heal. I screamed every time the doctor had to do that thing where they scrape off the burn."

His entire body shivered. "It's called debriding."

"It should be called excruciating instead." I checked to make sure the patch had adhered and then let go. "It hurt like hell. And afterward, when I healed, my skin itched like crazy. Do you hurt? Does your skin burn sometimes?"

He shrugged.

"It won't kill you to admit to the truth."

"I've got patches on my back that are totally numb." He paused. "The dryness and irritation drives me crazy. Sometimes I feel like I'm burning."

The silence that followed frightened me. I kept applying the lotion, but my stomach lurched like a jet ski on rough water.

"Seth?" I said. "Look at me, please. What did I do wrong? Am I doing something wrong right now?"

His head came up slowly. His eyes made contact with mine in the mirror. What I saw shocked me. Pain, profound and raw, gleamed in his stare. This brilliant man who came across proud and indomitable, ached, inside and out. He was also somehow ashamed, self-conscious and uncomfortable under my touch, and he didn't know how to deal with any of it.

"You haven't done anything wrong," he finally said. "Sorry if I was short with you. These days, I have trouble with change and…"

"And what?"

"I guess I'm not used to anybody touching me, that's all."

My heart stuttered and a flare of heat flushed through my body. The look on his face said it all. He hadn't allowed anyone else to touch him since he'd been hurt. It was hard for him, but he was allowing me to touch him now. Me and only me.

The joy. It took me completely by surprise. I soared like an eagle in the sky. Why was his trust so moving to me?

A primal need to soothe and console him overrode all of my fears. It felt like the most natural thing in the world. I put my arms around his waist, pressed my body against his back and kissed the scar on his shoulder. Time slowed down to show me the image of us on the mirror, sharing in the moment's intimacy. The expression on my face was raw as I held back from kissing and exploring every inch of him. His eyes sparkled and I swore he was holding back an impulse to do the same to me.

His hand fisted around the knot that held the towel around his waist. His belly tightened beneath my palm. The cream terrycloth tented over his erection's unmistakable bulk. The need I spotted in his eyes matched the passion challenging my resolutions, softening my knees and blazing in my lower belly. A vision from our first night together flashed in my head, a memory of me, lost and found in his arms.

The fragmented vision fed my fire. The look in his eyes didn't help. I'd never wanted another human being the way I wanted Seth Erickson right now. The flush burned through me like wildfire. My impulse was to jump into his arms right then and there. Instead, I unwound my arms from him and forced one foot to step back and then the other.

"We'll put another patch on you tomorrow," I mumbled, trying to conceal the fluster. "I'm off to the kitchen. It's omelets this morning."

I more or less ran for the door.

"Summer?" he said, holding himself very still against the bathroom counter.

"Yes?" I hit the pause button to freeze the scene of my harrowing escape.

"Thank you."

"Oh." I gulped. "Don't mention it."

I closed the door behind me, leaned against the wall,

and let out a long breath. My blood swooshed in my ears. Whatever had happened to Seth, it must have been a terrible ordeal. And yet none of that eased my craving for him. On the contrary, I admired the will that powered his recovery and I didn't want him to hurt anymore. Instead, I wanted him to moan in pleasure as I made love to him.

NINE

"WHAT DO YOU mean nothing?" I stared at Spider's face on my screen. "Are you telling me we're dead in the water?"

"I'm telling you that, right now, we've got no clue of who the guy on the clip is." Spider fidgeted on his chair. "I even ran the pics with my FBI contacts. Zero. Nobody knows who that fucker is."

"Now you got me worried."

"I know," Spider said. "The fact that he's not on anybody's radar is concerning."

"Not a petty criminal or a thug," I said. "A professional."

Spider nodded. "It ups the stakes for sure."

"We'd be talking big money."

"For sure."

If there was a professional out there stalking Summer, then she was in even more danger than I'd originally thought. It pretty much eliminated any theories that entailed mistaken identity.

"Here's what we're going to do," I said. "I want a full background investigation on anybody who could conceivably have an interest in Summer's death and the means to hire someone to do it."

"Okay, dude." Spider hesitated, then just came out and said it. "But I have to remind you that our resources are heavily invested on the Alex investigation right now.

I worry about distractions. The board meeting is coming up and you need to keep an eye on that motherfucker."

I opened my mouth to snap at Spider then thought better about it. He made a good point. I couldn't afford to lower my guard now, not when I knew Alex was making a run for my position.

"I'll keep my eyes on Alex and so will you," I said. "Bring on some additional assets so we can deal with both investigations. It's all on me, not out of the company's budget. Got that?"

"Got it." Some of the tension ebbed from Spider's face.

"Start with Sergio De Havilland," I said. "Summer refuses to discuss him. I can't tell you exactly what went down between him and Summer, but I can tell you he's a major asshole. Find him. I don't care if he's on a different planet. Find out if he's an asshole with a motive. Stick a tail on him. I want to know where he is at all times, who he's talking to and about what. If Summer's name so much as crosses his lips, I need to know."

"Okay," Spider said, taking notes as I spoke.

"Check out the stepmother too. Send someone down to Miami to ask questions, get me some impressions. Maybe from there we can come up with a list. Take a look at Carrera and Associates as well, disgruntled coworkers, for example. And look at the crazy sister too."

"We're searching for her all over Alaska."

"Dig into her background as well. Maybe she has a grudge against Summer. I want you to go all out, Spider."

"On it," Spider said, before the screen went dark.

I let out a long breath. I'd attended too many remote meetings today, answered hundreds of emails and messages and reviewed the draft of E&E's annual report twice. I'd also delivered the eulogy at Danny's funeral in his home state of Montana, albeit remotely. It'd been a hard day, but it was this last conversation with Spider that had my head throbbing, my lungs cramping and my scars feeling tight all over.

I needed a good cooldown. Instead, I grabbed my tablet from my desk and walked out of my office. Something changed when I spotted Summer stretched out on the hearth's granite bench. I drew in a deep breath. The air in the room felt lighter, cooler and fresher. She was here. She was safe.

She wore silk thermals and one of my MIT sweaters, which hung down almost to her knees. She lay on her belly, crossing and uncrossing her feet, fingering her screen at dizzying speeds as she moved lines and objects on the blueprints displayed on her touch-screen laptop. Music blared from her earphones, a woman belting out some powerful notes. Adele or maybe Alicia Keys?

Summer cozied up to the fire as if she couldn't get enough warmth. Her craving for heat made me jealous. Christ. I remembered this morning in the bathroom, the look on her face, the enormous amount of restraint I'd had to muster to keep myself in check. Something had shifted the moment she touched me. The connection between us had flared and, in the midst of the power surge, something inside of me tripped. She wasn't Alex's plant. She'd never been. The last of my doubts scattered on the spot. Originally, I'd wanted her to stay to learn more about her and, most importantly, to ensure that she was protected. But right now, I had to be honest with myself. I wanted her to stay so that I could make her mine again.

I stared at the woman by the hearth. All of a sudden, the fire seemed to burn too hot. I had a vision of the blue-tipped flames, reaching out for her like malignant little fingers. My skin prickled with memories of pain and I cringed. Was that sweater flame-retardant?

"Summer?" She couldn't hear me.

My pulse pounded in my ears. A sheen of sweat broke out over my lip. I took small breaths, trying to control the anxiety, but I couldn't resist the impulse. What the hell. I stepped up to the fireplace and scooped her up.

She squealed, pulling out her earphones in midair. "What are you doing?"

"You're way too close to the fire." I deposited her on the cowhide chaise.

Her eyes rounded on me. It didn't matter if she thought I was nuts. I wasn't going to let her burn. I wasn't afraid of the fire. I was afraid of the pain it could cause her. I retrieved her computer and settled it on her lap.

"Thank you, I think," she said. "But maybe I was cold."

"Your blood freezes at sixty degrees." I dragged the chaise—with Summer on it—and parked it alongside the fireplace.

"Now I'm going to be warm on one side and cold on the other."

"No, you're not." I settled down on the chaise and cozied up to her, shoulder to shoulder.

"Oh." Damn those probing eyes.

"Warm?" I asked.

She wiggled against me. "Like a slice in the toaster."

Her smile ignited the need in me and left me struggling to suppress my cock's rapid reaction. This had gone better than expected. I couldn't remember the chaise being this comfortable before. I couldn't remember being this close to another human being since coming back from Afghanistan, either.

"How much longer do you have on your project?" I asked.

"Two, three hours," she said, "but dinner's in twenty minutes."

The door chimed and Jer strolled in as if he owned the place. When he saw us sitting together on the chaise, he screeched to a stop, gaping like a goddamn idiot.

"Jeremy!" Summer leapt to her feet and welcomed him with a hug. "I'm glad you came."

"Yeah, me too," I said, but not sincerely. "What the hell are you doing here?"

"Summer invited me," Jer said in a defensive tone. "She said the three of us could look at the lodging project together."

"I hope it's okay I invited Jeremy," Summer said. "I wanted to thank him for his help and he wanted you to look at his project. Maybe I should've asked you before I opened my big mouth?"

"It's fine." I didn't mind Jer, I just wanted Summer all to myself, but obviously, that wasn't going to happen right now. "Let's take a look at those plans."

I got up from the chaise and marched to the kitchen counter, where the three of us clustered around Jer's blueprints. Our lively discussion introduced me to Summer the professional, a gifted, forward-thinking architect with valuable insight whose ideas got me all excited and not just physically. Not for anything, pretty women were nice to look at, but gorgeous women with huge brains, uttering sexy tech talk?

Irresistible.

In a short time, we made a lot of progress, except on one front. The solution for the tundra-friendly pylons continued to elude us. My belly's growls announced the end of the discussion.

"Somebody's hungry." Summer's smile teased all my senses.

"Make that two of us," Jer said.

"What are we having for dinner?" I asked.

"Can't you smell the deliciousness in the air?" Jer said. "Something Italian."

"Lasagna." Summer opened the oven and grabbed the potholders. "I make a mean one."

I looked in the oven. It was indeed a mean-looking dish, bubbling and steaming like the very mouth of hell, capable of scalding her to the bone.

"Jesus." I snatched the potholders from her and reached into the oven. "I'll do it."

"Be careful." She hovered over me, mouth pursed.

Balancing the broiling dish in my hands, I carried it and settled it on the bamboo mat on the table.

"Looks amazing," Jer said.

"I got this recipe from my Italian gourmet class," Summer said, rummaging through the kitchen drawers until she found a spatula.

"Do you take cooking classes often?"

"I love taking all kinds of classes." She came over to the table and cut into the dish, releasing a cloud of steam likely to vaporize flesh on contact.

"Let me do that." I took the spatula from her and dished out the portions.

"Thanks." She sat down on the chair Jer pulled out

for her. "I take a class every night of the week when work allows it. French. History. Art. Cooking."

"Sounds more like an addiction." Jer laughed. "What do you do for fun?"

"Weekends are all about the beach and the Discovery Channel. Love that stuff."

I recognized the strategy. If every moment of her day was busy, she didn't have a lot of time for fear, anxiety, or regret, or for venturing out beyond the safety of her scheduled activities and her door chain. Yep, I knew all about the Discovery Channel/exhaustion strategy.

I uncorked a Chianti I'd set aside for a special occasion.

"None for me." Summer covered the top of her wineglass when I tried to pour for her.

"A tad won't hurt," I said.

Her eyes scoured my face, probing my intentions. "I shouldn't."

"You'll be fine," I said. "I promise."

The look she gave me told me she believed me. Her hand wilted away from the glass. I poured her a couple of ounces. My heart drummed when her lips met the glass rim. Her eyes confirmed that she, who trusted no one, trusted me. The tug in my groin announced my cock approved. A cheer went up in the back of my mind.

Summer's lasagna tasted delicious. Jer and I ate like barbarians. It was the first time I'd had anyone at my table since I'd built the house. The atmosphere was downright cozy. Summer had dimmed the lights and lit some emergency candles I kept in the pantry. They pulsed in the middle of the table like tiny hearts. By dinner's end, I discovered in shock that I'd been having an excellent time.

Jer stretched out on his chair. "Bro, we should've done this before."

Summer's eyebrows quirked. "You mean Seth has never had you over for dinner?"

"Seth's a loner," Jer said. "We get together for a beer every so often, but he likes his space."

"You don't have to explain me as if I were exhibit A."

"Sorry, bro," Jer said, "but sometimes I do have to explain you to people. It's true you like your space. Isn't that why you moved out of the big house in the first place?"

"The big house?" Summer said.

"The family house," Jer said. "Hasn't he told you?"

Summer shook her head.

"Of course not." Jer tsked. "This is Seth we're talking about. His communication skills measure low on the Cro-Magnon scale."

"Hey!"

"The Ericksons live down the road a ways," Jer said. "We all keep rooms at the big house, except Seth, of course. He's antisocial. He'd rather live alone out here."

"Is that true?" Summer perused me as she sipped on her wine.

I shrugged. "I like my privacy and I enjoy having my own place. Besides, Jer forgot to tell you that the Ericksons—including him—are a pain in the ass."

She giggled at that. *Do-re-mi-fa.* Her laughter messed with me.

"I'm beginning to imagine a litter of puppies yapping away in the yard," she said. "Who are these famous Ericksons anyway?"

Jer jumped at the chance. "Let me tell you the story..."

"Oh, come on," I said.

"I'll make it short," Jer promised.

"Jer here wanted to be a filmmaker when he was a child," I said. "But Dad made him promise he'd be an engineer. Storytelling is his way to avenge too many hours of calculus."

"Please?" Her little pout struck me as extremely provocative. "Let him tell his story."

How could I resist those lips or the smile that reshaped them? Jer nodded eagerly. Two against one. I'd lost this one. I inclined my head in defeat.

"Our great-grandfather landed in Alaska in 1902, following rumors of gold," Jer began. "He found little gold, but he prospered, acquiring lots of land in the bargain. His only son, my grandfather, Olav Erickson, turned twenty in 1950 and needed a proper Norwegian wife. So he sent for one. Take one: my grandmother Astrid arrives in Alaska."

I propped my chin in my hand. "This is going to take a while."

"Fast-forward to 1959," Jer said. "Alaska becomes a state and Olav and Astrid have two strapping sons, Arthur and Benjamin. Entrepreneurs at heart, they start their own construction company early on. Foreseeing the growth coming to Alaska, they began to acquire land and build infrastructure. When the oil companies arrived and the pipeline was built in the '70s, they needed services, food, lumber, construction crews, the works. Take two, Arthur and Benjamin's partnership grows into an immensely profitable venture."

"Spill it," Summer said. "Which of the brothers is your father?"

Jer smiled cryptically. "All will be revealed in time."

"You'll be an old lady by the time you find out," I put in. "I'll be a fucking corpse."

"In 1976," Jer continued, "Arthur goes to New York on a business trip."

I huffed. "Are you really going to tell *that* part of the story?"

"It's the best part," Jer said. "While in New York, Arthur meets a shrewd investment banker. 'You know how to make money,' he's told. 'But you know squat about making money off your money.' The irreverent investment banker has ideas about multiplying the brothers' cash holdings. Most importantly, the banker has other important assets."

"Assets?" Summer frowned.

"Assets." Jer outlined a twin set of curves in the air, wiggling his eyebrows.

"Ooh." Summer grinned.

"You see," Jer said, "Arthur Erickson is smitten with none other than the brilliant Alice Hallis, a trailblazer investment banker. Take three: Alice marries Arthur and gives birth to three fantastic kids: Seth, the amazing Jeremy, and Ally."

"So Arthur is you father?" Summer said.

Jer's smile wavered. "Was."

"Oh." Summer looked to me. "I'm so sorry."

"But before we get to that," Jer said. "Arthur and Alice became inseparable. Together with Benjamin, they cemented the Erickson fortune and diversified the company. Unfortunately, Benjamin didn't have much luck in the love department. He favored gold diggers, married three times, and had ten children. The oldest of these is Alexander. He's Seth's age. Have you heard about Alex?"

Summer flashed me a curious look. "Only a little."

"Let's not talk about Alex in my house," I said, drawing the line.

"Okay," Jer said, "Mum on Alex, who's a son of a bitch. Take four: the year's 2001. Arthur, Alice, and Benjamin are in a meeting at the E&E's headquarters at the World Trade Center in New York. The date is September eleventh."

"Oh, God." Summer reached for my hand and squeezed it. "The three of them?"

I clung to her fingers and nodded. "The three of them."

Summer's mouth twisted into a sad grimace.

"Precocious Seth was twenty-one and already in his third year at MIT," Jer said. "My grandmother, Astrid, took on the company's guardianship, until Seth graduated. She remained as the chairman of the board, but as specified in the brothers' joint will, Seth took over as CEO of E&E and has been at it ever since. He's grown the conglomerate into a global giant."

Summer squeezed my hand again. "That's a lot of responsibility."

"So there you have it," Jer said. "The tale of the Ericksons in a nutshell."

It wasn't an easy tale to swallow, but if Summer kept holding my hand, I was game to hear about our ancestors all the way back to the dawn of mankind. Unfortunately, she got up from the table. On the upside, she returned carrying a delicious-looking apple pie.

"So," she said, cutting out a generous piece and parking the plateful before me. "This Alex cousin of yours is giving you guys trouble?"

"He's giving Seth problems," Jer said. "He took over as interim CEO when Seth went to Afghanistan. I guess he liked his stint at the top, because now he wants to be in charge. Since he can't persuade the board to elect him, he's tried all kinds of tricks."

"Really, Jer?" I said between bites. "Is that what we're going to talk about over the best pie I've ever had?"

"Glad you like it," Summer said, licking the sweet apple filling dripping from her fork.

The sight of her pink tongue swirling over the syrup and sliding over stainless steel had me doubling over the table. I had to suppress a groan when my dick throbbed. Christ, she was killing me, and she didn't even know it.

"Please, Jeremy, go on." She put down the lucky fork. "It's a fascinating story."

"See?" Jer poked my arm. "She thinks *I'm* fascinating."

"Nothing wrong with your self-esteem," I muttered, trying to put a lid on my overactive dick. *Focus on something else.*

Eating maybe. I pressed my fork on the china and gathered the last crumbs of pie from my plate. Summer sneaked in another slice onto my plate. The conspiratorial grin she flashed me had my heart doing somersaults and completely sabotaged my self-control efforts.

"Alex wants the power," Jer said. "To get it, he's promised his brothers and sisters a lot more dividends each year, money Seth sets aside for research and development, which accounts for the company's explosive growth. Alex also thinks that the company should be broken up and sold in pieces to generate cash for the voracious side of the family."

"Let's not talk about this anymore," I said. "It puts me in a bad mood."

"Okay, then." Jer put his fork down and pushed his plate aside. "Don't shoot the messenger, but I've been asked to remind you. The benefit is the week after next. You better not disappoint."

I'd hoped to avoid the affair altogether. "I'm really busy. I've got to finish the negotiations with the governor for the construction of the new highway and I need to inspect the North Slope field operations."

"No excuses, bro," Jer said. "You need to show up. You weren't there last year or the year before. The cousins have hardly seen you lately. People don't remember what you look like."

"The company's earnings are up," I said. "I get business done."

"Of course you get business done." Jer picked up the wine bottle and began to refill our glasses. "You're a damn workaholic. But it's not about the amount of work you're putting in, or the profits. It's about appearances. You need to address the rumors."

"What rumors?" Summer gathered the dirty dishes and started to get up.

"Sit," I said. "You cook, I clean."

"Fair enough." She set the dishes aside and stayed in her chair. "You mentioned rumors?"

"He knows what I'm talking about." Jer set the wine down. "People say he's a hermit. They think he's antisocial. You need to be seen."

"Sounds like wise advice." Summer toyed with her wineglass. "A little sucking up goes a long way with family and friends. Alex might be an ass, but what about the rest? And wouldn't this get-together be the perfect time to talk to them about your ideas for the company?"

"Now see?" Jer lifted his glass in the air. "She gets it."

I sipped on my wine. "I'll think about it. Okay?"

"Wait, I've got a great idea," Jer said. "Why don't you come to the benefit with us?"

"Me?" Summer's hand landed on her chest. "Oh, no. I'll be long gone by then."

Shit.

"In that case," Jer said. "Why don't you come stay with us at the big house for a few days? There are plenty of rooms over there. We can work on the lodging project together and you won't have to bother Seth in the least."

I repressed the urge to pummel my own brother. "She's not bothering me."

"It's a great idea," Jer said, ignoring me. "If you come and stay at the big house, you'll have everything you need and Seth will have to ditch his hermit status and come over and visit."

"Jer?" This time my voice hinted a warning. "She's fine. I want her to stay here."

Summer's brow furrowed. "If I'm bothering you…"

"Now see what you've done?" My brother had single-handedly undone my earlier work. "You keep going and she'll end up sleeping under the bridge for fear of inconveniencing the bears in their dens. Summer's fine here, she's staying with me and that's final."

After Jer left, Summer settled down on the chaise

with her laptop. The girl had grit. She stayed up late until she finished her redesign and sent it off to her boss and clients. But even as she worked, she seemed uneasy. I caught her stealing looks at me several times. I was beginning to understand how her mind operated. She was used to taking care of everyone around her and, right now, that included me.

When the time came to go to bed, she was jumpy as hell.

"Seth?" she said, after I came out of an ice-cold shower, decently dressed in sweats and a T-shirt. "I think I should sleep on the couch."

"Why?" I said, toweling my hair. "Do you find my bed uncomfortable?"

"No, your bed is actually very comfortable, which is why I think you should sleep in it and let me sleep on the couch."

"No can do."

"Why not?"

"Look around you," I said. "What do you see?"

She examined our surroundings. "Kitchen, living room, fireplace?"

"I see drawers full of sharp weapons, tripping hazards galore, doors, jagged glass, and fire dangers. You on that couch? I don't think so. I want you in the bedroom, behind locked doors, with that brawny door chain engaged, sleeping without worries and safe in bed."

"But…" She grappled for words. "What about you?"

"What about me?"

"That couch doesn't work well for you."

"You may be right about that." My heart revved up. "What do you suggest we do?"

"Maybe I should've gone to a hotel, or to the big house, like Jeremy suggested."

"Too late," I said. "I'll be fine."

"But you're not fine," she said, getting to her feet. "Jeremy said you ache when you don't sleep in your bed and you get cranky when you don't sleep well."

"Did he now?" I hung the towel over my shoulder. "Don't believe everything Jer says. I travel on business all the time and I do fine."

"But I do worry," she said. "I want you to sleep in your bed."

Talk about an opportunity I wasn't going to waste. My best hope was that I'd read Summer right. It was either takeoff or crash and burn, nothing in between. What the hell. I pulled on the collective and pushed on the cyclic. I was going a hundred percent for takeoff.

"Summer," I said, "the only way I can see me sleeping in my bed tonight is if you're in it next to me. But by the look on your face, I don't think you like that idea?"

"Um…" She hesitated. "I didn't say that."

"So what are you saying?" Hope teased me like the smile tickling my lips. "Summer Silva, did you just ask me to sleep with you?"

"No!" she said and then, "I mean, no, not in that way."

"Yeah, I got *that* message loud and clear."

"Oh, it's not that, it's just that… What if…you know…" She tripped over the words. "What if I tried to seduce you again?"

"Is that what has you all worried?" Relief. She wasn't rejecting me, not yet anyway. "I made you a couple of promises and I intend to keep them. If you get up, this time around I know what to do. I'd guide you back to bed like the doctor suggested. The question is: Are you willing to trust me?"

"Um…" Her eyes did a hit and run. "I don't know… it sounds…risky."

"And you're completely risk-adverse." It was a statement not a question.

"I must not be completely risk-adverse." She stared at her tightly clasped hands then back at me. "I'm here, am I not?"

"Excellent point." I stepped up to her, cupped her chin, and tilted her face until her eyes met mine. "Perhaps we could minimize the risks."

"H-how?"

"I think we'd be better off accepting what's happening here."

"And that is…?"

"That I want to kiss you." I hit the point of no return. "And that you want me to kiss you."

Her voice was a hoarse whisper. "It's not true."

"It's true and you know it." I ran my thumb over the soft expanse of her cheek. "So I propose that I kiss you now and get it out of the way. One kiss. Then we go to sleep and I mean just that, sleep, together, on my bed." I held my breath. "What do you think? Is it too much to ask?"

She opened her mouth and closed it. A storm brewed in her eyes. She wasn't sure. I knew it was a long shot, but I wasn't one to hold back for fear of failure. Her nostrils widened, taking in my scent as if sniffing for danger. The seconds ticked by, minutes, hours, centuries. And then…surprise. She nodded ever so slightly.

I didn't wait for her to change her mind. I kissed her,

a connection that my body celebrated with fireworks. I put my arms around her waist and tasted her lips, her tongue, her breath. Glory. My body resonated with the memories of our night together.

I kissed her, as I'd wanted to do for two days, and the kiss confirmed that the connection that tugged on my senses was real. I held her face between my hands and kissed her some more until we were both out of breath and I hovered at the edge of no return. I made a huge effort to climb out of a very steep drop before I screwed everything up.

"Christ," I rasped when I finally managed to tear my lips from hers.

Her breath came in short gasps, her eyes sparkled and her face flushed as if she had overexerted herself.

"Hell, I could kiss you all night." I tucked a strand of hair behind her ear before letting go. "But this little taste of you is going to last me 'til morning." Body screaming in protest, I took a step back. "Now go in there, get in bed, and don't be scared. Okay? I'll be along shortly."

Her lips wavered, then a new smile birthed in her eyes and spread to her face, a mischievous grin that turned those luscious lips up at the corners and warned of all kinds of trouble.

She leaned into my space and, approaching me slowly, delivered her own kiss to my lips. The kiss was like an arctic wallop, but scalding; like a blow to the senses, but soft. Her tongue swiped a little taste of me. I gasped when she cut me off without warning, leaving me reeling, rock hard and without a trace of oxygen flowing to my lungs.

"Erickson?" she said before she sauntered off. "I don't think you understand."

"Understand what?"

She halted at the threshold and looked over her shoulder.

"I'm not scared of you anymore," she said. "I'm scared of *me* when I'm with you."

TEN

FOUR DAYS LATER, I opened my eyes and there he was, the very man I'd been dreaming about, propped up on the pillows next to me, sharing his bed with me, illuminating dawn with the gold in his eyes. He was already dressed in dark slacks and a striped shirt, a marked departure from his usual informal attire.

"Going somewhere?" I said.

"Hey, there. Morning, beautiful." Seth set his tablet aside, turned on his side and, propping his head on his hand, smiled. "Got to go into the office today."

My smile faltered. He wasn't going to be around. I hid my disappointment and asked him the question I'd asked him first thing every day since I'd been staying with him.

"Did I?"

"Nope." The tips of his fingers trailed over my cheeks. "No dream chasing to report. Been waiting all night. Can I?"

I nodded. I loved that he always asked me before he leaned over and kissed me, a touch of lips that lingered just long enough to awaken the rest of my body. I closed my eyes and enjoyed the moment, the feel of his mouth against mine and his hand, immensely strong but also incredibly gentle as he ran his fingers through my hair.

A dream, this had to be a powerful dream. For the last few days, this had become our private routine, a show of trust, for both of us. But it was also a harsh test for my body. It was as if he were daring me with his self-control, tempting me like the devil himself. And me? I was having lots of trouble keeping my she-devil in check.

My body melted against his. My heart drummed against his heart. My fingers ran over his shirt, craving the skin beneath the fabric. I knew what he wanted, what his body needed, but I couldn't, wouldn't. I pressed myself against him, teasing my senses, testing him, knowing he wouldn't budge and neither would I, even if I secretly wished he'd forget about his promise and find a way to defeat all my objections.

"Trial by fire." He quit my mouth and got up from the bed with a groan. "You're tough, girl. But I'm tough too. I was just waiting for you to get up before I left. I've got meetings in Anchorage all morning. As for you, you should get some exercise, make sure our routine keeps working."

Our routine. It had a lovely ring to it, didn't it? Seth was right. It was working. I hadn't sleepwalked at all since that first night. Talk about a shift.

I sat up on the bed, reached for my laptop and clicked on my email to check for news of Tammy sightings, watching Seth behind lidded eyes, as he moved about the room. I admired his body's elegant stride and the way in which his slacks hugged his hips and cradled his ass. God and his freaking saints, help me. He'd seduced me, completely and absolutely bowled me over, had me panting after him like a smitten fool. No way around it. But even though I longed to give in, I couldn't. I'd come to Alaska to find my sister. I wasn't suited for this place. I had a life, responsibilities, four thousand miles away.

On the other hand, a girl could get used to the view, and I wasn't talking about the landscape that dazzled my eyes when Seth threw open the curtains.

I scrolled through my emails. My heart skipped when I saw that I had a response to one of my inquiries about Tammy. My fingers froze on the keyboard. What if I found Tammy today? What then? No more Seth. No more sleeping in his bed. My good mood plummeted. These days every gain was a loss and my emotions felt completely bipolar. I forced myself to read through the email.

"Somebody has information about Tammy in a place called Cooper Landing," I called out to Seth, who was knotting his tie in front of the mirror. "I'm going to drive over there. I may not be back in time for dinner."

"Kenai?" Seth marched into the bedroom and, adjusting his tie, scanned the email over my shoulder. "How do you plan to get there?"

"Car rental," I said. "Time to venture back on the road."

"I don't like it," he said, looking through his drawers. "That guy could be out there, waiting for you."

"Not about me, remember?" I said. "How many times do I have to tell you?"

"I'll be satisfied when we find the SOB and he tells us it was a mistake in his own words." He pulled out a leather-edged sweater from the dresser. "Kenai is pretty far from here. Why don't you come with me? I can give you a ride after my meetings. It'll be a hell of a lot quicker and it won't involve punctured brakes or you, car-skating all over Alaska."

As he pulled the tan sweater over his head, I found

myself imagining that instead of putting it on, he was undressing for me.

Seth fixed his yellow eyes on me. “Summer?”

Crap. I got myself under semi-control.

“Sooner or later I have to deal with the roads,” I said. “Besides, I’ve already imposed on you enough and I don’t have any fair way of reciprocating your help.”

“Reciprocating, eh?” He chuckled, a sound so sexy it curled my toes. “That’s a big word. Well, if you really want to ‘reciprocate,’ let’s make a barter. I give you a ride to Kenai and you come with me to the benefit next Thursday. Tit for tat.”

Me? Go out with Seth? To a party? In my current state of permanent lust, it sounded like a sure formula for disaster. “I thought you didn’t want to go to the benefit.”

“On selected occasions, I’ve been known to listen to good advice.” He fit his foot into a fine leather chukka boot. “I’ll go, but only if you come with me.”

Talk about pressure. His invitation hovered really close to emotional blackmail. I wavered. I had to find Tammy and Hector continued to pressure me to return to Miami. But I’d also learned from Jeremy that it was important for Seth to be at the benefit. And that knowledge seemed to overtake all of my other reservations.

“Okay,” I said. “If I’m still around next week, I’ll go with you.”

“Deal.” He tightened his laces. “Can you be ready to leave in half an hour?”

“Sure.” I set the laptop on the night table, threw the covers aside and rose from the bed.

It was only as I made my way to the bathroom that I realized what Seth had done. He’d gotten himself a date. With me. Note to self: people with tons of smarts and extraordinary grit managed sneak attacks under the radar with impressive cool.

I halted by the threshold. “Smooth, Erickson,” I said. “Very smooth.”

“Yeah.” He grinned. “I thought so myself.”

THE ROAR OF the helicopter announced the beginning of our newest journey. It touched down on a square landing pad not forty feet from the house. I knew nothing about helicopters, but this had to be the most striking machine I’d ever laid eyes on. The fuselage was a work of art and the modern, sleek lines of the metallic-gray aircraft bedazzled my eyes.

I swallowed a gulp of fear.

“What’s wrong?” Seth said.

“Have I told you?” I stared at the magnificent contraption. “I’m afraid of flying.”

“Now you tell me,” he said. “Have you flown in a helicopter before?”

I perched my fist on my hip. “Are you mistaking me for Kim Kardashian again?”

He laughed. “You’re going to like flying with me.”

He took my hand and together we approached thc helicopter, buffeted by the rotors’ gusty wind. Seth opened the door. I braced my foot on the boarding step, climbed on the flight deck and sat down on the left front seat. Seth strapped me in, shut the door, and strode around the helicopter before he took the pilot’s place in the cockpit.

“Thanks,” Seth yelled over the roar before he shut the door.

The man waved and made his way to the E&E truck

that came up the driveway to pick him up. Seth put on his helmet and strapped on a kneepad with a tablet. He went through his checklist, tested the instrument panel, checked the radar, and programmed the route into the computer. He handed me a headset and motioned for me to put it on.

"Ready?" His voice came crisp and clear over the com.

"As ready as I'm going to be." I sunk my fingernails into my seat.

He placed his feet on the pedals, held the stick between his legs with his right hand, and gripped the throttle mounted on the lever with his left. The roar of the helicopter increased as it lifted from the ground. It hovered in place for a moment, shuddered slightly and then moved forward through the air, gaining speed and altitude. Eyes hidden beneath his aviator sunglasses, Seth flashed me a reassuring smile, transitioning us into full flight.

The knot in my stomach eased as we gained altitude. I took in the cabin's plush interior, which reminded me of a high-end luxury yacht, complete with lots of leather, polished woods, and an exceptional-looking instrument panel. A quick glance revealed that the rear cabin was even more luxurious, outfitted with a two-toned bench and a couple of plush bucket seats. This wasn't so bad. Slowly, I let go of my seat.

"What kind of helicopter is this?" I asked.

"There isn't another one like it," he said. "The basic bones are an adaptation of a Sikorsky S-70C Firehawk, which is the commercial version of the Black Hawk. Are you familiar with the Black Hawk?"

"Familiar? No, but I've seen it in movies."

"This is a cutting-edge version of it, upgraded for high performance and customized to my specs."

"Very nice," I said. "Is this what you fly for the National Guard too?"

"Close enough," he said. "I fly the Sikorsky HH-60 Pave Hawk for the Guard, which is also a Black Hawk, but adapted for insertion, recovery, search and rescue."

"Impressive, Erickson," I said. "Where are your guns?"

"No need for guns on this one." He smiled. "The battles I fight these days involve mostly salvos across the desk."

"This must have cost you a pretty penny."

"It was pricey, but I saved some bucks by partnering up with the company to produce it as a prototype. They're hoping to market the concept to companies in the private sector."

"Smart bear," I said. "It must be a coup for E&E to own this piece of equipment."

"It's not E&E's helicopter," he said rather forcefully. "It's *my* private aircraft."

"Oops," I said. "Why do I feel like I just stepped on your sore tail?"

"I paid for my Firehawk. I run the company like a business, not like a piggy bank for a bunch of rich kids."

"I take it this is a touchy subject?" I said. "Let me guess: Cousin Alex?"

"I don't care if he wants to buy a Ferrari collection," he said. "As long as he pays for it, he can do whatever the hell he wants. I hold myself to the same standard. But enough about Alex. Look out your window."

The day was sunny and clear. The magnificent mountains flanked us on both sides, summits frosted with shimmering white. Vast swatches of uninterrupted forest flowed in every direction. The sound rippled beneath us, a smooth, blue carpet. Seth banked the helicopter. Three points sliced the water like knives.

"Oh, my God!" I squealed. "Are those…?"

"Orcas," Seth said. "We've got several pods that patrol the sound."

"They're spectacular," I said. "This is amazing!"

"And look at three o'clock." He circled over the mouth of a river. "That's a brown bear, fishing for salmon. Grizzlies, they call them in the lower forty-eight."

"It's like the Discovery Channel." I pressed my nose to the glass. "No, it's even better than the Discovery Channel!"

His laughter flowed over the coms, quiet, crisp, and rich. "Look closely as we fly over that little lake. There's an old moose that hangs out on the east shore."

"There it is!" I squealed. "Do you see it?"

"Every time I do this commute," Seth said. "The wildlife is just one of the reasons I love Alaska."

On a day like today, I could understand the attraction. I could feel the place seeping into my veins, awakening my numbed senses to the myriad details that dazzled and thrilled. The landscape's expansive proportions defied imagination. Sitting next to Seth, with the helicopter roaring beneath my seat and Alaska at my feet, I felt like a queen on my throne.

I glanced at him and recognized him for the extraordinary being he was. Up here, he was in harmony with his environment, part machine, part wildlife, free to soar. The helicopter was like an extension of him, connecting mind and machine by his body's subtle movements. It was obvious: he loved to fly. He belonged in the sky just as much as he belonged to Alaska.

He gripped the stick lightly, as if persuading the aircraft to dance with him. And suddenly I wanted to yield to his touch, to be the stick in his hand, to soar like the helicopter at the whim of his body, to fly him to places only I could take him.

"What?" he said, when he caught me looking.

"Nothing," I gnawed on my lips. "If you'd told me two weeks ago that I'd be in Alaska, flying in a helicopter, seeing bears, moose, and killer whales in the wild, I might have laughed in your face."

"And now?"

I smiled. "I'm glad I came."

ELEVEN

WE LANDED ON a helipad next to the parking lot of a sizable industrial complex overlooking the Cook Inlet and Knik Arm. An extensive set of understated historic buildings, warehouses, wharfs, and storage lots composed the E&E complex. Seth shut down the helicopter, took off his kneeboard and helmet and, after unstrapping his seat belt, came around and helped me to get down.

"That was amazing," I said.

The smile he gave me warmed my soul.

A BMW pulled up. The driver, a very attractive woman, got out of the car and went straight for Seth, hugging him as if she owned him. I refrained from peeling her off by an act of pure will, but I had to grit my teeth.

"Summer," Seth said, "this is my sister, Ally."

"Oh." I felt instantly better and not a little foolish. "Nice to meet you."

"Likewise." Ally flashed an open smile that reminded me of Jeremy.

Seth's brows quirked. "Who did you think she was?"

"Oh, well, I—I didn't know."

"I see." Seth flashed me a grin that said he was on to me. "I asked Ally to show you around Anchorage this morning."

"You don't have to trouble yourself. I can wait. No problem."

"It's no trouble," Ally said. "Come on. Let's leave Seth to do his thing. I've got a whole morning planned for us girls."

She was a platinum blonde version of Jeremy, with sparkling blue eyes, delicate features, and a round mouth that reminded me of a ripe strawberry. Like Jer, she was fun, bubbly, and vivacious and, unlike Seth, she was a prodigiously fast talker.

I soon learned that she lived in Anchorage with her husband, a Texan who was an emergency room doctor. She worked at E&E but was playing hooky today. She zipped me around Anchorage in her Beemer as if she were a NASCAR racer, shifting with the joy of a natural-born driver. The backseat driver in me cringed at every turn.

After a glorious morning and a thorough tour of Anchorage, she turned into the parking lot of what looked like a high-end boutique. "Shopping time," she announced, turning off the ignition. "Seth said you needed a dress for the benefit next week."

He hadn't said any of that to me, but I'd made a deal with him. He'd help me find my sister and, if I was still around, I'd go with him to the benefit. It was fair and square and I intended to stick by it…*if* I was still around by then.

I followed Ally into the store, where the two of us had a blast trying on dresses. I don't know why, but I had assumed that any Alaskan party would be informal. Apparently, I was wrong. Ally informed me that I needed fancy cocktail attire. I found a dress I liked for a price I didn't. I had to get an overcoat with it, as well as some shoes and accessories. My credit card was about to scream, but when I went to pay, Ally insisted she had strict orders from Seth.

"He's buying," she said.

"No way." I handed my credit card to the clerk. "It's not right."

"Of course it's right." Ally plucked my credit card from the clerk's hand and gave her another. "He's my big bro and he spoils me rotten. He'd like to do the same with you."

"I don't need to be spoiled."

"Come on." She wiggled her very fair brows. "Every girl wants to be spoiled."

"Not me." I'd learned the hard way that guys who pretended to spoil girls sometimes wanted your dignity in return.

"Give the guy a break." Ally dropped my credit card in my purse. "If he wants to give you a gift, let him! You didn't come to Alaska expecting to go to fancy parties. So, I think it's only fair he pays for your stuff."

"Seth has already done a lot for me," I said. "The last thing he needs is one more person sucking the life out of him."

"Seth is a giver for sure." Ally's pale blue eyes took a new measure of me. "I'm glad you're able to see beyond the tough exterior. But if you have any objections to his plan, kindly take it up with him. I have no desire to face his wrath."

She flashed me a sparkling smile that displayed the stubborn streak she shared with her brother. These people were nearly as pig-headed as my people.

"You're really something else." Ally took some of the posh garment bags from the clerk and motioned for me to do the same. "You're like the opposite of a gold digger."

"Excuse me?" I followed her out of the store.

"Sorry." She opened the trunk and settled the bags in it. "I don't mean to offend you with a compliment that's also an insult, but you need to understand. Gold diggers are the norm when you're an Erickson."

The Erickson money would make Seth a target for fortune-seekers wherever he went. His good looks would only add to the equation and his generosity, combined with what I was discovering was a very big heart, would be the icing on the cake. But Ally had me all wrong and, as I got into the car, I rushed to correct her misconceptions.

"Your brother and I aren't…you know." I swallowed a dry gulp. "I suppose I don't want to give you the wrong impression."

"Oh, please." She pushed on the ignition and peeled out of the parking lot. "I don't need to know the juicy details."

"I'm going back to Miami as soon as I find my sister."

"Sure." She smirked, speeding down the busy street. "If he lets you."

What did she mean by that? "Could you, please, um, slow down?"

"He's smitten with you," she said, blunt as her brother.

"He's *not* smitten with me."

"Oh, yes he is," Ally said. "I can tell by the way he looks at you. I don't know you very well, but I think you're smitten with him too."

"Stop," I said. "We've only known each other for a few days."

"I'll stop." She hurled the car into a tiny parking space and screeched to a stop. "But only because this lovely place is where we're having lunch."

The charming restaurant was perched on a cliff overlooking Cook Inlet. Cargo ships sailed in the distance and low-hanging clouds cast moving shadows over the stunning vistas.

"Best caribou burgers in Anchorage." Ally ordered for me. "Served on hot sourdough."

I'd never had caribou, let alone caribou burgers, but the one the waiter parked before me was delicious. I managed to put down a great portion of it. Ally's slim figure disguised a voracious appetite. She washed down her burger with a handcrafted ale.

"I don't think you're such bad news," she said when she was done dispatching her meal.

"Me?"

"Yes, you." She wiped her mouth with a napkin. "Seth would hate me for saying this to you, but he deserves a little happiness in his life. He's been through a lot."

I put down the remains of my burger. "What do you mean?"

"When Mom and Dad died, Seth's youth got cut off at the knees," Ally said. "The full yoke of E&E fell squarely around his neck. He's been an ox ever since, the family's work beast. He never got to enjoy being young and carefree, so you've got to excuse him if he's a little straight and square."

Straight and square—plus sharp like a right angle—described Seth all right.

"Jer and I tried to help," she said, "but we were too

young back then to fend for ourselves. Seth was like a dad to us."

"He's not that much older than you and Jeremy."

"He's only two years older than Jer and four years older than me," Ally said. "He used to help me with my homework. Even when he was in college, he'd call me every night to make sure I was doing okay. If I was blue or missed my parents, he'd fly out for the weekend, just to be with me. Seth gave me away at my wedding. A girl couldn't ask for a better brother."

Why wasn't I surprised at all?

"Think about it," she said. "He's barely thirty-four. Not only has he grown the company tremendously, but he's managed to do it while helping his community and serving his country. Did you know he holds the record for the highest-altitude helicopter rescue in North America?"

"No."

"He's a phenomenal pilot, the guy you want to pluck you out if you're in danger," Ally said. "He was the XO of the Alaska Air National Guard's 212th Rescue Squadron when they went to Afghanistan."

"He didn't mention any of that." But of course, he wouldn't. I gave in to my curiosity. "Ally? What happened in Afghanistan?"

"They were extracting a group of special ops out of the mountains. They were ambushed. An RPG blasted through the helicopter and killed one of Seth's crew and the other pilot."

"Holy shit."

"Yeah," Ally said. "I read his commendation letter. The helicopter was on fire, and so was he, but he managed to put the helo down and saved the lives of the rest of the crew and the five special ops guys he'd picked up. He was 'grievously wounded,' but he dragged three wounded out of the burning helicopter and then organized the survivors' defense. He held back the attackers for hours, until backup arrived."

Talk about the definition of heroism. "Wow."

"He's incredible," Ally said. "But he was pissed when he came back from Afghanistan, angry and depressed. Sometimes, I think he still is. They gave him a whole bunch of medals and decorations, but he never talks about any of that. My heart still hurts when I remember how sick he was when they shipped him back."

"Was it really bad?"

"Awful," Ally said. "He was in terrible shape. He broke his back in two places. His lungs were scorched. He couldn't breathe on his own for a while. And the burns. God. I cried when I saw him, which was the wrong thing to do, because for months after that, he wouldn't let any of us visit him at the hospital."

I had a flashback of his reflection in the bathroom mirror that first time I'd tended to his back. My stomach clenched. It had been so hard for him to accept my touch.

"The doctors weren't sure he would recover," Ally said. "But he did and look at him now. When he came out of the hospital, he moved out to the cabin. Sometimes, when I think of him, alone in his house, I want to pull out my hair. I was ecstatic when he called me up and asked me to take you around. I haven't seen him excited about anything or anybody for a long time."

Oh crap. I was the wrong thing to get excited about. I was such a mess, barely able to take care of Tammy and Louise, due out of Alaska anytime, struggling with my own problems…

And yet when I thought of Seth, something in me heartened. Here was someone who'd gone through so much more than the rest of us, whose daily challenges dwarfed mine, and yet he wasn't daunted by much. I liked his courage. I liked him. I craved his body too.

Crapola. I was in way over my head.

"Now we've got a little time to take care of you," Ally said after paying the bill. "If there are some other errands you'd like to run, I'm game."

"I suppose that if I bought a few things for myself I'd be sparing your wardrobe from Seth's 'borrows.'"

Ally laughed. "I don't mind, but let's go get what you need."

"And there's this compounding pharmacy here in Anchorage." I looked up the address in my cell and showed it to Ally. "Do you know where it is?"

"Seems easy enough to get to," she said as we got up from the table and walked to the car. "Why do you need to go there?"

"I spoke to the pharmacist this morning," I said. "I asked him to mix a medical moisturizer for Seth from a formula I got from the Burn Center at Johns Hopkins. Perhaps we could pick it up?"

"Sure." Ally said as we got in the car. "Why didn't I think of it?"

Probably because Seth would never admit to pain or discomfort to her or to anyone else for that matter and, unlike me, she hadn't caught him taking icy showers or rolling in the snow when he thought I wasn't looking.

We picked up the lotion then went on to get a few things to augment my limited wardrobe. I bought myself a jacket—on sale, which explained why I settled with the very loud pink—and a few other practical things.

"Have you seen this woman by any chance?" I held up my cell for the cashier. The screen displayed a picture of Tammy. I thought maybe the enormous store was a place my sister may have visited if she needed suitable gear for Alaska.

The cashier examined the picture. "Of course I have."

"Here?" My heart skipped a beat. "When?"

"Her picture is plastered all over the employee break room," the cashier said. "She's that silly girl who ran away to Alaska with a guy she met on the internet. How stupid can she be? Her sister is looking for her."

Great. Wonderful. Fabulous. I had succeeded at broadcasting my sister's flaws all over Alaska while failing miserably at finding her. I pinched the bridge of my nose and groaned.

"Chin up," Ally said. "You'll find her yet. You'll see."

We went to the supermarket, where I splurged buying ingredients to cook for Seth. I watched as the clerks packed my food order. Because so many people who worked in Anchorage lived away from the city, they packed the cold stuff in iceboxes, sealed for easy transport.

Ally's cell chimed as we loaded the groceries. Obediently, we drove back to E&E headquarters. Seth waited for us by the helicopter. He flashed me a smile when he opened the car door for me. My knees faltered.

"Did you have a good time?" he asked.

"Your sister is a fantastic tour guide," I said. "I had caribou for lunch."

"Impressive." He tugged at my new jacket. "Pink?"

I lifted my arms in the air and twirled. "Warm *and* on sale."

"That explains it." He laughed.

I really liked it when he laughed like that. The lines on his face softened and his eyes sparkled like gold coins. I wanted to hear that sound more often.

He took my hand and gestured to a distinguished, dark-skinned, sober-faced gentleman. "Summer, this is Robert, the big house manager."

The elegantly dressed man scrutinized me from head to toe while the ground crew transferred my purchases to the helicopter. He, too, had a load to add to the helicopter. I surmised he'd been shopping for "the big house."

Robert inclined his head formally. "Miss Silva."

"Nice to meet you," I said.

Just then, a black, unmarked sedan pulled onto the lot, followed by an Alaskan Wildlife Trooper. The tires screeched to a stop right in front of us. Seth's body tensed. He let go of my hand, planted his feet apart and set his hand on his hips. Two men got out of the car.

"Seth Erickson?" one of the men said.

"Who's asking," Seth said.

"I'm Agent Dobson, this is Agent Stevens." The man flashed a badge.

Seth examined the credentials. "Feds?"

"We need you to come with us," Agent Dobson said.

"And if I don't want to?"

"Then we'll show you the warrant."

My eyes shifted from the agent to Seth. The lines on his face were frozen into an unreadable expression. His yellow eyes fixed on the agent.

"Explain," he said.

"I think it'd be best to sort this out elsewhere." The agent landed a hand on Seth's arm.

Seth's stare settled on the other man's hand. "Don't. Touch. Me."

The agent's hand wilted from Seth's arm.

By now, a little crowd had gathered around us, the crew tending to the helicopter, workers from the dock, security, and a few employees detoured from the parking lots. Judging the mood, I had a feeling that, if Seth gave the order, those agents would be kicked out of the premises and not kindly.

"Mr. Erickson," Agent Stevens said. "We don't want any trouble. Please come with us."

Seth rumbled. "I'd like to see that warrant of yours first."

"Officer?" the agent called on the patrolman.

The officer strolled over.

"Will?" Seth said. "What's this about?"

"Something about a water pollution charge," the trooper said, without much conviction.

"E&E, polluting the water?" Seth scoffed. "We're the most environmentally responsible company in Alaska, but you know that."

"Sorry, man." The trooper shifted on his feet. "I'm not sure what's going on here, some rubbish about state-Fed cooperation. I don't like it, but I've got to do what I'm told."

"Understood." Seth took the warrant from the officer and read it.

"A spill at Star Lake has created a huge fish kill and an extensive dead zone," Agent Stevens said. "We have evidence that suggests that your company is in violation of the Clean Water Act."

"Let me get this straight," Seth said. "There's a fish

kill on Star Lake and you think E&E's lumber operation is responsible for it?"

"Apparently so."

"I fish on that lake," Seth said. "What evidence do you have?"

"That's not something I'm authorized to discuss with you."

"Who made this complaint?"

"I'm afraid I can't share that with you either," the agent said. "The complainant is under whistle-blower protection laws."

A news van pulled up to the chain-link fence and raised its portable satellite. A car screeched to a stop behind it. The window whirled down to reveal a photographer with a high-power lens. Seth gave them a cursory look then scrutinized the agents before him.

"Let's recap," he said. "You can't name my accuser and you have no evidence, and yet you're willing to launch a criminal investigation on the whims of a whistle-blower's complaint. You've also managed to leak the news to the media in a bid to broadcast this reality show for the whole of Alaska."

The men stared at their feet.

"This is not about pollution," Seth said. "This is about politics. Ally, call Jer. Have him call our attorneys. Summer? Get in the helicopter with Robert. He has instructions and will make sure that you're safe and comfortable. One of the pilots will fly the two of you home."

I started to speak. "But—"

"No buts," Seth said. "Do as I say. Stay at my place. You'll be safe there."

Why was he thinking about me when he was the one in trouble?

I rose on my toes and, winding my hands around his arm, whispered in his ear. "To bad weather, a brave face."

"I like that saying." His fingertips traced the line of my jaw. "Now get in the helicopter. Make sure you use the door chain tonight. Robert will take care of the rest. You'll be fine."

Of course I'd be fine. On the other hand, he wasn't going for a ride in the park.

"Promise me you'll be home soon," I said.

"I've got a good incentive to rush back." He gave me a quick peck on the lips and turned me in the direction of the helicopter. "Go."

"Ready?" Agent Stevens said.

"In a moment." He turned to look at me. "Let me see you get in that helicopter. Go on."

It took all I had to climb onto the helicopter. I flopped on the plush leather seat with a demoralized sigh. I put on the headset. Tears of frustration burned in my eyes, useless tears. Seth Erickson was a good man and this was a setup if I'd ever seen one. If only I could have a go at those arrogant agents.

Robert sat next to me and strapped on his seat belt. With a somber face, he nodded at Seth. A pilot rushed to the cockpit. As he went down his checklist, I met Seth's gaze across the tarmac. I sensed his strength in the tilt of his chin and resolve in his body's poise. He was neither afraid nor defeated. He was a warrior on the way to battle and he was going to kick some ass.

It was only after the rotors began to spin and I lifted a hand in good-bye that Seth waved back at me, got into the black sedan and left with the agents. My stomach plunged with a sudden sense of loss. I'd been around him for only a short time and yet, in his absence, I felt incomplete. Worst part? I was afraid for him. The lump in my throat was about to choke me. I had a bad feeling about this one.

TWELVE

The helicopter roared. The landing skids separated from the asphalt. I took in the black sedan, accelerating through the main gates, the media gathered by the fence, the little crowd surrounding Ally, and Jeremy, who came rushing out of the building.

"Stop!" I shouted into the headset. "Down, let me out of here, now!"

The startled pilot hovered only a few feet from the ground. He looked back at me, confused. I unclipped my seat belt, ripped off the headset, slid the door open, and hopped out of the helicopter. I landed on all fours, crept away from the whirlwind, and ran to Ally and Jeremy.

"What the hell?" Jer said, when I reached them.

"Summer?" Ally hugged me. "What did you just do?"

"I can't go," I rasped. "I just can't."

Behind me, the helicopter landed again. A flustered Robert caught up with me as the roar of the engines quit.

"Master Seth wouldn't approve of you jumping out of a moving helicopter," he said in a resounding English accent. "I'm sure of it, miss."

I looked to Ally and Jer. "Does he always talk like that?"

"Yes," they said in unison.

"Summer, that was crazy," Ally said. "You could've gotten hurt!"

"Never jump out of a helicopter." A glint of utter astonishment lit Jer's gaze. "It's not safe."

"I know that!"

"Then why the hell did you do it?"

"Because!" I didn't know quite how to explain it. "I'm not leaving. Period."

"Seth said you had to go," Ally noted.

"You must follow Master Seth's directions," Robert said.

"He's right," Jer agreed. "Around here, things work best when we do what Seth says."

"If the lot of you want to follow Seth's almighty commands, then do so," I said. "As for me, I'm here to stay. Did you call the attorneys?"

"They're on their way," Jer said.

"Miss Silva," Robert said. "We must leave."

"You go," I said. "If you don't mind, make sure the groceries get put away. I'm staying and we could all waste a lot of time talking about it, so let's not."

"Master Seth put you under my care."

"And I'm relieving you of the burden."

"Master Jeremy?" Robert said. "I must return to the house. Mistress Astrid is bound to find out about this unfortunate occurrence. When she does, she'll require my assistance."

"Boy, those Feds don't know what's coming," Jer muttered under his breath. "Grandma will have them roasted alive. Go ahead, Robert, go back to the house. Tell her what happened."

"And let vengeance rain upon them," Robert added scornfully. "What about Miss Silva?"

"I'll keep an eye on her."

"But Master Seth will be angry with me, with all of us!" Robert said.

"Hopefully he'll take it up with the proper party."

Jer's gaze, along with Robert's and Ally's, fell squarely on me.

JER PACED SETH'S OFFICE, a grand space illuminated by tall art-deco windows and furnished with dark mahogany pieces. He talked on one phone and texted and emailed on the other. I sat on the couch next to Ally, who was also working her cell, calling every contact on her list. I felt useless. Beyond the glass windows, the sun began to set over the mountains. Seth had been gone for hours and we knew nothing.

"The attorneys are still at it," Jer said when he hung up the phone. "They haven't been allowed to meet with Seth yet."

"Surely Seth asked for a lawyer right away," Ally said. "How can they keep him isolated all this time?"

"They're going to milk this for all it's worth." Jer's mouth twisted in anger. "They're probably waiting to disclose his location so that the courts are closed and he has to spend the night in jail."

Seth in jail? My mouth soured and my stomach squeezed.

"A night in jail will add to the scandal," Ally said somberly.

Jer agreed. "Seth's going to be majorly pissed."

"Who's doing this and why?" I asked.

"The who is easy." Ally scoffed. "Alex, of course."

"But proving that is an entirely different matter." Jer raked his fingers through his hair, a gesture that reminded me of Seth.

"I don't understand," I said. "Alex has a vested interest in E&E. Why would he want to hurt his own family?"

"Remember how I told you he wanted to sell off parts of the company?" Jer said. "Well, he wants the lumber division sold for a hefty profit, which probably explains why he fixated on the lumber mill at Star Lake. A public scandal like this will help him convince the board that the mill needs to be sold and that as the CEO, Seth has neglected his job and needs to be fired."

"But how did Alex manage to manipulate the system?" I said. "Those agents showed up with a freaking warrant for God's sake."

"Alex is a political animal," Ally said. "He's worked hard to make friends in high places. He has the connections."

"It doesn't even matter to him if the charges against Seth stick or not," Jer pointed out shrewdly. "It's a mudslinging campaign. Alex's goal is to undermine Seth's ability to run E&E. Seth is negotiating a huge contract with the governor, and Alex will do anything to stop him. And unless Seth can prove his complete innocence, this episode, no matter how it turns out, will hurt his reputation."

I shook my head. These people needed a lesson in family 101.

The door opened and one of Seth's administrative assistants walked in. "We're on the news." He grabbed the remote and turned on the flat-screen TV on the far wall.

We were on the news all right. The anchorwoman reported E&E's alleged involvement with the spill at Star Lake while the images of all of us, huddled around the helicopter, played on the screen. A wobbly camera shot focused on Seth as he talked to the agents. I caught a glimpse of me as the camera panned out. Outrage distorted my face.

The phone vibrated in my hand. It was Hector again. I didn't care what was happening at work. I couldn't spare the time. If Hector wanted to fire me, then let him. The only number I wanted to see on my screen was Seth's.

"The courthouse just closed." Jer grimaced, reading a text from Seth's attorneys. "They managed to get a copy of the criminal complaint right before it did."

"What evidence do they have?" Ally demanded.

"The complaint is very weak." Jer perused the document. "It's all based on the whistle-blower's statement. Water quality tests show only small traces of the pollutants prohibited by the EPA and, due to public health concerns, the health department ordered the dead fish burned before they could be tested for evidence."

Ally huffed. "No self-respecting Alaskan judge will accept a complaint without evidence."

"Unless he's bought and paid for," Jer noted.

"But isn't the lack of evidence good news for Seth?" I asked.

"Yes and no," Jer said. "It weakens the complaint, but not knowing what pollutants were used to kill the fish also weakens Seth's ability to prove his innocence. And I know my brother. I guarantee that he's going to want to clear his name."

"What will he need to prove that he's innocent?" I asked

"Conclusive water tests would've been nice," Jer said. "But the fish kill is over a week old. The poison is probably diluted by now. Fish would've been even better. Traces in the flesh would've given us an idea of what pollutants were used and for how long. If we knew that, we'd have some serious leads."

We waited for news all night. Jer and Ally stretched out on Seth's couches and got a couple of hours of sleep. Unwilling to risk a sleepwalking episode, I survived on coffee and paced up and down the building's long corridors. Many of E&E's employees kept vigil with us. In talking to them, I discovered that they liked and admired Seth immensely.

Early in the morning, Jer found me in one of the conference rooms, contemplating the huge topographical map of Alaska that occupied the center of the room. Something had been bothering me all night, and now the idea began to coalesce in my mind.

"News?" I said, as soon as he stepped into the room.

"None yet." He knuckled his eyes and yawned. "It's too early."

"Jer," I said. "Where's Star Lake?"

"Right here." Jer traced the star-shaped edges of a large blue puddle on the map.

"Where's Seth's house?" I asked.

"Here." Jer pointed.

I noticed that, as the crow's flies, Star Lake wasn't that far from Seth's house. I frowned. Could it be?

"Is Anya Golov's homestead on Star Lake?"

"Yes," he said. "Why do you ask?"

His phone rang before I could answer. Memories of my visit with Anya flashed before my eyes. *He's got the boys at the mill riled up*, she'd warned Seth about Alex. *He's promised them all sorts of goodies if they stick with him.*

I wondered if Seth remembered. Was this an inside

job? Was the mysterious whistle-blower one of the mill employees, working for Alex? And one other thought. Whatever had happened at the lake, it had happened a week ago, maybe longer. Anya. All that fish. *More fish than she could ever use*, Seth had noted.

Maybe there was a way to prove Seth's innocence after all.

Jer hung up. His somber expression spoke for itself. "We're going to court today."

"*You* are going to court," I said. "*I* need to be somewhere else."

ALLY'S CESSNA SKYHAWK glided onto Star Lake with the elegance of a ballerina easing onto the stage. She flew her small plane in the same forceful way in which she drove, which made it a terrifying experience for the backseat driver in me. I might have sweated a few quarts of fear along the way, but at least we had arrived.

There was an unusual amount of air traffic over Star Lake, mostly news planes and helicopters getting ready to contribute to Seth Erickson's spectacular slander. We dodged quite a few of them on our way to shore. We were in a hurry. The forecast called for snow, the radar showed the storm approaching and Seth's hearing was on the schedule for early afternoon. We needed to get back before then. As soon as we taxied to shore, Anya met us at the dock, with her rifle on hand, of course. This time, she didn't shoot. Best news? She was wearing her hearing aid.

"It's a busy day around here," she said as Ally and I tied down the plane. "The lake's had more visitors in one day than the rest of the year put together."

Anya didn't leave her homestead very often. She

didn't have TV or cell reception. She hadn't heard about Seth. I told her the whole story as we walked back to the cabin. She listened, nodding every once in a while. By the time I got to the end of the story, we were in her living room.

"I warned Seth," she said. "I told him to watch out."

"I don't think he believed Alex would stoop this low," Ally said.

"Anya," I said, holding my breath. "Did you keep any of the fish from the kill?"

She clucked and gave me one of her looks. "Good thing I watch out for my boys." She kicked an old rug aside and lifted the trapdoor below it. "Follow me."

"Where are we going?" I said. "Can you help?"

"Not an ounce of patience," Anya muttered, climbing down the steep ladder. "Not even a gram. But at least you've got a half a brain, which is more I can say about most people. I'm not so decrepit yet as to be careless. I knew something was—well—fishy at Star Lake." The light of a match ignited an oil lamp and illuminated the chilly cellar. "What do you girls see?"

"Winter provisions?" Ally said. "Canned goods?"

My gaze fell on the neatly organized, labeled, and dated jars on the shelves. "I see a whole lot of pickled fish." And hope, for Seth. Unless… "Anya, when you pickle things, do you erase all traces of other chemicals present?"

"Mostly? Yes. But…" Anya's face split into a mischievous grin.

"But what?"

"The problem with preconceptions is that it leads to some awful misjudgments," Anya said. "You think of me as an old, decrepit wild woman."

I shook my head. "No, no, I—"

"Apologies accepted." She stepped on a little stool, picked out a jar from the top shelf, and cradled it against her bosom. "You think your sister is running around with the equivalent of an Alaskan hillbilly. But you're wrong. Nikolai is a good boy and I was a chemist once. I did 'pickle' these fish from the kill, but I pickled them in my special formula…my chemist formula."

I gasped. "You are a chemist?"

"You preserved the dead fish?" Ally said.

"Things don't move very quickly out here, so when I saw the fish kill and those crews burning the carcasses in a hurry, I said, 'Anya, something's wrong yonder.' So I preserved some of the fish, just in case the fish kill ever needed to be scientifically explained."

I clapped, jumping up and down, and so did Ally.

"Thank you God," I said. "And thank you, Anya!"

She handed me the jar and pulled out a cell from her shirt's front pocket. "The boys gave me one of these for my birthday. We've got no reception out here, but I do love to take pictures."

It was mind-boggling, but standing in a cellar that was probably a hundred years older than I was, illuminated by the antique miner's lamp, Anya pulled up her pictures and displayed them for us. Two men stood by the lake, face covered by their hoods, rolling oil drums down the shore.

"I don't know for sure," she said. "But I reckon that the whistle-blower and the perpetrators of the fish kill could be one and the same."

I hugged the old woman until she couldn't breathe.

"You'll have to come with us," Ally said, "to court, to give your testimony."

"I don't like the city," Anya said, "but for Seth, I'll go."

It didn't take her long to dress for the trip. She came out of her room wearing a beaver trapper hat, a neon-orange jacket, beaded fur gloves, and curly lamb mukluk boots.

"What are you staring at?" She grabbed her Kate Spade handbag from the mantel and hooked it over her shoulder. "I always get cold in courthouses."

Right.

We hurried down to the lake and boarded the plane. Ally turned the ignition. Nothing happened. There was zero noise and the propeller didn't spin.

"What the hell?" Ally tapped on the instrument panel. "Don't you dare give me trouble, not now!"

She tried again several times to no avail.

I pointed to the red flashing icon. "What does this mean?"

"We're out of gas?" Ally cursed. "Impossible! I know we had to circle several times before we landed, but we fueled up before we took off!"

The leaden clouds were drifting in and the first flurries of snow danced in the wind. We could've radioed for help, but by the time someone came to get us, it would be too late. The weather would be too bad to fly and the hearing would be over.

"I can't believe it." Ally groaned. "I've never miscalculated my fuel before. Talk about horrible timing."

"At least you're not in the air."

Anya's observation gave me the shivers.

"Dammit." Ally turned to me. "All the other airplanes are gone from the lake. Why is it always feast or famine? What are we going to do?"

"Do you have a truck?" I asked Anya.

"It's parked fifteen miles away by the gravel road," she said. "In summer I get to it on my ATV. In winter, I go by snow machine."

Some days, Alaska was one humongous, cumbersome chore.

I opened the door and, jar in hand, clambered out of the Cessna. "Come on, people." I started up the hill. "Which will be faster, the ATV or the snow machine?"

"It'll have to be the ATV." Anya led us to the shed. "The snow machine is out of gas and the snow is not very deep. One problem." Anya threw open the door of the shed, to show a small single-rider Kawasaki. "We might be able to fit two of us on there, but not three."

The world conspired against me.

"You go with Anya," I said to Ally.

Ally shook her head, whipping her ponytail in the air. "I'm not leaving you here by yourself."

"She needs to travel to Anchorage in order to testify," I said. "If you don't leave right now, the weather will turn bad and we'll all be stuck here. You need to go with Anya on the ATV, get her truck, and drive to your family's hangar, wherever that is. Once there, you'll get another plane or a helicopter to take you to Anchorage. It's the only way Anya will make it on time."

"But I don't want to leave you behind," Ally said. "Besides, Seth won't like it. He'll kill me."

"Then let's make sure he's free to kill you, and me, if he wishes." I herded her to the ATV. "If Anya gets to the hearing, he's sure to go free."

"You go," Ally said. "I'll stay."

"You're the Erickson," I said. "They'll give you an airplane, not me or Anya. And who's going to pilot that plane if no pilots are about?"

Ally let out a disgusted groan.

"She's right." Anya straddled the ATV, dug the key out of her designer bag, and turned the machine on. "If we leave now, we've got a chance. Come on, Ally. Get on."

"Dammit." Ally hesitated. "You need to stay put, Summer. Don't go anywhere. Okay?"

"Where the heck am I going to go?" Not to the outhouse, that was for sure. I planned to run to the cabin, pee in a bucket, and stay inside for good. No bears for me. Or moose. No, thank you.

"Don't move from this location." Ally put on her knit hat. "If it starts snowing, make a fire. Can you make a fire?"

I'd never tried. "Sure, yes, get going."

"Don't burn down my house." Anya waggled a gloved finger in the air. "And don't make a mess either."

"Will do."

"I'll come get you as soon as I can," Ally said, stuffing her hands in her gloves. "If the weather gets really bad, it may be a day or two."

"There's food in the pantry," Anya said, "and pickled fish in the cellar."

Great. "I'll deal with it."

"Here." Anya pulled something from her purse and offered it to me.

"A handgun?" I'd never held a gun before and I didn't think it was a good idea to start today. As clumsy as I was, the chances of me shooting my nose off were way too high. How come everyone in Alaska carried guns everywhere?

"Do you even know how to shoot?" Ally said.

"It doesn't matter," I said. "I won't need it."

"All you have to do is take off the safety, like this." Anya demonstrated. "Cock the weapon, point and shoot. Got it?"

"Got it." I tucked the thing in my jacket pocket. "Please, just…go!"

Anya revved the engine. Ally squeezed in behind Anya. I handed her the jar of pickled fish.

"Don't drop it," I said.

"I won't." She flashed me a crooked smile and waved. "Be back in a cinch."

Anya pushed the throttle and off they went, bouncing over the rough terrain. As soon as I lost sight of them, I made for the cabin and closed the door behind me. I also barred it for good measure. There were no door chains on Anya's house. I'd never dealt with door bars before. I tied them down with some nylon ropes I found under the sink, then crossed my fingers hoping that if I fell asleep, I'd be a klutz at unraveling them in my sleep.

I hung my jacket on the rack and picked up a book from Anya's shelf, *Athabaskan Tales from Alaska.* I said a little prayer that the weather would hold off, that Anya and Ally would make it on time, and that Seth would be all right. Then I settled on the couch for the wait, however long it was going to be.

THIRTEEN

I MUST HAVE fallen asleep, because I woke up on the couch to the sound of the wind rattling the shutters. The weak, whitish light announced that it was late afternoon and the snow had begun falling. In contrast, a dark figure leaned over me. A quiet click echoed in the cabin and the cold barrel of a gun pressed against my forehead. The blood chilled in my veins.

"Who are you?" My voice sounded calm and collected, even though I was anything but. "What do you want?"

"Get up," the man said.

I got up from the couch slowly. My senses kicked in. Was this man a burglar, looking for money, food or gear? Was he a rapist or psychopath?

I forced myself to function. "Why are you here?"

"Be quiet," he said. "Just do what I say. Are you armed?"

I leveled a defiant gaze at him. "Why would I tell you if I were?"

"Don't play games with me." He tapped his gun's muzzle against my belly. "Spread 'em."

I inched my feet aside and raised my arms. He patted me down, running his hands up my legs and squeezing my breasts with unnecessary harshness.

"Nice." He leered. "Too bad I can't use you, but this one's strictly about the job."

The job?

The picture of my punctured brake lines walloped my mind. I'd never given much credit to Seth's concerns about an assassination attempt, mostly because I could think of no possible reason why someone would want to kill me. Until now. I forced myself to pay attention.

The man facing me was average in every way, early fifties, fit, brown eyes, clean-shaven, hawkish nose, and a neutral accent. He wore a beanie, a black jacket, and dark snow pants, similar to the attire of the thug from the grainy clip that Seth had showed me. The shiver that prickled my spine resonated in my body like a fire alarm. My gut turned to ice.

"Who put you up to this?" I said.

"Wouldn't you like to know?" He sneered. "Get your coat."

"My coat?" I glanced out the window. "Are you crazy? It's snowing."

"Shut up and do what I say."

"But—"

He barked. "Just do it!"

His breath gusted over my face. I imagined a rotten caribou carcass stunk less. I gulped, but I had trouble swallowing. I moved slowly toward the coat stand, keeping my eyes on him. I made a slow show of putting on my coat.

"How did you know where to find me?" I said. "Did you follow me here?"

"I watch the news," he said. "Following you was the easy part."

So he'd known about Seth's troubles. Seth had been right. I'd been safe and out of reach while at his house. But with Seth out of the way and me out and about, I'd become easy prey. The thug had followed me to Star Lake, perhaps in one of the airplanes we saw on the lake. I decided to take a chance.

"Look, if somebody is paying you to do this, I can do better."

"Doubt it," he said. "You've got next to nothing to your name. I did my homework."

The tone. The look. The research. This man was indeed a professional.

Had he disabled Ally's Cessna in order to force our party to split up and strand me in this isolated place? Of course. He'd tampered with my rental car. It made perfect sense that he'd messed with the plane as well. Not only was he a hired killer, he was a competent hired killer, who did his research and planned carefully. And he'd been paid to kill me. Why?

I had no clue, but one thing was for sure: from where I stood, things weren't looking good.

I bolted down the hallway, fumbling with my front pocket. I pulled on the zipper, but it jammed. The damn thing wouldn't budge. The man caught up with me and slammed me against the wall. The pictures of Anya's seven sons fell and the frames shattered on the floor.

"Don't." He held me against the wall. "I don't want any unnecessary bruising."

"For me or for you?" I slammed my knee between his legs.

The man crumpled on the ground. I ran, but I had to slow down to untie the rope on the door bar. *Hurry!* I glanced behind me. He came after me, face set with fury, eyes watering with fresh pain. I undid the last knot, hurled the two-by-four at him and sprinted out of the cabin, running into the beginnings of a blizzard, still fumbling with my jacket's stubborn zipper.

He tackled me. I fought back, but he was too strong. With a punch to the midriff, he knocked the breath out of me. Hard to fight back without air in the lungs. I squirmed on the deck like a fish out of the water.

"Be still." He held me down while he tied my hands behind my back with the zip ties he pulled out of his pocket. "You were supposed to be a soft target."

He didn't know me if he thought I'd be a soft target. I might've told him that if I could, but it was hard to speak when you couldn't breathe.

He grabbed me by the collar and dragged me down the path toward the lake. By then, the sun had set and fast-moving clouds obscured the light of a shy moon. The chilling air didn't make it any easier to inhale. The wind hauled a mournful warning to my ears.

I wrestled with the ties around my hands, trying to make some sense out of his actions. If he was going to kill me anyway, why take the trouble of putting on my coat and dragging me out of the house? Why didn't he just shoot me instead?

He didn't want my death to look like a murder. That's why he didn't want any bruising. It also explained why he hadn't raped, strangled, or shot me in the cabin. Whoever had paid him to kill me wanted my death to look like an accident.

One moment I was onshore, the next moment I landed face-first in the lake. The sting of the icy water startled whatever little breath I had left in me. The water was so cold that it hurt. I kicked. I struggled. I tried to wiggle my hands out of the cuffs. I resisted with all I had.

But the man held me down in the water. Star Lake

flowed into my nose and mouth and, like a cascade, poured down my throat. Bright lights exploded before my eyes. My senses started to ebb. My body began to lose strength. My mind went into a dreamlike state.

I was drowning. Like my mother. She'd drowned too. She'd walked into the ocean in her sleep and sunk to the bottom. A liquid version of her face materialized before me as the water gushed down my gullet, weighed down my stomach and clogged my lungs.

"Fight, Summer!" she said. "Fight! Don't let it happen again. Not again!"

Not again?

An image formed in my mind, the details of a little girl's purple-walled bedroom—my bedroom at my family's Fountain Way apartment. I realized I was seeing the room through my little girl's eyes. A whiff of fresh paint tickled my nostrils as I got up from the bed. We had moved in just days earlier. The sounds of an argument came from the living room.

I peeked out from behind the door and saw my mother, standing against the far wall, facing a man who had his back to me. A third voice came from somewhere to my right, a deep voice whose owner I couldn't see from where I stood.

"You had to do it," the man said. "You had to poke your damn nose in other people's business and push the envelope. You leave me no choice."

"Wait!" My mother's lips made a sound I couldn't hear. "Please, don't do this."

"Too late," the man said. "Finish this."

The click of a door closing announced that the first person had left. My mother's attention focused on the other man in the room.

"You don't have to do this," she said. "Please. I won't say anything, I promise!"

"It's as good as done," the man replied. "Shame I'll be vacating my nice digs by the end of the night."

My heart faltered as my mother's assailant stalked my mother across the living room. It was him! The same man who was drowning me now, younger back then, but easily recognizable.

"Summer!" My mother's eyes widened with terror when she spotted me behind the door. "Get back to your room. Lock the door!"

"A locked door won't stop me." The man blocked the way between me and my mother. "The girl's seen me. She's got to go too."

"No, please," my mother begged. "She sleepwalks, just like I do. She won't remember a thing in the morning."

"Is that so?" The man's dark eyes gleamed with a new idea. "In that case, I'll let her live. But you've got to come with me. No fuss. No crying or screaming. If you come with me right now, I'll spare the whelp."

"How do I know you won't come back here and hurt my daughter?" my mother said.

The man showed her the key in his hands then pitched it out the balcony, sixteen stories down. "The little sleepwalker doesn't need to die today."

"Go back to your bed, sweetie," my mother said on a sob. "Go on. Mommy loves you."

My feet obeyed my mother's voice, but I could feel her fear seeping into my soul. She must have known she was going to die that night.

"I didn't want to leave you," my mother's voice whispered in my mind. "I wasn't chasing a dream that day. Somebody was chasing me."

"Who?" I mumbled underwater. "Who?"

And I knew. Whoever wanted me to die had built my death to mimic my mother's. *Another sleepwalking disaster*, I could almost hear the coroner's verdict. Another careless parasomniac who ventured too far. A dream chaser who chased her life away.

But mine was not an accidental drowning. It was murder. As my mother's face flickered in and out of focus, I realized what she was trying to tell me. Had she been murdered too?

"Wake up, Summer!" My mother's voice startled me. "Don't let him win. Fight him!"

The vision dissolved in my mind. I was back, struggling under the water and much closer to drowning. I ran out of oxygen. My body went into a state of biological desperation. I heard my mom's quiet good-byes smothered beneath the sea as surely as I heard my muffled shrieks echoing in the lake's dark waters. I was the last thought in her mind before she died.

I forced myself into alertness. My stomach hurt, loaded with too much water. My lungs weighted me down. I was no match for the thug holding me underwater. My mind sputtered a number of options, but only one seemed to make sense.

I stopped fighting. I gave in to both my attacker's brute force and the water. I looked up and, under a fleeting ray of moonlight, watched the last string of bubbles deserting my body. It seemed like forever. Eventually, the pressure on my back eased. The zip ties were suddenly gone from my wrists. I floated listlessly in the water as my assailant cast me off into the lake.

I dug into my jacket and ripped off the zipper. I thrust my hand in the pocket. Anya's quick lesson replayed in my head. *Click.* I turned in the water, dug my heels in the mud, cocked the gun, pointed and shot.

The shot blasted my ears and jerked my arm. I wheezed, a terrible aspiration of air that collided with the water ruling my lungs. The man staggered in knee-high water and turned, face frozen in surprise. I shot again. His arms flailed in the air. He fell in the water, dragged himself to shore and crept out of the lake. I shot until I couldn't see him anymore and no more bullets came out of the gun. Then I dragged myself out of the lake.

I knew I had to run. I just couldn't. I was shaking too hard. He could return any minute, but I just lay on the shore, retching torrents of foul-tasting water. The gun was stuck in my grip. Shivers rattled my body. The cold burned, inside and out.

I had to get indoors. Back to the cabin. Build a fire. But it seemed so far away. I couldn't move. The snow fell all around me. The cold iced my bones and froze my muscles. All I could do was close my eyes and shiver some more.

A grunt shocked me out of senselessness. A hot, slimy slap warmed the side of my face. A dank stench startled me. I opened my eyes. Liquid brown eyes stared at me.

"Get up." The huge bear spoke with my mother's voice. "You're going to die, unless you get up."

I was hallucinating. I had to be. The old bear would surely maul me if he found me. The creature's lips never moved and yet the sound echoing in my head came from it. Oh, yeah, and my mother was gone and dead. Drowned. Murdered? Absurd. This bear-mother combination was hilarious. A hysterical giggle bubbled in the back of my throat. My frozen mind was a hoot.

"Summer Silva," the bear said in my mother's sternest tone. "Move. Crawl if you have to. They will not succeed."

They?

"You will not die tonight," my mother said. "Follow me."

The bear's paws rustled softly on the new snow. It took a few steps, then sat on its hind legs at the trailhead as if it was a big, ratty dog, waiting for me.

"Coward," the bear said, this time in my father's voice. "I didn't defy a dictator, cling to a raft for three days in the Florida Straits and fight off sharks for you to die in Alaska."

"Daddy?"

"All those years without a life," he said. "And now that you have a shot at one, you're giving up?"

What did he mean?

"You're wasting time," my father said. "You're squandering opportunity. You're wasting the one good thing you've found in Alaska."

"My life was fine before I came here," I mumbled through numb lips.

"But was it really?" my father said. "Every night you set up the door chain, locked in your fears and locked out your future. Is that the life you want?"

No, but I hadn't been able to trust anyone…until Seth.

"Get up," the bear said in my mother's voice. "Survival is the best revenge. Claim your life. You like him. You crave him. You love him."

How could I love someone who I had just met?

"Because you trust him," my mother said. "Him, you can trust."

Could I?

I'd stayed in his house. I'd slept in his bed, next to him, all these nights. I trusted him already and he, he'd proven my trust right.

"He'll be sad," my mother said. "He'll burn inside all over again."

I didn't want that for Seth. No more suffering for him.

I tried to get up, but my legs refused to move. "I don't think I can do this."

"Try," my mother said.

"I can't!"

"Can I eat your liver then?" the bear said in a low rumbling voice. "I really like liver. I ate a human not long ago. The meat was bland but the liver was yummy. Should I start now?"

"You wouldn't dare," I said. "I'll scratch your eyes out if you come near me."

"Follow me," the bear insisted. "Follow me or I'll eat your liver."

I tried crawling, but it didn't work very well. "I might be done."

"No way," the bear said, this time in Seth's voice. "I've got your back. Nothing bad will happen to you under my watch. Always remember: you're way too stubborn to let Alaska kill you."

Seth. My mother was dead and so was my father. But Seth? He was alive.

I crawled up the trail, following the bear.

"Cold," I grumbled. "Hate cold."

I couldn't figure out if I was awake or sleepwalking.

It was hard to think with a frozen brain. No, I wasn't asleep. I didn't feel pain, cold or discomfort when I sleepwalked, whereas right now, I was feeling plenty of all of that. On the other hand, I was following a bear. A bear, for God's sake! Give me a break. I might not be sleepwalking, but I was definitively hallucinating.

"Come on," the bear said. "Chase your dreams. Chase me."

I dragged myself up the path by the force of my elbows. I sank one elbow on the ground and then the other. I lost all sensation in my hands and feet. I had no concept of time. It seemed that I'd been dragging myself for days when my head hit on wood. I looked up. The bear sat at the top of the stairs. The deck. The cabin's deck.

I crawled up the steps. The door couldn't be too far away, but I ran out of steam. I was so cold I couldn't move anymore.

"Keep moving," the bear said in my mother's voice.

My body refused. I sprawled on the deck, watching the pile of snow growing next to me, snowflakes landing like butterflies without a sound. Pretty. The door. Where was it? Fire. I really wanted a hot fire. A roar. The deafening sound interrupted the silence and shook the cabin and the deck. It wasn't coming from the bear. It came from the sky instead.

"Almost there," the bear said.

"Good night, bear," I mumbled.

"Night, beautiful." An image of an eagle flashed in my mind. "Go chase your dreams."

FOURTEEN

How the hell had I managed to walk straight into Alex's trap? How was I supposed to protect those I cared for if nobody followed my instructions and everybody did whatever the hell they wanted?

The helicopter bucked in the air. I fought another wind gust, determined to get to my destination despite the weather. The forecast wasn't exactly conducive for flying and the ride quality was crap. Visibility was zero, surface winds exceeded forty-five knots, and the wind shear was giving the helicopter hell. My brain rattled in my skull like a marble in a can. I kept my eyes on the main rotor indicators. Severe turbulence led to rotor flapping which in turn led to blade stall, altitude deviation, and mast bumping. I didn't have time to deal with any of that tonight.

The helicopter's searchlights broke through a patch of heavy snow to illuminate the icy waters of Star Lake. At least I was close. I followed along the north shore of the lake's short finger on the GPS. A memory of today's debacles had me reeling. After twenty-four hours with my ass parked in a goddamn interrogation room, the hearing had been surprising enough.

There was the press, of course, always making a clusterfuck of things, but also Grandma, marching in with the governor, a senator, several members of the legislature and the tribal governments, and even a state supreme court judge. Anya and Ally showed up near the end.

Once Anya presented her evidence, the judge, who was already raving mad, threw a fit. He ranted against federal abuses in Alaska and ended the hearing on the spot. Alex hadn't succeeded at buying this judge. The Feds left the courtroom with their tails between their legs. The charges against me were dropped. Alex, who made an appearance in the courtroom, swore to Grandma that he had nothing to do with whole thing.

The hell with Alex. I gritted my teeth. Wait until I was done with this one.

I fought through a particularly violent bout of turbulence. The helicopter pitched and rolled. It plummeted a good thirty feet and so did my stomach. Good thing I had no civilian cargo. Otherwise, I'd need a barf cleanup crew, which I almost needed myself earlier today, when I found out what Summer had done.

I'd walked out of the courthouse a free man, only to have to deal with the public relations fallout, the storm that had grounded most flights, and Spider's news. He'd called me on my cell while I was on the way to the helipad. Dammit. I hadn't liked any of what he had to say.

"Found your guy, Sergio De Havilland," he'd announced without preamble. "He's having a good time in Rio."

"And?"

"He's in the import export business," Spider said. "Some sort of scheme peddling luxury cars to the rich and famous. The odometers are reset along the way."

Confirmation that the guy was indeed a bag of shit. "Did you get close like I asked?"

"Of course." Spider's voice sharpened with a mix

of affront and amusement. "Our guys on the ground bought him a few drinks."

"And asked him some good questions I hope?"

"It took some doing, but they got him talking about his ex."

"Go."

"According to De Havilland, Summer was a saint, the best woman ever."

"And the reason for the divorce?"

"He was young and foolish, she was the one who got away, yadda, yadda, yadda."

Interesting. Summer didn't want his name mentioned in her presence and yet he was all nice and lovey-dovey.

"Anything else?"

"Drugs," Spider said. "He keeps it really hush-hush, especially from his father, but the little shithead hits cocaine like a snorting machine."

Now we were getting somewhere. Summer wasn't likely to put up with that.

"Our guys put him to bed and checked out the rest," Spider said. "His accounts are maxed out and most of his efforts are centered on raising capital for his little adventure. Problem is, his mobster partners are likely to come after him if he doesn't pay for the merchandise. He's got a friend with international banking connections trying to throw him a lifeline. I'm no bean counter, but for what I saw, his business sense? Zero. Long story short, he needs money. He's going down fast."

Red flags snapping everywhere. "Does he have any insurance out on Summer?"

"None that we've found so far. I know what you're gonna say, you want us to look some more."

"Right on."

"Hacking insurance companies all over the wide world takes time."

"It's a thankless task, I know, but it's got to be done," I said. "While you're at it, check for policies where the beneficiary is the stepmother. What's the status on her?"

"Nothing new," Spider said. "Yes, she's up to her eyeballs in credit card debt, but her liabilities aren't out of whack with the average American. Everybody who we'd talked to in Miami said she was loud and shrewd, but not criminal in nature. We also canvassed work associates at Summer's office."

"And?"

"They fucking love her at Carrera and Associates. The people who work there think she's awesome, the glue that keeps the place together. Carrera relies on her for everything and everybody we talked to had nothing but praise for the woman."

Why wasn't I surprised?

"And the sister?"

"I have some interesting news about her." Spider launched into the specifics.

I'd listened carefully. The information he shared and subsequent communications put me in a precarious position. Even now, I hadn't decided what to do about it. And then there was Ally's astonishing story of what had gone down at Anya's.

Yes, I'd thought about Anya at the lake while I was "visiting" with the Feds, but I'd had no way to convey my thoughts to anyone useful. And even though I was grateful to Summer for her help, I would've much preferred to know she was safe under Robert's supervision and not alone in the middle of the damn Alaskan wilderness.

Jer and Ally had wanted me to wait until the morning to fetch Summer, but they didn't know her like I did. She was trouble in the flesh and prone to disaster. Grandma actually forbade me to fly and the storm almost grounded me for good. The only reason I was able to take to the air is because my Firehawk was equipped with a state-of-the-art ice protection system that used automatic electrothermal heating to prevent ice from forming on the main and tail rotor blades. The hell with the storm. I needed to get to Summer.

At last, the searchlights brushed against the outline of Anya's cabin. I spotted no lights inside and no smoke coming out of the chimney. Why hadn't Summer built a fire?

I attempted a landing, but the wind pummeled me again. Scrap that. I was testing the Firehawk tonight. The wind blew fiercely, the snow came straight at me, and I couldn't see squat. I had to get this bird on the ground, before the wind did it for me. I hated to leave the helicopter out in the elements, but what choice did I have?

I made another low pass over the cabin, watching the wind indicators, looking for an opportunity to land. I caught a break in the snow. The searchlights reflected a flash of snow-speckled hot pink. I did a double take. Jesus fucking Christ. I knew that jacket!

My heart shot to my throat. My pulse pounded in my ears. Was Summer lying on the deck, exposed to the elements? I forced the helicopter down and hover-taxied into position. A stiff crosswind buffeted the bird like a giant fist. The LTE alarms went off. The helicopter lost tail rotor effectiveness.

Oh, shit.

The Firehawk rotated to the right. I added left pedal,

but got zero response. I clipped one of Anya's rust piles with the tail. I drifted fast into the house. Fuck. I smashed the pedal to the floor, spun the nose around, and slammed down the collective. The helicopter hit the ground with a bang. I was less than seven feet away from the cabin, but at least I was down.

Go, go, go.

I powered down, tucked my gun into the back of my pants, grabbed the emergency kit, and bolted to the back deck. My boots crunched on the snow. My breath came in visible puffs. I sprinted around the corner so fast I almost ran into the bear. I skidded to a stop not five feet from the stairs, where the old bear sat wearing a little pile of snow on its head like a crown.

I reached for my gun. My stomach pitched. Had Summer walked out into the open while asleep? Had the bear attacked her? Was it about to attack me?

With a muted groan, the bear padded down the stairs. I clambered up to the deck and vaulted over the railings, keeping my eyes on the beast. The bear paid me no heed. It ambled toward the trail and got lost in the woods.

I tucked my gun away and landed on my knees next to Summer. Panic slammed into me. She shivered, pale as the snow and icy to my touch. Her pulse was faint. The ends of her hair had frozen and shallow puddles of snow gathered in the folds of her clothes. In her hand, she gripped a gun.

A gun?

I pried the gun from her blue-tipped fingers, opened the cabin door, and dragged her inside. I shut the door. For a moment, I didn't know what to do. In all my years flying search and rescue, insertions and extractions,

I'd never ever lost it like this. It was as if my mind had called it quits and my heart weighed a ton in my chest. Then my training kicked in.

For the second time in my life, I found myself taking off her clothes, boots, socks, pants. This time around, it was a lot worse. Would I find her dead the next time? What if she died on me?

I couldn't let that happen. No fucking way. It wasn't going to happen. I gritted my teeth and forced my shaking hands to work. The wet layers came off one after the other, until I'd taken everything off. I dried Summer off then wrapped her in a thick bundle of blankets I lifted from Anya's couches. Her teeth chattered. Her lips, ears, fingers, and toes were blue.

But shivering was good. People who succumbed to hypothermia stopped shivering before they died. If Summer was suffering from an extreme case of hypothermia, if her temperature had dropped beneath a certain level and her organs had shut down, she may not survive.

"You better not die on me." I had no idea how long she'd been wet and exposed. I hoped it hadn't been too long.

Her blue-tinted eyelids opened. Her sparkling green eyes fixed on my face. Her lips pursed but her mouth couldn't make out words. She pawed at my hand, but she couldn't grab it. I rubbed her fingers between my palms.

"I'll get you warm," I said. "I'm going to build you a fire."

In record time, I had a roaring fire going in Anya's hearth. I also lit the old stove. I laid Summer on the couch and pushed it closer to the fireplace. I was very careful not to jar her. Sudden movements could trigger irregular heartbeats in hypothermic patients. I placed a cushion beneath her head. She curled up with her knees against her chest and tried to speak again, but I couldn't make out what she was saying.

"Hush, baby." I stroked her face. "You're going to be fine."

I started several pots with water at the same time. I rummaged through my emergency kit, pulled out a bag of saline, and dropped it in the water as well. I tore the place apart until I found a collection of old rubber water bottles beneath the sink. I filled up the bottles with hot water and tucked them against Summer's chest and belly, under her arms and against her groin, trying to warm her internal organs. This time, when she tried to speak, I recognized my name on her lips.

"S-Seth?"

"It's all right," I said. "This too shall pass. I'm going to hook you up with some warm saline. It should help restore your body's temperature faster. Okay?"

I tested the saline solution. I needed it to be about a hundred and nine degrees, but I didn't have a thermometer, so I winged it. I had trouble finding a vein on Summer's arm. My hands were shaking and her veins seemed to have disappeared from her body. I took a deep breath and kept trying. *Dammit, Erickson, just find the fucking vein.*

After a few minutes, I located a vein in the crook of her arm and, stilling my trembling hands, inserted the needle. Okay, we were in business now. I hung the IV from the couch and rushed to brew a pot of hot tea. I managed to feed her a few sips.

"C-careful," she rasped. "H-he came."

"Who came?" I said, feeding her more tea.

"K-killer."

"Killer?"

"Brakes," she mumbled. "Car."

It hit me like a ton of bricks. "You mean the man who tampered with your brakes? He was here?"

"L-lake."

"Lake?" I stared at her, stunned. My mind raced, working out the different scenarios. "He tried to drown you? Is that why you were soaking wet? Is that why you had a gun in your hand?"

"S-shot him."

Jesus fucking Christ.

"Are you telling me that the son of a bitch showed up here, marched you down to the lake, and tried to drown you?" I was going to kill the bastard. "Are you telling me you fought him off and then, wet and freezing, made your way back here?"

"F-follow the bear," she said.

"The bear?"

She nodded, something that required body coordination, a sign that her temperature was rising.

"The bear," she said. "It spoke. My mother came."

"Okay, sure." She was probably hallucinating from the cold.

"She comes," she insisted. "In my dreams. All the time."

I couldn't ignore the certainty in her eyes. "She does?"

"She told me," she said. "About you. That first night? She said. Trust you."

"Is that why you believed me?" I grappled with the odd notion. "Is that why you were so sure I was telling you the truth?"

"Only comes…when I need her." She shuddered. "Always tells…the truth."

It was a tough act to swallow for a skeptic like me, but I hadn't believed Summer when she first told me about sleepwalking and yet it was true. I examined the facts. Summer wasn't crazy. On the contrary, she was one of the strongest, sanest people I knew. Whether her mother really came to her or Summer's intuition did all the work in her dreams, it didn't matter to me. Summer believed it. Besides, I liked that I'd earned her mom's seal of approval, even if she wasn't around anymore.

"No accident," Summer muttered.

"I know," I said. "The killer tried to drown you."

"My mother," Summer said. "He killed her."

Was she saying what I thought she was saying? "Look, baby." I brushed her hair away from her face. "You've been through a lot tonight…"

"You don't believe me." Her fingers clutched my sleeve. "It's true. He killed her!"

"But why?"

"Don't know. But I was there. I saw him!"

"Are you sure he was the same man?"

"Positive," she said, still shivering. "Need to tell you. Everything. What I saw."

"You're too tired now," I said. "How about tomorrow?"

"Now," she insisted. "Before I forget. Don't want to forget."

I knew how much she hated the fact that she couldn't remember her sleepwalking episodes. I wasn't sure what to make of all of this, but if it was important to her, then it was important to me. Slowly, hesitantly, as she warmed up, she described everything she'd seen while that son of a bitch tried to drown her.

The details. They were incredibly vivid. Her eyes were haunted. The story filled me with rage. Her voice cracked as she spoke, but she kept going and, when she was done, I was determined to look into every aspect for clues that would help us understand her mother's death and find her would-be killer.

"If I forget," she said, her temperature a lot warmer than before. "Will you remind me?"

"I've got it all here." I tapped my temple. "Your story is safe. Now you need to rest. Tomorrow, we'll work on this."

I needed to think about everything she'd said. If her dreams were right, then the likelihood of Sergio De Havilland being involved in this dropped to almost zero. He would've been a kid back then. But the guy was a fucking troll and every time I heard his name, my hackles bristled. On the other hand, her dreams went way back to her childhood, which meant I had to take a look at the players back then. That is, if I found a way to confirm that Summer's dreams were more than the sum of her fears and anxieties, true recollections.

I kissed the top of her head. "Christ, Summer, you're the toughest girl I know. You shot the bastard. Did you get him?"

"Not sure." Fear gleamed in her eyes. "Dangerous. He could still be around."

"Got it," I said. "I'll be right back."

I secured the doors and windows, including the one I found broken in the bunkroom, the killer's point of access. I borrowed some weapons from Anya's case and loaded them with ammunition. I set the weapons next to the couch, chambered a bullet in my gun, refilled the water bottles, and replaced them.

"Are you still cold?" I asked.

She nodded. I stripped my clothes and, inserting myself between her and the back of the couch, pressed my body to hers. She still felt cold, but not icy like before. I rubbed her arms and massaged her fingers.

Lying next to her, I took a deep breath. My lungs could benefit from a stint of oxygen therapy just about now. Or maybe it was my heart underperforming, failing to send enough blood to power my brain. Hell, I'd almost lost her. I dipped my nose in her hair and inhaled her scent. She smelled like coconut ice cream.

"S-Seth?" she mumbled. "The hearing?"

"Anya and Ally made it." I couldn't believe she was half-frozen and yet worrying about me. "The case against me was dismissed."

"Are you okay?"

No, I wasn't okay. I was raving mad and fit to howl at the moon. I had too many blips on my radar. I wanted to rip into Alex and unmask his game. I wanted to yell at Summer for defying my instructions and risking her life. I wanted to lecture her on the dangers and shake her until her brain fell into the right slot in her thick skull. At the same time, I wanted to go out there and hunt the motherfucker who'd tried to kill her. He was gonna pay. I'd be waiting for him if he made the bad decision of returning here. I took a deep breath and tried to calm the rage within.

"Sleep now." I hugged Summer against my body. "You need to rest."

"Stay with me," she mumbled. "Don't go out there. Promise me."

"I'm not going anywhere."

She closed her eyes and, for the first time ever, did exactly as I said, at least for a little while.

A FEW HOURS LATER, in the depth of the night, Summer came awake. I knew because I'd been watching, taking her pulse, monitoring her breathing, estimating her temperature. I'd just taken her off the IV when her gaze fell on me.

"How're you feeling?" I said.

"I can feel every part of me." She turned on the couch and laid her head on my shoulder. "That's good, right?"

"Very good," I said. "Are you still cold?"

"A little."

"Let me get you some more tea."

"No more tea." She tilted up her face and kissed me. "The only thing I need is you."

Her kiss jolted me to the core. My body stiffened beneath her touch. Every part of me relished those lips. My cock jerked with instant need.

"Wait a minute." I broke away from her mouth. "What's this all about?"

"You're not going to believe me," she said. "The bear made it clear."

I narrowed my gaze on her. "The bear again?"

"It spoke like my mom. It spoke like my dad too. It told me not to waste this opportunity."

"Opportunity?"

"Us."

She kissed me again and for the first time in hours, the panic encasing my heart began to crack. She was alive. She was well. And she was in my arms. I could deal with the rest.

I had to make a huge effort to break off the kiss. “Maybe you were sleepwalking.”

“I wasn’t asleep,” she said, “but I don’t think I was awake either. I was in a state in between, a place of heightened awareness. My dad was right. For years I’ve locked my fears in and the future out. I couldn’t trust anyone. It wasn’t the life I wanted, but it was the only life I thought I could have. And then you came into my life. The bear said… Oh, my God. I sound nuts. Please, forget it.”

“I don’t want to forget it,” I said. “Explain.”

She took a deep breath. “The bear spoke like you too, and I could feel you were already with me, in here.” She tapped her chest over her heart. “Last night, I understood what I haven’t had the courage to admit.”

“What’s that?”

“That I already trust you.”

With those simple words, she blew up my world. My heart boomed in my chest. Confirmation. *She* trusted *me.*

“So,” she said, sliding her hand beneath the covers. “I’m not wasting any time, Erickson, and neither are you.”

I caught her hand in mine. “Inasmuch as I really dig your newfound philosophy, we’re not doing this right now. You’re not well and I won’t wake up tomorrow to tears. I can’t handle that, not ever again.”

“I’m fine.” She pushed herself up on her elbow and kissed me, enveloping my senses with the simple touch of her lips. The lethal combination of her desire and my need flattened my objections. Her hand brushed over my belly, sank to my groin and wrapped around my sex.

"Wait." I stammered like a fool. "I found you half-frozen to hell not five hours ago."

"I feel good." She stroked me until I could barely think. "I learned on the Discovery Channel that vigorous activity helps with moderate hypothermia."

"Not this kind of activity."

"Precisely this sort of blood-pumping activity."

"Summer Silva, you're breaking your own rules."

"Good." She kissed my neck, my chest, my belly and pushed the blankets aside to kiss the tip of my cock. "Because I don't need them silly rules anymore."

She traced my cock with her tongue, unleashing chaos in me. I groaned and shuddered, raked by waves of overpowering need. Shit. I was losing this argument and I knew it, but still, I tried to hang back because I had promised myself that, the next time, it was going to be perfect.

"How about we wait till we get home tomorrow?" I said in a strangled voice.

"No more waiting," she said in between playful licks, her voice determined, her eyes fast on my face. "I'm awake. Fully awake. That was your first condition, was it not?"

I croaked. "Yes?"

"On to your second condition." She kept hold of my cock as she came up on her elbows. "You said you'd wait until I asked you. Right?"

"Right."

"Well then." She threw her leg over my thighs and straddled my hips. "Seth Erickson? I'm asking."

She was stunning. Illuminated by the light of the fire, she rose above me, long legs bent at either side of me, back straight, proud, beautiful breasts enticing me with a succulent offer of deliciously stiff nipples. She settled over my cock and rubbed herself up and down my erection, oiling me with her need, provoking me with her passion. Her eyes were bright with desire, but not translucent or glazed. I wanted to pinch myself. Instead, I pinched her, a quick nip on her bum.

"Ouch!" She flinched and rubbed her ass. "What was that for?"

"Just making sure you're really awake."

"I'm awake," she said. "I'm very awake."

The smile wavered on her face. The light flickered in her eyes. Doubts clouded her gaze and for an instant, I glimpsed the vulnerabilities that haunted one of the strongest women I'd ever met.

Her lower lip trembled. "Do you not want me anymore?"

Had I heard right? Was she really asking me if *I* wanted *her*?

She had no clue of the effect she had on me, no idea of the power she had over me. She didn't know that over the last few days, I'd gotten used to living in a constant state of lust. She didn't understand that beyond wanting her, I wanted to consume her like the air I inhaled into my lungs and convert her into the oxygen that powered my life. She had no idea that she already circulated through my bloodstream and pumped through my heart, fully integrated into my biology.

I threw my head back and laughed. She looked down on me, startled, and yet I couldn't stop laughing. The irony of my situation was almost too much to bear. I'd been craving this woman like a goddamn addict since day one. I'd flown through a superstorm to get to her. And now she wondered if I wanted her?

"Summer Silva," I said. "I want you all right. I don't care if you walk in your sleep. I don't care if you have visions in your dreams. I've wanted you since the day I met you. But you've got to know that. On the other hand, you better be damn sure about this, because I don't know what will happen if I get another taste of you."

"I know." Her lips shifted into a warm, caring, trusting smile. "I want you in me right now."

It was the same thing she'd said to me that first time, only she was awake now. It was the moment I'd been dreaming about since our first night together. No more waiting.

I lifted her off my hips at the same time I got to my knees. In one swift motion, I scooted her to the end of the couch and, pressing her back against the upholstered arm, parted her legs.

She squealed. "What are you doing?"

"This time, we're doing it *my* way."

I perched her heel on the back of the couch and planted her other foot on the floor. She tried to press her knees together, but I rumbled.

"Don't you dare close your legs on me." I kissed her knee and then planted a row of little kisses along her thigh's soft underside. I met her wide eyes and smirked. "When you wake up tomorrow, you'll have exactly zero regrets."

"Oh, my God!" She gasped when my lips landed on her clit and my tongue dipped between her folds. "Oh, please, God help me."

Her nails dug on the cushions as I tasted her body's handcrafted brew. She was almost too modest for my appetite. I bore down on her until I had her drenched and squirming on the couch, back arched, legs flexed, hip bones jutting, fingers entwined through my hair.

"Seth!" She gasped. "Stop, I'm going to come!"

"Not yet, baby," I mumbled, mouth full of her taste. "In a moment."

"Ooh." She moaned when I thumbed her opening. "What are you doing?"

"I want to give you something to come on." She was moist but she was also skittish, high-strung, and tight.

"I want you," she rasped. "You!"

"Oh, you're going to get a whole lot of me." I smiled between her legs, heady with her sexual scent, drunk with her flavors. "But first, I want to watch you come."

I stroked her while I worked my tongue over her clit. It puckered between my lips like a tiny nipple. Her breath quickened. A quiet whimper drifted out of her lips, a sound that combined agony and bliss and made me mad with want. I ached to be in her body.

"Come on, baby," I murmured, rubbing her spot. "Come for me."

Her entire body contracted around my finger in a convulsive fit. It was just like the first time, quiet but intense. The little vein popped up on her neck. The flush expanded from her face, blushing her skin and traveling down to her chest, where her breasts swelled with the force of her breaths and her nipples stabbed at the air. The shudders that racked her body rattled her limbs and deepened the curve of her back as her body bent backward over the arm of the couch in a sublime pose. A moan rumbled in the back of her throat and escaped her lips as I watched her, enthralled.

Her pleasure shoved me to the edge of my need. My blood roared in my ears and my cock turned granite hard. I waited until she collapsed on the couch and, keeping her legs apart, knelt in between. She moaned when I slid into her.

"I know you're really sensitive right now." I braced myself above her and kissed her. "I want to take advantage of that."

My cock glided into her deliciously lathered body, widening her as it went. Fuck, she felt as good as I remembered—no, better. It was as if her pussy had been configured to my specs. She opened her mouth to my tongue and I double-dipped, enjoying her body's silkiest surfaces and her depths' exquisite moisture.

She wrapped her legs around me and ran her hands over my back with greed that matched mine. Her affection enveloped me like a thermal blanket. Her fingertips brushed over my scars. Her touch felt fantastic to my skin. No longer was any part of me numb or tight or prickly. On the contrary, every one of my cells was renewed with a fresh kind of thrill.

"This is just the beginning," I murmured.

"I know," she said.

"Let me know if it's too much."

"It isn't."

"You want more?" I jostled more of me in her body. "How's that?"

She groaned. "I want all of you."

She wanted all of me, the lust, the greed, the need; the scars, the baggage, the bitterness I carried in my soul, and the crammed seed stored in my body. She wanted me.

I plunged all the way and watched her eyes widening, matching her sex's delicious expansion. I moved in and out of her, relishing every inch of her body, every extraordinary sensation surging through my body. Firmly connected, my cock transmitted pleasure to every part of me. I wanted to stay in her forever, to stretch the moment, to build on that connection until there was no boundary between her body and mine. Her reaction drove me to insanity. She rolled her hips and urged me into a stern pace that had both of us smarting with pleasure.

I lowered my lips and suckled her nipples, first one, then the other. My tongue slid over her flesh, testing her nipples' phenomenal texture, stretching them with my lips, raking them gently with my teeth, pressing them against my palate.

A surge of pleasure tested my endurance. My body had suffered enough restraint for a lifetime. I held back, but only barely. My eyes met hers. There was a reflective quality to her gaze, power that ruled my emotions.

"Are you awake?"

"I'm awake," she whispered. "Dreaming, but awake."

"Summer, look at me." I encased her face in my hands. "Can I come in you?"

"Yes," she said. "Yes!"

Jesus. I could hardly hold back.

"When I do," I said, "I want you to come with me. Do you understand?"

"Yes," she said.

"Soon after we're done," I said, "I'm going to need you again and I'm going to have to have you as much as I need to, in order to get through this."

"You can have me," she whispered. "You can have me as much as you want to."

I kissed her. "I don't think you understand."

"Erickson?" She lifted her head from the cushion.

"I understand. Got that? Now stop trying to hold back and fuck me, because I need you and I need you now."

I laughed and flattened over my irreverent vixen until she started to cry out and I started to come. As she required, I gave her a powerful orgasm, all the seed in my body and much more. I gave her my soul.

FIFTEEN

I WOKE UP to the sun shining through the cabin's curtains and the sound of a vehicle motoring in the distance. Seth curled around me, breathing softly on my ear. I felt good, a little sore around the middle, and pleasantly tender elsewhere, but whole, hale and completely satisfied. So this was what living and loving was all about.

The fire crackled in the hearth, the blankets were strewn all over the floor, and the kitchen looked like it had been looted. The couch smelled exactly like me; like lust, sex, and Seth. I remembered the last few hours of my life, the pleasure I'd discovered in Seth's arms. My entire body flushed with the memories.

"Seth?" I shifted around and, laying my head on his shoulder, shook him gently. "I think someone's coming."

"I hear them." He didn't open his eyes but he shoved a hand into the couch's cushions, dug out an impressive black gun and settled it on his flat belly. "I'll shoot any fool who attempts to come through that door."

"Please, don't shoot anybody." I kissed the lines radiating from the corners of his eyes, the space between his brows and the corners of his mouth, which turned up in appreciation. I drew little lines on his chest, rising and falling beneath my hand with powerful breaths, and traced the seams of his scars with my fingertips. He was such a beautiful man. And now, he was mine.

"Seth?" I kissed his ear. "It might be time to get up."

"Hmm," he mumbled. "Can I get some more butterfly kisses?"

I trailed more kisses along the line of his stubble-covered jaw and down his neck. "Come on, Seth. Get up."

"I can't get up." He tightened his grasp around my waist and pressed me against his side. "I don't think my legs will hold me. I'm drained dry. You did me in last night."

"*I* did *you* in?" I laughed. "You had nothing to do with the debauchery?"

He opened one eye and smiled. "That giggle of yours is just what I wanted to hear this morning. I'd wake up to you laughing any day. Morning, beautiful."

He lowered his face to mine and kissed me. Good thing I was lying down, because my knees, like the rest of me, liquefied on the spot. The contact wiped all the thoughts from my mind. How could he have this mind-altering effect on me?

He cupped my ass with his hand and, turning on his side, pressed his growing erection against my underbelly.

"Oh, my," I said. "For a man who's been drained dry, you seem rather full today."

"And you're about to have a busy morning." He kissed me some more.

The door rattled with a forceful set of knocks. "Seth, Summer!" Anya's voice came from the outside. "Open the door!"

Seth swore a string of obscenities. "Why is it that people are set on disrupting my life?"

"Maybe it's because we're in someone else's home?" I clambered down from the couch and rushed to get my panties, which Seth had hung to dry on the antlers mounted above the mantle like a flag on a pole. I had to jump up several times before I got a hold on them.

Seth crossed his hands behind his head and watched me, grinning. “Christ, you’re beautiful.”

“Right,” I said, slipping on my panties. “I’m a mess, that’s what I am.”

“You’re the sexiest mess alive.”

“Come on.” I picked up Seth’s underwear from the ground and tossed it his way. “Get dressed.”

“If we didn’t have to catch a son of a bitch, I’d never open that door.” He groaned and sat up on the couch. “All I want is a few hours of peace and quiet alone with you. Is that too much to ask?”

“The hours you got.” I clasped on my bra and shoved my legs into my jeans. “The peace and quiet? Not so much.”

The banging on the door drowned his laughter.

“Open up,” Anya shouted. “Right now!”

“Just a minute,” I yelled. “We’ll be right out.”

I took in the mess we’d made in the cabin while Seth got dressed. Anya wasn’t going to be happy. I picked up the water bottles from the floor, put the tea mugs in the sink, and cleaned up most of the glass from the broken frames. I dashed around in an effort to straighten the rest of the place. Seth caught me as I hurried past him.

“Got you.” He kissed me, a knee-weakening experience that left me longing for more. “Are you officially dating me now?”

“No, silly.” I kissed the tip of his nose. “We went straight to the fucking part.”

His smile widened. “I’m good with that.”

“That’s because you’re an overachiever.”

"You're no slouch," he said. "So that we're clear, I'm claiming an exclusive."

"What's good for the goose is good for the gander." I planted a kiss on his lips. "And so that you're clear, I don't share what's mine."

God, I loved the way he laughed! I craved that sound as the background music for my life. Unfortunately, Anya's patience was at an end and life lurked beyond the doors, along with the man who'd tried to kill my mother and me.

"Open up right now!"

I headed for the door. "Ready to rejoin the human race?"

He let out a blustery sigh. "If we must."

I lifted the bar and opened the door. Anya stepped in, nose sniffing the air, eyes scanning the place as if she knew exactly what we'd been doing inside for hours on end.

"Smells like a brothel in here," she said. "You two owe me a bottle of Febreze."

"I'll send you a case." Seth greeted two of Anya's sons, who lingered by the door. "I owe you a new window too."

Anya set her hands on her hips. "Now why would you be so careless to break my window?"

"I didn't break it," Seth said. "Neither did Summer, so don't look at her like that. It's a long story. I'll send someone to fix the window today. And so that you know, as soon as I get on the radio, you'll have the state troopers all over this place. So make sure there's nothing around here that can get you into trouble." Before Anya had time to ask more questions, he added, "How much for that couch?"

Anya frowned. "Why would you want that old thing?"

"How about two thousand bucks?"

"Sold!"

"Boys?" Seth said to Anya's sons. "Mind helping me carry the thing out?"

"What are you doing?" I said.

He winked at me. "We'll talk about it later."

The "boys," grown men by any account, helped Seth carry the old couch outside. They parked it next to the helicopter on a pile of new snow. I put on my coat, gloves and knit hat and followed them outside. All of us set out to clear the snow from the helicopter. Together, we dug it out. I'd never realized how strenuous shoveling snow could be. I was out of breath after three shovelfuls.

Once the snow was cleared, Seth climbed into the helicopter, got on the radio and notified the Alaska state troopers of what had happened last night. Anya and her sons listened to the story, trading startled looks. The tale sounded implausible, like something out of a movie. I still had trouble believing that it had happened to me.

When Seth was done talking with the police, he and the other men rigged a hoist to the couch. Anya padded over to me, eyes wide with concern.

"That was some awful business," she said. "Are you all right?"

"I was cold last night, but I'm good now."

"Are you sure?" she said. "You seem unsettled to me."

"I'm fine." I stared at my hands.

"You saw something, didn't you?" She lifted my chin with a finger and studied my face with her shrewd little eyes. "Something that puzzled you."

"I read some of your Athabaskan tales before I fell asleep." I shrugged. "Some of the stories probably messed with my mind."

"Oh, my." Anya stared. "You did see something, something your mind can't accept but your heart wants to embrace."

"A bear." The words just blurted out. "A bear led me to safety. How could it be?"

"The Athabaskans believed that in the beginning all animals were men," Anya said. "They thought animals could speak and shift shapes, and we were all one together with nature. The bear must be your clan animal. You are of the bear *yega*."

So much to digest in one great gulp. "What's a yega?"

"A yega is the outer spirit," Anya said. "It's like a picture of the self, like your shadow. Death came for you last night, but you were strong and so was your yega. The bear spirit offers powerful protection. You survived."

A shiver fringed my spine. The hair on the back of my head stood up. Was it even remotely possible that what Anya believed was true?

"The bear spoke to me," I said. "It used my mother's voice, and my father's. It even talked like…him." I motioned with my head to where Seth stood.

"It's you, silly, your shadow soul," Anya said. "It knew you. It knew your heart."

"This is so…confusing."

"Matters of the spirit are often confusing." Anya patted my shoulder kindly. "But you're strong, like your shadow soul. You'll be all right."

Seth called out. "Ready to go?"

"I'll be right there." I waved at him and returned my attention to Anya. "Sorry about the mess."

"No worries," Anya said. "I'm glad you're alive."

"Me too." The smile on my face felt crooked.

I started toward the helicopter, but stopped when I remembered something else.

"Anya?" I said. "The bear talked about eating my liver. Is there any significance to a shadow soul eating one's liver?"

The web on Anya's forehead deepened. "If I recall right, in the old days, one's animal protector was charged with avenging one's injury and death. If you killed someone, you could prevent revenge from an opponent's yega by eating a part from the dead person, usually the liver. But that's just talk, you know. Go on. The golden-eyed eagle boy is waiting for you."

"Who?" I said.

Anya sighed. "Seth. Standing right over there by the helicopter? Remember Seth?"

"Is the golden eagle his shadow soul?"

"How should I know?" Anya said. "I'm a shaman, not a witch. Ask him. And do try to be happy."

"I'll try." It was a pledge to myself. "Thanks for your patience, Anya."

"Patience, pfft." She waved her hands in the air as she waddled to her cabin. "You've got little of that and I've got none."

I made my way to the helicopter, considering everything I'd learned. Shadow souls. Bear spirits. Eagles. My mother, murdered? And the final, unavoidable truth: someone really wanted to kill me.

Talk about a freaking mess.

Seth was inspecting the aircraft, a model of efficient movement and elegance in motion. I remembered last night and went liquid inside. He helped me to climb up into the helicopter and strapped me in himself. Every time we made eye contact, I flushed. I had to suppress an urge to go for his mouth. I could tell he wanted me too. I'd fallen hard for this guy and I had no idea of what came next.

Seth powered up the helicopter and talking over the radio, maneuvered the tricky takeoff. I put on my headset and watched the couch take to the air below us.

"This is crazy," I said. "Why on earth would you want that old thing?"

The look he gave me curled my toes. "Do you really have to ask?"

BY NOON, TWO Alaskan state troopers arrived at Seth's place to take my statement. The senior officer was a grizzled veteran wearing a skeptical frown. Stocky, square, and thickset, he reminded me of a Pug. The other officer was fair, younger, and excitable, more like a Golden Retriever. He gaped at Seth and the house as if he stared at God in the flesh and heaven in this world. Seth sat next to me and held my hand, while the officers asked questions. I told them everything the man had said, everything I could remember.

"I'm sure it was the same man that was caught by the security camera at the rest stop," I said as I finished my story.

"His name is George Peterson," Officer Pug said. "We have information that suggests he's done murder for hires before in the lower forty-eight."

I looked at Seth. "Did you know about this?"

"I found out this morning, when I talked to Spider, my chief of cyber security. It took us quite some time to figure out who he was, but we caught a break late yesterday and we finally matched the face to the name."

"Oh." I was slightly miffed. "You should've told me."

"We're looking into Peterson's bank accounts as we speak," the trooper said. "We hope the money trail will help us find out who hired him and why. What makes you believe there's a connection between the attack last night and your mother's death years ago?"

Seth answered for me. "Her mother drowned."

Evidently, dreams and visions were not something he wanted to share with the troopers.

"Peterson tried to drown Summer in a similar way," Seth added. "I don't believe in coincidences."

"We'll look into it," the trooper said.

"Can we tell her now?" If Officer Golden Retriever had had a tail, it would be wagging.

"Tell me what?"

"The troopers have some news that might be unsettling to you."

I stared at Seth. "Unsettling?"

"I don't want you to get upset."

"I can handle it." Did he think I was an idiot? "Just tell me whatever the hell it is you have to tell me."

"They found George Peterson in the woods by the lake," Seth said. "He's dead."

"Oh, my God." I squeaked. "Did I kill him?"

"One of your bullets hit him in the leg," Officer Pug said in a solemn tone. "The wound slowed him down, but it was a bear that killed him."

"The bear?"

"It must sound strange to someone from the outside," Officer Golden Retriever said. "But this is Alaska."

"Wait." My mind was stuck. "Did you just say that the bear killed him?"

"The coroner hasn't completed the autopsy yet," the other trooper said, "but the evidence suggests that a bear attacked George Peterson as he tried to reach a rented hydroplane he'd anchored a couple of miles away from the Golov homestead. The man was alive when he met the bear."

Not a single word made it through my strangled throat.

"Breathe." Seth squeezed my hand. "Come on, take a breath."

I tried, but the air felt too heavy to inhale.

"It explains why Peterson didn't return to finish the job," the younger trooper said. "The bear didn't feed much on the corpse, except for the liver. He only ate the man's liver…"

I could see the officer's lips moving, but I couldn't hear the rest. The bear had killed the man and eaten his liver. His liver.

"Summer?" Seth's face floated into my frame of vision. "You look sick."

I grappled with the notion while I struggled to keep the food in my stomach. "You…um…you said bears don't usually attack humans."

"They don't, usually."

"Remember what I told you?"

"Yes," Seth said.

"What is she talking about?" Officer Pug asked.

"Summer saw the bear too," Seth said. "It wandered along the trail to the cabin."

I rested my hand on my belly and focused on breathing.

"I think she's had enough for today." Seth got up

and gestured for the troopers to do the same. “I’ll walk you out.”

Anya’s old bear friend, the same animal that had spoken in my loved ones’ voices and led me from the lake to the cabin, had stalked my wounded assailant, killed him and eaten his liver, the only part the bear in my dream/hallucination/vision had relished. My shadow soul, my bear yega, had eaten my enemy’s liver, presumably to avoid his yega’s revenge?

It was a bit too much. Never again would I pick up a book of Athabaskan legends. Period. My imagination was simply too fertile to deal with such vivid stories.

“Excuse me?” I croaked as the men ambled toward the front door. “I have a question.”

“Yes?” the veteran officer said.

“What happened to the bear?”

“We haven’t found it yet,” the trooper said. “We’ve got people looking, but we’ve found no traces of it.”

It was the most relief I’d felt all day.

SIXTEEN

By the time Seth came out of his office later that afternoon, I'd forced myself to tackle the present, where Tammy was nowhere to be found, my clients needed immediate changes to their plans, Jer's project required lots of research, and my boss and stepmother vied for my head. Seth found me at the kitchen bar, parked in front of my laptop.

"Hey." His strong hands kneaded my shoulders. "How are you holding up?"

His touch felt so good on my knotted muscles. "Jer's tundra-friendly pylons haven't been invented. Darius now wants the sixth floor redesigned. Hector demands I come back to Miami, even more urgently than before. Meanwhile, Louise thinks I'm in cahoots with Tammy to drive her insane."

"I'm telling you," Seth said, "your stepmother is off."

"Seth!"

"No disrespect intended."

"Right," I said. "If all of that wasn't enough, I talked to the innkeeper in Kenai. She has no idea where Tammy and Nikolai were going next. I swear I must have talked to every hotel, campsite, and bed-and-breakfast in south Alaska. It seems I've hit another dead end."

"Too bad," Seth said. "Maybe she'll turn up again soon?"

"She better." I got up from my stool and went to the

fridge, where I pulled out my latest creation and settled it on the counter in front of Seth. "Here, I baked you a flan."

"Wow." He eyed the dessert and grinned. "When did you have time to bake me a flan?"

"I bake when I'm stressed." I sliced the flan and spooned it onto a plate. "I'd rather abuse the oven than drugs and/or alcohol. It's the lesser vice, don't you think?"

"Absolutely." He grabbed a spoon. "You won't hear any complaints from me."

"Let's see if you like it." I parked the plate in front of him.

He dug in. "Hmm." His delight trickled down my spine and softened my center. "Awesome."

I ignored the little pangs of need coursing through my body, scooped myself a piece and tasted my creation. It'd turned out really good. I swallowed another bite. "I've extended my search for Tammy to the interior and the panhandle," I said. "Maybe I'll get something productive that way. Your guy hasn't come up with anything, has he?"

"Nothing helpful," he mumbled around a mouthful.

"I can't stick around forever," I said. "My job is on the line."

"You can't leave," he said between gulps. "There's Tammy, of course, and the police investigation. They want you to stay until they figure out why George Peterson wanted to kill you."

I poked at my flan. "I wonder how George Peterson got access to Fountain Way. Back then, it was a new building with great security. A guy like him in Fountain Way? Doesn't make sense."

"I thought the same thing," Seth said. "I had Spider

and his team dig out the list of owners for the period. Peterson's name wasn't on any of them, which means he must have been staying with someone else. The question is, who?"

"Maybe I should go back to Miami and take a look."

"No way." Seth set down his spoon. "You're not safe out there right now. You can't leave."

"I can't linger here forever. Someday, I have to go back to the real world."

"This is the real world too," Seth said.

"The idea that someone wants me dead still seems crazy to me."

"We need find out who hired him and why," he said. "Meanwhile, I've added some security measures. You're safe here."

I knew Seth. I knew he meant what he said. After last night, I also understood that the danger was real and I was grateful for his precautions. But I couldn't put my life on hold forever. Could I? I had responsibilities, obligations. I owed it to my mom to find her real killer. I also had to find Tammy.

My phone chimed. I looked at the screen. Hector. My stomach began to churn. What was I going to tell him now? Not that I'd had a run-in with an assassin for hire. He'd never believe me.

I clicked on the cell. "Hello?"

"When I gave you a job, I expected you to be at your office and carry the load," Hector said in a tone that curdled the flan in my belly. "I also expected you to answer your phone."

"Sorry," I mumbled. "I was out of range."

"I didn't expect you'd leave for weeks at a time and abandon your projects."

"I'm trying my best," I said. "I've kept up with the Darius project. We're on budget, on target and on schedule."

"I'm tired of excuses and family emergencies," he said. "Between Louise and Tammy, you've got a full-time babysitting gig."

"But—"

"I did you a favor," Hector said. "I hired you out of the goodness of my heart, because your father was my partner once. I gave you time off to go to Alaska because I know Tammy and Louise and, frankly, I think that they're both living impaired. But if you're not in my office by tomorrow at five o'clock, you'll never work as an architect in Miami again."

"You must understand," I said. "I can't leave until I find Tammy…"

"This goddam idiot is fixated on you." Seth plucked the cell out of my hand and spoke into the phone. "Hector Carrera? My name is Seth Erickson. I'm the CEO of Erickson & Erickson Enterprises. Look me up if you'd like, but don't interrupt me."

"Seth?" I groped for my cell. "What are you doing?"

Seth kept a firm hold on the phone and ignored me.

"We're currently in the process of accepting design bids for a milestone, multi-million-dollar portable housing project," he said to Hector. "The bidding process is by invitation only. Miss Silva has some innovative thoughts on the project. I'm inviting her—and only her—to submit a bid on behalf of your company."

"Seth," I muttered. "Give me my cell back!"

Seth put his hand over the speaker. "Hush, Summer, let me take care of this."

Hush, Summer?

"Carrera and Associates may have a shot at the project," Seth continued. "But only if you stop hassling Miss Silva and allow her to do her research. Obviously, she'll need to stay in Alaska to liaison with our people here. Are you interested?"

I imagined Hector's excitement on the other side of the line. Of course he'd be interested! It was a milestone project that would enhance his reputation worldwide and line his pockets. The bidding would be unavailable to him any other way and, even if he had to send me to Mars, he'd never turn down a multi-million-dollar project.

"Excellent," Seth said. "We'll get the paperwork rolling. A good day to you too." He clicked off the phone and handed it to me. "That's done."

The look on my face must have given him a hint of my emotions, or else the smoke billowing out of my ears gave me away.

"What's wrong?" he said.

"What's wrong?" I glared. "That was *my* boss you just talked to!"

"Yes, so?"

"Hector was *my* problem."

"Please." Seth rolled his eyes. "The son of a bitch was out of control. How the hell did you end up working for a jackass like him anyways?"

"I came out of grad school in the middle of a recession," I said. "I was lucky he offered me a job."

"He treats you like dirt," he said. "He won't do that again."

"Because you promised him a bidding invitation to a multi-million-dollar contract."

"I didn't lie to him," he said. "Your work on this project is top-notch. You've made more headway on the specs than anybody else. I want you on the project."

Was he crazy? "I have a full-time job in Miami."

"You can have a full-time a job here, too."

I rumbled inside. "Don't do this, Seth."

"Do what?"

"Mix the mayo with the ketchup."

He frowned. "What the hell are you talking about?"

"Don't try to cram our private and professional relationships into the same bucket," I said. "I might seem dumb to you, but I'm not completely clueless."

"I thought you said you didn't want to get fired."

"My job, my decision."

"Stop doing that," Seth said.

"What?"

"That thing where you frown, stick out your chin and flick your hair." He pointed at me with the spoon. "It means trouble, and I don't need trouble with you. The bid offered a solution all around."

I stomped my foot. "You can't keep me here by offering me a job and you can't go around bribing people to keep me on. I'm skilled. I don't need you to create an artificial position for me!"

"It's not an artificial position," he said. "You are very much needed on this project."

I narrowed my stare on him. "Did you interview me for the position?"

"I didn't need to," he said. "I saw your work."

"Did you interview other candidates and measure me against their qualifications?"

"No, but—"

"The only reason you want to hire me is because we're sleeping together."

He scowled. "I wouldn't have offered you the position if I didn't think you were qualified."

"I'm qualified, that's true, to get myself a new job if I need to." I cleared the dirty dishes from the counter and dumped them in the sink. "If I want to find work in Alaska, I'll apply for a job in Alaska. And that's not all. You told the police not to tell me about George Peterson's death. You thought I was going to fall apart."

"I didn't want you to get upset. What's wrong with that?"

"It would be normal for someone to be upset in a situation like this," I said. "The guy came after me and then the bear ate his liver…his liver!"

I still couldn't get over that one.

Seth came around the counter and put his arms around my waist. "Baby, I…"

"No, Seth." I pushed him away. "I can deal with my own problems. I get to make my own choices. I can take care of myself."

"Perhaps," he said cryptically.

I wheeled on him. "What do you mean 'perhaps'?"

"Personally," he said, crossing his arms and leaning against the counter, "I think that for a girl who claims to be risk-averse, you take too many risks."

"What the hell are you talking about?"

"Let's take the day before yesterday, for example," he said. "I told you to go home with Robert. What did you do instead? You jumped out of a damn helicopter."

"It was low to the ground."

"You don't do crap like that." His stare grew stern. "You could've been hurt. If that wasn't enough, you ignored my instructions, set out on a wild chase, and exposed yourself to incredible danger."

"I did not!" My temper flared. "I had a theory based on logical expectations and—surprise!—it panned out and you're free."

"I don't mean to be an ungrateful son of a bitch," he said. "But I wouldn't have minded a few more hours with my ass parked in detention in exchange for your safety."

"I minded!" I said. "I didn't want you in jail. And how on earth could I've known that man was going to come after me?"

"Contingency thinking," he said. "It's what I do for a living. I'm fairly good at it, if only you'd trust me. You would've been safe, had you followed my instructions."

"Okay, well, maybe, but you need to know I'm not very good at following instructions." I cocked my fists on my hips. "In fact, I flunked kindergarten because I couldn't follow instructions. So get over it, Erickson."

"No, you get over it," he said. "You want to live in Alaska? You better listen to me."

"Who says I want to live in Alaska?"

He winced and I knew right away that I'd scored a blow below the belt. In all honesty, I wanted to find a way to be close to him too, but I had a lot of stuff to work out in my mind and some of it was complicated. I hadn't planned on coming to Alaska, let alone to linger out here. I hadn't planned on Seth either. The way I felt frightened me. My life was in Miami. My family too. I was responsible for Louise and Tammy. If I didn't take care of them, who would?

Seth modulated his voice with visible effort. "The

first time I met you, I had to pick you up from the pavement."

"I slipped on the ice!"

"Last night, I had to shake icicles from your hair."

"Not because I was careless or reckless."

"You said the punctured brakes weren't about you," he said flatly. "But you were wrong. It was about you, about your mother. Someone wants to kill you and whether you're ready to accept that or not, you've got to own up to the fact that you are in danger."

"I have!" I said. "And that's why I need to go back to Miami and figure out what this is all about."

"Going back to Miami is not the answer," he said. "Let the police do their work. Let us finish this investigation before you go anywhere."

"But—"

"What's going to happen the next time?" he said. "Am I going to have to scoop parts of your brain back into your thick skull?"

"Oh, come on. Don't you think you're being overly dramatic here?"

"Dammit, no!" he snapped. "Last night? For a whole half an hour, I thought you were going to die."

"But I didn't die, right? That should count for something."

"If something were to happen to you..."

The anguish in his stare blew me out of the water. I had no doubt that his emotions were honest. Had the situations been reversed, I might have felt the same fear. Oh, God. What a mess.

"Don't ever lie to me," I said. "Don't keep things from me and don't run interference. You're powerful, I get that. You've got resources. Great. You're brilliant, smart, and capable. Fantastic. But I want a shot at my life. Do you hear me?"

"Loud and clear." He plopped down on a stool. "But promise me you'll stay here, in Alaska, until we find who's behind all this."

"I'll stay until I find Tammy," I said. "That was our deal. After that, we'll have to see where we are."

"Okay, fine." He kneaded his temples. "Now, can you please stop fighting with me? You're giving me a headache."

"Who's giving who a headache?"

"Not too many people fight with me."

"That may be because you act like a bully sometimes."

"Me?" He scoffed. "You're like a pit bull from hell when you're mad."

"I am not!"

"Oh, yes, you are." He reached out, caught my wrists in his hands and pulled me into the space between his knees. "I'd rather take on ISIS any day. I don't like it when you're mad at me. It feels wrong. Besides, I've got to be out of here in twenty minutes."

My stomach squeezed. "Where are you going?"

"I've got a dinner meeting in Fairbanks."

"Oh?" I slumped. Did I think that his world would stop spinning just because we'd slept together?

"It's in and out on the Learjet. I'll be back tonight." He gathered me against his chest. "Truce?"

"Fine." I put my arms around him and planted a little kiss on his mouth. "Truce."

"Let's go downstairs then."

"Downstairs?" I eyed him suspiciously. "Why?"

He brushed his lips against my knuckles. “I need to make peace with you before I go.”

“In the garage?”

“What, have you forgotten?” He grinned. “That’s where the couch is.”

SEVENTEEN

MY MEETING IN Fairbanks turned out to be productive but not necessarily helpful. It also left me in a shitty situation. Perhaps I should've shared my findings with Summer, but then again, I'd made an agreement in exchange for information and I always kept my word. Priority number one was Summer's safety. The rest was peripheral and incidental and we'd have to hash it out later, when she was no longer in danger.

Summer was asleep by the time I got back, which was probably a good thing. I'd cradled her in my arms all night, feeling goddamn lucky to have her safe, hale and whole in my bed. Still, every time I thought about what had happened at Star Lake, the rage barreled through my veins. Worry and sleep didn't go too well together, so morning found me at my desk, working, the best way I knew how to blow off steam, other than making love with Summer, who needed her rest. Yeah, I was definitively operating at a higher, nobler level these days.

I spent the next two days negotiating with the governor, preparing for the upcoming board meeting, and doing some more internal sleuthing on Alex. I made some progress. This morning, I was on my third cup of coffee, chewing on my pen and studying the numbers on my laptop when my online coms beeped. I accepted the call and Spider's face appeared on my screen.

"Morning, dude," he said in a flash of fangs. "Hey, you never told me. How was Fairbanks?"

"Interesting," I said.

"I bet," Spider said. "Are you gonna share?"

"Negative."

"Damn, dude, I do all the ground work and you leave out the juicy parts?"

"I'm on it, okay? That's all I'm going to say. Status report?"

"Oh, man, do I have some goodies for you today." Had he been a fox, I would've gone straight to check on the chicken coop.

"Anything new on the Peterson investigation?"

"Still tracing his whereabouts seventeen years ago," Spider said. "Working on the insurance angle and keeping track of everyone under surveillance."

"What about Sergio De Havilland?"

"He's still under surveillance as well," Spider said. "But I thought you'd eliminated him from the equation, on account of dudette's early memories."

Memories, dreams, I wasn't sure, but it made no difference. "I haven't eliminated anyone, especially not him. He did something wrong to Summer. She managed to eject him completely out of her life. He needs money. Those reasons are motive enough. Keep working his angle."

"Will do." Spider smirked. "Can I tell you the good stuff now?"

"Go."

"First to the Star Lake mess," Spider said. "The lab reports are in on Anya Golov's pickled fish. The substance that killed those fish is a very efficient designer poison, active only for a span of a few hours. There are only two laboratories in the world that produce it. One of them delivered an order to the E&E lumber mill on Star Lake. The fool who signed for that order is one of the two men in Anya's pictures, the shift supervisor."

I tapped my pen on the desk. "What's his connection to Alex?"

"He's been employee of the month for seven months in a row," Spider said. "You should see the bonuses he's getting. Apparently, Alex delivers the award personally each month."

"We'll need a full confession for the board meeting and the Feds. What else?"

"Big news." Spider's lips and cheeks vibrated with a pretty good drum roll imitation as he beat an imaginary pair of crash cymbals in the air. "I found them. You were right. Alex's accounts are in Luxembourg. Under an assumed name, mind you, but he's got them. And boy are they hefty."

"Are you sure they're his?"

"Positive." Spider held a finger over the keyboard. "I'm sending you the trail of accounts…now."

I clicked the files open and took a quick look. Jackpot. The son of a bitch was mine.

"Spider, you are top-of-the-line shit-hot stuff," I said. "Alex's brothers and sisters are going to have a cow when they learn that their big brother has been dipping into their piggy bank. You're worth every penny."

"We've got the accounts, but we haven't actually caught him in the honeypot yet."

"The hell we haven't."

Spider gawked. "Are you holding out on me?"

"I've been doing my own hunting over here."

"Damn," Spider said, shaking his head. "I forgot how much you like to hunt."

"At the end of the day it's all simple math," I said. "Want me to give you *the* number?"

"You're a brainy son of a bitch," Spider said. "Shoot."

"Sixty-three mil, over the last two years, give or take a little."

Spider stared. "How the hell did you do that?"

"You don't want to know."

"That's about the balance in those accounts I found," Spider said. "Remind me never to step on the wrong side of your line. How come the auditors didn't catch it?"

"The mill's books are cooked," I said. "Alex had a good racket going, fake vendors, dummy companies, and kickbacks funneled through the lumber division. The fucker set up shop the year I went to Afghanistan."

"I wanna be a fly on the wall at the board meeting."

"I can't imagine you're not."

"Dude, you're hurting my feelings." Spider clutched his chest. "Do you think I'm a freaking spy?"

"The best there is," I said. "It's why I hired you. Thanks, Spider. Fantastic work."

I clicked off and returned to work right away, updating my board meeting notes on pen and paper, as I usually did. Some things were too sensitive to put on a device and I trusted my house's cutting edge security system. I'd just finished when Summer burst through the door.

"It's Tammy." She stood across from my desk, face flushed, eyes sparkling like glaciers. "I found her!"

"You found her?" How could it be? "Are you sure?"

"I'm sure, Seth. She's at Denali National Park!"

My gut activated a burst of acid reflux. “That doesn’t sound right.”

“Of course it does,” she said. “Anybody trekking all the way to Alaska and skipping Denali is brain-dead.”

“If you say so.” I had to think on my feet. “But how do you know that they’re there?”

“I just talked to a ranger at Denali,” she said. “Tammy’s name is on a list for a backcountry permit, along with Nikolai’s.”

Damn. It was plausible, if not on my timeline.

“Denali is a huge place,” I said cautiously. “It’s over six million acres, larger than Massachusetts. It will be impossible to find them in the backcountry.”

“That’s what’s so great,” she said. “The permit specified a destination. They were heading to a place called—hang on, let me see—” She checked her notes. “Kantishna?”

“I know Kantishna,” I said, considering my options. “It’s a pretty isolated outpost, especially at this time of the year. It doesn’t sound right. Besides, no Alaskan in his right mind would take a tropical girl without hiking experience bushwhacking in October.”

Summer’s face crumpled. “Why aren’t you excited for me? I found my sister!”

What to do? I was torn in opposite directions.

“Come here,” I finally said, patting my lap. “I don’t mean to burst your bubble, but a hiking trip to Denali at this time of the year is just…unlikely.”

“But, Seth.” She eased down on my lap and put her arms around my neck. “I’ve got to go. I looked into it. The air taxi can pick me up right here. The pilot said…”

Shit. “You talked to an air taxi pilot?”

“He said he could fly me there and back today.”

"The weather can be tricky around the Alaskan Range in October."

"He assured me that the weather is perfect for flying over the Range today," she said. "I've got to go now."

Damn the cocky ass bush pilot.

"Baby…" I was the most wretched jerk on the planet and I knew it. "You can't go. I won't let you."

Her body tensed on my lap. Her eyes sparked with fury. If all of that wasn't ominous enough, her chin stuck out and her hair flickered with an imperious toss of her head.

Uh-oh.

"You can't go with just any rent-a-pilot," I said, "and why would you need to pay for a rookie who drives an air scooter when you've got your own personal expert who knows those mountains better than anyone else?"

She stared at me, blinking in surprise. "You want to fly me to Denali?"

What option did I have? "Sure."

Her fury was instantly appeased.

"It's very sweet of you." She kissed me, a tickle of soft lips that resonated deep in my groin. "But you're so busy finalizing that contract with the governor and you've got to prep for your big board meeting."

"Contract is nearly finalized." I tapped the notes on my desk. "Prep's done."

"Really?" She gave me the narrow-eyed look that said she didn't believe me. "What about the Alex thing?"

"Now, see, that's a little more complicated, because although we've made tremendous progress, Alex is a sneaky bastard."

Her lips compressed with worry. "Do you think he's setting up a trap?"

"I know he is. I just need to figure out when and how."

"Then you're better off staying here and working on that while I go find Tammy."

"That's a negative," I said, "as in you're not going out there without me. In any case, I need a break. Fresh eyes do the job best."

"Really?" She examined me closely. "Are you sure?"

"Really." I tucked the notes in the drawer, then reached around her and, with one hand, punched on my keyboard to pull up the latest weather report. It wasn't half bad. "I wouldn't want people to say you were brain-dead."

"Me?" she said. "Brain-dead?"

"Only the brain-dead come to Alaska and skip Denali."

She grinned. "I do recall saying that."

I planted a quick kiss on her lips. "Shall we fix the oversight?"

"Only if you really have the time for it."

"Forget this shit." I threw my pen over my shoulder. "Let's go flying, baby."

AS I EXPECTED, we didn't find Tammy and Nikolai in Denali. I was good with that, in more ways than one. The flight wasn't a waste of time. I loved having Summer all to myself and I seized the chance to show her Alaska's wonders. Even though she was disappointed that we didn't find her sister, she squealed when she spotted the Dall sheep on Stony Dome and the herds of caribou crossing the Toklat River. And her face when she spied Mount Denali towering over the Range? Priceless.

Our flight path back took us on a south by southeast

course over Talkeetna, Highway Three, Denali National Park, and the Alaskan Range. The mountain's high altitude and deep canyons complicated the flying in these parts. The weather was fickle and the wind was known to shift without patterns.

Fortunately, I knew the Range like the back of my hand. I'd trained in this theater exhaustively. To this day, my reserve squadron trained and assisted with Denali's air rescue team several times a year, which was also why we'd been so goddamn effective in the high mountains of Afghanistan.

As I mounted the spine of the Range, I checked the radar for west to east traffic and clicked on the radio. "Mountain Traffic, this is Firehawk, Alpha-niner-niner-Victor-Romeo, Great Gorge, 8000 feet, Gateway."

"Copy that, Firehawk, niner-Victor-Romeo, this is Mountain Traffic South. Long time no see. Welcome home, Eagle."

"Thanks, Pete," I said, recognizing the voice. "Glad to be back."

"Who was that?" Summer asked.

"One of my old flying buddies."

"Why did he call you eagle?"

"Eagle was my call name with the National Guard."

Her eyebrows quirked. "Was?"

Was, is, I wasn't sure, so I shrugged.

"When was the last time you flew up here?" she asked.

"It's been a while."

"Have you flown a Pave Hawk since you came back from Afghanistan?"

I flashed her an irritated glance.

"Oh, come on."

She wasn't going to let up.

"If you have to know," I said, "unofficially, yes, I have."

"Unofficially?" She thought about that. "Oh, I get it. Somehow, you've been flying Pave Hawks with people from your squadron. Am I right?"

"I can't confirm or deny that," I said. "People can get in serious trouble for doing shit like that. I've been up several times and I did fine, if that's what you're ruminating."

"Good going, Erickson. I'm impressed. So if all systems are a go, why aren't you back on active reserves?"

Excellent question. "I've been busy."

"Ha." She flashed me another glance. "Try again."

"I don't have the time."

"Yeah, no," she said. "I don't buy it."

I glanced at her. "What's it to you?"

"Good question." Her gaze lingered on me for a second too long. "When I think about you on active duty, my stomach feels sick with worry."

"Because you think I'm going to crash again?"

"You didn't crash, Seth. Your helicopter was hit by an RPG. I doubt there's a lot of those zipping through the air in Alaska. But I know there are lots of risks. Honestly? The whole active reserve stuff scares the bejesus out of me."

"Then why the hell are you riding my tail so hard about going back?"

"Because you love it," she said. "And you miss flying those Pave Hawks. You miss your friends at the squadron, too. You're happy when you're up here. You're busy, but you could make time if you wanted to. Something else is holding you back."

"Something like what, Miss Know It All?"

"I think you're punishing yourself."

"What?" Where the fuck had that come from?

"You're punishing yourself for the loss of your friends' lives."

Blindsided. Her words slammed into me like a punch to the gut. I went into a tailspin. I almost doubled over the stick. *Focus, Erickson.* I wasn't going to lose it at this altitude. I glanced over at Summer. The compassion etched on her face left me reeling. Jesus fucking Christ. Was she right? Had I grounded myself to atone for my friends' deaths?

"Enough punishment." She stared at me with those relentless eyes. "You've served your sentence. It's time to let yourself out of prison."

She was right. Any idiot could see that. How the hell had she figured out what I hadn't been able to see for myself? I was holding back, out of guilt, grief, and despair. I couldn't make sense of what had happened. Why the hell was I alive? Did I have a right to happiness when my friends were gone?

Summer's voice hoisted me out of the darkness. "It's called survivor's guilt. I looked it up. It's not uncommon. I don't know that anybody gets over stuff like that, but some people learn to live with it."

My throat tightened. Behind my shades, a watery film blurred my vision. I had to blink several times before I could read the instruments. I focused my attention on the radar and adjusted the collective. Hell no, there was no way could I talk about this, not now, maybe never. *Just fly the damn helicopter.*

"Your friends loved flying, didn't they?" Summer said.

"They did," I admitted reluctantly.

"Then flying is how you celebrate their lives," she said, "and every time you fly with your squadron, you honor their memories. In fact, you're honoring them right now."

She was spot-on. Jonesy and Shawn would've loved it. I could think of no better tribute to my friends than a successfully executed mission. Why hadn't I thought of that?

I glanced over at the woman beside me. She smiled at me, a kind, soothing gesture that pierced through the gloom that enveloped me whenever I thought of my fallen friends. She was beginning to know me better than I knew myself and, now that she'd gutted my grief and dragged out my sorrows into the open, she did me a second favor: she dropped the subject and swiftly moved on.

"There it is," she said as we flew east of Mount Denali. "I've got no words. It's like the mother of all mountains."

"North America's tallest." I cleared my throat, thankful for the distraction. "It's so big, it makes its own weather."

"Have you climbed it?" she asked.

"Several times."

"And you summited every time, didn't you?"

I shrugged. It was in the record books, so no need to boast.

She flashed a proud smile. "So you're good at climbing ginormous mountains too?"

"I've had a lot of practice and a good technical education." High-altitude mountaineering had been a passion of mine, right up there with flying. "I'm okay."

"You're probably a lot better than okay. Are we near to where you saved that hiker?"

I glanced at her. “How do you know about that?”

“Ally told me you held the record for the highest-altitude helicopter rescue in North America. So I looked it up.”

“It wasn’t a big deal.”

“What happened?”

“The hiker got stranded on a ledge. There was some weather coming in—hell, this is Alaska, there’s always weather coming in. I plucked him off a ledge on the south side. The guy sends me a Christmas card every year.”

“I bet.” She flashed me a knowing smile. “He’s alive because of you.”

“We got lucky, that’s all.”

The sun set a fiery death behind the mountains. The sky turned into a gorgeous tone of luminescent indigo before the first stars began to play peek-a-boo with our eyes. I switched the helicopter’s setting to night flight. A soft glow illuminated Summer’s face. We talked a lot, about her childhood, my upbringing, and growing up in Alaska.

“Do you want to know what I think about this feud you’ve got going with this Alex person?” she said.

“Go ahead.” Not even divine intervention would stop Summer from giving her opinion, but honestly? I wanted to hear what she had to say. “Don’t hold back on my account.”

“I think you should reach out to your cousins,” she said. “Just because Alex is a jerk doesn’t mean the rest of them are too. They’re your family, you know.”

“In name,” I said, “but not in substance.”

“You’re not around them much,” she said. “They don’t know who you are.”

“I don’t think they like me much these days.”

"So what?" she said. "You don't stand by your family because you like them. You stand by them because they're your family."

The way she thought about family made me wish she was part of mine. But my family was a total clusterfuck and I didn't have the time, patience or inclination to tackle that can of worms.

Summer's next question came out of left field.

"Would you consider living somewhere other than Alaska?"

I glanced at her. "Somewhere else like where?"

"Oh, I don't know." She squirmed under my scrutiny. "I guess you'd melt in Miami."

"Miami?" What the fuck was going on in her head? "It's hot as hell in Miami."

"You're right." She slumped on her seat. "For a guy who craves ice, Miami would be unbearable."

By the way her eyes dimmed, I kind of got her heading.

"Hey," I said. "Just because our body temps clock at opposite ends of the thermometer doesn't mean we're doomed."

She met my eyes. "You think so?"

"We grow tropical orchids year-round in the Erickson greenhouses."

"We've got air-conditioning in Miami."

She was as stubborn as I was and we weren't talking about the weather anymore.

"I bet you don't have this in Miami," I said.

A diffused glow lit up the sky to our west. A flutter of green light tiptoed across the sky then disappeared. Her eyes narrowed, peering into the night. A curtain of translucent green unfurled across the night, a luminous veil flickering against the sky, shifting, changing, breaking up, and reassembling into fantastic new combinations.

Summer's eyes sparkled with the lights. "Is that…?"

"Aurora borealis," I said, "performing tonight for your enjoyment."

"Wow." Summer took in the spectacle. "Incredible. How does it work?"

"One theory is that solar winds flowing by the earth bring charged particles that interact with the atmosphere's geomagnetic components."

"So it's raining speckles of sunlight on us tonight." She gazed at the sky. "How marvelous is that?"

Her wonder powered my grin. "It's pretty cool."

"Do you know what the Northern Lights remind me of?" she said. "A neon billboard, flashing a message from the universe."

"What's the universe advertising tonight?"

"Life is beautiful? The universe rocks? Welcome home?"

"I really, really like that last one."

The smile she gave me had me roaming for a landing spot. I needed a quickie. I'd just turned on the searchlights when a call came through in my private channel, derailing my best plans. Well, fuck me.

"What's wrong?" Summer asked when I switched off the searchlights and banked on a southerly heading.

"Got to go," I said. "Trouble in Prudhoe Bay."

"I hope it's nothing serious."

"We'll see." I should've made it over there days ago. "But don't worry, you'll be safe while I'm gone. I promise."

"Erickson?" She flashed me one of her looks. "I wasn't worried about me. I was worried about you."

"Don't be," I said. "Troubleshooting is what I do for a living. I'll take you home, fly out in the jet, and be back in a cinch. You'll be fine."

"Yeah, I'll be fine," she said, "as long as trouble doesn't shoot back at you."

EIGHTEEN

I CLUTCHED MY coffee and watched the sun setting over the mountains. As sunsets went, Alaska's were spectacular. Light crowned the mountains in royal purples and the world seemed to take a last breath before plunging into the night's mysteries. I set down my cup and loaded up two thermoses I found in the pantry with coffee. I put on my pink coat, stepped out on the deck and, leaning over the railing, called out.

"Hey, you, down there, come out where I can see you."

Nothing.

"Come on, power ranger," I said in a singsong voice. "Or is it ninja turtle? Assassin's Creed?"

Nary a rustle from beneath the deck.

"You've been there all day," I said. "Come out and talk to me. Or if you prefer, I'll come down there to meet you."

"Don't." A man wearing camo stepped out into view. "No one is supposed to know we're here and you're to stay inside at all times."

"Ah, we're playing the princess in the tower game, are we?" I waved the thermoses in the air. "This one's for you and this one's for your friend over there in the woods. I realize I have no chance of getting you guys to come upstairs, so catch."

"Thank you, ma'am." The man hooked his weapon

over his shoulder and caught the thermoses I dropped into his hands. "We've got strict orders."

"Of course you do," I said. "Far be it for me to get you guys into trouble, but it's really cold out here, so I unlocked the side door to the garage. Please feel free to come in and defrost at regular intervals. I know you burly Alaskan types have thick hides, but it'll make me feel a lot better if I knew my shining knights weren't frozen in their armor."

"Yes, ma'am." The guy grinned. "Thanks again, ma'am."

"And just in case you people need an incentive to avoid frostbite, I left a plate of homemade cookies on the shelf. I'd be heartbroken if I found leftovers in the morning."

"Cookies?" The guy put his fist over his chest and bowed. "You've got a champion for life, my lady."

I laughed and waved, scurrying inside on frozen toes just as my cell chirped. I fished it out from beneath the pile of blueprints that Jer and I had been working on earlier. I recognized the number on the screen.

"Princess Silva, speaking," I said. "Live, from her perch atop Erickson's fortress."

A long pause and then, "Are you mad at me?"

"Nah," I said. "I miss you too much. You're growing on me, Erickson."

"Damn." He sounded surprised. "Must be my lucky day."

"I don't know that a camouflaged army is really necessary to keep intruders out and me in, but if it gives you peace of mind, I'll just have to live with it."

"It's just a few operatives trained to watch over priority assets."

"In shifts, I'd like to add." I paced along the windows. "When exactly did I transform from a person into an asset?"

"You're sharp, I get it," he said. "But I'm not taking any chances. Maybe I should've told you about them before I left."

"Now you're learning."

"You seem surprised."

"An old Spanish proverb says you can't teach an old parrot new words."

"Maybe this old parrot can learn."

"I'm happy to have a myth disproven," I said. "How are you doing? Did you put on the lotion I got for you? Is it working?"

"It works a hell of a lot better than what I was using before."

"Excellent." I did a little dance. "Does that mean you're not competing with the polar bears for fresh patches of snow?"

A few moments of silence and then, "You know about that?"

"I'm not entirely clueless, Erickson," I said. "How are things on Planet Pluto?"

I could hear the smile on his face. "It's Prudhoe Bay and so that you know, it's different from Planet Pluto."

"Poor Pluto," I said. "He's a planet off and on these days. How would you feel if one day you're a planet in all your glory and the next day you're nothing but a mass of stinky gas?"

His laughter tickled me down to my toes. "Man, I miss you real bad."

"Are you sure you're not just missing that old couch you like so much?"

"The couch is nothing without you on it."

It was my turn to smile and reminisce about the very wicked pleasures I'd discovered on the couch in question.

"Did Robert stop by?" Seth asked.

"Three times so far."

"Did Jer talk to you?"

"He was here too," I said. "We've been making progress with his project."

"Excellent." He paused. I could almost hear his mind working on something.

"What's wrong?" I said. "Why are you worried?"

"I don't think I'll make it back today, either," he said. "Things got complicated out here. I might have to stay a few days in order to set things straight."

"Unpredictability is a part of interstellar travel." I tried to hide my disappointment. "If you're worried about me, please don't. I've got the Erickson brigade watching over me and, even if you don't believe me, for the last twenty-nine and a half years, I've managed without you."

"Ouch," he said. "Never one to miss the chance to take a bite."

"Watch out," I said. "My people came from the islands. We evolved from a fierce line of sharp-toothed sharks."

"That explains it." He laughed then sobered up. "Seriously now, I've got it covered. I need you to feel safe in the house."

"I feel super safe and you should feel worry-free."

"Do me a favor," he said. "Be sure to engage the door chain."

"Always do."

"And lock the door when you're ready to go to bed. The door lock will activate the house security alert system and the motion sensors, which will in turn notify me via satellite if anyone tries to enter the house or if you start wandering in your sleep."

"Stop. *Pare*. Halt," I said. "Now you're scaring the living shit out of me."

"Why?"

"You've gone over the top."

"How?"

"Seth," I said. "I've managed all my life with this disorder. I haven't needed remote monitoring, motion sensors or satellite security alerts. The door chain helps. The rest is overkill."

"I don't agree but…"

"But what?"

"I guess you'll want the indoor cameras off then?"

Oh. My. Freaking. God. "There are security cameras inside this house?"

"I do travel a great deal and—"

"Erickson!"

"I know, over the top, I get it," he said. "I'm trying over here. Bear with me. Okay? How about I trade you a mea culpa for a break?"

I suspected him immediately. "What kind of a break?"

"I want to leave on the volume so I can hear you breathe."

I squeezed the bridge of my nose. The line between sweetness and obsession was iffy, but I could hear the struggle in his voice. He was trying hard. His honesty echoed in my heart.

"All right," I said. "You want to have the audio on?

Fine, but on one condition: I get to hear you breathing too. I sleep a lot better when I feel you near."

"You want to hear me snoring?" Beyond encouraged, he sounded thrilled. "Deal. I'll set you up with a connection to my laptop for tonight."

"Good," I said. "For future reference, it's only fair if it goes both ways."

"Got it." I heard another voice in the background, calling his name. "Ah, hell, I've got to go."

"Good luck with the conquest of Pluto," I said. "Don't forget to wear your gas mask."

He laughed. "Talk to you later."

"Good night, Erickson."

"Good night, beautiful," he said and then, "Love you."

"Love you back."

It was only after I hung up that I realized with a start what we had said to each other.

NINETEEN

THE MANSION THAT presided over the Erickson estate appeared at the end of a long drive like a magnificent vision. It rose on a sprawling promontory overlooking the sound, framed against the Alaskan Range's dramatic backdrop. Built in the traditional New England Shingle Style, the big house could've been in Kennebunkport or Hyannis Port. And yet it belonged in Alaska as surely as the spruce forest surrounding the expansive compound and the red fox that caused my driver to swerve as it strutted across the road.

An army of uniformed valets kept the line of cars ahead of us moving. Sitting in the backseat of the Suburban that Seth had sent for me, I noticed a number of hydroplanes landing on the water and taxiing to the dock. People were coming from everywhere for this event.

Seth had been gone for the last three days. It felt like forever. I'd spoken with him every day, several times a day, but seeing his face on a screen wasn't the same. He'd made me promise I'd meet him at the benefit today. Every particle in my body buzzed with the excitement of seeing him again.

It wasn't as if I'd had a lot of time to pine for him. Between the Erickson and Darius projects, Hector Carrera kept me busy 24/7. If anything, he was even more high-strung than usual these days, keeping close track of me, a boss on steroids. In addition, I'd spoken to a hotel manager in Talkeetna who said he'd talked to Tammy. He told me that Tammy and Nikolai had stayed at the hotel after a day hike at Denali. He said they'd mentioned they were heading north, but he didn't know where.

Based on the new information, I'd extended my search to Fairbanks and the Dalton. I'd also had to deal with yet another meltdown from Louise, who now wanted me to file kidnapping charges against Nikolai Golov. Right. Like Tammy had nothing to do with her own disappearance. I'd spent countless hours on the phone, but so far, the weak lead was all I had. Alaska had swallowed my sister.

As the attendant opened the door and helped me out of the car, I fought the surge of nerves that weakened my knees. Talk about being a fish out of water. I didn't know anybody here. I hoped Seth had already arrived.

I stepped out of the car into a flawless Alaskan day, blue skies, crisp air, and a balmy fifty-eight degrees. Perfect day for a festive luncheon. I joined the steady stream of guests passing through the front doors. An attendant took my coat. I straightened my dress. It was cream lamé embroidered with a blush pattern, with a pleated skirt and a scooped back. Ally and I had paired it with pearl chandelier earrings and nude pumps. I hoped I looked okay.

"Miss Silva?" Robert greeted me.

"Hi, Robert," I said. "Is Seth here?"

"Not yet, miss, but soon," he said. "Please, follow me. The mistress will see you now."

The mistress?

I tripped over my feet. Did he mean Seth's grandmother, the famous—or infamous, depending who you asked—Astrid Erickson? I had a moment of total panic. Where the hell was Seth when you needed him? Alternatively, how about a stiff drink?

I had a vision of me, shaking off my heels and bolting. Robert must have spotted the impulse in my eyes. He grabbed my elbow and guided me up a majestic set of stairs into an extraordinary room. An enormous bank of windows lined the far wall, overlooking the water and illuminating a massive two-story library, framed by sweeping mahogany balconies.

"Wait here," Robert said. "The mistress will be with you shortly. Good luck," he added before he disappeared behind a pair of double doors.

Good luck? Why? Was I going to war? On safari? To the casino?

I swallowed the lump in my throat and studied the library. I didn't know my art as well as I should, but I was pretty sure that a massive Renoir presided over the huge fireplace, flanked by a wall of European classics, Alaskan landscapes, and Native American art. A collection of fine ceramics adorned the shelves everywhere. Were those original Ming Dynasty? The mounted animal trophy heads added a touch of the macabre to the eclectic decor. Glassy eyes stared down on me with hackle-raising intensity.

The quiet click of a door opening came from upstairs. I looked up. Astrid Erickson stood on one of the balconies, looking down on me.

"Let me see you," she said, voice tilting with the distant echoes of a Nordic accent. "Step up to the light. Come on, we don't have all day."

I walked deeper into the library, until I was able to crane my neck and take in the woman above me. She was tall, almost as tall as me, lean, erect, and strong in contrast to my obviously misguided idea of an octogenarian. A full and fashionably styled silver mane framed a striking face with high cheekbones. She looked stunning in a light blue silk suit that matched her wolfish eyes.

"Not bad," she said flatly. "I supposed Seth could do better, but I approve of the dress and pearls are always a sensible accessory."

Wonderful. "Thank you…I think."

She snapped her fingers. "Devon, Daemon."

Two Giant Schnauzers galloped out of the shadows, the tallest, blackest dogs I'd ever seen. I might have run, but I'd learned something from my bear encounter. My heart lurched to my throat, but I stood my ground. Ears forward, jaws agape, the dogs circled me like a pair of sharks at sea, sniffing my legs, poking my groin and backside with their enormous muzzles.

The witch on the balcony wanted to see me flinch. I was willing to get bitten by her devil dogs before I let her. "Sit." I pointed at the floor. "You too."

Much to my surprise, the dogs obeyed me.

I let out a discreet breath and looked up to the balcony. "Is the test over or will you be bringing in a pack of wolves next? If it's a grade you're looking to give me, I prefer questions in written form. Essays are fine, but if you're pressed for time, multiple choice will do."

The woman's mouth lifted at the corners to form the most condescending smile in the history of condescension. "You're not easily intimidated, are you?"

"Yeah, right," I mumbled under my breath. "If you want to talk to me you need to come down from your heights. Or else I can come up. Your pick. My neck is killing me."

Astrid let out a sigh and came down the circular staircase regally, like a woman used to being admired. Her eyes were on me every step of the way. Her heels clicked on the hardwood like a ticking clock. It was unnerving, but I clasped my beaded clutch purse, straightened my back and squared my shoulders. She reached the library's main floor and sauntered to a paneled wall lined with formal portraits.

"My husband, Olav." She gestured then moved on to the next two portraits. "My sons, Arthur and Benjamin. Arthur, he found Alice, but Ben, the poor thing, wasn't so fortunate."

I took in the pictures on the wall. The Erickson DNA was powerful stuff. It replicated itself with uncanny accuracy from one generation to the next. Arthur and Benjamin could've easily been Seth and Jeremy, except for Seth's eyes. They belonged to the woman on the next portrait, Alice Hallis-Erickson.

"She was the last interesting woman I met." Astrid contemplated the portrait. "Don't get me wrong. I've met some formidable women in my lifetime. Competent too. But interesting? Not so many."

The look she gave me implied I was none of those things. I might have said something, but I saw no point in being snarky to Seth's grandmother. It was an act of pure will, but I kept my eyes on her and my tongue firmly in check.

She sauntered over to the windows and looked down on the people sipping champagne on the lawn. "Why do you think they came here today?"

"Because you invited them?"

"Of course I did." Her lips flickered with irritation. "But they came as one of two sorts: they're either spectators or competitors. I'm wondering: Which kind are you?"

I shrugged. "A third kind, maybe? The accidental guest?"

"Really?" Her she-wolf grin said she didn't believe me. "Do you ski, my dear?"

"Ski?" I'd never had the suicidal inclination of strapping two pieces of wood to my feet and flinging myself off a mountain. "No, there aren't too many snow-covered slopes in Miami."

"Do you like to snowshoe?"

"Don't know," I said. "Never been."

"Do you fish, hunt, hike or ice climb?"

"Can't say I do."

"I'm an old woman and yet I do all of those things."

What could I say to that? "Good for you."

Her eyes mocked me. "I imagine you're more of an indoor girl. Perhaps clubbing is your thing?"

Christ give me patience. "I like dancing, that's true, but I also like the beach a lot. I swim, surf, paddleboard, and kayak. Why are you so interested in my hobbies?"

"Oh, no, dear." She tittered delicately. "I'm not interested in your hobbies at all. I was just assessing if you were Alaska-suitable."

"Alaska-suitable?"

"I can see you're the tropical type. I always imagined Seth would go for a local. He himself is so—well, how should I put it?—Alaskan."

Queen bitch just kept getting bitchier, but by some miracle, I kept my cool. "Is there a point to this conversation?"

"You want a point?" She smiled icily. "Allow me to make a good one: Erickson men don't fall in love very often. Oh, they like women, don't get me wrong, and they like sex. Lust, yes, but love? It doesn't come easy to them."

Was this woman serious?

"Honestly?" I said. "I don't want to have any conversation with you that includes the subjects of sex, lust, or love."

"It's a pity you don't pick the themes I wish to discuss." Smoothing her skirt, Astrid sat on a high-back chair. Queen bitch didn't offer me a seat. Well, kiss my ass. I squared my shoulders and drew taller. She snapped her fingers again. The dogs ran to her side and huddled at her feet. I wondered if she expected me to do the same.

"Let's cut to the chase," she said. "My grandson is not a piggy bank with a nice face. He's a catch in every sense of the word."

"Agreed," I said. "Seth is an amazing human being. That doesn't mean he doesn't have his share of seriously freaky hang-ups, like the rest of us. But it does mean that he has a right to his own life and you should stop interfering in his private affairs."

"I watch after my grandson," she said briskly. "You need to understand that, *if* you have the slightest hope of being part of the Erickson family."

"Woo, whoa, wow." The room reeled around me like a carousel at high speed. "Lady, are you freaking insane? Who says I *want* to be part of your seriously fucked-up family? From what I've seen so far, I'd rather have my liver eaten by a bear."

Her eyes widened. "Are you telling me you're not interested in marrying Seth?"

"*Marrying* Seth?" She might as well have punched me in the gut. "I don't want to marry anyone!"

She eyed me skeptically. "Any other woman in the world would jump at the opportunity of securing an Erickson marriage."

"I guess I'm not any other woman in the world," I said. "Look, if you have to know, I think the world of Seth. But I'm *not* looking to marry. Period."

"But…" She grappled for words. "What about the children?"

"Children?"

"You can't have legitimate children without a marriage," she said. "If you are with Seth, we expect you to fulfill your duty and bear offspring in order to continue the Erickson line."

Oh. My. Freaking. God.

"If you don't mind," I said, strangling the purse in my hands. "I'd like to add marriage and children to my list."

"What list?"

"The list of topics I refuse to discuss with you."

"But—"

I lifted a hand in the air. "You've said your piece, so let me say mine. No wonder your grandson can't find happiness. No wonder he moved away from this place and lives alone like a hermit. You talk about him as if he was some sort of genetic occurrence instead of his own person. I mean, what woman in her right mind is going to put up with this?"

"Whatever do you mean?"

"This!" I threw my hands up in the air. "You! This conversation?"

"It's my job to vet my grandson's suitors."

"Good luck with that." I angled for the exit. "Now, if you'll excuse me, I need to leave, because frankly, Mrs. Erickson, you're pissing me off."

"You haven't been dismissed."

"Why, I don't need to." I marched across the room. "You see, I'm not your servant, your dog, or your family, which you treat all about the same."

I made my way toward the doors with as much dignity as I could muster. My dad had not fought in a revolution, defied a dictator, clung to a sinking raft for three days and fought off the sharks so that I could roll over and fetch.

I was almost to the doors when they opened and Robert came in.

"Master Erickson has arrived," he announced formally.

I stopped dead in my tracks. These people really did watch too much *Downton Abbey.* Sure enough, in strode the source of contention in the flesh, the only man in the world who managed to weaken my knees with a smile. And boy did he test my knees now, not to mention my pumping heart's endurance.

Wearing a three-piece suit, Seth looked phenomenal. A tailored black jacket with silk lapels fit his body's fine lines to perfection, showcasing his shoulders' width. The striped amber-and-brown tie and the silk kerchief peeking from his pocket enhanced the elegant look. A patterned amber vest over a crisp white shirt echoed the gleam in his eyes and the gold in his hair, which had been trimmed and styled away from his clean-shaven face. I had to will my mouth to close.

"Grandma," he said, but he made a straight line for little old insignificant, DNA deficient, Alaska-unsuitable me.

The world straightened the moment his arms enfolded me. His body's heat enveloped me in a protective cocoon. I couldn't remember why I'd been mad or the reason I'd been about to leave Ericksonland. For a full fifteen seconds, I couldn't even remember my name.

"You look amazing," he murmured in my ear.

I felt amazing when he held me. "You don't clean up too badly yourself."

He knuckled his fresh shave. "Date worthy by the rules?"

"Date perfect."

He winked at me. "More on that later?"

"Deal." I locked my wobbly knees and fought an urge to cling to him. "I'll wait for you outside."

"No, please, stay." He led me to a chair, gestured for me to sit down and then went to his grandmother and kissed her on the cheek. "Happy birthday."

I hadn't realized that it was Astrid's birthday today. I felt bad—okay, maybe not bad, but a little naughty. I hadn't been particularly nice to the birthday girl. But then again, the bitch had made niceties hard the moment she sicced her dogs on me and tried to manhandle me into a conversation I wasn't ready to have.

Seth took a small bundle from his pocket and, sitting next to Astrid, put it in her hands. I recognized the little package. It was the one Anya had given him the first time we'd gone out to her homestead. I'd been so jealous when I'd thought he had a girlfriend.

Astrid opened the package and gasped. "Is it…?"

"The old man carved it especially for you," Seth said. "Anya got it during her last visit."

"That old fox." Astrid signaled to Robert. "Magnifying glass, please."

Robert rushed to retrieve it from the desk.

"It's divine." She stared through the glass at the miniature totem pole she held between her fingers. "Oh, Seth." The warmth in her smile shocked me. "This is wonderful, the best birthday present. Thank you so much, dear."

"You're very welcome." He smiled at her in return and I caught a glimpse of the boy he'd once been, of the young man who'd strived to please the demanding grandmother he no doubt adored. Perhaps I'd been too harsh on her. After all, she was his family and he loved her.

"Mistress?" Robert said, after conferring with the attendant who came to the door. "The governor has arrived."

"In that case," she said, rising to her feet, "I suppose we should greet said governor."

She took a moment to find a place for her gift on one of the shelves that held a fine collection of miniature totems. "Perfect," she said, before she appropriated Seth's arm.

"Robert?" she added. "Please escort Miss Silva to the hall. Seth and I will attend to the reception line."

"Summer can stand the hassle." Seth offered me his other arm. "Will you?"

Astrid's smile wavered on her lips.

"I don't want to get in the way." I took Robert's arm. "I'll just mosey around, make new friends."

"Are you sure?" Seth said. "You're welcome to stand with me."

"I'm sure." I conceded the small victory to the birthday girl. "See you later, alligator."

His smile tampered with my knees. "That's a promise."

THE PARTY WAS in full swing. Cocktails were served in the main hall, an atrium that spanned the entire length of the house and opened up to the expansive veranda. There must have been a thousand people in the lavish mansion and the gardens. Armed with a watered-down mimosa, I found a secluded corner that allowed me a good view of the reception line and settled down for a hearty session of people watching.

What the hell was I doing here, so far away from home, surrounded by such a dazzling display of wealth, fashion, and power, in an environment that defied the little I'd known about Alaska prior to my arrival?

My eyes fell on Seth, who'd turned on the charm and was enthralling his guests like a battle-seasoned veteran of the social scene. He had so many facets to his personality. He could morph on the spot, from CEO to pilot, from soldier to civilian, from hermit to socialite, from business genius to family man, to just my guy.

My guy?

I choked on the damn mimosa. I slapped my chest until I stopped coughing. The way I felt about Seth frightened me. I'd fallen for him too fast. It wasn't like me. I'd always been cautious and, after my disastrous marriage, I hadn't expected to find someone who could accept me with my hang-ups. Someone who despite my inconvenient disorder, I could trust. I'd come to Alaska looking for Tammy. I hadn't found her yet, but I'd collided with Seth.

"Excuse me?" A young man with gray eyes, a freckled face, and two glasses in hand interrupted my thoughts. "Are you Summer?"

"I am," I said. "Who might you be?"

"I'm Stuart." He offered me a fresh mimosa. "Ally's husband?"

"Ah, yes, Stuart, the doctor from Texas. Nice to meet you." I set my empty glass on the windowsill and accepted the drink. "Perfect timing."

"Ally sent me to the rescue," Stuart said.

"Oh, I can manage," I said. "You don't have to rescue me."

"But I do," he said, flashing his infectious smile. "Seth told Ally and Ally told me. Double Erickson orders. Those have to be followed or I risk catastrophe."

I had to laugh. "I think I know what you mean."

"Ericksons spend an inordinate amount of time manning long reception lines at parties," he said. "I'm afraid my company will have to suffice for the moment."

"What about the other family members?" I asked. "Don't you spend time with them?"

Stuart waved a finger from side to side. "We do not fraternize with the enemy. We stick by the good Ericksons and we don't go to the dark side, ever."

"The dark side?" I said. "You mean Benjamin's side of the family?"

"The Alex faction," Stuart said. "That's him over there. The one with the dark curls? He just weaseled his way between Seth and Jeremy. Did you see that? Ally just gave him *the* look."

"*The* look?" I said.

"Yes, you know, the Erickson look?" Stuart said. "The narrow-eyed, straight-lipped glare that burns a hole in your skull and activates your acid reflux?"

"Ooh," I said, laughing. "Yes, of course, the radioactive look."

"Radioactive is right." Stuart grinned. "You've got to have guts to stick with an Erickson. You've got to have gastric endurance."

"Stop terrorizing me," I said. "Astrid already did enough of that for a day."

"Astrid?" Stuart grimaced. "Ouch. Do you want me to call the ambulance?"

"I'll live."

"Sorry you had to go through that," Stuart said. "I wish I could tell you it gets easier to climb the Astrid glacier, but there isn't a pair of crampons sharp enough to conquer those heights. Did you see that?" Stuart elbowed me. "Alex just spoke to Astrid. She spoke back!"

"Um…is that unusual?"

"It's a bit surprising, after what Alex did to Seth last week with that Star Lake mess," Stuart said. "On the other hand, she's got no proof that Alex was behind the hoopla and Astrid is the neutral element, Switzerland on steroids. She will not favor one grandson over the other without solid proof."

"She did lose two sons," I said. "I'm sure she loved them both."

"But think about it," Stuart said. "She must be partial to Arthur's kids. After all, she brought them up single-handedly. Seth, Jer, and Ally were orphaned. Whereas Ben's children still had mothers to care for them, even if Ben's wives were all certifiably insane."

"Alex's mother too?" I asked.

"Alex's mother especially." Stuart downed his drink. "She is greed in the flesh and she taught it to her son, who worships the mighty dollar. Alex is the most rapacious of the Ben lot."

"Sounds like a reality show."

"An Erickson reality show would be all drama," Stuart said. "I don't know what more proof Astrid could want. Alex has been jealous of Seth all his life. Ally says Alex was always trying to throw a wrench in Seth's plans. He even stole Seth's girlfriend when Seth was sick. Talk about a low blow."

Girlfriend? My antennae perked up. I was about to ask Stuart for details when Astrid and her brood broke out of the reception line. She headed for the balcony overlooking the atrium and waited for her family, the governor, and her most notable guests to arrange themselves behind her. The crowd broke into applause. Seth stepped up to the podium, welcomed everybody and wished his grandmother a happy birthday. Then Astrid took to the mike, thanked the crowd for their contributions to the Alaskan Conservation Fund and invited them to proceed to the dining tents.

"Twenty thousand dollars a person," Stuart said, as we flowed with the crowd out the terrace and down to the lawn. "That's how much an invite to this lovely party cost these folks. I don't know about you, but where I come from, that's an obscene amount of money. She raises millions a pop. No wonder she's the queen of queens."

Or the empress of all queen bitches. I bit my rebellious tongue back and, wedged next to Stuart, made it to the proper table, where my name was engraved on a silver placeholder, next to Seth's. I had to say good-bye to Stuart, who was assigned to the opposite side of the incredibly long VIP table. I took in the fresh flower arrangements on the tall silver stands, the vintage bone china, and the crystal chandeliers. I guess I knew what to expect if I ever donated twenty thousand dollars to a cause.

Eventually, Astrid led the VIP procession. She took her place at the head of the table, escorted by Jer, who sat next to her, along with the governor and his wife and a host of celebrity guests. Ally joined her husband somewhere north of me. Several chairs south from me, Alex pulled out the chair for a red-haired hottie, whose long curls provided a lot more coverage than her minidress.

I found myself glancing at the woman. So this was the girlfriend Seth had been with when he got hurt, the one who left him for Alex. Wow. She was so different from me. In every way. What had Seth seen in her? What could he possibly see in me? How would he want to be with me when he'd been with her?

Seth was the last one to come to the table. Undoing his coat's top button, he took his seat next to me, reached out for my hand, and leaned over my shoulder.

"Did Stuart find you?" he said.

"Yes, sir," I said. "And he did his duty. He welcomed me to Ericksonland."

He quirked an eyebrow. "Ericksonland?"

"It's more than a concept, you know."

He broke out into a fit of quiet laughter. "I love it."

The smile on my face widened. I felt as if I'd been deprived of joy when Seth finally sobered up.

"Sorry about the solo grandmother encounter," he said. "Was it bad?"

"It was like fumbling into a tigress's cage wearing a raw steak gown."

"Damn," he muttered. "I know how Grandma can be."

"I'm so glad she doesn't own wolves instead of dogs."

"Oh, fuck." Seth grimaced. "Please don't tell me she did that thing where she set Devon and Daemon on you?"

"Okeydokey," I said, rolling my eyes. "I won't tell you."

He swore under his breath. "I know this has been a dud so far, but we just have to get through dinner and then we're home free. Bear with me, will you?"

"I shall try." I sighed as the first plate of the fourteen-course meal outlined on the printed menu was set before me. Only thirteen courses to go.

DINNER WAS AN endless affair and, even though some courses held only microscopic samples of rare delicacies, fourteen courses was a lot of food. My favorite part of the meal comprised a trio of gigantic crab legs. Seth had to get the meat out of the armored shell for me, but once I tasted it, I was in food heaven.

After dinner, we tried to recuse ourselves from the table, but the governor wanted a word in private with Seth. I drifted back to the atrium, where several bands took turns entertaining the crowd. I watched the people dance, took a self-guided tour of the house and ended up at one of the bars on one of the grounds' overlooks. By then it was getting colder, which was not a problem, since attendants dressed in Andean costumes made an appearance, distributing exquisite merino shawls to the partygoers.

I wrapped myself in a fine cream shawl and enjoyed the stunning views. A pair of otters played in the surf and several eagles fished along the coastline. I leaned over the railing and spotted a lighthouse at one end of the property, a straight white tower standing like a sentinel on the rocky shore.

Out of the corner of my eye, I tracked Alex Erickson, assessing me from afar. I had no interest in meeting him, so I straightened my spine and bristled with hostility, letting my body language do the talking. Either the idiot couldn't read my not-so-subtle cues or he chose to ignore them altogether. Next I knew, he leaned on the railing next to me.

"My great-grandfather had that lighthouse built in the 1930s." The breeze toyed with his curls. "It was before Alaska became a state in the union. My father used to keep an apartment out there, for when he was out of sorts with his wives."

"I suppose that would make your father Benjamin." I glanced at him. "And you are, of course, Alex Erickson."

"At your service." He appropriated my hand and kissed it. *"Enchanté."*

"I'm afraid I can't say the same in reference to you," I said, retrieving my hand from his clutch.

"Don't tell me a beauty of your caliber has already chosen sides." He flashed his version of a seductive smile, which struck me as fake and faulty at the same time. "From what I'd heard about you, I gathered you'd give a guy a fair chance."

"Please," I said. "No need for flattery here."

"Flattery?" He flashed a phosphorescently white

set of teeth. "Surely, you haven't looked in the mirror lately."

Really? Was he making a pass at me, right here, in broad daylight?

I shot him a cutting glance. "It won't work with me."

"What won't work with you?" he asked.

"Your shameless flirting."

His shrewd stare took me in. "Feisty, aren't you?"

"I've been called worse."

Alex pulled out a monogrammed case from his pocket and eyed me as he put together the halves of an electronic cigarette. I got the clear sense he was trying to figure me out. He had the poise of a proper Erickson plus a set of swarthy looks that must have come from his mother's side. A head of curls topped a wide forehead and framed a narrow face that reminded me of the painting of Napoleon I'd just previewed in the gallery.

"Everybody in the family is talking about you," Alex said.

"Glad to be pulp for the rumor mill."

"You've got spunk." He puffed on his e-cig and released a cloud of vapor. "You and I may be able to get along."

"Not for anything, Mr. Erickson, but I'm not looking to get along with you."

"Please, honey, call me Alex." His eyes perused my face. "Don't be so fast to take sides. The differences between Seth and I aren't personal. We have diverging business visions. You might be surprised to know that I think Seth did a good job with E&E, at least before he left for Afghanistan."

"I'm shocked, really."

"It's a shame that he couldn't do the same after he

returned," he said. "But war changes people. It changed Seth and now E&E is suffering for it."

Seduction hadn't worked, so he was on to persuasion. "Is that your full script?"

"And here I thought I had the makings of a storyteller." His confident smirk irked me to no end. "Everybody can see it. You should see it too. The wounds. The burns. They've affected his capabilities to run the business."

My fingers tightened around the railing. "How?"

"Isn't it obvious?" Alex said. "He's lost his leadership abilities. He suffers from post-traumatic stress. He's lost himself."

"And how do you know all of that?"

"Gina?" He called to the red-haired stunner, who stood nearby talking to a neighboring group that looked decidedly like part of the dark-haired Erickson clan.

She trotted over like one of Astrid's dogs. "Yes, Alex?"

"Tell Summer the things you learned when you were with Seth."

Gina leaned over, as if confiding in me before she recited her lines in an annoying, shrill, nasally voice. "He has a bad temper and is as cranky as they come. He's no fun anymore. He's a hermit and he's violent sometimes. It's why I had to leave. Besides, he can't do it anymore."

"It?"

"You know what I mean." Gina clutched her little silk purse and wiggled it flaccidly between her legs. "*It* doesn't work anymore."

For Pete's freaking sake. I looked from Gina to Alex. Talk about an all-out defamation campaign. As if a person's business abilities were somehow tied to his sexual prowess. It was an outdated, stupid, asinine slur that a, was a big huge lie—as I knew very well—and b, didn't have any bearing on anything, but I bet it could do harm in certain circles.

"Why are you telling me this?" I asked.

It was Alex who answered. "Because you can help unmask Seth and de-mystify this legend he's built around himself. You can let others know the truth about who he really is. And because there are plenty of rewards available to you if you do precisely as I ask."

Crafty son of a bitch. He'd gone from seduction to persuasion to bribery in four minutes flat. He was a piece of work and as bold and arrogant as they came. The SOB wanted me to help Gina spread the dirt around and he was willing to pay a fee for the job. Fourteen courses revolted in my stomach. He must have thought that I was as pliable, or at least as buyable, as Gina was.

I tried to keep my cool, I really did try hard.

"What about you, Alex?" I said calmly. "Have you suddenly grown the management skills necessary to run E&E? The experience? What about the cojones? Or are you planning on operating on pure and naked ambition?"

"Don't get your pretty little head all riled up," Alex said. "You don't need to pretend with me. I saw how Seth looked at you today. You're in a great position to play the game. Why not try to make the most out of it?"

Easy, Silva.

No need to rip his eyes out. "What do you mean?"

"The lines are drawn," he said. "The board meeting is coming up. There will be winners and losers. You're a latecomer to the show, but you could still stand to benefit, as long as you do your part and stick with the winners."

Now I wanted specifics. "And how would I do that?"

"I'd love to be able to anticipate Seth's approach to the board meeting," Alex said. "You get me the information I need and I'll take care of you. You'll go back to Miami in a different income bracket, if you get my drift. You're a smart girl. Surely you want to capitalize on your short time in Alaska?"

What a fucking lying, worthless piece of shit. He thought an awful lot of himself if he thought he could persuade me into doing something so nasty and low handed. And one other thing. He knew freaking squat about me if he thought I'd go for it.

"Think about it, Summer." His hand slithered down my spine and flirted with my ass, right in front of his dimwitted girlfriend no less. "You could come out of this with an improved net worth."

Don't smack him.

Not yet.

"You Ericksons." I sighed, gazing at the seagulls rioting over the ocean. "You think the whole world is after your money. And maybe that's true, I don't know. Your answer is a big fat no." I grabbed his wandering hand and slapped it on the railing. "Now bug off and leave me alone."

Alex's jaw dropped. I don't think anyone had ever spoken to him as I did. Gina didn't know how to react, so she looked to Alex for direction. Muffled laughter drifted in from the audience next door. It was obvious that the Erickson cousins had been eavesdropping on our conversation. Now they pressed even closer. They fit squarely into Astrid's spectator category and not in a good way.

I was furious, teetering at the edge of a major Silva rage. I caught a glimpse of Ally and Stuart coming down the steps. Ally looked absolutely gorgeous in the emerald green dress we'd bought together, but her mouth tightened in alarm when she saw me with Alex. Dragging Stuart along, she set a straight course toward us.

"Summer?" she said. "What are you doing? Why don't you come have a drink with us?"

"You mean what am I doing with these two?" I said loudly enough for the spectators to hear. "I was actually about to conclude a fascinating conversation, comparing notes with poor Gina here, whose experiences with Seth were so different from mine."

Ally frowned. "What on earth are you talking about?"

"Don't pay any heed to Summer." Alex put away his e-cig. "She's upset. She misunderstood something Gina said."

"I didn't misunderstand a thing," I said. "My ears work quite well, thank you very much. See, Ally, Alex is trying to convince me that Seth is not fit to lead and Gina here says that Seth was moody and violent with her."

A deep flush crept over Ally's face. "Really?"

Gina fidgeted with her purse. "I didn't mean it like that..."

"She said that's why she had to leave Seth for Alex."

Ally crossed her arms. "Is that so?"

"Ally, Summer?" Stuart jumped in to defuse the tension. "How about some punch?"

"In a moment," Ally said.

I flashed my most ferocious smile. "I was about to tell Gina that Seth has been nothing but sweet and wonderful to me. He's the kindest, smartest, most gracious person I've ever met. I was about to confide to these folks, and to the rest of the family if it mattered to anyone, that Seth is an extraordinary lover. His stamina is exceptional. Sex with Seth? Extraordinary. I'm not big on counting, but last time?" I flashed seven fingers in the air. "In a row."

Ally's jaw dropped. Stuart had the decency to stare at his feet. Alex's murderous glare beamed on me, and the little crowd next door stirred with murmurs.

"Really?" Gina's eyes rounded to the size of saucers. "Seven times?"

Alex snapped. "Shut up."

"I'm sorry to hear you were not so fortunate," I said. "I hope you have better luck with Alex here. But honestly?" I ran my eyes up and down his body and scoffed. "I doubt he has what it takes. If you'll excuse me."

"Summer?" Ally trotted after me. "Please come with us."

"I'm good," I lied, widening my stride. "I feel like taking a walk."

"You know, missy," Alex said, loud enough for me to hear. "It never does anybody any good to slam the door shut."

"You're wrong," I said over my shoulder, trudging on. "Consider this door slammed in your face. Oh, yeah, and by the way, Alex? Rot in hell."

TWENTY

It was a day of traps. The harder I fought to get to Summer, the harder other people fought to get to me. No sooner had the governor and I finished talking, than the CEOs of several of the oil companies corralled me in the garden. I dealt with them as quickly as I could, but Grandmother waited for me at the fountain, the only way out of the rose garden. I considered jumping the hedges, then decided against it. Running from natural predators only triggered the chase instinct.

"How did it go with the governor?" She took my arm and walked with me, silver hair shifting in the wind, steps strong, mind sharp as ever.

"The contract is ready to go." I scoured the crowd for Summer. "We sign tomorrow."

"Lovely work." She waved a delicate hand to greet someone from afar. "I do like to see you in action. Are you ready for the board meeting?"

"Have I ever not been prepared for a meeting before?"

"No, but there's a lot going on," she said in her best didactic tone. "This meeting is very important. I don't want you to succumb to distractions."

"Distractions?" I realized what she meant. "You're talking about Summer, aren't you?"

"You tell me," she said. "Aren't you looking for her as we speak?"

I took the fifth on that one. I hadn't been able to stop thinking about Summer since I'd met her. The attraction intensified with each hour that passed. The last few days had been particularly difficult. When she was far, I felt deprived, as if the air lacked enough oxygen to power my lungs. Talking to her on the phone or seeing her on a screen wasn't nearly as satisfying as touching her or breathing in her scent.

Christ, I was screwed. I got hard just thinking about her. I wanted to be in bed with her right now, kissing her mouth, drinking her pleasure, plugged into her body, charging my need with hers. My craving for her was distracting, overriding, overpowering. For the past few days, I'd been miserable knowing that she was in my home and I wasn't. And now, it drove me insane that she and I were in the same location and yet we weren't together right this minute.

"Is this Summer person something we need to worry about?" Grandma asked.

"She's not something," I said. "She's someone. She's also my business, not yours."

"Interesting." Grandma smiled at a group of guests as we passed. "Summer said something similar to me. She's not one to mince words. She's her own breed, very odd, outspoken. I find her…vexing."

"Vexing?" I stifled a laugh. "Yes, I suppose you'd find someone like Summer vexing, but I need you to be nice to Summer."

The look she gave me could've iced my bone marrow. "The most important board meeting of your life is coming up. You don't ask me to support your initiatives, pledge you my votes, or help you put to rest the assorted variety of rumors going around. Instead, you ask me to be nice to this Summer person who popped out of nowhere."

"You won't support anyone's initiatives unless you believe in them," I said. "You vote strictly on financial performance and you know the rumors aren't true. Why bother? I'm asking you to do something for me, personally, something you could do, if you wanted to. I'd like to have a fair shot at Summer. I can't do that if you scare the hell out of her."

"Oh, please." Grandma rolled her eyes. "Anyone wanting to join our family needs to have a backbone."

"Join our family?" Shit. "Tell me you didn't say those words to Summer."

"Why are you so upset?"

"Because anyone wanting to join our family would need to be certifiably insane." I glared. "Which is why I would really appreciate it if you didn't bring up the subject with my girlfriend. She barely knows me."

"And she isn't particularly interested in marriage, I know."

Why the statement stung like a lick of fire was beyond me. "She told you that?"

"Indeed," Grandma said. "She seemed quite spooked by the idea of it. If her attitude is any indication, we won't be seeing any green-eyed Erickson babies out of her belly anytime soon."

"Grandma!" I wanted to strangle her. "Please tell me you didn't mention marriage or babies to Summer!"

"I did nothing wrong," Grandma said. "I'd like to see you settled with a proper wife and a brood of children before I die. As to the rest, I do approve."

I more or less snarled. "You approve of what?"

"Of a girl that covets you and not your money," Grandma said. "Of a woman who doesn't want you for your name, but loves you."

The air rushed out of my lungs. Had I been flying, I might have crash-landed on the spot. I was stunned. Had my grandmother just said what I thought I heard?

"You think she loves me?"

Grandma's bright blue eyes sparkled with mischief. "Seth, dear, she's crazy about you. I'm certain of it. Your grandfather didn't marry me for my good looks only. She loves you. Why else would she defend you like a lioness protecting her cub? She flew all the way out to the Golov's to get a jar of pickled fish."

She had done that.

"A feisty soul like her, making a supreme effort to hold her tongue while facing a bitch like me, for as long as she did?" Grandma let out a throaty laugh. "It's a feat of love, I tell you, whether she knows it or not."

It was the best news I'd had all day and, coming from a reliable source, it was news I could trust.

"Sorry if I seemed cranky earlier," I mumbled.

"What I do for you," she said, "what I do for all of you is for your benefit only."

"I know."

She cupped my cheek in her porcelain-white hand. "But do you really know?"

My lips twitched. "I wouldn't put up with the bullshit if I didn't think it so."

"Seth!" Ally called out, scampering to meet up with us. "Where have you been? You're not answering your cell. I've been looking for you everywhere!"

"You found me." I reached out to steady her as she teetered on her heels. "Why are you in such a tipsy?"

"It's Summer," she said, holding her side and bending over her knees to catch her breath.

My mind went instantly on high alert. "What about Summer? Is she all right? Didn't I tell you to look after her?"

"It's not easy to keep track of Summer." Ally wheezed. "She doesn't follow instructions. If you look away for one sec, she's gone and in some sort of trouble."

"Oh, dear," Grandma said. "She does breed trouble, that one."

"Besides," Ally said, still gasping for air. "After dinner, I thought she was with you."

"She's not with me." I looked around us. "Where the hell is she?"

"She was down by the north overlook a few minutes ago," Ally said. "You're not going to believe what she did. Alex cornered her—"

"Alex?" My blood pressure shot up.

"He was looking for trouble," Ally said. "Gina was there too, saying all kinds of rude and inappropriate things. Alex was being a jackass."

Son of a bitch.

"But Summer, she told him—no—she told *everybody* that…" She looked at Grandma, hesitated then clammed up.

"What?" I said.

"Come on," Grandma said. "What did she tell Alex and the others?"

"You may not want to hear this," Ally cautioned.

"Don't be silly," Grandma said.

"What did Summer say?" I demanded.

Ally took a deep breath. "She told everyone you were sweet, wonderful, and smart."

"She did?" A stupid grin tickled the corners of my lips.

"That's not all," Ally said. "She also told everyone that you were an extraordinary lover. She told Alex you made her come seven times in a row."

Well, funny shit. Summer Silva had my back. The grin overtook my face and there was nothing I could do about it.

Grandma tsked. "Whatever happened to privacy, good manners, and polite conversation?"

Ally started to speak. "But Grandma..."

"Quiet!" Grandma snapped. "I didn't ask for your opinion. Seth, that Summer child is insolent, sassy, and...gutsy." She squared her shoulders. "That impertinent girlfriend of yours just scored a PR coup that money can't buy. Don't let it go to waste."

Hell, yeah. I agreed. From now on, there would be no more time wasted.

I THOUGHT OF myself as a simple guy. I was on or off, good or bad, smart or dumb. But as I made my way through the crowds in an effort to find Summer, my emotions broiled and my mood swung between joy, awe, and fear. Fear because in confronting Alex, Summer had risked his anger. Christ help me, she might never learn to assess danger's intangibles. Awe because her reactions to challenges never ceased to amaze me. Joy because she was on my side. It wasn't my imagination. Grandma had said so. A guy as lucky as I was, even one with thickened scars, singed lungs and numbed skin, ought to be able to do something with all of that.

I pulled out my cell and called Summer. No answer. Was she mad at me for abandoning her to her means? Hell, if she was, I couldn't blame her. At least I had some options. The big house was one of the safest places in Alaska, but just in case, I'd assigned a few security agents to watch over Summer at the party.

Status? I texted.

The reply came back in seconds. Lighthouse.

What the hell was Summer doing at the lighthouse? Was it even safe out there?

I shook hands and greeted guests as I made my way through the gardens, but I disentangled myself from any potential conversations before they began. I needed to find Summer.

I stomped down the old path and through the woods. I hadn't been at the lighthouse in years. I remembered going there when I was younger to visit with Uncle Ben. After the lighthouse had been decommissioned, he'd used it as his private retreat.

The tower rose from the rocky inlet at the end of the causeway. As I approached, one of my agents stepped out from the trees, smartly dressed and indistinguishable from the rest of the guests.

"Good afternoon, Mr. Erickson."

"Good afternoon," I said. "Everything in order?"

"The area is clear and the perimeter secured."

"Keep it that way." I marched across the causeway, where the surf rustled against the rocks and a heap of fat seals basked like bloated sausages under the sun.

I strode onto the ground floor. It was like stepping

back in time. Uncle Ben's furnishings filled the place, mid-century refined, dust-free, polished, and lovingly maintained. Robert's doing, I was sure, with Grandma's blessing. The comfy couch, the antique daybed, and the shelves full of mystery books were exactly as I remembered.

A door creaked upstairs.

"Summer?" I called out.

No answer.

I tackled the steep spiraling steps, all two hundred of them. The clang of my feet pounding on metal echoed in the hollowed heights. The fast climb made me suck in for air a little. The stairs ended at the top floor. I took in the circular room, where the glass windows showcased the spectacular three-hundred-and-sixty-degree views.

In his time, Uncle Ben had affixed a wood tabletop to the concrete stump where the light had once been mounted, converting it into a game table. I ran my fingers over the table, where an elaborate map of Alaska was finely etched in the wood.

One moment, my hand trailed the etching on the table. The next moment, it was Mom's long and delicate hand tracing the map as she, Dad, and Uncle Ben sat around the table, laughing over a game of cards.

The flashback took me by surprise. I remembered that day. I'd been around twelve. We were watching the whales bubble-net feeding in the sound. I'd been on lookout duty, working the binoculars, trying to identify my favorite whale by the markings on her fluke, a female born to the sound matriarch in the same year I was born.

"You'll find her," my mother said. "Have no doubt about it."

A second image from my past took shape, also reflected on the glass windows. I walked into the ready room in Afghanistan, where my crew was engaged in a fierce game of cards. Shawn, my copilot, and Jonesy, my flight engineer, were locked in a poker duel.

"Gents," I said. "I hate to interrupt, but special ops needs a chariot and we're it."

"Drop-off or pickup?" Shawn asked.

"Pickup," I said. "Hot zone, narrow canyon, going in dark."

"Sounds like a hell of a lot of fun," Jonesy said. "Wouldn't miss it for the world."

"Gear up," I said. "Let's go get our boys."

"I've got an awesome hand here." Shawn threw a couple of chips on the table. "I'm not folding."

"I'm not folding either." Jonesy upped his bet and set his cards facedown on the table. "I'll see you when we get back."

An explosion jarred my mind. My heart raced. My forehead broke out into a sweat. Simultaneously, a plane crashed into the North Tower and an RPG slammed into my Pave Hawk. When I next knew it, my heart lodged in my throat and my friends and families lay in a smoldering heap of ashes and smoke.

The images were so vivid they felt real. My lungs were on fire. I clung to the edge of the table and dug my nails into the wood, fighting to stay on my feet. The world as I knew it ended in a double whammy.

"Seth?" Summer's voice called out of the darkness. "Seth! Are you all right?"

I forced myself to inhale and focus. Summer stood by the glass door leading out to the metal platform, with her face flushed by the cold and a cream shawl wrapped around her shoulders. Her dress gathered the light streaming through the windows, showed off her slender figure and showcased her legs' elegant mileage. But it was her stare that shocked me. Her eyes reflected the grief in my soul. She couldn't see the images etched in my mind, but she could sense the sorrow in my heart.

She was on me in three steps. Her arms Velcroed around me. Her embrace felt like a bulletproof vest. The sight of her dispelled the smoke darkening my mind. Her scent, vanilla beans and coconut milk, challenged the stink of ashes and burning flesh.

"We can't do anything about the past," she whispered, her breath warm against my neck. "But maybe we can do something about the present."

I looked down at her. "Something like what?"

"Maybe we can make new memories," she said, "good memories, to replace the bad ones that show up in your eyes sometimes."

I liked the sound of that.

I clung to her until the memories ebbed. I hated myself for the weakness, but I was glad for both her company and her silence. Words were useless. Her embrace, on the other hand, soothed the old grief and gave me the time and space I needed to regain control of my emotions.

"I've been looking for you all over," I said, after a little while. "Why did you come out here?"

"I needed a break."

"Sorry." I gathered her hands and rubbed her cold fingers between mine. "But Summer, I don't want you talking to Alex. He's an asshole and he's not safe."

"I can handle Alex," she said. "I put him in his place."

"I heard about that."

She had the grace to blush. "I guess it wasn't up to Erickson standards, but Alex made me so mad! And that Gina witch. I swear, the things that came out of her mouth pissed me off majorly."

"I don't care what she said."

"But…"

"But what?"

Summer winced. "She's so beautiful."

The doubt in her eyes punched me in the gut. Summer was jealous. Jealous! Part of me was profoundly flattered. The other part was stunned. Summer was jealous of Gina?

"Gina might be flashy on the outside," I said. "But she's empty inside. That's why it never worked out between us."

"But the things she said about you…"

"I've heard them before and, if it helped her walk away, I can deal with it. If Alex wants that sort of hollowness in his life, by all means. It doesn't matter to me."

Summer's eyebrows spiked on her forehead. "Really?"

"Really." I brought her hand to my lips and kissed her knuckles. "If you could look into my head, you'd know by the sheer amount of real estate you occupy in my brain that there can be no possible comparison. I never wanted her, whereas you, I always want you."

Her eyes shone brighter than any lighthouse in the world. She bracketed my face with her hands, gaze filled with emotions that echoed the ones cramming my heart and squeezing my throat.

"Seth?" she said softly. "You don't say much, but when you do, you really know how to knock it out of the ballpark."

Were those tears welling in her eyes? "Then why the hell are you crying?"

"Because I'm so happy." She flashed a crooked little smile. "Because I'm so afraid."

"Afraid?" I said. "Of what?"

Her lips quivered. "Can *we* be?"

"Summer, baby." I traced the line of her jaw with my fingertips and followed it to her chin, which I tilted slightly to ensure a touch-and-go, the smooth, brief landing of my mouth over hers. "*We* are."

She ran her lips together as if savoring the quick brush. "Do you always know what to say?"

"Hell, no." I removed the shawl from her shoulders and set it aside. "But sometimes, I know what to do."

I kissed her, reacquainting myself with the full range of her flavors and rediscovering her mouth's vital warmth. The distance and the hardship of the last few days fell away. She was here, now, and she was mine. I'd had my doubts for quite a while but, if there was a God, I thanked him.

I couldn't wait any longer. I reached for her dress's zipper. It whirred down her back revealing a gorgeous span of soft, creamy skin and freeing her body to my touch. I pulled down on the dress, but she clung to it.

"What if somebody comes?" she said, wide-eyed.

"Nobody's coming."

"Are you sure?"

"A hundred percent," I said. "How about we make some of those new memories you promised me?"

She dropped the dress to the floor. "New memories for the lighthouse it is."

Cream stockings encased her long legs, topped by a pair of lace garters that encircled her thighs. A lace bra cupped her breasts and matched the sexy thong she wore. Jesus. She was a goddamn work of art.

"Me, so little clothes." She pouted playfully. "You, so many."

"You little tyrant." I pretended to glare but my lips turned up at the ends. "Is that a complaint I hear?"

"The least you could do is give up a piece of clothing or two."

"Not yet."

She rolled her eyes. "Who's the real tyrant now?"

"I am."

I whirled her around to face the window. I claimed her wrists, settled her palms against the glass, and kissed the nape of her neck, brushing my lips against the top of her spine. "Keep your hands on the window. Yes, that's good." I tapped on her heels with the tip of my shoes until she widened her stance then took a step back to admire my extraordinarily good fortune.

She looked over her shoulder and met my gaze. "What are you staring at?" She swung her hips provocatively. "A girl shouldn't have to wait around forever to get a little satisfaction."

"Is that so?"

"You've made me wait long enough." Her smile tugged at my cock. "Get to it, Erickson."

I was used to giving the orders around here, but for once, I wanted to comply. I stepped up to her and, wrapping my arms around her waist, nibbled at the line of her shoulder. "Do you think you can order me about?"

"You? I doubt it." She reached back with one hand and groped between my legs. "But I might stand a chance with this part of you."

Her hand caught my cock. Her touch launched me in a single-minded, straight trajectory. Her body swayed against mine, a slow, sinuous dance that enticed my every molecule. All the blood in my body rushed toward her fingers. I clenched my teeth and, defying my body's urgency, pinned her between me and the half wall, and rubbed my erection against her. "*My* lighthouse. *My* rules."

"Your lighthouse," she said huskily. "Your rules."

"See? You can follow some directions."

I planted a long line of kisses down her back, then rolled down her thong and cleared it from her feet. My body didn't allow for delays. All these days separated from her had taken a toll. I undid my pants and pressed myself against her.

"Too soon?" I asked.

"Not soon enough."

She was tight and her body resisted the pressure, but only for a moment. The instant her muscles yielded, I slipped in. She let out a quiet moan as I advanced. Christ, she felt good. I clutched her hips and held her in place until all of me was in her. It was only then that I let out a long breath.

"Gawd." Her voice quavered with her body.

"I know."

If heaven existed, this was it. After the long wait, I was exactly where I wanted to be. I had to pace myself. I moved inside of her in an excruciating sequence, retreat, advance, repeat. She leaned her forehead against the window, fingers splayed on the pane, frosting the glass with her breaths. Her body rippled with my strokes, echoing the pleasure I felt and the need that propelled me.

I reached over with one hand, unclasped her bra and pitched it over my shoulder. She whimpered when I leaned over, cupped her breasts, and trapped her nipples between my fingers. A compulsive need to reach deeper in her made me thrust faster and harder. A moan purred in the back of her throat, a sound that tested my limits.

Her voice, her scent, her body's movements, everything about her intensified the sexual creature in me. In that moment, I understood the savage forces that unleashed nature's epic mating seasons, the primal instinct that drives a male to fuck a female and cram her full of his seed.

"Summer?"

"Whatever you do," she rasped, "don't you dare stop."

Her eyes glimmered with untamed lust. Her body hummed with need. When her knees buckled under my thrusts, I wrapped my hands around her waist and shifted her over to the card table, where she landed on all fours over the map of Alaska. Standing behind her, I rearranged her legs and plunged into her again.

Jesus fucking Christ. This was so goddamn right. She felt hot like the summer sea and as torrid as the tropics. Who needed to go to Miami when the equator bisected her body exactly below her hips?

She met my charge with grit, rebounding from my strokes with quiet yelps. "Seth?" she called out. "Seth!"

I bore down on her and held her as her body went into orgasm. Her pussy squeezed, clinging to my erection. Her hair spilled like a curtain around her face. Her skin flushed, her nipples spiked and her lips glimmered, as moist as her sex. She couldn't stop coming.

"Oh, my God, Seth, Seth, Seth!"

I kissed her back and trailed her spine with my lips. "I know, baby. I know."

I waited for her orgasm to subside, basking in her body's warmth, taking in her primal scent—lush jungle after the rain. As soon as her respiration evened, I started to move in her again.

She murmured faintly. "I don't think I can do that again."

"You can," I said. "As long as my cock is hard, your pussy's got come power."

She breathed out a hoarse whimper.

I reached around and strummed her clit. "Do you want more?"

"You're making a glutton out of me." I caught a glimpse of green behind her lidded eyes as she pressed against me. "But what about you? I don't want to come again without you."

I smiled. She liked it all right. My good intentions wavered. Burrowed in her pussy all the way, with her body twitching and squeezing all around me, I almost came, but I got a hold of myself and recommitted to my mission, maintaining my body's discipline, thrusting in and out of her at a steady pace.

"Oh, God," she whimpered and I knew she was close to coming again. She craned her neck to look at me. "More? Are you sure?"

"More," I said. "I wouldn't want to make a liar out of you."

Her brow furrowed. "A liar?"

"Seven times in a row," I said. "Isn't that what you said to the others?"

"Seven?" Her eyes widened.

"I like it when you brag." I reached out, tilted her face, and kissed her with the full force of my need. "So, this time around, let's make it eight."

TWENTY-ONE

THE SOUND OF a horn startled me out of my stupor. From my perch on Uncle Ben's rumpled daybed, I looked up. My eyes followed the lighthouse's spiral stairs to the top, where far above, the windows reflected the sunset's orange glow. I listened to the distinctive call as it came again.

"What's that?" I said. "Is Ericksonland under attack?"

Lying beside me on the quilt, Seth rumbled with laughter. "No, they're not summoning warriors to the fortress's walls, if that's what you mean."

"Then why the ruckus?"

"That's the summons to the concert," he said, stretching out in the way I imagined a bear would stretch when awakening from hibernation.

"What concert?"

"The benefit concert," Seth explained, propping himself up on one elbow.

"You mean the festivities aren't over?"

"No." He reached out to play with my hair. "In fact, a lot of people would say that the best part is yet to come."

"How so?"

"The younger Ericksons are in charge of the evening fundraisers," Seth said. "I suppose it's Grandma's version of apprenticeships in philanthropy. The concert is open to the public. But I think we're done here. I want to take you home straight to my bed."

"From one mattress to the next." I sighed and grinned. "Is that the kind of life you envision for me?"

"A guy can dream." He cradled the back of my head in his big hand, strong fingers digging into my hair, lowered my face to his and kissed me.

I was completely immersed in the feel of his mouth on my lips when the metal door to the lighthouse rattled and boomed. I startled. He almost leapt out of the bed.

He groaned. "What now?"

"Open up, Seth," Ally shouted. "I know you're in there!"

Seth put his finger to his lips and mouthed, "She'll go away."

"I'm not giving up," she said pounding some more. "I'm as stubborn as you are. So open up, bro."

Seth looked at me.

I shrugged. "It's your damn DNA."

"Christ." He huffed. "What is it about me being with you that turns people into annoying dumbasses?" He got up, buttoned his pants and straightened his rumpled clothes, before he turned the locking wheel, opened the door and faced his sister. "What do you want?"

"Can you please tell your dogs to chill?" Ally said, cocking her chin over her shoulder. "They didn't want to let me through. They said you gave orders. They've got Stuart, poor thing, but I pulled Erickson rank."

Seth stepped out and signaled to someone I couldn't see, no doubt a member or two of the Erickson brigade. I sighed. After what happened at Star Lake, I understood Seth's precautions. I even understood that "asset protection" was a common concept in Ericksonland. But would I ever get used to the idea of having a protective detail? Not in this lifetime.

"Is Summer with you in there?" Ally dodged Seth and peeked in the door.

I scrambled to hide my naked self behind the shawl.

"Hi, Summer." She waved cheerfully. "Fancy finding you here."

"Oh, hi." I waved back, face glowing like a chunk of flaming coal.

"Are you ready?" Ally said to Seth.

"Ready for what?" Seth said.

"For the concert, silly." She grinned. "Didn't you hear the horn?"

"We were thinking about skipping."

"I was afraid of that." Ally pouted prettily. "You can't skip, Seth, you can't. It's my first year organizing the concert and I have a surprise for you."

"A surprise?"

"The headliners tonight?" She gave a little squeal. "Battle Dragons!"

Seth gaped. "You got Battle Dragons to come all the way out here?"

"They're your favorite band."

"Battle Dragons?" I wrapped the shawl around myself as it were a towel and padded over to the door where I joined Seth and Ally, who'd changed clothes since I'd last seen her and was now wearing blue jeans, thigh-high boots and a kickass red leather jacket.

"Battle Dragons is one of my favorite bands too," I said.

Seth cocked an eyebrow. "I never made you for a Battle Dragons kind of girl."

"What?" I said. "You don't think I like angst, dark and deep?"

"It's not that." Seth smirked. "I had no idea you had exquisite taste in music."

"Well, now you know," I said. "I've been keeping my eye out for Battle Dragons in concert for a while, but they hardly ever tour."

"Hell, Ally, I'm impressed," Seth said. "You pulled some shit-hot stuff, sis."

"I know!" Ally clapped excitedly. "I went through lots of trouble to get these guys to Alaska. I brought them here especially for you. Will you please, please come to the concert?"

"You're an amazing sister." I discreetly nudged Seth in the ribs. "I'm sure Seth really appreciates your hard work. Of course he's coming."

"Yeah, sure, of course," he said, belatedly. "We'll be there."

"Yay!" She gave her brother a hug. "But hurry up, guys. The concert starts in thirty minutes."

It wasn't going to be easy putting myself back together after two hours of crazy intense lovemaking. I was pretty sure that Seth would be able to restore his earlier splendor with a face wash and a comb, but mine was a different story. Not that I had any complaints, but sex with Seth was a cataclysmic event. It was like being sexually mauled time and time again, like being consumed and adored at once. I'd volunteer anytime.

My hair was tangled, my makeup was all but gone, and every part of me had been ruffled, kissed, and licked beyond repair. Standing before the mirror, thankful that Uncle Ben had seen fit to install a proper bathroom in the lighthouse, I wasn't exactly sure how I was going to make myself presentable. And then another knock on the door revealed the magnificent Robert, carrying a basket of neatly folded garments and shoes.

"Is he a mind reader?" I said, when Seth handed me a pair of skinny jeans, a fringed black top, and a pair of black booties. "Did he raid Ally's closet again? And how on earth does he know what I want to wear?"

"I texted him and asked him to bring us a change of clothing." Seth inspected the clothes Robert had brought for him. "Stop worrying. Robert has been taking care of us since we were kids. Ally's closet is like a department store and Robert's taste is impeccable."

"Unbelievable." I closed the bathroom door, ran the water and stepped under the shower. Maybe being an Erickson wasn't such a terrible thing after all. Maybe the perks made up for some of the aggravation.

After the shower, I dressed quickly, fixed my hair and put on a touch of blush and mascara that I carried in my little clutch. Seth waited for me with a knit hat, gloves, and my jacket. He looked hot wearing a black leather jacket, jeans, and combat boots. My knees did that buckling thing again.

"Warm enough?" he asked, as he zipped up my jacket.

"Hot like a steaming volcano when you're around."

He laughed the rich cackles I treasured. "Glad to be of some use."

He grabbed my hand and I followed him out to the causeway, up the hill and onto the ATV that waited parked by the trailhead.

"Ready?" He revved the engine and turned on the headlights.

"Full steam ahead." I squealed as we took off.

I braced my arms around his waist and pressed my cheek against his back, inhaling his jacket's leather scent. The sun had set and dusk gave way to a clear night with bright stars popping up by the minute. We drove past huge greenhouses and thick forest, until we arrived at a field packed with all kinds of vehicles, trucks, cars, bikes, ATVs, planes; you name it.

We made our way through the crowds streaming in. There must have been thousands of people lined up. Seth handed the ATV off to an attendant at the head of the line and led me down a set of stone-carved steps. The steps opened onto a cove, a rocky beach where the naturally graded terrain had been transformed into a rugged amphitheater.

I stopped at the top to take in the astonishing sight. Spotlights swept over the excited throng. Fire pits burned brightly to keep the crowd warm. An elaborate stage rose against the sound and the mountains' breath-taking background.

"My grandfather loved music," Seth said. "He built this place to share his passion with his fellow Alaskans. Come on." The spotlights began to flicker. "The concert is about to start."

The attendants led us to the roped-off section at the front of the mosh pit, where a whole bunch of Ericksons mingled with celebrities and notable guests.

Seth introduced me to some of the people crammed into our section, which included a lot of people from the 212th Rescue Squadron. I shook lots of hands, trying to remember names, enduring the scrutiny with as much grace as I could muster. After all, these were Seth's friends, the men and women he'd served with.

"Seth's girlfriend," I heard the murmur running from one person to another.

"Not bad," someone else said behind my back. "Her name is Summer."

"Summer in Alaska?"

I knew what came next.

"Boy, she's really late."

"Or maybe supremely early."

Laughter and then, "She's not from around here."

No I wasn't. For all practical purposes, I came from a different world. And yet Alaska had grown on me. In just a few weeks, I felt like a new person. Beyond that, I was someone's girlfriend. Oh, lord. If that wasn't a shock in itself, I was Seth's girlfriend. Seth Erickson. From Alaska.

Stick with the moment, Silva.

Don't freak out. I drifted toward a group front and center.

"Hi." I greeted a hunk of a guy sitting in a wheelchair. "I'm Summer and, yes, I've heard all the jokes about Summer in Alaska."

The guy laughed. "I'm Trevor and since you're not from here, I bet you no one has bothered to tell you the truth."

"About what?"

"About summer." The handsome devil smirked. "Thirty-five different species of mosquitoes, all of them bigger than your thumb. That's summer for you in Alaska."

It was my turn to laugh. "I'll make sure to stay away. Where are you from?"

"We come from all over Alaska," the guy said. "I work out of the Fairbanks office. We're with the New

Mission Project, you know, the one that Seth founded? We provide health and transition services to wounded warriors returning to civilian life."

"Of course." Seth hadn't mentioned a word about it, but it made perfect sense to me. He practiced his own silent brand of philanthropy.

"Hey, Summer!" Seth motioned me over. "Stop making gooey eyes with Trevor and stick with me. I know the guy's got game, but I wouldn't want to lose you in this crowd."

I took my leave from Trevor and made my way back to Seth. He encased me between his body and the rope, right in front of the stage. I spotted Alex and Gina among a gaggle of dark-haired Ericksons. I made a point to wave at Seth's cousins.

"Will Astrid come?" I asked.

"Hell, no," Seth said. "Not her kind of gig. She claims rock gives her migraines."

Just then, Stuart and Jer made their way to us, eyes shimmering with excitement.

"Cool, yes?" Jer said.

"Super cool!" I said.

"I told you, Ericksons know how to party."

"Oh, yeah."

"Here comes the star of my show," Stuart announced with a proud smile.

Ally made her way up the stage and grabbed the mike. "Hello, Alaska!"

The crowd greeted her back with a roar.

"Welcome, everybody," she said. "Welcome especially to all the military service members and their families who are our honored guests tonight. Whether you're on active duty, inactive, retired or reserve, we owe you big time. We love you!"

The crowd cheered.

"I want to give a shout-out to our wounded veterans tonight, who've given up so much for us," Ally said. "Tonight, we celebrate you."

"Thank you, thank you," the crowd chanted.

Ally smiled and motioned with her hands to tone down the noise. "This concert is dedicated to the heroes in our lives. Yeah, you know who you are. There's mine." She pointed at the mosh pit and the spotlight fell on Seth.

The crowd cheered. "Seth, Seth, Seth."

My jaw dropped. All those people. They knew Seth by name.

"The little twerp." Seth shaded his face with his hand, shrinking from the spotlight. "What the hell does she know of real heroes?"

"But you are her hero." I planted a kiss on his cheek. "Mine too."

He actually groaned.

"On behalf of a grateful nation," Ally shouted. "We thank you! And now, I give you…Battle Dragons!"

The stage went dark. The spotlights went crazy. Music blasted the air, together with alarms and a real flyby, ostensibly from the nearby air force base. A military ship lit up on the water, an amphibious assault vehicle that roared onto the beach and dropped the front gate to disgorge the members of the band, already strumming their guitars.

The crowd cheered. The band stormed the stage. The music blared, a mix of metal rock infused with a complex musicality. The lead singer belted out the first verse with a passion that echoed through my veins. Just as he went into the chorus, the stage unfolded and a full orchestra and a chamber choir emerged on elevated platforms. The crowd went insane.

"What do you think?" Ally joined us, flushed and excited, wearing a headset through which she monitored the show. "I expect we should raise a good chunk of change tonight."

"Sis," Jer said, "you rock."

Seth hooked his arm over Ally's shoulder and hugged her to his side. "Thanks for doing all of this for the guys."

The acoustics in the outdoor theater were extraordinary. I knew the lyrics to every song and I sang at the top of my lungs. Confined to the small space between Seth's arms, I danced to my heart's content, swaying against him, enjoying the feel of his hands encasing my hips, the subtle grind of his groin against my ass.

I was surprised when people started to leap high above the crowd throughout the amphitheater. "What's going on?"

"Blanket toss," Seth said. "Want to check it out?"

He led me to the edge of one of the circles, where a bunch of people held a thick hide blanket, tossing a guy who leapt up and down as if he was on a trampoline.

"Wow," I said. "He's going high!"

"The Inupiat used to toss hunters on walrus-skin blankets like these to spot the whales in the water," Seth explained. "They still use it to celebrate good whaling seasons. Want to give it a try?"

"Me? On that thing? Oh, I don't know..."

Before I could end my sentence, Seth picked me up

and tossed me into the recently vacated blanket. The blanket holders heaved in unison, launching me in the air. Up I went, arms and legs flailing, squealing like a madwoman. For a brief moment, I soared above the crowd, only to plummet like a stone, crash on my bum, and bounce again. By the third bounce, I knew enough to stay upright. By the fourth bounce, I was actually enjoying myself, laughing like a little girl, trying to do somersaults in the air.

The thrill. I felt alive. For the first time since my dad's death, joy gushed through me like a long-awaited flood. I forgot all about having to find Tammy. I forgot about Louise, my duties and responsibilities at work and at home. I forgot about my mother's murder and the attempt on me. I felt happy, carefree, hopeful. True, the star-studded sky and the powerful music helped me soar high into the Alaskan night, but it was Seth's smile, waiting for me at the bottom of every bounce, that thrilled me beyond belief.

Just when I thought that this grand night couldn't get any better, the spotlights illuminated the sea and I spied a spout breaking through the water's surface.

"Whale," I shouted and pointed. "Over there. Whale!"

The whale breached in the water, adding its primal majesty to the awesome spectacle that was Alaska. The crowd roared as one. Behind the stage, the ocean exploded with the impact. The blanket holders turned to watch. I fell a long way onto a slack blanket, but Seth was there. He caught me in his arms and set me on my feet.

"Spotting a first whale brings blessings for the season," he said, face flushed with excitement. "Good?"

"Extraordinary."

I threw my arms around his neck, dove for his mouth and kissed him. I rocketed up to the sky without the need for the walrus-hide blanket. I was sleepwalking while awake, caught in an extraordinary dream and unwilling to wake. As if on cue, the band began to play my all-time favorite song, "Slave to My Dreams." I couldn't stop kissing Seth.

"Get a room," someone called out playfully nearby.

"Oh, God," I muttered when I came up for breath.

"I know what you mean." Seth grabbed my hand. "The hell with it."

He led me under the rope. A mere look was all he needed for security to let us through. I thought we were going backstage, but instead of going upstairs, Seth ducked below the stage, where I followed blindly.

I stumbled in the dim space, surrounded by scaffolding, tripping over tangles of wires and cables. I dodged the metal braces that held the stage, which hovered dangerously close to the top of Seth's head. The scent of trampled seaweed and sea salt enveloped my senses, combined with a heady whiff of pot. Someone had used this hideout before us.

It was loud down here, deafening in fact, but as Seth crushed me against his body, the sounds of the music enfolded us in an acoustic cocoon, lending us a sense of intimacy. It was a totally false one, but in my current state of lust, I didn't care. I clung to Seth, devouring his mouth, exploring the shape of his body with eager hands, engaging him in a slow, grinding dance.

Seth braced himself against a metal column and cupped my ass. I lifted one foot on a pylon and dug the other one in the sand to give him berth. He angled between my legs and pressed me against his groin. The pleasure of that rasping contact left me breathless. The thrill of doing this, now, here, was an aphrodisiac.

I was so aroused that I couldn't think. There was a lot of freedom in not thinking. Intense and all-consuming need freed me from my mind's bondage. All of my body's resources were committed to fulfilling the primal craving aching and throbbing between my thighs. Seth's hands found all kinds of ways around my clothing, diving beneath my coat, dipping into my jeans, stealing into my bra and raking over my rigid nipples.

My hips curled in and out of his hands. My crotch rubbed hard against his jeans, riding his erection's wooden path. He felt so good! My own jeans contributed to the friction. The seam pressed against my clit. My sex smarted and chafed and yet I didn't want to stop. I rasped against him like a match on sandpaper.

It didn't take more than a song, maybe two. I cried out so loud, the whole of Alaska must have heard me coming. Seth roared in my ear. His fingers dug into my flesh. Pleasure struck us in unison, drove us to our knees and left us both shaking and sucking for breath.

The crowd cheered the end of the song at the same time that my body hailed a mind-blowing orgasm. I couldn't believe my staggering, newfound capability for sexual pleasure. It was Seth. He was like an accelerant to my fires. Together we were an explosion waiting to happen.

I kissed his mouth, his neck, the spot pulsing with his powerful heartbeats. I basked in his enthralling scent, spent male, come and sexual sweat. He gathered me on his lap and held me as if I were a part of him, his arm, his leg, his heart, as if he'd never let me go. We clung to each other for a long time, trying to catch our breaths. For all I knew, we were the only two people remaining in the world.

"Hell, Summer." He planted a kiss on my lips. "I think we made fire."

I was pretty sure I'd felt the flames.

Eventually, reluctantly, his arms loosened about me. "I guess we should get back out there. I don't want you to miss the grand finale."

"Didn't we just have one of those?" I said. "Wait, do you mean grander than that?"

The smile he gave me ignited me all over again. "Not that grand."

He planted another kiss on my lips then helped me rise to my feet in spite of my wobbly knees. We straightened our clothes as best we could. Together, we stole out from beneath the stage and back to our roped section, grinning at each other like fools, partners in naughty crimes.

The world streamed before my eyes like a high-definition movie. My overly stimulated body resonated with every single note. The light dazzled my eyes. For a girl who had shunned sex most of her life, it had been a day of sex and excess, and yet I couldn't regret it. My body savored Seth's essence. My sex quickened with the memories. My heart drummed in tune with my body's song. For once, my soul felt whole.

Back behind the rope, Seth put his arms around me and held me through this other grand finale. I leaned against him as we watched the fireworks light up the night. I craned my neck to glance up at him, feeling as close and intimate as I'd ever felt to another human being. Eyes wide, lips turned up at the ends, he looked happy.

The concert came to an end with an explosion of light and music. When the glorious sounds ceased and the band took a final bow, after the spotlights dimmed and the crowd began to disperse, we lingered behind. We held hands and talked with Seth's friends along with Ally, Stuart, and Jer, enjoying the concert's resounding success.

I waited while Seth talked to some of his crew. I couldn't help but notice that a few of his cousins hovered nearby in an isolated little group, as if contemplating approaching him. A little part of me empathized with their hesitation, since I still remembered keenly how intimidating Seth had been when I first met him on that frozen stretch of Alaskan road. As more of Seth's crew came over, he lingered greeting them. The cousins wavered. It looked like they were getting ready to leave. I knew the rule, the strict division between the Erickson factions, but, hey, I wasn't technically an Erickson and I didn't want to let the opportunity go to waste.

I took a deep breath, mumbled a little prayer and sauntered over to the group. It took some courage, but I introduced myself and struck up a conversation with some of the girls. They were a little leery of me at first, but after we got talking, I found out that they were curious about me and interested in anything I had to say about Seth. So I said a lot and all of it was true.

And then, something incredible happened. Seth came over and joined me. He actually engaged his cousins in conversation, asked them about their lives and even joked a little with them, reminiscing about their youth. One of the women actually asked him about what had happened at Star Lake. Seth told his side of the story and, as he answered other questions, began to share with them his vision for the company's future. His cousins listened. And boy, he was good. I was so proud of him. I melted into the background and enjoyed the magical moment when Seth lowered his drawbridge and allowed his family into his mind's formidable fortress.

Alex noticed. I watched him from the corner of my eye. His face set into a grim expression as more of his own brothers and sisters gravitated toward Seth. Never one to be upstaged, he countered Seth's move by approaching the folks from Seth's New Mission Program. One thing I'd learned during my brief time in Alaska was the people here relished strong views and the right to express them. Alex might have been born in Alaska, but he hadn't learned that lesson yet. He offered his hand to my new friend, Trevor, but Trevor's fingers tightened around his chair's wheels as he refused to shake with Alex.

Alex's face flushed a deep shade of crimson. "What's your problem? Don't you know who am I? Don't you want to meet one of the Ericksons that supports your little program?"

"I know who you are." Trevor spat on the ground. "I haven't forgotten what you tried to do last week. I also know the Ericksons that matter. You're not one of them."

"The hell with you," Alex said. "I can have you thrown out in no time. Who do you think you are talking to me like that?"

"He's Seth's VIP guest." I stepped in. "Why don't you move on, Alex?"

Alex sneered. "An imported slut like you wants to tell me what to do while standing on Erickson property?"

Trevor grumbled. "You shouldn't call a lady names if you're aiming for a punch-free night."

Alex snapped. "Shut up, wheels. She's no lady and what are you gonna do, trample me with your wheelchair?"

Seth was suddenly there, standing next to me. "What's the problem here?"

"No problem." I exchanged a pleading look with Trevor, who immediately understood the need to avoid trouble.

"Just waiting for my ride," Trevor said.

"You need to upgrade your taste in friends," Alex said. "Between this moron and that slut, you're surrounded by freaks."

Seth's body uncoiled with the speed of a viper. He lunged at Alex. Hand around his throat, he slammed him against the stage. I got in between the men, pried Seth's fingers one by one from Alex's neck and, planting my hands on Seth's chest, pushed back with all I had.

It was like trying to move a mountain. Trevor helped, wedging his chair between the men. People around us took notice. Jer and Stuart rushed to help me hold Seth back.

"What's going on?" Jer asked.

"Your hothead brother is itching for a fight." Alex fingered his neck and straightened his collar with an angry tug. "When you hang out with crap, you get splashed."

Seth rumbled. "I'm warning you."

"Come on, Seth," I said. "Let's go home."

"Run away, little boy," Alex taunted. "Hide behind your girlfriend just as you've always hidden behind Grandma's skirt."

"Is that what this is about?" Seth said.

"I don't need propping up," Alex said. "And I don't need the support of an old wrinkled crone to do my job."

This time it took more of us to hold Seth back.

"This is what he wants," I said. "He wants to provoke you, ruin your evening and show everybody that you're short-tempered and violent. Don't give him the satisfaction."

"Yeah, Seth, go home," Alex said. "Take your whore with you, see if she can squeeze more Erickson money out of your inert little dick. After all, there aren't too many whores willing to put up with a half-grilled coward who killed half his crew."

Alex had called me names. He'd insulted me in every possible way. He'd even messed with Trevor, someone he had no business irking. But it was his cruelty toward Seth that set me off. Before my mind registered, I was on Alex and my fist collided with his jawbone.

He staggered backward, stunned. "What the fuck?"

I stared at my fist, throbbing with pain. "Ow."

"You bitch!" Alex charged at me, face twisted with rage.

One moment Seth was standing behind me, held back by Stuart, Jer, Trevor, and several others. The next moment, a dark shadow flew at the edge of my peripheral vision, all of the guys sprawled on the ground, and Seth pounded on Alex with lethal efficiency.

Stuart and Jer tried to stop the fight, but Alex's brothers got in the way. The fighting expanded. The guys of Seth's squadron jumped into the fray along with his friends from the program. Within seconds, most people who'd lingered in the mosh pit were fighting, even if most of them didn't know why.

And that's how the best night of my life went to hell.

TWENTY-TWO

ROBERT ARRIVED AT the sitting room, carrying another silver bucket full of ice. He assessed our sorry lot and shook his head. "I can't believe that you were willing to put the mistress through this," he said somberly. "I might have expected this sort of behavior from others, but not from you. The troopers had to be called. The troopers!"

As he exited the room, his countenance left no doubt that he was disappointed in all of us. No wonder. Seth sprawled on the couch, pressing an ice bag to his eye. Jer leaned over a mirror, disinfecting the gash on his forehead. Ally iced Stuart's shoulder, while Stuart examined my hand. I opened and closed my fist for him. I was pretty sure none of my knuckles were broken, but boy, they hurt.

"Nothing's broken," Stuart confirmed, letting go of my hand. "You'll be fine tomorrow."

Seth didn't say anything. His face was blank. His silence spoke volumes. I was pretty sure he was livid with me. He held me responsible for the fight. Oh, hell, *I* held me responsible for the fight.

"Summer's got quite the hook." Jer winced when he dabbed his forehead with alcohol. "Really impressive. If we ever have to fight again, I want you on my side."

Stuart grinned. "Are you sure you're not from Texas?"

"You made that jerk whirl," Ally said admiringly. "He deserved it."

"I hope he's black and purple all over," Jer said.

"If you must know," Stuart said, "Alex is worse off than any of us, by far. Astrid asked me to check him out. His nose might be broken. I put his arm in a sling, and his clothing is in tatters." He eyed Seth obliquely. "He looks as if the wrath of God descended on him in lightning form."

"I don't know what got into me." I mumbled a bad attempt at yet another apology. "I'm really sorry. I've never hit anybody in my life."

"If you had to hit someone, you picked a good one," Jer said.

"I can't believe I did that." I dipped my face in my hands. "I lost my cool."

The sounds of an argument came from somewhere upstairs, a screech and a crash. Seth set aside the ice bag and sat up on the couch. "What the hell is that?"

"Master Erickson!" Robert's shouts rang through the house. "Miss Silva!"

Seth bolted out of the sitting room and tackled the stairs like a horse at a gallop. I followed on his heels and so did everyone else. Our feet hammered on the polished wood floors and thumped over the oriental rugs. Robert met us at the top of the stairs, face ashen, mouth set in a downward curve.

"What's wrong?" Seth demanded.

"It's the mistress," Robert said, "along with trouble like I've never seen before."

Another crash echoed from the library.

"Dear God." Robert grabbed me by the shoulder and

pushed me through the doors. "You have to fix this. Go in there."

I stumbled into the library and took in the scene. Astrid stood by the family portraits dressed in a silk kaftan, hands on her head, mouth gaping, eyes fast on the broken pieces of china scattered on the floor. The dogs whimpered, hiding behind her legs. I was distantly aware that there were other people in the room, but my stare was glued to the wiry woman with an awful lot of crazy in her glare who faced Astrid.

Nah. It couldn't be.

I took in the woman's teased, bleached blonde hair, her artificially enhanced pout, which was smeared in neon-pink lipstick, and her toasted brown-and-orange skin, wrinkled and freckled by too many hours spent under the sun.

I knuckled my eyes. Was I seeing right?

Standing next to the fireplace, her chest puffed out like a rooster in the fighting ring. The pair of artificial double Ds skewering the air dwarfed her scrawny frame. Leopard-print tights did nothing to suppress an overall impression of feral wildness. My throat constricted. Oh. My. Freaking. God.

I squeaked. "Louise?"

My stepmother didn't even bother to look at me. Her furious stare beamed on Astrid like a death ray. Her platform sandals crunched on the broken shards on the floor as if she were playing Candy Crush with her feet. And the filth coming out of her mouth. My nails bit into my palms. I wanted to be anywhere but here.

"Is that who I think it is?" Seth said under his breath.

"Yes," I muttered, "and she can't be around china when she's in a rage. Help me, please?"

"Got it." Seth peeled off to my right. "Go."

"Louise?" I edged my way forward. "Look at me. What are you doing here?"

"That bitch!" Louise growled in her best Brooklyn accent, adding a string of mortifying obscenities. "She set her dogs on me!"

"I know you're mad," I said, advancing slowly. "But you need to calm down."

"Who the hell does she think she is?" Louise grabbed a Ming vase from the shelves. "The queen of England? Nobody treats me like this. Nobody! I'm not trash to be thrown to them devil dogs. I'm not putting up with this stuck-up bitch."

"Louise, please." My eyes shifted between her face and the vase in her hands. "I know you're mad and you're right, Mrs. Erickson shouldn't have set those dogs on you. But this is her house and you have to get your temper under control."

"What about her?" Louise's face flushed with a surge of fresh rage. "She's the one stinking up this mausoleum."

God almighty. How on earth had I gotten stuck in this nightmare? Louise raved and Astrid sneered and all I could do was stare at those broken shards on the ground and think about the six-hundred-year-old vase in Louise's hands, which had survived war, natural disasters, raids, time, and greed only to succumb to clashing egos and my stepmother's legendary temper.

"This is no mausoleum," Astrid spat, incensed. "This is my family's home and you'd be well advised to behave in my presence!"

"Well, since you asked nicely," Louise said, "allow me to say… Up your ass!"

The vase went airborne at the same time that Seth tackled Louise from behind. I dove to the ground and caught it, not two inches from the floor. I lay there for a moment, knees and elbows smarting, catching my breath, balancing six hundred years of history in my quaking fingers, listening to Louise's foul string as she wrestled in Seth's arms.

"Mrs. Silva, please calm down." His voice broke through, even and neutral. "I assure you, we mean you no offense."

I got up on my knees and, holding on to the Ming vase, accepted the hand that came to my assistance. I'd been so focused on Louise and the vase, that, other than Astrid, I hadn't taken notice of who else was in the room. It was Alex who helped me up to my feet. His face looked deformed, his arm was in a sling and one of his eyes was swollen shut, but his other eye gleamed with amusement that irritated me to no end.

"Family rows are such a riot, don't you think?" He smirked. "Welcome to my world."

I couldn't share in his good humor. I snatched my hand from his and, after dusting off my jeans, returned the vase to the shelf and went to Seth's assistance.

"Let me go, you big brute!" Louise kicked his shins and stomped on his foot. "Is this what you call Alaskan hospitality?"

Seth winced, but he didn't let go. Instead, he asked, "How long will this last?"

I shrugged and gestured toward the balcony. "Maybe a breath of fresh air will help?"

"This way." Seth dragged Louise along while she kicked and screamed like a cranky mule. He glowered at his grandmother as he went by. "I'll be right back."

I straightened my back and followed Seth, aware of all the eyes fastened on me. I was so embarrassed. There was Astrid, of course, beaming her icy glare in my direction, and also Robert, who looked both shocked and appalled. Jer, Ally, and Stuart looked somewhere north of supremely uncomfortable. Alex's face was set on that stupid smirk. I tripped when I saw Hector Carrera, a tiny elf of a man, pale as a ghost and making himself even smaller in the corner by the door.

I frowned. "What the hell are you doing here?"

"It's kind of a long story," he said. "Tell you later?"

"Good idea." I pushed through the doors to the balcony and got walloped by a lungful of freezing air.

The Alaskan evening had the desired impact of cooling down Louise's temper. Seth let her go, but blocked the door to the library, just in case.

I crossed my arms and faced my stepmother. "What was that?"

"I'm sorry." Louise slumped, avoiding my eyes. "I don't know what got into me."

"Your temper got in the way," I said. "You know you're not supposed to react like a crazy woman every time somebody rains on your parade."

"I know, I know!" She looked wretched. "I tried, I swear, but that woman, she's got the worst case of the snobs I've ever seen, and you know how I feel about snobs."

I knew very well. I also knew that some situations challenged people like us worse than others. Case in point, I'd just socked Alex myself. Still, I wasn't feeling very sympathetic toward my stepmother at the moment.

"I've been doing better with my temper." Louise's

huge eyes leaked a few fat tears. "But I guess I didn't do too good today. I made a spectacle of myself, didn't I?"

"Un-huh." I gave a crisp nod.

"I promise," she said. "If it makes you happy, I'll go to Dirty Dog Pottery next week and make the witch another vase on my buck. Or five if she wants. Or maybe I should make her a turtle-shaped ashtray too?"

"Louise?" I said. "That vase you broke before I came into the library can't be replaced with something you make in your pottery class. It was probably really old and extremely expensive."

"I'll put it on my credit card, then."

I shook my head.

"Oh, dear." Now she looked sick. "Will I need to get a second mortgage on the condo?"

I took pity on her. "I'll figure something out."

"Thanks, you always do," she said in her hoarse, cigarette-husky baritone. She lifted her arms and wiggled her fingers. "Aren't you gonna say hello to your Mami?"

I tried to stay mad at her, I really did, but then I spotted the longing in her eyes, and yes, maybe even a bit of remorse, and I just couldn't.

She embraced me, poking her double Ds like concrete cones into my chest. I knew she was sincere. This was the same woman who'd cared for my dad when he was sick, the same loving soul who'd tried to be a mother to me after I became an orphan. Beneath her jean jacket, she was shivering. I took off my jacket and put it on her.

"Better?" I said.

"Better." Louise huddled inside the jacket. "Is it always so cold here?"

"As far as I know," I said, feeling the chill in my bones.

Seth had been quietly standing by the door, but now he came forward, took off his leather coat and draped it over my shoulders.

"Who's he?" Louise asked.

"This is Seth," I said. "Seth, this is my stepmother, Louise."

"Mrs. Silva." Seth gave Louise a curt nod.

"I'm very sorry if I hurt you." She winced when she spotted Seth's bruised eye. "Oh, geesh, please tell me I didn't do that."

"You didn't."

"Good—well, not good that you have a black eye, I didn't mean it that way." Louise twisted the golden rings adorning her thickened knuckles. "It's just that sometimes I get crazy when I'm mad. I'm not wrong in the head, you know. I just lost my marbles when that woman said that Summer was sleeping around with some Alaskan guy."

Seth's eyes narrowed. "Is that what she said?"

"Imagine that," Louise said. "Summer. Sleeping around. That broad doesn't know anything about my baby, and yet she implied my Summer was nothing but a cheap slut."

Seth's irises darkened. "Did she now?"

"Un-huh." Louise nodded. "She tried to feed me some yarn about Summer, hitchhiking, but she doesn't know Summer like I do. My Summer is as cautious as they come. Classy too. She'd never hitchhike. As to sleeping around. Ha! Not Summer. She doesn't sleep around. Period. I'm sorry, but could you stomach someone you loved being thrashed around like that?"

"Nope," Seth said. "If you'll excuse me, I need to set some things straight."

"Seth," I said. "Don't…"

His glower forbade me from saying another word.

"It's cold out," he said, before he went in the door. "I'll clear the crowd. You come inside as soon as you're ready."

"Boy." Louise whistled as she watched him go. "That guy reminds me of thunder booming over the ocean. He's something else, isn't he?"

"That he is." I took a deep breath. "There are a couple other things you should know about him."

"Like what?" Louise said.

"I did hitch a ride with him," I said. "And then I slept with him. A lot. And then some more. And now? I'm totally hooked on him."

BY THE TIMES things settled, the evening was late. Seth had disappeared with his grandmother, but Robert had obviously been instructed to keep us comfortable, something he did to perfection. I was surprised and grateful when he offered Hector and Louise rooms. After the spat tonight, I expected that the Ericksons would throw me out, along with anyone remotely related to me.

Hector looked dead on his feet and I really wasn't in the mood to talk to him. He accepted Robert's hospitality and followed the attendant who led him to his rooms for the night. I suspected he'd traveled all the way here to check up on me. With a multi-million dollar deal on the table, could I really blame him?

Louise, on the other hand, wasn't one to let go of a grudge so easily. She crossed her skinny arms and grumbled. "I'd rather stay at Motel 6."

"You're not in Miami anymore," I said. "The nearest hotel is far, far away."

"So what?" She wrinkled her nose. "These people give me the heebie-jeebies."

"Please, Mrs. Silva," Robert said in his British accent. "On behalf of Master Erickson, I strongly urge you to reconsider. He insists you accept his hospitality."

Louise gestured to Robert with her pointy chin. "Does he always speak like that?"

"Always," I said. "Louise, can we try to get along, at least for tonight?"

"Okay, fine," Louise said. "We'll do it your way."

We followed Robert to a luxurious suite on the third floor, appointed with all the conveniences, including a crackling fireplace and tray of hot tea along with a three-tiered platter loaded with finger sandwiches and tiny cakes.

"Not too shabby." Louise stuffed tiny cakes in her mouth as she moseyed around the room, taking in the elaborate wallpaper, the heavy drapery, and the massive canopied bed. She poked at the mattress. "To think that an old broad like me gets to sleep on a bed like this one."

I went around the room, collecting everything remotely breakable from the mantel top, the shelves, and the tables. After piling my findings on a tray, I handed them over to Robert. "Here."

He cocked an eyebrow.

"Better safe than sorry?"

"Ah." He inclined his head formally. "Excellent idea, Miss Silva."

Louise dropped into one of the club chairs by the fire, propped her feet on the ottoman and popped a tiny sandwich in her mouth.

"Will there be anything else?" Robert said.

"Sure, handsome," Louise mumbled through a mouthful. "How about a shot of whisky? I like a little punch in my tea, if you get my drift."

"I'll have a selection delivered to your room." Robert walked out of the room, trailed by Louise's brazen stare.

I groaned. "Louise!"

"What?"

"Stop staring at him!"

"It's not my fault that the waiter has a nice ass."

"He's not a waiter," I said, exasperated. "He's the house manager for the Ericksons and the man who helped raised Seth and his siblings."

"Don't think I didn't notice." Louise grinned. "Seth has a nice ass too."

It was going to be a long night.

I perched on the chair across from Louise. "Do you want to tell me what the hell you're doing here? And why didn't you tell me you were coming?"

"It was a spur of the moment decision," Louise said. "I thought about it and I did it."

Of course it was an impulse. That's how Louise and Tammy lived their lives, but I didn't say that aloud.

"To be honest," Louise said, "I was lonely without my girls. It's so boring without anyone around. I've got my bridge friends, but even those gals get stale like moldy bread. So when Hector showed up at my door, I said, 'What the hell. Let's go to Alaska.'"

"Hector showed up at your door?"

"You know he keeps an eye on us," Louise said. "He said you were working on a difficult project. I would've never dared to come out here on my own, didn't have the dough either. But Hector offered to pay for the ticket and so I came. We tried calling you, but your cell didn't answer. When we got to the house, they told us you were at a concert. Then that woman called us up to her throne room. Didn't know Alaska had a queen. But enough about that: Where's Tammy?"

I told Louise everything I'd done to find Tammy. I also told her a little about Seth. She asked a lot of questions, some of which I wasn't ready to answer just yet.

"Does the boy know?" Louise's eyes widened with expectation.

"Yes," I said, although I didn't tell her how he had found out that I walked in my sleep.

"Are you okay with him knowing?"

"I trust him."

"Holy cow, Batman." Louise stared. "I don't think I've ever heard you say that about anyone other than your dad."

No point in denying the truth

A discreet knock echoed from the door. I got up and answered. It was Seth, his face set in that terrifying, forbidding expression, his eye still bruised from the fight earlier. I stepped out of the room and, closing the door behind me, faced him.

"I'm really, really sorry," I mumbled.

He inspected my knuckles. "How's your hand?"

"Fine."

"Good," he said. "Let's go home."

"I can't," I said. "I should stay with Louise tonight."

Seth's jaw tightened. "I was afraid you were going to say something like that."

"There's a lot of expensive china in this house," I said. "Who knows what kind of trouble Louise will get into if I'm not around?"

"You're not her babysitter."

"What other option do I have?"

The door to Louise's bedroom cracked open to reveal her face and an apologetic grin. "How about you go sleep with the boy and let your old stepmom do her thing?"

"Oh, lord." I sighed. "Didn't we agree that listening to other people's conversations behind closed doors was a bad habit?"

"Sure," Louise said. "But I still like to do it."

I gave Seth a cursory look. Did I have the fortitude to face his anger tonight?

"We'll both stay here tonight," he decided, making no allowances for disagreement, texting on his cell as he spoke. "I'll have Robert send someone to fetch our things and I'll leave directly from here to Juneau tomorrow. You can be close by in case of a china emergency."

"Sounds peachy." Louise reached out with her scrawny arm and pinched Seth's cheek. "Smart and cute. Watch the temper, handsome, will ya? My girl is like an Easter cream egg, a hard shell outside, but all sweet and gooey inside."

I stomped my foot. "Louise!"

"Good night." She waved as she closed the door.

"Sorry," I muttered. "Welcome to Silvaland."

"Thanks." Seth started down the hallway. "Now we're even."

I FOLLOWED SETH to what used to be his old bedroom. Decorated in tones of blue, it was as posh and luxurious as the rest of the house. A bad feeling weighed me down as we entered the room. I was exhausted and I didn't know how else to apologize. I didn't know what

Seth was thinking, but by the stern tilt of his mouth, I figured it was nothing good.

I gasped when he took off his coat. Blood blotched the back of his shirt. "You're bleeding!"

"It's nothing." He shrugged, but I lifted the back of his shirt and examined his back.

"It's that stubborn spot that won't heal." Damn Alex and his vitriol. "It looks like it got torn in the fight. You should've told me you were hurting. We could've had Stuart take a look."

"I'm fine." He marched into the bathroom.

"You're not fine." I followed him. "You should see a doctor."

"Not necessary." He closed the door on me.

I knew how he felt about doctors. I also knew how he felt about other people looking at his scars. But he had to be hurting and I worried a lot about infection. The sound of the shower echoed from the bathroom. I was certain that the water coming out of the faucets flowed cold as ice.

He took a long time in the shower. He had to be burning in addition to hurting. Robert arrived, along with a steward who helped carry our things, laptops, and essentials. I thanked Robert and retrieved what I needed from Seth's carry-on. Then I changed for bed and waited some more.

When Seth finally came out of the bathroom, he wore pajama pants, hanging low on his hips. The shiner around his eye had darkened, but the swelling had actually gone down. He looked tired. I had the prescription ointment in my hand and a new silicone patch laid out on the night table. He gave the stuff a surly look.

"Please?" I said.

Without a word, he stretched belly down on the bed. I knelt on the mattress next to him and examined his back. The blood was gone now, but the lesion was ripped open and larger than before. I cursed under my breath. I should've socked Alex harder.

I dabbed on the medicine as gingerly as possible, cringing when he flinched. I placed a new silicone patch and applied some lotion over the scars on his back, trying to warm his cold skin and knead the tension that knotted his muscles.

"Summer?" he said while I worked on him. "We've got to have a serious talk."

My heart froze. My hands stilled over his shoulder blades. I knew what he was going to say. What I'd done tonight was unforgivable. I'd upset his grandmother. Meddled in his family's affairs. Endangered him and his friends. Messed up a really great night, possibly the best of my life.

I knew he must have other complaints, worries that haunted me too. My stepmother had to figure highly among them. She'd made such a racket. And the vase she broke. I had no idea how I was going to pay for it. Maybe Astrid would take me on as an indentured servant. God, what a mess. Tears swelled in my eyes. There were many, many reasons why this couldn't work out. Tonight was only one more.

"Summer?" He craned his neck to look at me. "Are you listening?"

"I'm listening," I said in a strangled voice. "Do you want me to leave?"

"Leave?" He flipped over and sat up, smearing lotion all over the bedcovers and the upholstered headboard. The scowl on his face iced my guts. "Why the hell would I want you to leave?"

"Because you haven't said much since the fight with Alex." The pitch in my voice rose steadily. "Because I come from a crazy family and I'm not Alaska-suitable. Because I started the fight with Alex and upset your grandmother. Because I'm a freak of nature and I walk in my sleep. Because things are moving too fast, things have gotten too intense, and you've had enough of me."

"Jesus Christ." He huffed and ran his fingers through his hair, leaving strands standing up like raised hackles. "Where do I begin to unravel all that crap? First, I haven't had a chance to talk to you all night with all these people around. Second, you didn't start that fight with Alex. It started a long while back, way before you were even on the horizon. Third, you're not a freak of nature and I don't give a rat's ass if you walk in your sleep. It's the rest of the stuff you said that really pisses me off. If you think we're moving too fast, then that's on you. Don't put it on me."

"You have to admit it." I stared at my hands. "It's a little unreal."

"Fine, I admit it." He got up from the bed and began to pace the room. "It happened real fast. But I can't control the way I feel. In fact, I can't help it. I don't know how to slow this down, and frankly, I don't want to. So what if it's too fast or intense? Does it scare the shit out of me sometimes? Yes. Do I want to end it? No. Do you want to end it?"

I swallowed a dry gulp. "No."

"Then this discussion is over." He sat next to me and hugged me against his chest. "You're not leaving and that's final."

My head ached. I buzzed with all kinds of emotions. I don't know what happened to me. The tears caught me by surprise. They just popped out of my eyes like hot kernels. I dipped my face in my hands and cried, because so much had happened in so little time and the emotions overwhelmed me.

"Oh, shit, don't cry, Summer." Seth gathered me on his lap, frantically kissing my forehead, my nose, my wet cheeks. "If I said something wrong, hit me over the head, take a hammer to my laptop, do whatever you want, but please, baby, don't cry."

"I'm sorry." I curled in his lap. "I don't seem able to stop right now. But Seth…my stepmother," I hiccupped. "She broke a freaking Ming vase!"

"Forget about the stupid vase," he said. "It's nothing. It wasn't a real Ming. Okay? Just…stop crying…please? Hell, tell me what you need and I'll get it done. I'm about to crap my pants over here."

"I'm fine." I took in a deep breath. "This is just emotion…fear…frustration. I came to Alaska to find Tammy. I haven't found her, but instead I found you. I wasn't expecting you. I hadn't planned on you."

"I know."

"I'm an architect." I wiped the tears from the corners of my eyes. "I design things. Buildings. Lives. It's what I do. But this, this didn't happen by design. It's just…a lot."

"Hush, baby." He lifted me gingerly, undid the bed covers and deposited me on the crisp sheets and against the pillows. "You're just tired and today was stressful all around."

He tucked me in and turned off the lights, so that only the glow of the fire illuminated the room. He settled next to me and gathered me in his arms. I laid my head on his shoulder and trailed my fingers over his skin, drawing little patterns over his chest.

"I know the concert ended badly but…"

"But what?"

"I'm going to remember tonight for the rest of my life. The lighthouse. The concert. The whale. Remember the whale?" I sniffed and gave out a little laugh. "It was fantastic. Oh, and I'll never forget making out under the stage under Battle Dragons. Many years from now, when I tell my grandchildren about today, I'm going to blow their minds. They're going to think I'm the coolest Grandma ever."

Seth's laughter rumbled against my ear. "It was a good day. I had fun too. I had fun because you were with me."

My heart soared, because the night's troubles hadn't eclipsed the day's gains.

I remembered something else. "Seth?"

"Hmm-hmm?"

"What did you want to talk to me about in the first place?"

"Oh, that." His chest rose and fell beneath my cheek. "You've had enough for one day. Maybe we should wait until tomorrow."

"Oh, come on." I cupped his chin and, meeting his gaze, cajoled him with a pout. "Now, Erickson."

"Okay, fine." His Adam's apple bounced as he cleared his throat. "I've been thinking about us, Summer, not just today, but for the last few days."

My body tensed in his arms. "Uh-oh."

"Just relax and listen to what I have to say," he said, his fingers pleasantly raking through my hair. "Please?"

"Okay." If he kept on scratching my head, I'd listen forever.

"It was unbearable."

"What was unbearable?"

"The time I had to spend away from you. When I went to Prudhoe Bay? It was excruciating." His fingers rubbed against my scalp. "I'd rather be shot down again."

"Don't say things like that."

"It's true." His hand stilled on my head. "You've got a right to your life. I get that. I know you love what you do and where you live. I'm not supposed to tell you what to do or how to go about your life, but I want you to think about what I'm saying."

"What exactly is it that I'm thinking about?"

"I'm not asking you to change, or to give up on the things you want," he said. "But we're going to have to do something differently, because I can't bear the thought of you leaving and I don't want to live my life away from you."

TWENTY-THREE

I WATCHED SUMMER set the blankets aside and get up. The fire illuminated her figure as her feet padded quietly on the plush carpet on her way to the door. I sprang from the bed, beat her to the door, and blocked it. Eyes wide and translucent, she turned around and moved on to try the bathroom door.

I should've expected trouble tonight. The stress of the day had created the right kind of scenario. Combine all that with fatigue and you had all the elements that precipitated Summer's sleepwalking episodes. It was precisely what I'd been trying to avoid all along.

I blocked her path to the bathroom, placed a hand on her shoulder and pointed her in the direction of the bed. She turned around again and went for the door as if I wasn't standing right there.

"I have to find her," she said.

"Not tonight," I said. "You need to go back to bed."

She hesitated on her feet, then went about the room. Should I wake her up? The doctor had said that waking a sleepwalker wasn't a good idea, so I followed her.

Her face wore a blank expression. Her feet glided on the floor. She moved as she did when she was awake, with grace and purpose. The blood curdled in my veins when she tested a window next. Had I not been there to anticipate her moves, she would've been outside by now.

She looked around the room, past me. Her gaze fell

on the desk, where her laptop idled. She stared at the laptop for a while, then her knees flexed and she sat on the chair. *Plop*. Her fingers landed on her keyboard. She began to type prodigiously fast, calling up complex formulas and design specifications, applying her calculations to the architectural designs popping up on her screen with mind-blowing speed.

I stood behind her and called out softly. "Summer?"

She didn't answer. Her behavior seemed different from the last time, more focused, more concentrated and less interactive. I suddenly wished I had Dr. Sanchez on speed dial. I tried talking to Summer, but it was as if she couldn't hear me.

"Summer, baby, don't you want to go back to bed?"

No reply. The minutes ticked by. I sat with her, but she didn't seem to be aware of my presence. Her eyes were bloodshot. Her lips looked dry. She was completely caught in what she was doing.

"Baby," I finally said. "Tell me what's going on. Tell me what you're doing."

Her fingers didn't stop typing, but her eyes considered me briefly.

"The tundra's delicate ecosystem is susceptible to temperature changes," she said in a flat monotone. "Temperature changes melt the permafrost, destabilizing structural foundations. Self-regulating pylons inspired by the ones in your house will support a solid structural framework that, designed to the correct specifications, will bear the living and working compounds."

I gawked at the blueprints popping on her screen. "Summer, this is brilliant." She'd designed a smart pylon *while* she slept. The doctor had mentioned a case where a sleepwalker, a mathematician by trade, had solved complex problems in her sleep, but this was extraordinary. I wouldn't have believed it if I hadn't seen it happen with my own two eyes.

But even with the pylon solution at hand, Summer kept at it, snared in some sort of sleepwalking rage, working herself to oblivion. Exhaustion etched her face. I had to do something.

"Summer," I said in a firmer tone. "You need to stop. Now."

Her fingers froze on the keyboard. Her hands dropped to her lap. Her head fell forward and her eyelids drooped. I realized she hadn't listened to me when I talked to her normally, but she had followed my commands.

Commands?

Summer would follow instructions, but only when she was asleep?

I tested my new hypothesis. "Summer, get up, please."

To my amazement, she pushed back on the chair and stood up.

"Go to the bed," I said and she did just so. "Get under the covers." I guided her gently. "That's it. Good."

I tucked her in, kissed her forehead and lay down next to her. Her eyes were open and fixed on the ceiling. I reviewed the night's lessons in my mind. She was as persistent in her sleep as she was when awake. She was prone to working frenzies while sleepwalking. She could engineer design solutions in her dreams and work herself to oblivion. She followed directions. The realization made me feel queasy. Would she follow anyone's directions?

"Summer?" I turned on my side and, propping myself up on my elbow, faced her. "I'm going to ask you some questions and you will answer them. Do you understand?"

"Yes." She fixed her gaze on me, pupils huge, green speckled irises translucent, ethereal and haunted.

"Have you always followed instructions when you sleepwalk?"

One shoulder came up, a fragile, uncertain shrug that reminded me she remembered nothing of her sleepwalking episodes and hated herself for it. "Daddy said I did. So did Louise. And Tammy."

"Did anyone else know?"

Both shoulders rose from the pillow this time around, a reluctant gesture that combined with her lips' subtle downturn set off my alarms.

"Well?" I insisted. "Who else knew?"

"Sergio."

Son of a bitch. Sergio De Havilland, her ex-husband. The bile roiled in my stomach. My mind churned, remembering everything I'd learned about the dirtbag and the times his name had come up in my conversations with Summer. *You will not mention his name in my presence ever again*, she'd said that first day when we drove to Anya's place. *For all I care, he's dead*, she'd added later when I pressed her. No love lost there. The dots began to connect.

Sergio must have known about her condition. Whether she told him about all that it entailed or whether he found out on his own, it didn't matter. By Summer's own admission, he also knew she followed instructions while she sleepwalked. That kind of power didn't belong to scum like De Havilland. Instead of helping her to cope, he must have betrayed her trust. How?

Summer never spoke of him. There was a good

chance she never would. I felt like a miserable worm, but I needed to know.

"I'm really sorry to have to ask you this," I said, stroking her hair. "Did your ex Sergio take advantage of you while you were sleepwalking?"

Her eyes went instantly liquid. "Yes."

My guts melted at the sight of her tears. "When?"

"When we were in college," she said, reluctantly.

This conversation was hard for her, even in her sleep. It was hard for me too. What I had to ask next was even harder.

"Tell me what happened."

"I was always careful," she murmured. "He lived in my dorm. I had a single with a door chain. We started dating, but I didn't want to sleep with him, not yet. I warned him about my problem. But one night, there was a party. He slipped something in my drink. I woke up two days later in his dorm room."

The sadness I spotted in her eyes launched a new surge of rage blazing through my veins. From my research, I knew that many drugs exacerbated sleepwalking episodes. Sergio must have used that knowledge to make her helpless and even more vulnerable.

I had to force myself to ask the next question. "Why did you marry him?"

"I didn't know what else to do." Her knuckles paled around the sheets. "At first, he wanted me to do all his schoolwork for him and take care of his—um—needs."

My nails stabbed against my palms. I had to make a conscious effort to ease my grip before I drew blood. The only blood I really wanted to spill belonged to that son of a bitch.

"Then he wanted more," Summer said in that even,

impersonal tone. “He told me he was going to show Daddy the pictures if I didn’t marry him.”

Pictures?

“Explain.”

“The pictures of me,” she said as if I should know exactly what she was talking about. “Doing stuff. Stuff he made me do. Commands he gave me. While asleep.”

Jesus fucking Christ. I sucked in all the air in the room. “He threatened to show the pictures to your father if you didn’t marry him?”

“Yes,” she said in a frail voice. “And after we were married, he said that, if I left, if I refused to do what he told me to do, he’d plaster the pictures all over the internet. I was mortified. What would Louise and Tammy think? Daddy was sick. Grief could kill him.”

Son of a bitch. He’d played on Summer’s weaknesses to manipulate and control her. He knew how much she loved her family, especially her father, and had used that against her. It was worse than I’d imagined and for Summer’s pain, the asshole was going to pay.

I wiped the tear that spilled from the corner of her eye and took a calming breath to smother my fury. When I could speak again, I asked, “How were you able to get out of the marriage?”

“It was hard,” she said, dodging the question, even in her dreams.

“Tell me how you did it.”

Her brows met in a furious frown. “I said to him, ‘You have pictures of me? Well I have pictures of you. If you make my dad sad, I’ll make your father mad.’”

It took me a moment to realize what she meant. Then I remembered what Spider had said about De Havilland. Sergio couldn’t afford to piss off his father, who’d only pay his expenses if the son behaved. A new question lurked in my mind.

"What kind of pictures did you have on Sergio?" I asked.

"The ones about the drug deals."

Of course. Spider had reported that Sergio was an addict, but his father didn't know that. It all came full circle and clicked nice and neat.

"Tell me," I said. "Who took those pictures?"

"I did."

I stared at the woman lying beside me, at the lines etched between her brows, at the sorrow reflected in her eyes. She'd taken a tremendous risk, following Sergio to his dealer and taking the pictures herself. It was typical Summer, brave to the point of recklessness. I could only begin to imagine what she'd gone through.

"How did Sergio react when he learned you had those pictures?" I asked.

"He was furious," Summer said. "He said I had to give him the pictures."

"But you didn't give him the pictures," I said. "What did you do instead?"

"I gave the pictures to an attorney," she said. "I told him to release them to Sergio's father and the press if something happened to me or if pictures of me surfaced on the internet. Then I demanded a divorce. Sergio didn't want to face his father's rage, so he signed the papers."

I was blown out of the water. What Summer had done was incredible. *He wouldn't dare mess with me*, she'd said that first day in my living room. *I made sure of that*. Indeed she had. She had single-handedly identified her opponent's weakness, devised the only possible strategy to resolve her problem, and executed it flawlessly. She'd managed to even out the odds and free herself.

I now understood why she'd been so reluctant to warn me before she passed out on the truck, why she'd been so upset the morning after and so alarmed when she'd thought I'd had pictures of our night together. My admiration for Summer continued to grow. She was fierce. The more I learned about her, the more I understood the depth of her courage. I was in awe of her, but I wanted to pound Sergio De Havilland to dust and send the troll to hell where he belonged. Still, I forced myself to think through my anger.

Could the pictures serve as a motive for murder? It didn't seem likely. If something happened to Summer, Sergio would be screwed. But tonight's developments merited further research and specific follow-up. I reached for my cell and typed a message to Spider. I was about to turn up the heat on Sergio De Havilland and he didn't know it.

I turned on my back, leaned my head on the pillow and hugged Summer to my chest. She lifted herself on her elbows, cased my face with her hands and kissed me, challenging all of my high-minded resolutions with the seductive gaze she beamed through her thick, dark, fluttering eyelashes.

"Oh, no, you don't," I said. "We're not doing this again."

"But you need me," she said, translucent eyes ablaze. "You want me."

"You're so right about that." I planted a quick kiss on her warm, plush lips.

"Your aura." She traced the lines of my face with her soft fingertips. "It's so beautiful. It's like a solar flare."

"Now you remember." Damn my rotten luck. Her light feathering touch was sweet and innocent and yet it tightened my balls and stiffened my dick into an aching rod.

"A taste," she murmured in between kisses that had me groaning with need. "Just a little taste?"

"Not while you're asleep." I hated to give my next command, but I opted to be the better version of me tonight. "Close your eyes, Summer. Go to sleep."

She laid her head on my shoulder. Her lids fell like curtains over her eyes. Her body relaxed against mine. Her respiration evened. I stared at the ceiling. Everything I'd learned tonight contributed to my worries. I'd known that Summer was vulnerable when sleepwalking, but I hadn't realized how vulnerable.

I didn't get to sleep for a long time. When I finally did, the nightmares came: the planes flying into the towers, the RPG punching through the helicopter, Summer walking into the ocean like her mother. And my life, empty all over again.

"MORNING, BEAUTIFUL," I SAID, as soon as her eyes opened.

She smiled and the day got a whole lot better as I appropriated her lips.

"I love waking up to you," she mumbled against my mouth.

"Me too."

I traced the edges of her face with my lips, pressing small kisses along the line of her jaw. Her eyes were slatted with traces of sleep. Her hair spilled all over the pillow. Lines from the sheets marked her cheek. Christ. Having her in my bed felt like a prize.

"Did I?" she asked.

I had to tell her the truth. "You did."

Fear flared in her eyes. "Did I get out?"

"Do you really think I'd let you get away like that?" I smirked. "Not under my watch. No worries, you were very active last night, but I fought you off my body with heroic flair."

"My hero." She giggled. "You must be exhausted after such an epic battle."

"You are the one who must be tired," I said. "You worked out a brilliant technical solution to Jer's pylon problem last night."

"I did?"

I planted another kiss on her mouth. "You were amazing."

"I want to see." She bounced out of my arms and off the bed, marched out to the desk and, returning with her laptop in tow, settled back on the mattress next to me. "Oh, my God! This could work." She scrolled down her screen. "If we can produce these, Jer's problems will be solved!"

"We can produce these," I said, looking at the screen over her shoulder. "We can manufacture the parts."

"I need to work in my sleep more often." She set the laptop aside. "Those specs must have taken me a while. Were you up all night with me?"

"It didn't take you all night," I said and it was true, although I omitted the rest of the story. What was the point in upsetting her all over again?

"You must be so tired." She brushed her knuckles

against my stubble. “And today you have to travel to Juneau to meet with the governor.”

“Tired?” I coiled my arm around her waist and brought her down on my chest. “No, more like horny as hell.”

“Well, well, well.” Her kisses traced my lips from one corner of my mouth to the other. “I can take care of that.”

My entire body reacted to her grin. “I was hoping you’d say that.”

SUMMER WAS TAKING a shower and I was in the dressing room, adjusting my cuff links, when my tablet chimed. I propped it up on the dresser and clicked on my secured com. Spider came online, his narrow face amplified on the high-definition screen. The tarantula look sharpened his features.

“Hiya,” Spider said. “I found something curious about Summer’s father.”

That caught my attention. “Go ahead.”

“Somebody set up a deferred life insurance policy with his name on it,” Spider said. “You know, the kind that fathers set up for young kids. Say I die now, but I don’t want my kid to blow the money before he grows a brain, so the money automatically goes into trust until the kid reaches a certain age—”

“I know what it is.”

“Well, there’s one of those set up under Miguel Silva’s name and by the looks of it, it must be large enough to matter.”

“Is Summer the beneficiary?”

“I don’t know.”

“What do you mean you don’t know?”

"I know that the policy exists because it's listed under the insurance company roster," Spider explained. "I haven't actually hacked the policy itself."

"Are you waiting for a printed invitation?" I said. "If Summer is the beneficiary of that policy, we've got motive for murder."

"We're back to the stepmother, aren't we?"

"Summer remembers another man in the room on the night her mother died, not another woman."

"The observation doesn't necessarily exclude the stepmother," Spider said. "I hear Louise Silva speaks in a hoarse baritone that could be easily confused with a male's voice."

Spider was on his game. Leave it to him to point out the obvious. I'd noticed too.

"Don't you think Summer would've recognized her own stepmother's voice?" I said.

"Not if she's not ready to accept a difficult reality."

Another excellent observation.

"Let's wait and see." I picked out a tie.

"The thing is…" Spider hesitated.

"What?"

"I have confirmed that Louise owned a condo at Fountain Way at the time that Summer's mother died." He shrugged. "Sorry, but I think we're getting close."

The damn tie tightened like a noose around my neck.

"I made sure we've got eyes on the stepmother while she's here," I said, "but we need proof. Summer's really protective of her family."

"Dude, you're about to stick your dick in a hornet's nest," Spider said. "Word on the street is you're into this gal."

"Is that so?"

"Yeah." Spider flashed a crooked smirk. "Word is she's cool and you're screwed."

I couldn't deny any of that.

"She socked Alex." Spider's smirk opened into a smug grin. "How cool is that?"

Did everybody know about that?

"If this pans out," Spider said, "she's gonna be mad as hell at someone, and that someone's gonna be you."

No two ways about it, if this lead turned into something solid, Summer's life was going to change and not in a good way. On the other hand, her life was at risk and I couldn't rest until the threat was neutralized and the danger gone.

"Do it," I said.

"Don't tell me I didn't warn you," Spider said before he signed off.

I studied my reflection in the mirror. The bruise around my eye was almost gone, replaced by a yellowish stain. I took in the neatly creased trousers, the crisp white shirt, the striped tie, and my father's silver cuff links. I'd come a long way from the mangled mess I'd once been. I felt as if I teetered at the edge of restoration. I'd be fine if I could convince Summer to stay. But how the hell was I going to do that if I had to break her heart first?

LOUISE SILVA OPENED the door in a polka-dot babydoll that did little to conceal her artificially enhanced chest. She leaned against the door and perched a hand on her hip.

"Why, hello, handsome." The end of her cigarette flared as she drew from it. "You're dressed for trouble today. I wasn't expecting you this morning."

"I'd like to speak to you before I leave," I said. "May I come in?"

"Sure." She exhaled a toxic cloud and gestured me inside. "Have a seat."

I followed her to the club chairs, fanning the smoke out of my way. If Grandma and Robert knew Louise was smoking in her room, they'd both have a cow. Me, I had to pick my battles. Thankfully, Louise slipped her scrawny arms into a robe before she sat on the padded chair across from me.

"Spit it out," Louise said. "What's bugging you?"

"Summer loves you," I said. "She thinks the world of you."

"But you aren't so keen on me, are you?" She unpinned one of the pink rollers that covered her head and released a multicolored curl. She dropped the roller on her lap before she moved on to the next one. "Let me guess. She's smart, gorgeous, and educated. She's tasteful, chic, and stylish—kind of like you. But she doesn't jive with crude, ordinary old me. I don't look right to you. I'm loud and obnoxious and I grate on your nerves."

"It's about Summer," I said. "I want her happy and safe."

"Then you and I have something in common." She dropped another roller on her lap.

"Do we?"

Her mouth set on a downward curve. Her acrylic nails tapped on the pile of pink plastic on her lap before she recovered. She unpinned the last roller, shook her head and combed her short mane with her fingers.

"I won't bite," she rumbled in her husky voice. "I lost my marbles yesterday, but I promised Summer I'd be good today. So say what you came to say. I don't like people who wanna play mind games."

I had to give it to Louise. She was smarter and more perceptive than I'd anticipated, which also confirmed her as my best suspect. I had to tread carefully.

"Summer has gone through a lot in order to find Tammy," I said. "She could've gotten hurt, but you didn't care. You sent her out here, all by herself, knowing about her challenges, without so much as a second thought."

She worked her throat, making a supreme effort to control her temper before she answered. "I'm a bit impulsive at times. Maybe I made a rash decision. But you think I'd mess up one child to get the other back. You think I love Tammy more than Summer, because Tammy's my biological daughter."

"You have to admit," I said. "It looks likely from the outside."

"I'm gonna tell you right now. I love both my daughters. Summer's just as much mine as Tammy. I worry about Tammy, that's true. She's got a wild streak about her. But I also worry about Summer."

I eyed the woman skeptically. "Summer's got a good head on her shoulders. Why should you worry?"

"Buried alive in her work, hanging on to her routine like a cat dangling from its claws, refusing to put herself out there for fear of betrayal." Louise paused. "What kind of life is that?"

"Do you know what happened to her?"

"Of course I know," Louise snapped. "I'm her mom. Who do you think picked her up from the bastard's apartment on the day she walked out without a dime to her name? Who do you think helped her find an attorney? Who do you think helped her keep the secret from her sick dad and nursed her when she wouldn't come out of her room for ten days straight?"

I bristled at the mere thought of Summer broken like that. But maybe Louise had ulterior motives in helping her stepdaughter. If she knew that Miguel Silva had made provisions for his daughter, perhaps she'd colluded to endear herself to Summer in order to get the money.

Time to up the ante.

"Did Summer tell you that someone tried to kill her here in Alaska?"

Louise flinched. "Come again?"

I'd known some great actresses in my time, but I didn't think any of them could blanch as authentically as Louise did now. The color drained from her face, highlighting the sunspots that blotched her complexion.

"Twice," I said. "A hired killer tampered with her brakes and, when that didn't work, tried to drown her in a lake."

The expression in Louise's gaze shifted from confusion to fury. "Who?" she demanded. "Tell me who, right now."

"He's dead now," I said. "His name was George Peterson. He didn't give up his employer's name. He tried to set it up so it looked like a sleepwalking episode."

Louise stared at me. "Summer's mother drowned while sleepwalking."

"Coincidence?"

"You don't think so." Louise's eyes tapered into slits. "You think Summer's murder attempt was somehow linked to her mother's death. Why would anybody want to kill Summer or her mother?"

"I thought perhaps you'd have some ideas," I said. "Can you think of anyone who might want to harm Summer?" I didn't add *other than yourself.*

"You think it was me." She glared at me, incredulous. "You think I hired someone to kill Summer's mother and then Summer."

I opted for silence.

Louise's chest rose and fell in a deep breath. She opened her mouth, closed it, then tried again. "You're wrong. You and your family know nothing about love. I didn't know Summer's mother before she died. And why would I want to kill my daughter?"

"You tell me."

"I married Miguel for love," she said. "He never had a dime to his name. The only thing he had when I met him was that condo in Fountain Way where we live now, a freebie from his last project. He was pretty much ruined when we got together."

"Strange." I tried to suppress the sarcasm in my voice. "Miguel Silva was such an innovating, successful architect."

"He was a great architect, that's true, but he knew squat about managing money," Louise said. "I'm not one to talk, but Miguel had no clue how much money he made or spent. Miguel bet all he had left in the Fountain Way project, but the real estate market caved, and after that, he was too sick to work. Hector was his best friend and partner and he was good enough to float Miguel some money. That's how we paid for the hospital bills. That's how we buried him. But to answer your question, no. I don't know of a single soul who'd want to harm Summer or her mother."

"What about Sergio De Havilland?"

"Summer made sure that idiot would want her alive and well."

"What about Tammy?"

"No!" Louise stomped her foot, a stubborn gesture that reminded me of Summer. "Tammy loves Summer. They're sisters."

Three very different women, three identical responses.

Time to throw in a twist.

"The evidence suggests that Peterson lived at Fountain Way or had free access to it."

Louise's painted eyebrows angled up. "So?"

"You lived in 16C, just a few doors down from Miguel Silva and his wife."

Louise's gaze shifted to the lamp between us. "Is that a Walmart special?"

"Nope," I said. "It's a Tiffany original."

"Expensive?"

"Priceless."

"Shit." The look she gave me could've turned me into ashes. "I don't like you very much right now, but I'm gonna tell you something, because I also like you a lot."

I frowned. "I don't follow."

"You're a son of a bitch," she said. "A ruthless, intimidating, self-righteous bully who thinks he can bulldoze over everyone else 'cause you have money and you know better. That's the part I don't like. But you care for Summer. You're trying to protect her. I like that, even if right now, the sight of you makes me wanna barf."

"I—"

"Quiet." She lifted a bony hand in the air. "I want you to go back and check me out some more."

"The research is done."

"Look again, genius," she said. "If you do, you'll find out that I bought my condo at Fountain Way the year before Summer's mother died, but rented it out until I moved down to Miami a year later. Until then, I lived in New York where I worked as a secretary for the public school system. Check it out. You'll see."

Could it be true?

"I'm telling you the truth." Louise clasped her hands on her lap and glowered at me. "Now, Mr. Erickson, get out, and don't come back until you've got your facts straight and the name of the scum who hired George Peterson to kill Summer."

TWENTY-FOUR

BY THE TIME I saw Seth off to Juneau for his meeting with the governor, Hector waited for me, anxious to talk about E&E's project. I deferred breakfast in favor of meeting with him. We met in an alcove at the main house, because I wanted to be nearby in case of a Louise china crisis, even though Hector insisted we'd get more work done at his lodgings in the lighthouse. Sometime mid-morning, I promised him I would meet him out there with the blueprints, after I checked on Louise.

I wandered about the big house, looking for my stepmother. She wasn't in her room. She wasn't in the dining room either. One of the maids mentioned she'd seen Louise in Astrid's library. I rushed up the stairs.

I erupted into the library, fearing another scene of destruction like last night's. Astrid's devil dogs made a line for me, but I didn't miss a stride. I snapped my fingers, commanded them to sit, and scoured the library for the site of the next skirmish.

The surreal scene that faced me didn't include broken china or brawling crones. The morning light poured through the windows to illuminate a card table set against the sound's dramatic background. Louise and Astrid sat opposite to each other, playing bridge in a most unlikely pairing. They teamed up against none other than a stone-faced Robert and Anya Golov, who waved at me before making her play.

"Hello there," Astrid called out cheerfully. "Might I offer you some tea?"

Astrid was offering me tea. Me. Tea. She was playing cards with Louise. My eyes wandered over the impressive pile of single dollar bills evenly distributed between Astrid and Louise.

God almighty. I pinched myself. Was I sleepwalking again?

Louise picked up a card from the pile and shot me a side-glance. "Cat ate your tongue?"

"Miss Silva hasn't had her café-con-leche yet," Robert put in. "Master Erickson says she won't function without it."

"Oh, that explains it." Anya reached for a platter from the sideboard and offered it to me. "How about some pickled fish to get your metabolism churning?"

It was my stomach that went into a churn. "Perhaps a little later." The bile soured my mouth. "Is…is everything all right?"

"Of course. Everything's fine." Louise pinched a slice of fish from Anya's tray, folded it into a little tube, and popped it into her mouth. "Not bad."

Sometime last night the universe had flipped over and the world had turned upside down.

Astrid smiled. "You never told me your stepmother was an accomplished bridge player."

"She's a cheater, that's what she is," Anya grumbled, setting the platter aside. "And so are you, Astrid Erickson. Together, you two are the scourge of the earth. So get off your high horse and prepare to lose your Depends. Robert didn't draft me out of the homestead to be roadkill for you two."

"Certainly not." Robert examined Louise's discard

before picking another card from the pile. "With all due respect to the mistresses, I expect we shall win this contest."

"That accent." Louise fanned her face. "It tickles my G-spot."

"Louise!"

She pursed her pink pout. "What?"

I stared at her, mortified. "You need to zip it!"

"Now, child, more respect." Astrid arched her silver eyebrows. "Louise, dear, if you ask me, you gave this one too much leeway with her mouth growing up."

"True," Louise said. "She was always fast with her tongue and hot with her temper."

"Still is," Astrid observed.

"Miss Silva is also unable to follow directions," Robert added.

"And she has no patience," Anya put in. "Not even an ounce."

Had I died and gone to hell?

"The problem with my Summer is that she's a worrywart." Louise tapped her acrylic nails on the green felt. "She worries about everything. She's too sensitive. Everything sticks. Her mind's like a cow, chewing cud. I tell her to chill all the time. She's gonna get an ulcer by thirty."

Anya winked at me. "Some people don't know when to stop chasing worries."

Time to get out of this place. I backed away from the table, because I wasn't about to turn my back on those four.

"I have some work to do," I mumbled, still in shock.

"Go ahead," Astrid said. "I'll be delighted to entertain your stepmother. She's really a talent, you know."

Enough surrealism for one day.

I hightailed it out of the library, afraid of breaking what had to be a powerful peacekeeping spell. I didn't know which of the witches in there was responsible for it, and I didn't care. Alternatively, they were playing charades, conspiring to throw me off. Surely, as soon as I left, Louise would throw up Anya's pickled fish on Astrid's lap and the bickering would begin. I donned a scarf and my coat, grabbed the blueprints from Seth's room and dashed down the stairs. I wasn't about to second-guess my luck.

On my way to the lighthouse, Alex ambushed me at the verandah. He stepped out from behind the door, cradling his tablet against his chest. His arm was no longer in a sling, but with his nose still swollen from last night's fight and with his eyes bruised, he looked like a giant raccoon.

"Why if it isn't our sweet, enterprising Summer." He blocked my path. "I've been waiting to talk to you."

I tried to sidestep him. "You and I have nothing to talk about."

"Au contraire." Alex shifted to block my path again. "We have much to discuss. About Seth. About your missing sister."

"Go try your tricks on someone else." I swerved around him. "I'm not up for your lies."

"Running off to the lighthouse again?"

His tone froze my steps.

"We all know what you like to do over there." He leered. "Got to keep that hot Latin blood of yours pumping, I suppose."

My face burned, probably beet red. So he knew. Alex had been keeping tabs on us. I don't know why it surprised me. He had the money and the resources to do so without suffering from any moral or ethical dilemmas.

Devil dogs or demon cousins, I wasn't afraid of either, and I was really tired of Alex's clumsy attempts to turn me against Seth. Since he hadn't gotten the message last night, it was time to set him straight for good. I wheeled on my heels and confronted him.

"I'm going to the lighthouse to meet with my boss, who's staying there, strictly for work. So stop spreading rumors and causing trouble. Think of your family."

"The family, yes." Alex drew on his e-cig. "The Erickson brood seems suddenly fascinated by your tropical essence. Everybody is talking about you. Seth's girlfriend is so real, they say. In a strange twist, some of my brothers and sisters find you appealing and even Grandma has taken an interest in the hottest season of the year."

"Please." I tried not to roll my eyes but failed miserably. "It would do this family a lot of good if you focused your energies on building it up instead of trying to destroy it."

"My problem is with Seth," he said. "Do you expect me to let him run the family as if he was God and emperor?"

"Seth's a good man, trying his best," I said. "You and he share the same blood. Give him a break. I mean, really, what is it about him that rankles you so much?"

"That would be a long list."

"Maybe things could change," I said. "You could stop undermining Seth and talk to him, one adult to another. He'll listen. I guarantee it. Seth can be trusted."

The grin on Alex's face chilled my belly. "You seem so sure about that."

I squared my shoulder and stuck out my chin. "I'm sure."

"Allow me to dispel a myth." His malicious smile widened. "My dear cousin Seth is not nearly as perfect nor as trustable as you think he is. His character is irreparably broken. Your trust is misplaced."

"See?" I pointed at him with the blueprints. "This is exactly what I'm talking about. You're always putting him down, undermining him—"

"He knows where your sister is."

I wasn't sure I'd heard him right. "What?"

"Seth lied to you." Alex's stare bore into me. "He knew where Tammy was all along. He actually talked to her and Nikolai, days ago. He just didn't want you to know."

"I don't believe you," I said. "Seth knows I'm worried about Tammy. Why would he keep her whereabouts from me?"

"Because he wants to control you," Alex said, palms up, as if it should be obvious to me. "Because he wants to control everything and everyone. Face it, Summer. He's a power hog, a control freak. He lies, cheats, and deceives people for a living. He always gets his way."

"And what about you?" I snapped. "Aren't you fighting for control right now? Aren't you trying to manipulate me with your lies as we speak?"

"I won't deny I have a dog in this fight," he said. "But I'm telling you the truth. Seth knows, has known for a long time."

I shot him a cutting glance. "You're making this up."

"My information comes from reliable sources," Alex said. "Seth knew that, if you found your sister, you'd get out of Alaska faster than he could blink. He didn't want you to be free to make your own choices."

My stomach squeezed and I suppressed the frisson of foreboding that crept up my spine. Could there be an ounce of truth in what Alex was saying? No, he was a liar and a schemer. Seth wouldn't keep the truth from me. He wouldn't lie to me either. We were good together. We trusted each other.

But deep down, I also knew that Alex was mixing lies with truth. Seth was used to having his way and he wanted me to stay in Alaska. He'd worked hard to keep me in his house and in his life. I wasn't a fool. But lying? No, he knew better. He wouldn't lie, not to me.

"I suppose you need proof." Alex grabbed his tablet, punched some keys and thrust the screen before me. "Here. Take a look at this message stream."

"I don't need to look at anything." I crushed the blueprints to my chest and made a point to look away, fixing my stare on the noisy gulls rioting over the shoreline. "Whatever you have, it's fake. Seth's systems can't be hacked."

"Agreed," Alex said. "Seth's systems are solid and even my best people don't have superpowers. But Nikolai Golov? Poor thing. His devices don't even have virus protection. Take a look." Alex offered me the tablet. "If you don't want to believe me, that's your problem. But you owe it to yourself to at least consider the evidence."

I didn't want to look. I didn't want to credit Alex's schemes with even the slightest consideration. I didn't want to doubt Seth either. Looking at that screen felt like betrayal. But refuting Alex's so-called "evidence" was also the only way to put an end to his lies. Surely, I'd be able to identify the discrepancies and establish that the messages were fakes, created by Alex to discredit Seth.

I snatched the tablet from Alex's eager hands. I perused the screen. And there it was, an involved exchange, allegedly between Seth and Nikolai. I read through the messages, first quickly and then more slowly. My eyes tripped over the ones where a purported Seth related to a purported Nikolai our first visit with Anya. It explained how worried I was and how I'd almost gotten shot when I found Tammy's blanket on the line.

The details. They were spot-on, recounted by someone who'd been present during the events. I recognized Seth's voice in the messages, his stark, succinct style, trying to convince Nikolai to get Tammy to meet with me. These messages weren't fakes.

The bile rose in my throat. Seth had known where my sister was. He'd lied to me. That's why he'd been so lukewarm about my leads. That's why his guy had never come up with anything helpful. That's why he hadn't wanted me to go to Denali in the first place.

The gull's cackles seemed to be directed at me. Something inside of me broke. Whatever part of me generated my capacity to trust shattered all over again. My heart ached and my knees faltered. I plopped down on the steps. Seth knew where Tammy was. He hadn't told me. He'd lied to me.

I clamped down on my lips and swallowed the tears. No crying. I dipped my face in my hands. Pain and fury collided inside of me. For a full sixty seconds, the battle within annihilated my capacity to think. How could he?

"I can take you to your sister." Uninvited, Alex took a seat on the stairs next to me. "I can fly you out there right now. She'll confirm that Seth has known where she was for a while."

"You must be deluded if you think I'm going anywhere with you." I might be mad and hurt, but I wasn't stupid and, no matter what, I wasn't going to conspire with Alex to destroy Seth. Never. "You're not doing this for my benefit. You want to cause trouble for Seth? Well, kiss my ass. I'm *not* going with you."

"The jerk lied to you," Alex said. "I'm your only chance to get to your sister, now, today, before she makes the mistake of a lifetime."

My head snapped up. "What do you mean?"

Alex took the tablet from me and pulled up some photographs on the screen. "Once we hacked into Nikolai's devices, I hired a pair of private eyes to track down Tammy. They've gone along on your sister's little adventure, sending me nice pictures along the way. These are from this morning. By the way, your sister's hot. She looks happy, wouldn't you say?"

I stared at the pictures on Alex's tablet as he scrolled from one frame to the next. Blonde and sprite-like, Tammy pranced next to a dark-haired man who must be Nikolai as they exited an official-looking building somewhere in Alaska. In the next frame, Tammy pumped her fists in the air, holding up what looked like a paper of some sort.

"Would you like to know what that document is?" Alex said.

I covered my mouth. Oh, no. No, no, no.

"It's a marriage license."

Had Tammy gone insane? What was wrong with that girl? I wanted to throttle my sister. If Louise found out, all hell would break loose. Oh, my God. I had to stop

Tammy from ruining her life. She must be on a high. A manic state was the only possible explanation for this. I knew what a bad marriage was like. I knew the humiliation and indignities she'd have to endure.

The ground opened up beneath my feet. I'd been fine this morning, more than fine. Now I was freefalling. I had to think through the pain.

I spat the words between my clenched teeth. "Where is she now?"

"That's the million-dollar question, isn't it?" The ass had the gall to smirk.

"Don't you dare get in my way," I said. "This is important. I have to get to Tammy. I've got to find her right now."

"Far be it for me to get in the way of two loving sisters," Alex said. "My pilot is on standby. You can have this whole thing in the bag by nightfall, that is, if you're willing to do as I say."

Of course he'd want something in exchange.

"I want to see Seth's handwritten notes for the board meeting," Alex said. "I need to know what he has against me, so I can make my own adjustments. Given his security precautions, you're the only one who can get those notes for me."

"No." I didn't even have to think about it.

"Don't be rash," he said. "We'll make a brief stop at his house. Security won't let me in, but you? They'll let you in. You'll find the notes, copy them, put them back exactly where you found them and then deliver the copies to me. Notes in hand, I'll fly you out to your sister, where I'll give you thirty minutes to dissuade her of her folly."

"I'm not doing any of that," I said. "It's out of the question."

"I take it you're abandoning your sister to her fate then?"

Crap.

"I'll make this easy *and* enticing for you." Alex grinned like the cat about to eat the canary. "Fifty grand up front, deposited in your bank account the moment you deliver the notes to me and double that upon you landing in Miami."

My mouth must have been wide open. No sound made it through my throat. Alex was willing to spend a hundred thousand dollars, today, for Seth's notes. It was a lot of money for me. A hundred grand would erase my student debt. Hell, it was a lot of money for anybody. But most importantly, the offer confirmed that his failure to pin the Star Lake mess on Seth hadn't dissuaded him from his efforts. Alex was willing to do anything—anything—to defeat Seth and, since the board meeting was only three days away, that meant that we'd entered the critical, last minute period of this twisted game.

I remembered what Seth had said about Alex setting up a trap for him. Seth didn't know where, when and how, but he knew it was coming. On the other hand, if Alex was willing to make me such a reckless offer, what else did he have up his sleeve? Who else had he bought along the way? Most importantly, what was the trap he'd set for Seth?

The hot ball in my stomach churned with fear and anxiety. Sure, Seth had lied to me, and I was angry at him, livid really. I didn't know how to tackle the lie that had shaken my trust in him. But first things first. Seth was in more danger than he knew and, despite his smarts and resources, he might not be able to figure out Alex's plan in time. The board meeting was around the corner and Alex looked too smug and confident for my taste.

I made up my mind right there and then. No matter what, I was going to protect Seth. I wasn't going to allow Alex to destroy Seth. It wasn't going to happen, not on my watch.

Alex mistook the resolve that hardened my mouth for temptation.

"Yeah, a hundred grand for five minutes' work is a good return on your investment." His little eyes scoured my face. "Plus, you get your sister in the bargain. You're a practical soul. I bet you people can sniff the almighty dollar all the way from the other side of the Rio Grande. From one capitalist to another, I admire a good businesswoman."

I was Cuban American but I didn't appreciate the dig against our southern neighbors. I doubted that Alex knew enough geography to distinguish Cuba from Mexico and I got that he totally meant to insult me with his compliment. It didn't matter. I had a better chance to figure out what he was up to if he thought I was really interested in the money. One other thing. He was right about me. I was a practical soul. I intended to kill two birds with one stone. I'd find Tammy and figure out Alex's plan to destroy Seth in one bold move.

"*If I* decided to do this," I stressed the *if* for effect, "what's the plan?"

"Smart girl." Alex beamed. "You do this job for me and you don't have to face Seth ever again. So, here's what we do. I fly you out to your sister. After you meet with Tammy and before Seth gets back from Juneau, I'll put you on a flight to Miami, first class, my treat."

Alex was no slouch, making sure I was nowhere around when Seth got back, but I didn't say that aloud.

"Oh, and before we go," Alex said casually, "when we go to the house to retrieve the notes? I want you to leave a little card on Seth's bed." He pulled out a sheet of stationery emblazoned with the Erickson seal. "You just have to write one word and pen your signature. Then we're in business."

This had been at the heart of Alex's plan all along. Destroy Seth on a personal level, make him feel betrayed and abandoned so that he would fall apart and falter at the board meeting. Alex was a cruel, underhanded rat. I had to hope he'd underestimated Seth's fortitude, because there was no doubt in my mind of what I had to do next.

"Fine," I said. "Take me to my sister first, then we'll tackle the rest."

"Yeah, sure," Alex said. "But first, I'll need your cell." He reached over, plucked my cell from where it stuck out from my jeans' front pocket and tucked it inside his jacket. "Don't worry, sweetheart, you won't be needing it during the next few hours."

Sweetheart? My teeth ached from clenching.

He flashed a grin, satisfied that he'd removed my only means of communication. "There are a couple of small details you should know. In the unlikely event that you may be considering deviating from my instructions, I have some insurance in place."

A twinge of fear penetrated my inner armor. "Insurance?"

"Insurance," Alex repeated sternly. "Should you

change your mind or decide against following through with our agreement, I have an agent among the servants, someone loyal to me, who's right here on the grounds. This well-placed person will tell your stepmother about your stepsister."

"So?"

"Imagine your stepmother's reaction." Alex shook his head in mock sorrow. "How many more Mings would you like to see destroyed?"

Talk about a guy with severe character deficiencies.

"The vase my stepmother broke wasn't a Ming." I sounded a tad too prim. "Seth said so."

"And you believed him?" Alex's laughter matched the gull's creepy cackles. "Grandma doesn't do fakes. You should know that by now. Even if that vase wasn't a Ming, it was a pricey one. I guarantee it. But Seth, he didn't want you to get upset and bolt out of Alaska, never to look back. So he lied to you. Again."

Oh, my God. Alex was right. An avid collector like Astrid wouldn't allow anything other than originals on her shelves. What was wrong with me?

"There will be no telling what your stepmother will do when she finds out about your sister's plans." Alex rummaged through his pocket and held up a thumb drive. "And to make sure everything goes according to plan, there's also this." He inserted the drive into the tablet. "I couldn't hack Seth's personal systems, so I had my people hack into his security company instead. It took a while and it cost me a pretty penny, but we hit the jackpot early this morning. They were able to salvage a single frame from the company's deleted surveillance footage to find this gem."

The grainy, black-and-white image on the screen imprinted on my retinas and pierced right through my heart. It showed me, naked on Seth's dining room table in a very compromising position.

"Inspired, don't you think?" He flashed his fangs like the lowlife vampire he was. "This is the only copy currently in existence, but it won't be, if you refuse to work with me."

"But..." The roll of blueprints crumpled beneath my fingers. "Seth...He swore there were no pictures."

"Third time in a row," he said. "Seth lied to you."

My past slammed into my present. The collision obliterated my senses. It was happening. Just like before. Alex had a picture. A picture! Just like Sergio. And like Sergio, Alex would use thc picture against me, unless I found a way to prevent him from doing so. I was caught in Alex's net and drowning.

Alex pulled out his cell and, keeping his eyes on me, clicked on a programmed number. "We're ready to go," he informed the person on the other side of the line. "Begin the disruption pattern."

Disruption pattern? I realized Alex meant to neutralize Seth's security precautions and shake off any tails Seth had put on Alex. Talk about a screwed-up family. And yet I couldn't even begin to imagine what would happen to the Ericksons if Alex succeeded. The family itself was at stake.

Alex put away his cell and flashed the smug smirk that irked and nauseated me at the same time. "I know Seth keeps close tabs on me. He's a paranoid son of a bitch and he's got eyes on you as well. But don't worry, sweetheart." He took the blueprints from my hands and dropped them into one of the verandah's plush outdoor sofas. "I've got resources too. We're about to blindside almighty Seth. By the time he figures this one out, you'll be long gone and he'll be done."

I forced my mouth shut and my feet to move. Suppressing an urge to claw Alex's eyes out, I gritted my teeth some more and walked with him. *Don't lose it, Silva.*

Not now. I had to find Tammy. I had to figure out the nuts and bolts of Alex's plan. I had to keep Seth safe. I had to do all of that, while preventing Alex from triggering my stepmother's wrath and keeping my naked pictures off the internet. I'd had only a few choices before. Now, I had none.

TWENTY-FIVE

ALEX HAD CHOSEN his Benedict Arnold perfectly, a fact clearly illustrated when the security guards saw me and allowed the Range Rover to drive into Seth's property without questions. The chauffer parked in front of the stairs that ascended to the front door.

"Let me show you something," Alex said before I got out of the car. He held up his tablet. It showed the empty spaces inside Seth's cabin. "This is what they call in the hacking business a ten-minute hijack. Nobody will ever know, but my tech experts have created a distraction and broken into the security company visual surveillance systems. For the next few minutes, I'll be able to monitor your activities."

Damn. Alex hadn't been able to compromise Seth's personal archives, but his experts had been able to penetrate the security company's defenses and hijack the live feed broadcast from the cabin's monitoring cameras. Crap. I'd hoped to leave a warning behind for Seth, but it wasn't possible if Alex was able to see everything I did inside the house. I examined the six frames on the screen. Correction. Almost everything.

"Don't speak to the guards and don't bother trying to use the phone or the computers," he warned as I opened the door and stepped out of the Land Rover. "The lines are temporarily out of service."

The rat was being thorough. "What's wrong, Alex?"

I said, mockingly. “You don’t think greed is enough motivation?”

“Greed is the best motivator, but I won’t take any chances with you. Hustle. You’ve got ten minutes. If you’re not back in ten, you’ll suffer the consequences.” Alex glanced at his watch. “Your time starts…now.”

I slammed the door and made for the stairs. My boots crunched on the frost on the ground. I waved and smiled at the security guards. Questions from them right now would be disastrous in all fronts. I trotted up the stairs, heart pounding in my ears. I punched the security code, ran the key card through the slot and raced to Seth’s office. If Seth’s systems were operational, he’d be alerted that I’d entered the house, but he wouldn’t be suspicious of my presence here.

Seth’s detailed notes for the board meeting were right there in his desk’s top drawer, along with the supporting documentation. He trusted his security arrangements and me, so he hadn’t even locked the desk. I knew where he kept his notes, but I pretended to look around, rummaging through several of his well-stocked drawers. While I did that, I stole a few useful things and concealed them in the sleeves of my jacket, before I turned to the right drawer.

I grabbed the notes, turned to the printer and started to make copies, scanning the succinct, bulleted sentences. Talk about a set of well researched and impressively laid out arguments. It was his vision of the company’s future that impressed me the most. Seth’s brilliance shone through on every point. Standing with my back to where I calculated the security camera would be hidden, the bulk of those copies ended up inside my coat.

The need for an emergency potty break was too real

to ignore. I turned around, faced the camera, crossed my legs, placed my hand on my belly and pointed at the restroom door, conveying the urgent message of my aching bladder, before I darted into the bathroom adjacent to Seth's study. My grueling years studying architecture had equipped me with a set of unusual, old-fashioned skills that came to my assistance now. Hard deadlines had built me into the quick, last-minute Houdini I reverted to inside the bathroom. I was also good at multitasking. A girl could work and pee at the same time. *Focus, Silva.*

You can do this.

I tossed the evidence in the trash. I toyed with the idea of leaving a notc in the bathroom explaining my actions but ultimately decided against it. Seth didn't use this bathroom much and the chances of his finding the note were low. Most importantly, I wasn't sure what he'd do if he came home and found the note before I could explain. I feared he might go after Alex with a vengeance and then I'd have an even bigger mess on my hands.

But that didn't mean I couldn't warn Seth somehow. I pulled out the monogrammed card that Alex had insisted I bring along from my now discreetly stuffed front pocket. Alex had made me pen the single word and the signature while in the car. Given the lack of time, I added a line, before I tucked it back into my pocket.

I took a deep breath and dashed out of the bathroom, back to prime time and the printer, where I organized, collated, and copied like the devil himself. When I was done, I returned the originals to the drawers. I made sure they were out of order, the only real warning I could leave behind for Seth. I had no idea if he'd even notice.

The clocks mounted on the wall of Seth's office

showed the time across the globe, New York, London, Tokyo, Dubai. But it was the rapidly changing digital display showing the local time that prevented me from further improvisation. The blue numbers announced I had less than two minutes left.

I raced to Seth's bedroom and placed that stupid card on his pillow. It was clearly my handwriting, even if the script looked crooked. My hand had been shaking hard when I wrote it. Out of time, I ran out of the house, leaving my aching heart behind, along with that note, and an invisible trail of grief.

I wondered if Seth would ever forgive me for leaving behind that note. I might not forgive myself. But it was necessary if the rest of my plan was going to succeed. And then again, he'd lied to me. Lied.

I felt like a zombie as I delivered copies of Seth's notes to Alex, numb but rotten to the core and falling apart piece by piece. Alex reviewed the copies. I swear, if he kept smirking like that, I might not be able to prevent myself from socking him again. As the Range Rover sped to the airfield, Alex instructed someone over his cell to transfer the money into my bank account. I felt like throwing up. The transfer established a hard trail of treason. Talk about breaking trust. That's how Seth would look at this.

I didn't know much about airplanes, but I learned a great deal during my brief visit to the Erickson hangars while Alex threw a monumental tantrum. Apparently, Gina had "borrowed" his jet for a shopping trip to Seattle and wasn't due back until later today. The kink in Alex's carefully laid plans enraged him. The obscenities that poured out of his mouth made his seasoned pilot blush. He and I traded suffering looks.

"I'm Joe Pilot," he said, shaking my hand.

Joe Pilot? Was he pulling my leg? "I'm Summer."

"Are you sure you want to hang out with this guy?"

"Zero alternative."

"Sorry," he said. "Some of us are just gluttons for punishment."

Joe Pilot interrupted Alex's tantrum to assure him that a turboprop would be a better choice for this particular trip anyway. The airport at our destination had a short gravel runway better suited for small aircraft.

Eventually, a suitable plane was found, a brand-new, shiny Beechcraft Baron Alex disliked on the spot because it had none of the amenities he enjoyed, like a full galley, a bar, and the affection of the flight attendant who was currently Gina's shopping companion.

Such were the problems of the rich and spoiled.

"You do realize that there's a low pressure system parked right off the coast?" the pilot said as we boarded. "It's stationary so far, but it's gathering strength and, if it starts moving, we'll have a small window of opportunity to get in and out."

"Go for it," Alex said, fastening his seat belt. "Get this clunker in the air."

The flight took two endless hours of banging and rattling. The new plane smell contributed to the sensory overload that fueled my pervasive case of nausea. My stomach lurched from my throat to my heels as the little plane negotiated the cloud cover. We motored through sun, sleet, rain, and snow as if riding a motorcycle in the sky.

Alex scoured the notes, his eyes ping-ponging over the papers, his sly grin getting wider by the page.

"Good stuff?" I asked.

"Excellent stuff," he mumbled, licking his finger before he turned the page.

"You think you got him?"

"I *know* I got him."

His certainty sent shivers down my spine.

I tried again. "Do you have a smoking gun?"

"Of course I do and these notes tell me he has no clue what's coming his way."

Crap.

His eyes lifted and his stare met mine, sparkling with amusement. "I bet you've got some other morsels for me. I'm happy to pay a little more for dirt that sticks."

He wanted me to give him dirt on Seth. On his character. Fat chance. I'd already given Alex all he was going to get from me. I deflected his latest efforts with small, meaningless talk, because if I sent him to hell like I wanted to, greed would no longer suffice as my cover for being here.

A burst of severe turbulence rattled the plane. My fear of flying returned in full force. I clenched my teeth and dug my nails into my seat.

Alex laughed his cruel cackles. "Not a frequent flyer?"

"More of a terrestrial animal." I gagged and tried really hard not to vomit in his lap. After that, he left me more or less alone with my thoughts.

I tried to keep panic at bay by focusing my attention on the radar. For the first part of our trip, we flew due north along Highway Four, high over Denali National Park and the Alaskan Range, a route I'd flown once before. After that, a few openings in the cloud cover allowed me to catch glimpses of the Yukon River below, as it weaved in and out of our path. At that point, the flight got so rough I had to close my eyes and hold on for dear life.

All I could think about was Seth. As soon as he found out what I'd done, he'd hate me. I'd given him enough reasons for him to think I'd betrayed him. And if he looked at my bank account…yikes. His rage would be fast and profound. I closed my eyes and prayed that, someday, he'd find enough reasons to forgive me.

My mind drifted. The memories of our time together soothed and tormented me at the same time. Seth's stingy smile, so rarely given at the beginning, so generously offered as of late. His body, warm and solid between my arms, his mouth so eager for mine, his hands, hot as they slid between my legs…

The fear of never seeing him again, combined with a memory of the grainy image of me naked on his table, uncorked a plug in my mind. Visions of our first night together burst through. The memories poured out, vivid, bright, and intense. For the first time ever, I remembered the sleepwalking episode in detail. It was…extraordinary.

My body tingled as I recalled the passion of Seth's first caresses, the need in his eyes. He'd been so kind and gentle, so intense and passionate. My pussy grew moist as I recalled the care that went into our union, the need that transformed our lives. I understood why the moment had been so important to Seth. It had been important to me too, but all this time, he'd carried the burden of that knowledge for both of us.

The sweet memories scattered when the plane plunged into another pothole in the sky. My stomach bounced to my throat and got stuck there. I groped for a barf bag but couldn't find one. Alex shot me a glare that said *if you vomit, I'll press the eject button.* I swallowed an acid gulp, forgave Seth for lying to me, and begged God to give me a chance to buy back all my sins. I was pretty sure I was going to die today.

From the air, our destination was but a tiny disruption in the tundra's immensity, a chicken scratch on the earth along the Dalton's lonely line. The landing was Joe Pilot's finest moment. The plane bounded on the gravel runway like a basketball then skidded to a stop. I stumbled out of the aircraft repressing an impulse to kiss the earth beneath my feet.

A decrepit sign announced our arrival at Coldfoot, Alaska, population ten. It comprised an old miner's cabin, a cluster of rusting buildings, and a rambling restaurant that served as post office, general store, tourist center, rest stop, and gas station. I had enough presence of mind to take in the details. The weathered marquee announced the highest gas prices in the United States along with a perverse ultimatum: *Next Services, 240 miles.* All of this next to one of the most prolific oil pipelines in the world.

Go figure.

Alex's cronies waited for us in the parking lot, two burly guys with scruffy beards and matching beer bellies. They started to give Alex a full report of their "monitoring" activities, but I wasn't in the mood to wait.

"Where is she?" I demanded, scouring the grounds. "Is she in the hotel?"

"She's hunkered over there." One of the men gestured at the huge truck parked on the lot.

I marched over to the gleaming freightliner, but whirled on Alex when he attempted to follow me.

"You didn't pay enough for a first-row seat," I

snapped. "This reunion is not for your benefit, so stay out of my way."

My fury must have been convincing. Alex fell behind, but he called after me.

"Thirty minutes," he said. "That's all you have. And not a word of our agreement to your sister. If I find out you've told her, you'll forfeit the balance of your honorarium."

"Scum," I muttered under my breath. As if I cared about the money. Honorarium my ass.

My head throbbed and the space between my shoulders ached, tight as a drum. I was literally at the end of my proverbial rope. But today was all about solutions and Tammy's problem was also going to get resolved, right now.

I climbed up on the driver's side door and, balancing on the steps like a monkey, banged on the truck. Within seconds, the window framed a dark-haired man with high cheekbones, a hooked nose, and a pair of striking eyebrows that spiked when he saw me. His thin lips set into a grim line. He motioned for me to get down.

"I'm not going away," I yelled. "So open the damn door!"

He lowered the window a tad. "If I open the door, I'll knock you off the steps."

"Oh." Fury and stress could make me stupid.

I climbed down, he opened the door and then I climbed up again.

"I'm Nikolai," he said, holding out his hand.

I ignored the man's hand and glared at him. "Where is she? You might as well tell me right now. I'm not moving until you tell me."

"I'm right here." My sister stepped into the cab from the back of the truck.

I'd been prepared to face Tammy in the midst of a manic state, eyes glimmering with madness, words firing out of her mouth in a furious rat-a-tat, hands gesticulating wildly. Alternatively, I had prepared to find Tammy in a profound state of depression, sad, disheveled, and inconsolable.

But the woman who faced me didn't show any obvious signs of bipolar disorder. She stood there, smiling at me, calm but alert, wearing a pair of killer jeans and a royal blue turtleneck that complimented her coloring and looked amazing on her.

"Please, sis." She pouted prettily. "Don't be mad at me."

It was hard not to succumb to Tammy's natural charm. With her creamy complexion and her sparkling hazel eyes, her beauty was irresistible to most people. But I made a serious effort to dislike her. Yes, sir, I did. I clung to my anger with all I had.

Tammy had put me through so much. She'd made me leave Miami and travel to Alaska. She was the reason I'd had to endure cold, discomfort, stress, and all sorts of new and unfathomable experiences, some of which I'd rather soon forget. She'd precipitated the events that had landed me in Seth's bed and then, because of her, I'd had to betray the only man I'd ever loved. I tried to be mad at Tammy. I really did. Then she smiled.

After all this time looking for my sister, after all the hassle, worry and anxiety, the fury just melted off me like butter on toast. I threw myself into Tammy's embrace.

"I'm sorry I worried you." She sniffled. "I didn't mean to make a mess of things."

"It's okay." I hugged her tightly, breathing in her familiar baby powder scent, spiced with a sharp note of...diesel fuel? I loosened my grip and, keeping my hands on her shoulders, pulled back a little to examine her closely. "Are you okay?"

"I'm doing great." She wiped a tear from my cheek. "I have so much to tell you!"

"Why don't we all have a seat?" Nikolai said. "Can I offer you some coffee?"

I looked to Tammy.

She nodded. "He makes the best café-con-leche."

"Second best," I muttered, locking stares with Nikolai.

What did I see in his black eyes?

Concern for my sister, to whom he seemed connected by an invisible cable, but also a desire to please her that appeased me a little. I spotted a bit of Anya in him as well, or was that a glimpse of his yega?

"Sorry," I mumbled. "I didn't mean to be totally rude."

He didn't miss a beat. "For Tammy, I can take all the rude you've got."

I gave him his first point on my mental scoreboard. "Coffee would be great."

Tammy and I sat on the convertible sofa in the back of the truck. Nikolai served a round of coffee and took a seat on a stool across from us. The truck's sleeping compartment turned out to be a nice but compact space, including a small desk, a kitchenette, and a tiny bathroom in addition to the seating area that doubled as a bedroom.

Tammy lifted her hands in the air and gestured around her. "You like?"

"Very nice," I said.

"It's fifty percent mine."

I jerked, spilling the coffee all over my lap. "What?"

"Don't get all bent out of shape." Tammy grabbed some paper towels and wiped up the mess. "Before you go berserk, let me explain."

"It's Louise who's going to go nuts when she hears about this."

"You might not scream, holler or break the china," Tammy said. "But you get really angry when things don't go as planned. Whether it's the silent treatment or the torture interrogation, you're truly terrifying. And, oh, the glare. It wilts flowers. I told Nikolai. It's the stuff of nightmares."

Seth had sort of implied the same thing. Was I really that bad? Me, the voice of reason in the Silva family, the point of balance?

"This is not about me," I said. "It's about you."

"Allow me to explain," she said. "I know I'm your little sister. You take care of me and I appreciate it, especially when I'm sick..." She choked. "I love you so much!"

I squeezed her hand. "You left so suddenly and we were so worried."

"I had to go, Summer," she said, "I was suffocating in my own breath. I know you and Mom love me. I know I suffer from a chronic disease. It's rough some days and it's not going to go away, but it doesn't mean I can't grow up and be an adult and run my own life."

"Of course not."

"So I grew up," she said with a certainty that left me spinning. "I took charge of my own life. It wasn't the chemical imbalance driving my decisions. It was me."

She eyed Nikolai, who sat quietly on his stool. "I need you to know. I've been talking to Nikolai for a long time. I didn't take off after a random guy I met on the internet like you told all those people."

I bit my lips and winced. "You know about that?"

"Who doesn't?" Tammy grabbed a wrinkled paper from the desk and showed it to me. It was a printed copy of one of the flyers I'd emailed to everybody and their mothers. "The whole state of Alaska knows I'm a dumb blonde."

"Sorry," I mumbled, a little embarrassed. "But you ran away with a total stranger..."

"I met Nikolai in an exclusive chatroom for truck aficionados." Tammy smiled at Nikolai and he smiled back. "Three years I've known this guy."

"Three years?" I swallowed the lump in my throat. Three years was a good, solid amount of time to get to know someone and a lot better than three weeks.

"He came down to see me in Miami. Last year. Remember when I went on that four-day cruise to the Bahamas with my girlfriends? Well, I didn't go with the girls. I went with Nikolai. We had a great time together."

"Knowing someone from afar is very different from day-to-day living."

"That's why I came," Tammy said. "Nikolai wanted me to meet his family. He wanted to make sure I could be happy in Alaska. We wanted to see what it would be like to live and work together."

I frowned. "Work together?"

Tammy nodded excitedly. "Yes, listen to this. I've already completed a six-month online program on commercial driving management. I got an A. Me. An A!"

It was hard to believe. Tammy had barely managed

to graduate from high school, flunked out of college and was never able to stick with her community college classes.

"Next week," she said, "I start a sixteen-day class to get my commercial freightliner driver's license. After that, I'm doing my internship. In this truck. With Nikolai, who's had a commercial driver's license for ten years. And after that, we already have a contract for long-distance cargo hauling, right here in Alaska."

I stared at Tammy, willing my mouth to stay closed. Tammy had committed to something. Tammy had completed a course. Tammy, my little sister, irresponsible, willful, impulsive Tammy who'd never earned a penny in her life, had lined up an employment contract and a way to make a living.

Wake up, Summer.

You're dreaming again.

Reality check. What if this was a different stage of her disease? What if this was a new kind of manic, a subversive, harder-to-detect symptom of her bipolarity, a tricky turn that would blow up in our faces?

"I know what you're thinking," Tammy said. "I'm not in a manic stage. I'm as balanced and stable as I've ever been. I feel great and I'm fully medicated. Ask Nikolai."

I glanced at Nikolai. "So he knows everything?"

"Of course he knows," Tammy said. "He's known for a while. He has to if he's going to be with me. He has a brother who's bipolar."

"Is that true?" I asked.

"My brother gets along fine when he's on his meds and so does your sister," Nikolai said. "Tammy's gotten really good at taking her meds. When she forgets, I remind her."

Reminding Tammy to take her meds had been my job. I was the one who counted her pills, organized them every Sunday and made sure she took them properly. I took care of Tammy. Correction. I used to take care of Tammy.

I took in Nikolai's face, the dark curls framing a strong nose. How did I really feel about my replacement? How did I feel about giving up my caregiver's role?

Empty. Scared. A little sad but also relieved. It had been such a large part of my life for so long.

"I'm thinking clearly," Tammy assured me. "Unlike you and Mom, Nikolai doesn't think that someone with bipolar disease is a cripple."

I cringed. Was she right? Was that how I'd thought of Tammy all these years? Out of love and fear, had I been too overprotective of my sister?

"Tammy knows what she's doing," Nikolai offered in his quiet way. "And she's a hell of a good driver. She's good even on sheer ice."

Unlike her idiot of a sister.

"Tammy's smart," Nikolai said. "She knows her mechanics. She's passionate about trucks, but you know that. I'm not at the top of the food chain yet, but I've got a stake in my family's homestead and a place of my own. I work hard, I make a good living and Tammy will never go without if she sticks with me. I love her. It's why I asked her to marry me."

"And I did," Tammy said. "This morning."

The blood drained out of my veins. My fingers and toes went numb. I'd known they had a marriage license when I came out to Coldfoot, but I'd hoped to stop them before they got married. But I was too late. Nikolai had asked Tammy to marry her and she had accepted. They were married now. Married!

"Marriage is such a…" Terrible state of slavery? Dreadful type of dependency? Trap? The words got stuck in my throat.

"I know you had a bad experience," Tammy said. "But I want to be married. I want children. Don't you want kids someday? Mom and Dad had a great life together. Why couldn't we have it too?"

Why indeed?

Because I was a biased, bitter, self-righteous, burned-out bitch who measured other people's lives by my own failures.

I took a deep breath. "Why didn't you tell me that this is what you wanted?"

"Would you have believed me?" she asked. "Let's not even talk about Mom. She would've forbidden me to come. Tell me the truth, Summer: Would you have allowed your sick little sister to go chasing after her dreams?"

She was right. I would have said no a thousand times. I'd come here to save my sister from Nikolai and return her safely home. Instead, I'd discovered my own prejudices. In trying to help Tammy, I'd done more harm than good. I'd failed to see that her happiness depended on her abilities rather than mine. I'd suffocated her with my care. I'd tried to design her life when she wanted to draw up her own plans. She had a right to chase after her own dreams. It was all very hard to take, but it was the honest truth.

Something changed at that moment. In my mind, I opened my fist and let the wind flow through my fingers. The knot that had tortured my stomach for the last three weeks dissipated. My sister had turned into a woman, capable of making her own decisions. She didn't need me anymore. And it was okay.

"I knew you were looking for me," Tammy said. "But I needed the time away to make sure this was the right thing for me. I thought I was done for when Seth Erickson found us."

So Seth had found Tammy, like Alex said, and then decided not to tell me. "When did he find you?"

"He tracked us down smack in the middle of the Star Lake mess," Tammy said. "His chief of cyber security located us. He contacted Nikolai and patched Seth through. Seth drilled Nikolai. Boy, that guy's relentless. We had several conversations."

The sting burned hotter than ever.

"Please, don't be mad at him," Tammy said. "I begged him not to tell you where I was. He told me how worried you were."

"I was scared," I said. "You left your blankie behind."

"I don't need it anymore," she said with confidence that blew me away. "That's why I left it. Seth tried everything to persuade me to contact you. He even flew out to Fairbanks one night to meet with us."

Fairbanks, yes, I remembered that trip.

"He said he needed to lay eyes on me to make sure I was healthy and happy. I'm pretty sure he would've forcibly flown me back to you if I hadn't been a hundred percent. He did good by me, Summer. Promise me you won't hold him responsible for my actions."

"He lied to me." It was impossible to overlook the fact or ignore the violent way in which my stomach lurched every time I thought about it. "How can I not be mad at him?"

"I made him swear not to tell you," Tammy said. "I wanted a few more days so I could come to you, commercial driver's license in hand and make you proud. Seth was so nice to us. He even arranged for that contract to drive for E&E."

Sounded like Seth all right, always arranging everything for everybody, always agenting people's successes.

"He went out of his way to help us," Tammy said. "He must really like you."

After today, "liked" was probably the better word.

"Tell me the truth," Tammy said. "Do you like him?"

"What kind of question is that?"

"A good one," Tammy said.

"I'm mad at him right now," I said. "It's sort of complicated."

"Come on, Summer, tell me."

"Maybe I like him a little bit." I held my thumb and index finger close together. "But only when he's not lying to me."

"You love him!" Tammy squealed, jumping up and down on her seat. "Nikolai, my sister is finally in love!"

My face had to be glowing red.

The truck door rattled, startling us. Alex, I was sure. Nikolai went up front, lowered the window, and talked to him briefly.

"That jerk wants me to tell you that your thirty minutes are up," Nikolai said. "What's he talking about and why are you hanging out with the one Erickson I can't stomach?"

"It's a long story," I said. "I'll have to tell it to you some other time."

"He says there's weather coming in," Nikolai said. "If you're going to fly, you have to leave now. But you're welcome to stay. You can ride with us if you want to."

Ride with them. It was tempting. Ride the road without worries, live in the present without concerns, chase a dream, any dream, perhaps even my best dream, the one I'd found in Alaska.

But inasmuch as I'd have loved the opportunity to escape my choices at the moment, I couldn't afford the luxury of a quick getaway. I had to go back. I had work to do. I had to find out what Alex had over Seth.

Tammy and Nikolai walked me to the airplane.

"You better take care of my little sister," I said to Nikolai.

"Done." Nikolai stopped a few feet behind us to give Tammy and me a little privacy.

"If you need anything," I said to Tammy, "if you need me to give that new husband of yours a kick in the ass, just call me, okay?"

"Promise," Tammy said. "Summer?"

"Yes?"

"Do you know what I like best about Nikolai?"

"What?"

"He doesn't see me as a sick person," she said. "He's not blind. He sees my disease, but he looks past it, to see me, who I am, what I'm capable of doing."

"You chose well, then." I hugged her tightly, imbuing her with my love, my blessings and my honest wish that, in this new adventure, she'd find the happiness she deserved.

"What about you?" Tammy said. "What do you like

best about Seth Erickson, mind you, when you're not raving mad at him?"

I didn't have to think about it long.

"Same as you," I said. "Same thing exactly."

A LIGHT SPRINKLE of snow fell from the leaden sky and a gust of wind snapped the weather sock at the end of the runway as we taxied.

"The front is on the move," Joe Pilot announced. "We're cutting it close."

"We have three whole hours before the storm hits," Alex said, dismissing the pilot's concerns. "Plenty of time to get this young lady out to Anchorage and on to Miami. Let's get out of this hellhole."

By the self-satisfied expression pasted on his face, things were definitely going his way.

On the way back, the clouds closed rank, but the ride was a million times smoother. The calm before the storm had arrived. We flew sandwiched between two dense layers of clouds in a pocket of smooth air. Every so often the clouds would break. A few times, I thought I saw an eagle flying nearby. I couldn't stop thinking about Seth. His kindness to my sister warmed my heart, yet he had still decided to lie to me, his girlfriend. Could eagles fly this high?

The peaks of the Alaskan Range poked through the clouds like islands in the sea. I turned my attention to my next goal. I didn't think Alex was simply going to tell me about his trap for Seth. The way I saw it, I had one chance at finding out. If I hadn't figured it out by the time we got to Anchorage, I'd refuse to get on the plane until he told me. I'd make a scene if I had to and I was willing to risk the consequences to get the information I needed. Alex needed me out of the way, so I had a shot.

We were roughly at the halfway point when the indicators on the instrument panel went offline. The radar quit. Joe Pilot flicked his fingers against the panel, but nothing came back on.

"Mountain Traffic, this is Beechcraft Baron, Eight-Romeo-Papa," he reported over the radio. "Come in, Mountain Traffic."

Nothing.

"We must be having some sort of electric short," the pilot said. "The instruments are playing hooky and the radio is off. Switching off to visual."

I had no idea of what that meant, but I didn't like the way it sounded. Neither did I like the coughing fit that rattled the propeller outside my window.

"Uh-oh," Joe said.

Uh-oh? It wasn't a sound you wanted to hear from your pilot when flying over the Range.

"What's happening?" Alex demanded.

"Stand by." Joe executed several different maneuvers to restart the stalled engine with little success. The propeller outside my window sputtered some more and then stopped spinning altogether.

"I suppose we're just going to have to find us a place to land," Joe muttered.

I croaked. "A place to land?"

"We can't land in the middle of nowhere," Alex said. "There's a storm coming!"

"Since you insisted we had to fly today, we have no choice." The pilot's jaw tightened as he clicked on the inert radio. "Mayday, mayday, mayday. This is..."

My ears stopped processing. I got stuck on the word

"mayday." I'd watched enough movies to know I didn't want to hear those words mid-flight. I tightened my seat belt and started to pray.

"The weather is closed in behind us," Joe said. "But we've got a break ahead."

The aircraft punched through the opening in the clouds. I spotted the luminous blue glimmer of a glacier below us. A vertical rock face topped with sharp spikes rose on one side. On the other side, a sheer wall of snow and ice cased us into a narrow canyon. The fuselage shook as wind streamed down the canyon and pummeled the plane. Alarms blared. We rattled like peanuts in a can. My mind was both blank and numb. I prayed some more.

The remaining engine held. The pilot banked sharply, dove and aimed for the snow-covered flat ahead. The airplane swooped down, coasting over the terrain, losing altitude in a controlled descent. The pilot fought to keep the plane straight. My eyes registered the long valley at the bottom of the mountains. We were going to make it.

A burst of wind grabbed hold of the plane and rocked it to one side then the other. Joe compensated for the first tilt, but the second burst was too strong. Jagged spires of granite tore off the right wing. The door went with it. With a groan and a screech, the fuselage crumpled around me like aluminum foil. The cold wind punched into the cabin and hit me in the face. I was distantly aware of Alex screaming, but my eyes were fixed on the white face of the mountain, coming straight at us.

TWENTY-SIX

THE MEETING WITH the governor went well. The signing happened without a hitch and the flight back took a little less than two hours in the Learjet. Spider reached me while in the air.

"I've hit the jackpot," he announced on my screen without preamble. "I hacked into the policy and confirmed a few things after that. You're not going to believe it."

My gut twisted. "Hit me."

The stream of information unfolded in images before me as Spider explained his findings. One by one, the pieces of evidence connected, creating a complicated but complete puzzle which revealed who was responsible for hiring George Peterson and most importantly, why. Jesus Christ. My jaw was about to break. I should've seen it before. Summer was not going to like it. I bristled but kept my cool. We'd done the fieldwork; now it was time to bring in the authorities.

"You have enough to justify a warrant," I said. "Notify the troopers. Have them meet me at the house this afternoon. I want to be there. I'll contact Robert so he knows what to expect."

"Got it," Spider said.

"Anything else?"

"One small thing," Spider said. "Report on Summer's ex."

"Go ahead."

"Sergio De Havilland was the victim of an unfortunate crime in Rio yesterday. His Ferrari's tires were slashed in a public parking lot."

I sighed. "When I said retribution, I didn't mean petty stuff like that."

"Oh, that was me being petty, not you." Spider grinned. "You actually blocked the multi-million-dollar loan that the bank was going to give Pretty Boy in order to cover the deficits in his father's account."

I suppressed a smile. "You weren't supposed to know about that."

"It was way too interesting not to follow," Spider said. "Your international leverage is impressive. Now Sergio will have to face his father's wrath. I hear the old man's anger is Machiavellian, kind of like yours. If at any point you decide to forgive this guy's trespasses, you need to let me know."

"Why?"

"So I can take him off the no-fly list."

"You grounded him abroad like a terrorist?" Not bad. "I like it."

"I thought you would," Spider said, grinning. "This guy is going to be wondering where his luck went for the rest of his life. Remind me never to piss you off, okay?"

"Done," I said. "I'll let you know how the takedown goes. Thanks, Spider. You've been a real asset."

As soon as the Learjet landed, I headed straight for home. I'd received security notifications that showed Summer had returned to the cabin earlier in the day. I didn't blame her. She probably needed a break from Ericksonland. It worked for me. We had a lot to talk about.

Besides, I was looking forward to our time alone and craving her like crazy.

But Summer was not in the cabin. She wasn't answering her cell either. When I contacted Robert, he said he hadn't seen her since mid-morning. Additional inquiries showed she wasn't with Louise or Hector Carrera. I grilled Carrera over the cell. He mentioned she had promised to return to the lighthouse with the blueprints for the E&E project and yet she hadn't. It wasn't like Summer. Instant worry.

I dialed security while I scoured the house. As soon as the agent on duty picked up, I barked into my cell. "Where the hell is she?"

"Miss Silva left from the Erickson hangars earlier today," the agent reported.

"Why didn't you notify me?"

"We did notify you, right away, sir."

"What the hell?" Had I missed the notifications? I halted in the hallway and scrolled through my messages. "I've got an automatic notification from the cabin's security system at ten twenty-four. I've got nothing from you."

"Sir?" Confusion wasn't a trait I relished on any of my staff. "We had several communications back and forth with you, where you acknowledged our coms and authorized the subject's movements."

I stared at the goddamn cell. "Come again?"

"I've got the messages right here." A keyboard clicked on the other side of the line. "I've got your replies as well."

"I didn't get your damn messages," I muttered into the cell. "Whatever instructions you received, they weren't from me."

"Let me run a systems check," the man said. "The only other alternatives involve a communication breach, system security failure, or some sort of an intercept."

Intercept?

I growled. "Give me a rundown of the original communications."

"Subject left the big house at about ten hundred," the man recited. "Arrived on-site twenty-two minutes after that. Cleared security. Entered the house. Remained in the house for approximately ten minutes, rode out to the hangars and boarded E&E's Beechcraft Baron, Eight-Romeo-Papa, destination Coldfoot, Alaska."

Coldfoot, Alaska?

"Who transported Miss Silva to the cabin and the hangars?" I demanded. "Who authorized the use of the airplane?"

"As reported in our original communications," the man said. "Miss Silva left with Alexander Erickson."

Son of a bitch.

"Mr. Erickson?" the security officer said. "According to our records, you were informed of this and you authorized Miss Silva's actions."

"The hell I did."

I clicked off the cell and marched into my bedroom haunted by a horrible sense of déjà vu. My heart pumped in my throat and my stomach clenched. And there it was. The monogrammed card. Right on my pillow. Only it wasn't from Gina, whose betrayal hadn't been unexpected or mourned. It was from Summer, whose betrayal set me ablaze.

I was in the Pave Hawk's cockpit. Alarms blared. The cockpit was on fire. Shawn was gone, leaving behind only gruesome, smoldering remains. Screams came from the cabin. Smoke choked my lungs. I couldn't see. The helo spun into a death spiral, plummeting to the ground. I fought the dying machine with all I had, lungs burning with heat, body screaming with pain, mind focused on the emergency maneuvers drilled into my brain. The ground was too close, too close. I didn't know if we could survive the landing…

My knees hit the floor next to the bed. The heat burned through me with the zeal of fire. Sweat broke out on my forehead and pooled over my lip. I didn't want to read that note. I didn't want to crash and burn all over again. But I braced myself for the worst, gritted my teeth and snatched the note from the pillow.

The note was identical to the one Gina had left, down to the Erickson seal embossed on the linen stationery. Only this time, Summer's signature appeared at the bottom instead of Gina's inconsequential one. Another difference glared at me, a single line inscribed below the signature like an afterthought. *You lied to me.*

She knew. Summer knew. That I had found her sister.

How?

Alex. Son of a bitch. It had to be him. He was the only one with the motivation and the resources to orchestrate the sophisticated maneuvering needed to pull this off. I punched a message into my cell. *We've been compromised.* I texted Spider the single command that would neutralize Alex's technological attack for good: *Seek and destroy.*

With that taken care of, I got up to my feet and I tramped to the office. My meeting notes were scattered in the drawer. They'd been compromised as well. I understood the gist of Alex's plan.

The fury burning through my veins paralyzed me. I

sat down on my chair, crossed my arms on the desk and rested my forehead on my arms. The phone vibrated in my hand. *Shut the fuck up*. I had to think. I didn't want to talk to anyone. The cell kept buzzing with annoying, humanlike stubbornness. I glanced at the screen. I had several 911s from Jer, Spider, Robert, my office, you name it. I didn't care. I just sat there, caught in a vortex of rage and confusion, clutching that card until my hand ached.

Like the cell, the damn landline wouldn't stop ringing. My senses were distantly aware of the racket. The doorbell chimed and somebody pounded on the front doors. I'm not sure how much time passed before Jer burst into my office.

"Bad news," he said. "You've got to come with me."

"Not now," I said. "Get the hell out of here."

"But—"

"Fuck off." I lifted my head and glowered. "Whatever it is, I don't give a shit."

Jer's jaw tightened. "We've got an emergency."

"You handle it."

"We need you," Jer said. "Everyone is waiting for you."

"Tell them I don't give a flying fuck."

Summer was gone. Summer had left me? Knowing her, it seemed impossible, implausible, and yet the reports were clear. She'd gone. With Alex. It was all I could think about.

"So you know?" Jer said. "You know what happened?"

Of course I knew. Alex had persuaded Summer to betray me and Summer, after finding out I'd lied to her, had left. Maybe she had good reason to leave me. Perhaps I deserved this. But she could've called me. She could've asked me to explain. A huge part of me rebelled at the deliberate cruelty she and Alex had built into their actions.

"Surely there's something that can be done," Jer was saying. "The pilot said they were alive when he left the site hours ago."

I had to cut through a thick haze. "What pilot?"

"The pilot who was flying the Baron when it went down!"

The Baron?

"You mean E&E's Eight-Romeo-Papa?"

"It's bad, Seth." Jer shook his head. "A rescue is simply not possible. The darkness. Hurricane-force winds. They crashed in the Range and there's a storm about to hit."

"Crashed?" Had I heard that right? "The Beechcraft Baron crashed?"

"So you don't know?" Jer's eyes widened, his mouth twisted with grief. "The plane crashed. Alex was on it. And Seth? There's something else you need to know." He paused then forced out the words. "Summer was also on that plane."

TWENTY-SEVEN

My head throbbed and the warm blood running down my face hued the world crimson. I wiped my eyes, groped around and released my seat belt, only to plummet headfirst a short distance, onto what had once been the roof of the aircraft. Somehow, I found my knees, righted myself on all fours, and crawled out of the wreckage.

A white expanse tilted at a sharp angle before me. The front of the aircraft was gone, along with one of the wings, ripped off the fuselage. The back end of the plane perched precariously on a crag, shadowed by a snow ledge and overlooking a small hanging valley.

The wind cut through me like a frozen blade. I forced my mind to work. Alaska 101. Get warm, Silva. Stay dry. I zipped up my coat, groped through my pockets and donned my gloves, scarf, and knit hat. We had crashed. Unbelievable. In the Alaskan wilderness no less. What were the odds?

"I'm *not* going to die here." My dad hadn't fought in a revolution, defied a dictator, clung to a raft, fought off the sharks for three days in the Florida Straits and become Miami's foremost architect for me to die in this frozen expanse.

I ran my hands over my limbs. Arms and legs were there. Check. Fingers and toes intact. Check. Heart beating, lungs breathing, brain churning, albeit slowly. Check.

A spot stung at my hairline under my beanie, but other than the pain across my chest where the seat belt had held me in place, I seemed to be okay.

A burst of movement caught my attention. My eyes focused on the blinding whiteness. I spotted parts of the plane, crumpled metal strewn across the slope. A dark shadow trudged toward me through an ocean of deep snow. I peered into a slanting horizon. I recognized Joe Pilot as he came closer. I waved both arms in the air. I was so happy to see him.

A groan came from somewhere behind me. Alex. Where was Alex? I crawled back into the wreck. Alex hung upside down from his seat. As I reached out to try to help him, his seat belt gave way. He crashed next to me, screaming in pain.

I leaned over his crumpled shape. "Are you okay?"

"My leg." He groaned and grabbed me by my coat. "Help me!"

"Easy now." I extricated myself from his hold. "Let me take a look."

I ran my hand carefully over his right leg. The lower bones yielded like broken twigs beneath my fingers. The leg was severely fractured and any attempt to move it could result in more damage and shards breaking through the bruised flesh.

"Is he going to make it?" It was Joe, crouching right behind me, wearing a pack on his back. A bruise darkened his face and a nasty cut slashed the side of his head from ear to chin, but otherwise, he seemed calm and focused.

Alex, on the other hand, was about to lose it. "Am I going to die?"

"You're going to be all right," I said with fake certainty. "We just need to put the leg into a splint and stabilize the injury."

How the hell did I know that?

Thank God for the Discovery Channel. I took in small breaths to slow down my racing heart. And now, for the small details. "Do you perchance know how to splint a broken leg?"

Joe shrugged. "I can try. There should be some sort of an emergency kit somewhere in the back. There should be an emergency booklet with it."

"Hang on," I said to myself as much as to the other two. "I'll be right back."

I crawled to the back of the plane, reached up, opened the compartment beneath the bench seat and retrieved the emergency bag. I unzipped it and examined the contents. It included several thermal blankets, water boxes, self-heating ready-to-eat meals, and a decent supply of bandages, painkillers, and disinfectants.

I fed Alex the painkillers, then the pilot and I got to work on his leg, using the bandages from the kit and a piece of paneling we ripped from the cabin. It was difficult. Alex cried the entire time and, even with my gloves on, my fingers were stiff from the cold.

When we were done, I wrapped Alex snug in the blankets. The pilot rummaged through the emergency supplies and selected a compass, a flashlight, and a few other things, all of which he dropped in his backpack.

"The storm was moving at a good clip," he said. "It will be here in no time. We need to leave now."

"Leave?" I squeaked. "To where?"

"There's a mountaineering school that keeps summer headquarters nearby." He zipped up the backpack and clutched an axe in his hand. "Depending on the weather, we might be able to reach it in a few hours. The school is already closed for the season, but if we get lucky, we could break in and use their radio equipment to call for help."

"Wait," I said. "Isn't rescue already on the way? Don't they know we went down? Isn't this plane equipped with a locator beacon?"

"Yes, the plane is equipped with an Emergency Locator Transmitter and, provided it wasn't damaged in the crash, it should be operating right now. But…"

"But what?"

"It's satellite based." His gaze studied the sky. "We're pretty well encased in the mountains and that's a thick cloud cover above us. It's only bound to get thicker as the storm arrives. There's a good chance someone heard our mayday, but the towers won't know our exact location, only our last coordinates before they lost track of us."

Crap.

"What about these?" I held up a bright orange, radio-like object I found in the emergency bag. "Can't we use these to communicate our position?"

"This is a SPOT, a global beacon." Joe took it from me and switched it on. "It's designed to transmit our location and call for help, but it's satellite based too. See the red light? It's not able to hook up. But just in case, we'll deploy it as a backup to the ELT. Pass me the strobe light as well. We should mark this location as well as we can."

He stepped outside the wreckage and duct-taped the tracker and the emergency strobe light to the crumpled fuselage, before he returned to crouch next to me.

"Our best hope is to reach the mountaineering school," he said.

"What about me?" Alex whimpered. "I can't walk, let alone trek through deep snow."

"You'll have to stay here while we go for help." The stone-faced pilot donned the backpack and fixed his eyes on me. "Are you ready?"

I wished we had a different option, but Joe was right. Alex was in no condition to attempt a descent, let alone a long hike through the deep snow. We had to get out of here and soon.

"I pay your salary," Alex said with mind-boggling arrogance. "I forbid you to go."

"You can forbid me all you want," Joe said. "But we'll all die here if we stay put. Daylight will be gone soon. The temperatures are about to plummet. The weather will become lethal. If we're not out of here by then…" He left the rest unsaid.

"I swear," Alex said. "If you leave me here, I'll fire your ass!"

"No need," Joe said. "The hell with this job."

Alex opened his mouth to shout, but Joe lifted a gloved finger in the air.

"My best advice is to you is to stay warm and be quiet," he said. "You are on borrowed time. If you look outside, you'll see a protruding lip of snow and a chute, both prone to avalanches and very sensitive to noise. Need I say more?"

The wreck. The storm. The plummeting temperatures. The avalanche threat. It was too much to take in. There were too many ways to die out here, and all of them applied today.

"You can't leave me behind," Alex pleaded. "You can't leave me all alone here."

"It's the only option," the pilot said. "We'll send help

as soon as we can. Summer? We need to get going. We have to make the best use of the daylight."

Get going, Silva. I tightened my boot laces and rose to my feet. *Time's ticking.* I wrapped my scarf around my face and followed the pilot. A stiff wind buffeted me as soon as I stepped out of the wreckage. As I took in the white desolation, the doubts pummeled me too. The odds of survival got worse with every second I hesitated. On the other hand, I was—well—me, and like it or not, Alex was Seth's family.

"You go." I lowered the scarf on my face. "I'll stay with Alex."

"Bad idea," Joe said. "He's really not worth your life."

Who knew whose life was valuable and why?

I had to stay, but a new concern had me second-guessing my decision. What if Seth found out about the crash? What if in a moment of monumental stupidity, he made the wrong decision and came after us?

My stomach clenched. Was there any danger of that happening? Seth would be really pissed at me right about now. With my actions today, I'd pretty much written myself out of his equation. God, he probably hated me.

But I couldn't overlook his nature. He'd consistently displayed a propensity for trouble and a habit for heroism. He was a seasoned pilot and he knew the Range, but he wasn't crazy, was he? What if he tried and then got hurt trying to get to us?

"Joe, listen to me very carefully," I said. "When you get to the school and radio for help, tell them we're okay. Tell them we're prepared to wait out the storm. We've got food and supplies. Under no circumstances are they to attempt a rescue while the storm is raging. It's too dangerous."

"You don't understand," Joe said. "The conditions will only get worse."

"I'll do everything I can do keep us warm and safe," I said. "But I don't want anyone else hurt because of us." Especially not Seth. "And if perchance, you have to face Seth Erickson, and if at any time he expresses even a remote wish to mount a rescue attempt, tell him to stay put. Okay? In the unlikely situation he insists, give him a message from me. Tell him that I said no. Flying a helicopter into a superstorm is even more dangerous than staying here. Don't let him come. Send rescue only *after* the storm passes. Will you please make sure that Seth stays safely on the ground?"

"You're a brave one." The pilot shook his head. "Foolish, but brave. Given this terrain, I can't drag you out of here against your will. Are you sure?"

"Yes."

He started to walk away.

"Hey, Joe?" I said. "Is Joe Pilot your real name?"

He shrugged. "With a name like that, what else could I be but a pilot?"

"You're a good one."

"Only you would say that, considering the circumstances."

"The three of us are alive when we shouldn't be." I waved. "Good luck, Joe Pilot."

I watched him work his way down the face of the mountain, cringing every time the snow rushed after him in small avalanches. The sun set at about the same time he reached the valley below. I lost sight of him beyond the snowdrifts.

Alex gawked when he saw me. "Why the hell are you here?"

"Don't be a knucklehead." I crouched next to him and rummaged through the emergency bag. "I thought you and I could bond over some s'mores. In the absence of graham crackers and marshmallows, my company will have to suffice."

I handed him some water and food rations, before I climbed out of the wreckage and located the luggage compartment. Stored in there, I found a couple of tarps, no doubt used to protect the airplane against the weather. Using what remained of the duct tape, the tarps, the seat cushions, and anything else I could find, I created a small cocoon for us in the very back of the plane. Moving slowly, I dragged Alex as far in as I could and made him as comfortable as the circumstances allowed. It was still cold back there, but at least we were out of the wind. I studied the mountain through the back window. If the slope held, we had a chance.

"Jackpot," I said, when I found a few packages of chemical hand warmers in the bag.

I opened a pack and handed them to Alex before I inserted the next pair into my gloves in an effort to defrost my fingertips. I kept Alex busy for a while with an inventory of our supplies. We found a fire starter in the kit, but the strong odor of fuel and the leaking tanks dissuaded us from using it.

As the sun set, the storm arrived in full force. The wind pummeled the fuselage and seeped into our little shelter, chilling my bones. I turned off the flashlight to conserve the battery. In the darkness, we huddled together under the thermal blankets, listening to the wind howling outside. *To bad weather, a brave face.* Easier said than done when the weather turned deadly.

"We're going to die," Alex muttered, shivering next to me. "If an avalanche doesn't get us, the cold will kill us. We're going to freeze like Popsicles."

"Hey, I'm trying to stay positive over here." I rubbed my arms and legs to keep the blood flowing.

"You are such a fool." Alex scoffed. "You could've hiked your way to safety."

"And if the situation had been reversed," I said. "Would you've left me behind?"

"Absolutely yes." He snickered in the darkness. "Until a couple of hours ago, I had no reason in the world to like you, none whatsoever."

"And here I was, suspecting you liked me from day one."

His snickers petered off into a coughing fit.

"Allow me to dispel a myth," he said after a while. "There will be no rescue for us today. Nobody in their right mind would take to the air tonight, not with this monster storm raging. The airspace will be closed. A rescue is simply not possible."

"Then they'll come tomorrow," I said. "After the storm."

"We'll be a pretty pair of ice sculptures by the time they find us."

"Think good thoughts." I closed my eyes. "Right now, I'm imagining Seth lying on the cowhide chaise by the fireplace." A little flame burned inside me when I visualized him safe and sound.

"You really do love him," Alex said.

"Is that really so hard to believe?"

He exhaled a pained breath. "I guess not."

A little honesty from Alex. How refreshing.

"Why do you hate Seth so much?"

"You wouldn't understand."

"Try me." I rubbed my gloved fingers together.

"It'd be a waste of time."

"Time's something we have at the moment."

"True." He hesitated. "All my life I had to prove myself against Seth. It gets tiresome after a while."

"Prove yourself?" I said. "How?"

"In school, he was always the genius with the high grades," Alex said. "In high school he was the honor student who was also the quarterback. Fishing, hunting, mushing, hiking, he excelled at everything he tried. The girls liked him and the boys respected him. Nobody ever tried to bully Seth Erickson. Alex Erickson? Maybe. Seth had to pound a few jerks on my behalf in middle school. Everybody liked Seth. Including me."

"So you liked Seth way back when?"

"What was there not to like?" Alex squirmed next to me. "We had fun together. We even talked about going to MIT together. He got in on his first try. Me? I barely managed to get into a third-rate college and only because my father made a sizable donation."

"Please don't tell me you hate Seth because he got into MIT and you didn't."

"Nah."

"What changed?"

"Life changed," Alex said. "Did Seth ever tell you the story of AEE?"

"No," I said, blowing into my cupped hands to warm my nose. "What does it stand for?"

"Alex Erickson's Enterprises," he said, voice shivering. "A few years ago, I started my own business. I modeled it after E&E's business plan. I wanted to give Seth a run for his money and show everybody else that I could do better than Seth at the helm of my own company."

"What happened?"

"I went broke, of course." A note of inevitability dulled Alex's voice. "I was up to my eyeballs in debt. Do you know what the SOB did to me?"

"What?"

"He went behind my back and paid all my debts out of his own pocket before the bankruptcy became public knowledge. He didn't tell anyone, not even Grandma. Then he offered me my old position back at E&E."

Yep, just like Seth.

"Some people would've been deliriously happy with an outcome like that."

Alex scoffed. "It was humiliating. But then I saw my chance when Seth had to go to Afghanistan. I ran the company for almost a year. Sure, he supervised my decisions remotely, but I did fine. Just when I was getting the hang of things, the guy comes back, physically destroyed, but mentally? He was all there. It stunk. I had all this power and authority. As soon as Seth was back on his feet, it was all gone."

It was just like Alex to blame Seth for a harrowing recovery. Something was broken inside of Alex, his ability to measure reality, his capability to empathize with others, his compassion meter. What could cause someone to ignore the pain of others and focus only on themselves?

"Seth always comes up with the winning play," Alex said. "He helped me so he could feel morally superior to me."

God. If he kept talking like this, I might just take my

chances with the storm and hike out of the Range just to get away from the weasel.

"I think Seth tried to help you because you're his family and he cares." I refused to give Alex a pass. "Which is why I find it so strange that, instead of being grateful, you take every opportunity to harm him. You even tried to frame him for the spill at Star Lake."

"Ah, that." Alex snickered. "Almost got him. It was well done, don't you think? I might have succeeded outright if it wasn't for the Golov woman and you."

"You sound so proud of yourself."

"I was going to win in the end," Alex said. "I was all set to end Seth's tenure."

"I doubt that."

The skepticism in my voice did the job, needling Alex's ego.

"This time, it was going to happen," he said with audible glee. "I would've loved to live long enough to see Seth's face at the board meeting when he realizes that he's still caught in my web. Do you think Grandma will postpone the board meeting until after the mourning period is over?"

Alex just couldn't stop thinking about himself. Right now, he was taking perverse pleasure in imagining his family grieving his death. I suppressed the sudden image that flashed in my mind of Louise and Tammy crying over my grave. No self-pity allowed. Instead, my ears perked up. I concentrated on something Alex had just said. We might be stranded, freezing and in mortal danger, but if there was a chance for me to identify the trap that Alex had laid for Seth, then I was going to try.

"What do you mean with that bit about Seth still being caught in your web?"

"I suppose there's no harm in telling you now," Alex said. "You and I, we're history. Seth thinks he has proof against me for bribing the lumber mill's supervisor and purchasing the poison. But by the time the Feds finish their investigation, they'll be able to trace the money, not to my accounts, as Seth expects, but to his own accounts. Wait until everybody gets a load that dear awesome Seth is stealing from the company. Seth doesn't know it, but he's a dead man walking."

Had I really stayed behind with this poor excuse of a human being?

"You are a piece of work," I muttered. "I hate you right now."

I closed my eyes, wrung my hands and wished I had a way to warn Seth of the next trap awaiting him. I wished I had the strength to pummel Alex to oblivion. But my limbs were weak and my core temperature matched that of a freezer's. My head hurt and a heavy haze settled over my senses, until all I wanted to do was go to sleep.

"Stay awake." Alex shook me. "You won't wake up if you fall asleep. Keep talking. It'll help you stay alert."

"You're a snake," I mumbled. "A freaking dirtbag. I still don't understand why you hate Seth so much. All this talk, and not a clue."

"Right." Alex said. "Let's see how you'd feel if your own father, in his last will and testament, chose your cousin over you to run his precious company."

And there it was. The simple reason that fueled Alex's primal hatred for Seth. Alex's father had agreed that Seth was the better candidate to run E&E. It wasn't something Alex could forget or forgive. And since Alex's father was dead, Seth had to pay the price, because revenge was the only force powering Alex's miserable life.

I mustered my strength to move my lips. "I'm sorry."

"For what?" Alex said.

"For your grief," I said. "I know you miss your father. But competing with Seth isn't going to bring him back. Neither would it change the choice that your father made many years ago. All your efforts, all that scheming and plotting, they were for nothing."

"There you go again." Alex slurred his words. "Psychobabble."

Things seemed crystal clear to my frozen mind.

"It's too late for you to make your father proud," I said. "But you could make your grandma proud, and your family too, your future wife, your kids. Hell, I bet you could make Seth proud of you if put your mind to it."

He snorted. "Why would I want to make Seth proud?"

"Because deep down inside, you respect and admire him."

Alex went silent. A long time passed. At least it seemed that way to me. God, it was cold! The wreckage trembled with wallops from the wind. The snow blew in horizontal layers outside. The slope was fat with accumulation, perfect for avalanching. I clutched my frozen hands and prayed that the storm passed quickly, because otherwise, we weren't going to make it.

"It's too late," Alex murmured next to me.

"Too late for what?"

"To change anything," he said. "Seth will fall into the trap. Without Seth and with me gone, the company will eventually fall into the hands of strangers. I won't care. I'll be dead."

"Would you do anything differently if you survived?"

"Maybe," he mumbled. "I don't know."

"Promise me," I said. "Promise me that if you survive, you'll make peace with Seth."

He grunted. "Like you'd believe anything I'd say."

"Blame the present circumstances for my ingenuity."

Alex was quiet for a long time. I thought he'd gone to sleep. A mercy. I was shivering too hard to think. My limbs were numb. My eyelids grew heavy. My mind entered a wooly world where dreams offered a much better alternative to the present. At some point, Alex's hand groped for mine. I woke up. He placed a hard object between my fingertips, the thumb drive that contained that awful picture.

"I mean to die better than I lived," he mumbled, voice barely audible. "I swear," he added, before he fell silent.

IN MY DREAM, Aurora Borealis illuminated the landscape with green and purple swipes of her long, shimmering mane. I stood at the top the Range beneath the glowing skies like a lonely figurine atop a magnificent tiered cake. The snow tasted sweet as icing between my lips. The wind was gone. The cold was but a distant memory.

I followed a fresh set of tracks on the snow, the prints of bare feet, which ended at the edge of a cliff. From those prints, my mother emerged, black hair garnished with a crown of icicles, eyes glimmering with the Northern Lights' reflection.

"You found me," she said. "After all this time, you've come to the end of the chase."

My eyes met hers. "All this time I've been chasing after you?"

"You've been chasing me," she said, "in order to get to the truth."

"What truth?"

"Look inside."

When I next knew, I stood at the Fountain Way apartment, a little girl hiding behind the door, listening to my mother as she pleaded for her life. I peeked out and saw her, standing against the far wall, facing a man who had his back to me. A third voice came from somewhere to my right, a deep baritone whose owner I couldn't see from where I stood.

"You had to do it," the man said. "You had to poke your damn nose in other people's business and push the envelope. You leave me no choice."

"Wait!" My mother's lips made a sound I couldn't hear. "Please, don't do this."

"Too late," the man said, opening the front door. "Finish this," he added as he left the room.

The scene rewound in my mind. It played in slow motion several times, until I could see and hear even the smallest details.

"Wait, Hector!" This time, my mother's voice came through clearly. "Please, don't do this."

I caught a glimpse of Hector Carrera as he walked out of the apartment, leaving my mother to die in Peterson's hands.

Hector Carrera. My heart hammered my chest. My father's partner? My family's benefactor? My mother had found out something that threatened Hector and because of it, Hector had had her killed. And now he wanted me dead too?

I couldn't understand why he'd want me dead. I'd been good for his business. I'd worked hard. But whatever the reason, it had started a long time ago and it explained his behavior in the last few weeks. He'd been so mad when I left Miami. And after Peterson failed at

Star Lake, he'd been so eager for me to go back. He'd come all the way to Alaska. My God. Had he come to kill me himself?

The truth. The memories in a dream. The reason why my mother had to die. That's what I'd been chasing all this time.

"Wake up, Summer." My mother's face lit up the sky with a dazzling flash that awakened my senses, then disappeared with the Aurora.

The wind screeched in my ears and tore into me with arctic teeth. My feet ached. My hands did too. The cold. Oh, my God. It was back with a vengeance. I made a huge effort to lift my eyelids. The world exploded with white light. It hurt my eyes. Where was I?

I was no longer tucked inside the wreckage with Alex. I was out in the elements! Had I been sleepwalking?

The night spun around me in a white maelstrom. In a swirl of snow, a strange figure, the source of that bright light, stood before me. My brain couldn't make a rational connection between the sight and my senses. It made a huge leap. The yeti maybe?

Dreaming, yes, I was dreaming. About the yeti? I giggled a little and tiny puffs of condensed breath steamed from the top of my scarf and brushed against my cold cheeks.

Growling. Pushing. I was too cold to be afraid, too woolly to make sense of anything. But the creature was bossy. It barked over the howl of the wind as it turned me around and shoved me forward.

I should've been afraid, only I wasn't. I was beyond fear, beyond cold. I was totally numb, past reason and logic, past the grasp of terror, standing at the very edge of oblivion, where nothing mattered anymore and things just looked and sounded…funny?

In less than four steps, I stumbled through the tarp and into our precarious shelter. Relief. At least the wind wasn't hitting me straight on. A beam illuminated the small space. Alex lay beneath the blankets, covered by a thin layer of frost. Slow breaths puffed out of his nose in tiny bursts of vapor. He was still alive.

I knuckled my eyes. Yes, I must have been walking in my sleep. But I remembered the dream. I usually didn't remember anything when I sleepwalked. Maybe I'd been somewhere in between dream and reality, like when I'd been under the water at Star Lake, at the boundary between life and death where knowledge meets awareness.

I looked down at my gloved hands. No flashlight. Where was the light coming from? I whirled on my knees. There it was again. The yeti. Wearing a blinding headlamp. But mythological creatures didn't wear subzero protective clothing, goggles, boots, the works. They didn't carry a huge pack, or coils of ropes and carabiners strapped around their waists, or ice axes and flashlights.

The creature knelt before me and lifted the goggles from its face. From the slits of a black facemask, yellow eyes flecked with brown and gold pierced through me. I recognized those eyes.

He couldn't be here. It was impossible. Was I still dreaming? I put my gloved hand over my mouth and giggled. Yes, dreaming. That had to be it. God knew, Seth made frequent guest appearances in my dreams.

"Keep it together." Seth's arms closed around me. He held me against his chest while I giggled hysterically. "It's all right, Summer. It's going to be all right."

"Am I hallucinating?"

"I'm here," Seth said, pulling up his facemask. "But we've got to move quickly. The lip above can cave anytime. Do you understand?"

I undid my scarf and pinched my frozen face. Perhaps I felt something beneath the numb skin. I was awake. Seth was here. My stomach lurched. Oh, no. No!

"Tell me you're are not here," I begged. "Tell me you are far away from here."

"Sorry."

"You are going to die!" I said. "Why would you do something so foolish as to try to rescue us?"

"Rescue you?" He gave me a skeptical look. "On a night like this? Are you crazy? Who said anything about a rescue?"

I frowned. "So you're not here to rescue us?"

"No, ma'am," he said. "I'm not so deranged as to think I could."

"Then why on earth did you come?"

"Oh, that." He smiled. "I've got an idea."

TWENTY-EIGHT

I TOOK STOCK of Summer first, then Alex. Summer was banged up and extremely cold, but she was alive, alert, and mobile. Consistent with Joe Pilot's report, Alex couldn't walk and nothing I could do would change that. I eyed the slope shifting in the wind, gathering more snow as the storm continued, and looked at my high-tech mountaineering watch. Time to get moving.

I opened my pack and systematically laid out the highly specialized gear I'd selected and hauled up the mountain.

"Put that on." I handed Summer an arctic-rated overcoat, sub-zero-tested gloves, a pair of high-performance hiking boots, a facemask, goggles, a helmet with a headlamp, and a set of crampons. "Don't leave any part of your skin exposed. Understand?"

"But..."

"Summer?" I unpacked more gear. "Hustle. No time for explanations."

"What about Alex?" Summer said, donning the gear.

I grumbled. "Wouldn't mind leaving him behind."

"Seth!"

"But I won't." I crouched next to Alex and shook him gently.

Alex came out of hibernation groggily.

"You're here?" His eyes focused on my face. "But... how?"

"Questions later." I gave him a shot of morphine and, careful not to jostle his leg, fitted him into an arctic-rated sleeping bag. I tightened the hood around his face. "Hike time."

"But I can't..."

"I know." I unpacked the extra-light rescue sled I'd attached to my pack and folded it out. "We're doing this the old-fashioned way."

"Oh, fuck." Alex grimaced.

I worked quickly. With Summer's help, I strapped Alex into the sled, bundled him up and secured the pulling ropes in place. Next, I put Summer into a harness and clipped it through a length of rope to my belt. She wasn't going anywhere without me.

I did a last systems check and shouldered my pack. "Here we go."

"Are you sure?" Summer said, lowering her goggles over her eyes.

"Affirmative," I grabbed the lines of Alex's sled. "The slope is unstable. The worst of the storm is yet to come. According to the radar, there will be a slight break in the weather in..." I checked my watch. "Three minutes. It's now or never."

"And if we get down?" she asked.

"*When* we get down," I said, "we'll tackle the next set of challenges. For now, I need you to concentrate on putting one foot in front of the other and following my instructions. Got it?"

Her throat swallowed, but to her credit, she nodded, pulled up her neck guard, and followed me out of the wreckage. I lowered my goggles, covered my face, and pulled the sled to the nearby outcrop. I'd taken the time to set up the ropes during my ascent. It had been a grueling, time-consuming process, but in the darkness, without the ropes, the descent could not be managed.

Once at the outcrop, I secured the sled in place and hooked Summer to the vertical rope system. The wind had died down some, but it was hard to relay proper instructions.

"You go first," I shouted.

"I want to go with you," she shouted back, voice muffled by her facemask.

"Need you down there," I shouted. "To receive Alex."

It was about the only way she'd agree to go first.

I belayed Summer down the slope as fast as I dared. My heart beat in my throat every time I lost sight of the light of her headlamp. She did well. By the time she signaled that she had reached the bottom with a flare, we'd made good time.

"Your turn," I said, rigging the sled into the vertical rope system.

Alex's goggles cased the darkness below with obvious fear. "What if I fall?"

"I won't let you fall."

Belaying the sled proved to be a lot more challenging than belaying Summer. The sled got stuck in the snow a couple of times. The second time, I had to belay myself down half the slope and re-rig the sled. I relied on my technical skills to bridge the transition. My own body challenged the process. The cold took a huge toll on my strength. My biceps ached, my back strained and my thighs burned like hell.

The temperature had dropped tremendously by the time the sled finally arrived at the bottom. I climbed down the last of the slope. The wind clobbered me as if I were a punching bag. It almost knocked me off the slope a couple of times. My crampons found level ground at about the time that the storm regained full strength. Alex had passed out and Summer was on her knees. Time for a quick gear change.

I unstrapped the snowshoes from my pack, helped Summer put on the smaller pair and then secured the larger pair to my feet. I detached the four collapsible poles I'd hooked to my pack, lengthened them and handed Summer her pair. I worked fast. Every minute that passed counted against our lives. But without the equipment, we had no prayer to make it across the valley. Finally, I slipped on the sled's pulling harness over my shoulders.

"Get up," I shouted. "Come on, on your feet, I need you to walk with me."

"I'm too cold." Summer shivered on her knees. "I can't."

"You're made of better stuff than that," I said. "Get up. Your father didn't cling to a raft for three days in the Florida Straits for you to die here."

Her head snapped up. Her lamp lit me up. She hesitated for a moment, then clung to her poles and pulled herself up. She planted a foot, then a pole, then the other foot. I had to admire her grit. We made slow but steady progress. The wind pummeled us from behind. At times, it almost flattened us to the ground. Despite the snowshoes, the snow caved beneath our steps. Summer tripped and fell several times as we crossed the flat, and yet every time, she got up again.

The pulling strained my heart. It was hard, much harder than I remembered from my arctic training. My pack weighed a hell of a lot less without all the equipment I'd doled out, but the sled slowed me down, much heavier than the pack had ever been.

I kept looking over my shoulder, anticipating the avalanche that could bury us alive, but under whiteout conditions, visibility sucked. Every so often, when the wind eased, I caught a glimpse of the emergency strobe light on the high ridge.

The grueling trek required every ounce of energy I could muster. I'd expected it to be so, anticipated the conditions and planned for them, but expecting, anticipating, and planning were not the same thing as bearing the brunt of nature's worst. My heart ached from the effort. My lungs cramped. My strength ebbed. Failure wasn't in the range of my options, so I huffed and puffed as we mounted the hill at the end of the valley.

We were roughly halfway up the hill when a fearsome sound overtook the sounds of the storm. *Crack*. It sounded like a strike of lightning and then a roar. The earth shook. In the darkness, the strobe light that had once flashed atop the wreckage plummeted from the mountainside and disappeared. A few seconds later, a wave of snow flowed by our feet, hissing like a giant snake.

I grabbed Summer's arm and, dragging both Summer and the sled, rushed farther up the hill. It wasn't until we crested the knoll that I slowed down to catch my breath. In between furious swirls of snow, I spotted the tip of a wing, sticking out of the ground, flapping in the wind as if it was built out of rubber. I gave myself a mental high five. I'd read the area's topography correctly and chosen the only geographical feature that offered some protection from the massive avalanche that had just buried the wreckage.

Summer leaned on her poles and, puffing bursts of vapors through her facemask, shouted. "Avalanche?"

"Affirmative," I shouted back. "Keep going."

She peered into the blowing snow, where she caught a glimpse of the spectral shadow looming there. “What’s that?”

“A few more steps,” I shouted. “Almost there.”

“Helicopter?” Her goggles aimed at the sight ahead. “Seth, is that your Firehawk?”

My Firehawk, yes. No time to explain. No energy either. I motioned Summer on and together we trudged through the last few steps, dodging the steel cables that fastened the helo to the frozen ground.

A good three feet of snow had already piled around the helicopter. No wonder. It had taken me hours to secure the Firehawk, make my way across the hanging valley, set up the rope system, climb up to the wreckage, and reverse my steps with Summer and Alex. I’d had to sacrifice time in exchange for safety, but it had been the only plausible way.

I slid open the Firehawk’s side door and manhandled the sled into the helicopter. Summer tried to help, but she was pretty much done. I was done too, but I managed to boost Summer into the cabin, where she sprawled on the floor next to the rescue sled, heaving and shivering at the same time. I climbed behind her and, fighting for breath, slammed the door shut. I went to my knees. Somehow, I switched on the battery-operated space heater. Then I collapsed. I lay on the deck, with my heart pounding in my ears, unable to move, waiting for the heart attack to kill me.

“SETH?” SUMMER’S PLEA radioed over from a different dimension. “Please, Seth, wake up!”

I opened my eyes and waited for my senses to pull together the sights floating above me, the headlight, shining on my face, the glimmering green eyes, the stubborn jaw, the lips, cracked and dry and yet somehow still appealing to my senses. A tentative, crooked smile welcomed me back to the world of the living.

"Thank God!" Summer took off my hat, goggles, and facemask and, holding my face between her hands, examined me closely. "Are you okay?"

"Fine," I rasped. "You?"

"Defrosting."

She'd taken off her face's protective gear. Under the light of my headlamp, her cheeks and the tip of her nose glared red, but I didn't spot any obvious signs of frostbite. Talk about a miracle. She was whole and hale and for the first time in the last twelve hours, I could breathe without fighting the dread weighing me down.

"Are you sure you're not hurt?" A tear escaped from her eye. "I came to, and I thought you were dead."

"I'm alive." I took stock of our situation from the comfort of her lap. "It's just my lungs. And my heart. I left them out there somewhere. Alex?"

"Breathing," Summer reported, before she lowered her face and kissed me.

The fear, the rough, dangerous flight, the cold, the arduous trek up and down the mountain, it was all worth it to feel the way I did right now, full, ecstatic, and exhilarated beyond relief. The best alpine gear in the world could only go so far in protecting human life from conditions like the one we'd experienced, but Summer's kiss shoved my body firmly into thawing range.

The kiss ended all too quickly for my taste. But as long as she was willing to kiss me, I could fix the rest. That's what I was. Right? An engineer by training, a problem solver by vocation. That's why I'd come.

Summer caressed my face. “I sent you a message. I told Joe Pilot to tell you not to come.”

“He told me.” I kissed her hand, then planted elbows on the ground and sat up with a groan. “In fact, the man was very convincing.”

“So why didn’t you do what I said?”

I smirked. “So now you think you’re the boss of me?”

“What’s wrong with you?” She slapped me on the shoulder. “You should’ve listened!”

“Since when has either one of us been good at following directions?”

Now that she was with me, she could glower all she wanted. I took off my gloves. My hands ached. My fingers were stiff as hell and white or purple at the tips, but none of the ten looked like they were about to fall off just yet. I stumbled to my feet, rummaged through my supplies and found the camping lamp. I turned it on and hooked it up to the ceiling, before I switched off my headlamp and set it aside.

Next, I found the food stores and located the thermoses that Robert had prepared. Hands still shaking, I poured a cup of hot, high-protein broth for Summer, then put the thermos to my lips and guzzled the rest down, flooding my gullet with an awesome trail of heat.

Summer downed her drink, green eyes fixed on me. I set the thermos aside and, knees cracking, muscles still aching and quivering from the effort, knelt next to Alex and checked his pulse. Strong and even. Good.

“You ditched your Firehawk.” Summer switched off her headlamp and took off her helmet. “You crash-landed your precious helicopter in the middle of nowhere. Why?”

“I knew I had a good chance of getting in.”

She squeaked. "A good chance?"

"Forty-six percent probability to get into the Range to be exact."

"Oh, God." Her lips crumpled. "You also had to know that there was zero percent chance of flying out of this hellhole tonight."

"Yeah." I unpacked the medical supplies and unzipped Alex's sleeping bag. "The probabilities for a survivable takeoff were not good."

"So why on earth did you come?" She set her drink aside, took off her gloves, and handed me the scissors.

"Three reasons." I cut open the layers of Alex's sleeves. "One, I promised you that I wouldn't let Alaska kill you. Two, I always keep my promises. Three, I knew I could make a difference."

"For God's sake." Summer glared. "This has to be the most reckless rescue attempt in the history of aviation."

"Correction." I set the scissors aside. "It was never a rescue attempt. My goal was to provide suitable shelter against the elements."

"By ditching your helicopter?" She ripped open a pack and handed me the alcohol swabs.

"Affirmative." I palpated Alex's arm, found a vein, and disinfected the spot. "Suitable shelter drastically increases the odds for survival."

"You are crazy," Summer muttered.

"Crazy people don't spend time making careful and deliberate plans."

She huffed her disagreement and handed me the IV, a combination of hydration, antibiotics, painkillers, and muscle relaxants that I'd had Stuart prepare based on Joe Pilot's information to address Alex's injury.

"You love your Firehawk," she said. "You'll never get it out of here in one piece."

"Of course I will." I paused to stick the needle in the vein. "Next May or June."

"May or June?" She groaned. "I can't believe your family allowed you to do this!"

"They don't know I'm here." I finished hooking the IV. "Well, Jer, Robert, and Stuart know, because I needed their help to expedite the preparations. I didn't want to worry the rest."

"Of course not." She scowled some more. "You've got to be the most reckless man in the galaxy."

"I wasn't reckless." I put the medical supplies away. "Some of Alaska's most accomplished pilots and mountaineers participated in organizing this operation. I spent a lot of time planning my steps, packing my gear, studying the terrain, selecting my routes, and anticipating the contingencies."

"Ah, yes, contingency thinking," she said. "That's what you do for a living and you do it quite well, if I remember right."

"Exactly."

I checked on the battery-operated space heater. It was a small piece of equipment, nothing to write home about, but it had a huge impact on a small space. From the moment I'd requisitioned it from the hangar, I knew it could be the difference between surviving the night or not. The temperature inside the cabin was far from toasty, but it was warm enough to keep the killer cold at bay. I checked my watch. Eight hours to go.

Alex's eyelids fluttered open.

"Home?" he muttered.

"Not yet," I said. "But you're safe for the night. Try to get some rest."

Summer fed Alex some warm broth. We tried to make him as comfortable as possible. We had some space to work with, since I'd had the bucket seats removed from the cabin before takeoff. We didn't want to move Alex any more, so we kept him on the sled and piled up some additional blankets. The medications began to kick in right away.

"I can't believe you came," Alex said.

"You had to know that I would at least try."

"For Summer, right?"

"For Summer." Goddammit, would it kill me to say what he needed to hear? "For you too, but I'll deny that in public."

"Me too," Alex mumbled, somewhere between lucidity and oblivion. "Summer made me promise."

"Summer made you promise what?"

"I'd make peace with you," he said. "*If* I survived."

"Ah." I glanced at Summer. "She's crafty that way."

Summer lifted a shoulder as a way of apology.

"The bribe money," Alex muttered. "It's connected to your personal accounts."

"I know."

Alex's eyes widened. "But…how?"

"I mapped the money trail," I said. "I discovered how you connected it to me, then connected the bribe back to you. I also found your accounts in Luxembourg."

Alex sighed. "The next board meeting is the end."

"Up to you," I said. "You've got time to make things right."

"*If* I make it."

"We're going to make it," I said. "No ifs or buts. Consider it done."

Alex groped for my hand. "Peace, man."

I squeezed his hand. "Peace."

Alex closed his eyes. His features relaxed and his respiration evened. I took his pulse. It was strong. I didn't like the fucker much these days, but he was still family and I didn't wish him pain and suffering. I tucked his hand beneath the blanket and checked on the IV. At least he'd rest comfortably for the next few hours.

"His father chose you to run the company over him," Summer offered from her perch, huddled with her chin on her knees next to the space heater.

"Is that what this was all about?"

She shrugged. "Simple and yet complicated."

It was hard to believe but when I thought about it, I recognized the truth. Would I have felt differently than Alex if my father had chosen him over me?

The anger drained out of me. All those years of rivalry and rage seemed like an awful waste of time. I crawled over Alex and settled next to Summer, casing her between the heater and me. "I should've known."

"You're smart," she said, "but you're not a mind reader."

"I should have figured it out."

"Perhaps next time?" Summer said. "After all, you don't expect Alex to grow up all of a sudden, do you?"

"You're right." I had to chuckle. "One day at a time."

Summer's gaze fixed on me. "What now?"

"Now we wait for the storm to pass." I located the protein bars and, after handing one to Summer, tore into one myself. "Eat up. You need to replenish your energy. The storm is supposed to last another eight hours or so, but we've got a reliable heat source and enough food and water for a few days if need be. The rescue squadron is aware of our location. They'll mount a proper rescue when it's safe to do so."

Summer nibbled on the protein bar, looking as exhausted as I'd ever seen her, but also rugged as hell. She'd survived. My tropical orchid had survived the worst that Alaska had to offer with the grit of a native species.

"How did you find us?" she asked between bites.

"Joe Pilot gave me thorough directions and coordinates." I chewed on my protein bar and swallowed. "Once I flew into the valley, I caught the signal for the plane's emergency beacon. The strobe light and the SPOT's signal helped guide my ascent."

"What you did was very dangerous," Summer said. "I had it under control, you know."

I smirked. "You were going to freeze your ass solid."

"I didn't need your ass to freeze along with mine," she said. "I wanted you safe at home and far away from here. You were willing to die."

"Hell, no," I said. "I didn't come here to die. I came here to live. No more dying for me or for you. We've got to learn how to live, Summer, and I mean it, beyond working like hell and taking care of other people, both of us have to get better at enjoying our lives."

She grumbled under her breath. "That hero complex of yours got the best of you."

"Bullshit," I said. "You were the one trying to play heroine."

She rolled her eyes. "Oh, please."

"You could've hiked out with Joe," I said. "That

might have been a sensible decision. But no, oh no. You had to stay. Who's the one with the hero complex?"

"I hate that you came." Her green eyes brimmed with emotions. "But I'm also glad that you came. I know, I sound loony. I'm not making any sense."

"You make total sense to me." I put my arm over her shoulder and hugged her to me.

"Are you mad at me?" She cuddled against me.

"Raving mad." I kissed the top of her head. "Cross-eyed mad. Furious, livid, and enraged."

"Sorry," she said. "So much has happened since I last saw you. I don't know where to begin."

"Pick a subject," I said. "Any subject."

She hesitated before she asked. "I was sleepwalking when you found me, wasn't I?"

"I think so." I shuddered when I imagined what could've happened if she had stepped off the cliff, or been swept off by an avalanche, or frozen right there on the high ridge…Christ. That heart attack still lingered close at hand. I had to stop thinking like that.

"I saw the killer in my dream," she said. "I know who he is."

"Hector Carrera."

Her mouth fell open. "How—how do you know?"

"Spider hacked into a life insurance policy purchased by your father years ago," I explained. "The policy was drawn against the balance of the stock your father owned in his partnership with Carrera, the only asset he had left back then. At the time, the stock wasn't very valuable, but over time, its value has grown tremendously. That led us to further investigate the partnership."

"And?"

"We discovered that Carrera was swindling your father when they were partners. Your father did most of the work, but Carrera embezzled the profits. Your mother must have discovered Carrera's fraud. That's why he had her killed. As the developer of Fountain Way, Carrera had access to the building. He shared that access with Peterson, who he hired to murder your mother first, and then you."

"All these years, Hector pretended like he cared," Summer said. "He even gave me a job."

"He needed to keep you close at hand," I said. "The policy was coming due next month. You were the benefactor. With the shares realized, it would've given you half stake in Carrera's firm, plus the value of the policy. But if you were dead, the stock would return to him along with the money. He wanted it all for himself."

Her eyes widened. "God."

"There's more." I took her hands in mine. "State troopers executed a warrant on Carrera this afternoon. They found a stash of sleeping medications in his luggage. It would have aggravated your sleepwalking episodes and rendered you helpless. With Peterson dead, Carrera came to Alaska to kill you himself."

"That's why he insisted I bring the plans to the lighthouse." Her hands fisted in my grip. "That's why he wanted to be alone with me."

"That's also why I'm going to make sure he will rot in jail for the rest of his life."

It was a lot to handle, but Summer took it all in with the resignation of someone who already knew the truth. In fact, she'd figured it all out in her dreams, where her unconscious mind tackled complex problems with astonishing results.

"I..." Her fingers softened against my palms and her gaze found me. "I don't know how to thank you."

"You did most of the groundwork," I said. "We just followed your lead. That sleeping disorder of yours is a liability, sure, but it's also an incredible asset."

She considered the idea. "I never thought about it that way. You may have a point."

"While we're at it," I said, "I might as well tell you. Your stepmother is raving mad at me."

"Why?"

"I may have implied that she was behind all of this."

Summer grimaced. "You're in deep trouble. I told you she wasn't involved."

"If it's any consolation," I said, "she didn't break anything else. Do you think she'll ever forgive me?"

"A little sucking up goes a long way with Louise," Summer said. "It won't be easy. She's as cantankerous as they come. But, given time, you're likely to grow on her, Erickson."

I laughed. Summer flashed me a crooked little smile, but her eyes glimmered with that haunted expression that got my gut churning. I could almost hear her brain working inside her skull.

"Seth?" She hesitated. "Why did you come after me? After I left you that note, and handed over your board meeting notes to Alex? And don't you dare give me those lines about keeping your promise or providing suitable shelter. Knowing you, all of that was just the means to an end."

"Fair enough," I said. "You're right. I had another good reason to come all the way out here. I wanted to ask you a question."

"You flew through a superstorm, ditched your beloved helicopter, and risked your life to ask me a question?"

"Yep."

"You are unbelievable," she said. "The most obtuse man on the planet. You know that?"

"I'm dense, that's true."

She fixed her eyes on me. "So?"

I had to fight the lump blocking my throat. "I guess Alex forced you into doing his bidding."

"He wanted to pay me for your notes, deposited money in my account, but..."

"Hang on," I said. "Give me a chance here. I want to come clean. I'm sorry I didn't tell you about Tammy."

"I talked to Tammy," she said. "She told me she asked you not to tell me. I don't like it, but I understand that lying to me wasn't your first choice."

"In hindsight, it was a very bad idea," I said. "Also..."

"What?"

"That vase your stepmother broke?" I winced. "It was a pricey one. I lied to you because I didn't want you to obsess about it."

"I don't obsess—"

"Oh, yes, you do," I said. "You obsess about people and things all the time. You're easily consumed with worry."

"Tammy said the same thing." She puffed a long breath. "Maybe you guys are a little right. Alex told me about the vase. Knowing Astrid, I should've been able to figure it out on my own."

"I'm sorry I lied to you twice," I said. "I know you must have felt betrayed. But still...why didn't you call me? Why didn't you at least give me a chance to explain before you went off with Alex?"

"Seth?" Her green eyes studied and caressed my face at once. "I couldn't call you because I didn't have the means. Alex took my cell. But most importantly, I *wanted* to go with Alex."

"What?" I frowned. "Why?"

"To find out what he was planning," she said. "To figure out how he meant to trap you."

"So you went with Alex for me?"

"Of course, silly."

"For Christ's sake, Summer." I grappled for words. "The things you do."

"I wasn't going to let him hurt you," she said, sticking out that little stubborn chin of hers. "I just…wasn't."

The thaw raged through me, out of season and yet complete. Every frosted part of me warmed and melted. I lowered my lips to her mouth and kissed her. My body's reaction confirmed that my skeptical, fucked-up mind had had to work through the possibility of Summer's betrayal, but my body had never believed it.

"I have to admit that I was mad at you for lying at me," she mumbled against my lips. "And the picture frightened me at first. It really threw me for a spin."

I frowned. "What picture?"

"The picture of me? On your dining room table? That first night?"

"There were no pictures." I'd made sure of that. "I deleted the footage from the security cameras."

"But Alex hacked the security company's deleted files," she said. "He managed to retrieve one image. He paid big bucks for it. He swears this is the only copy."

She pulled out a thumb drive from her pocket. I took it from her and crushed it in my fist. It was, of course, a symbolic gesture, but it helped combat the revulsion in my gut. Later on, I'd make sure the gesture became reality.

"I hate that you had to live through this again," I said.

"So you know?" she said. "About Sergio and all of that? Your investigators found out?"

"You told me," I said. "When I asked you. In your dreams."

"Oh." Her lips compressed into a grim line. "I…I had a hard time getting over that."

I squeezed her shoulder. "I know."

"But something else happened when I saw the picture." Her mouth relaxed and hints of a smile matched the light that returned to her eyes. "Later. In the plane? I remembered that night. I remembered everything."

My heart tripped. "You did?"

She nodded. "I was at ease in the picture. I was happy and I wanted you. What happened that night was beautiful. From the very beginning, I trusted you, in my dreams."

And I had trusted her.

"So," she said. "Are you going to ask the question you came to ask?"

"Okay." I took a deep breath. "When you wrote the word 'gone' on that note you left on my pillow, did you really mean it? Were you going to leave me—I mean—Alaska?"

"Yes."

The storm outside roared, even more ferocious than before. The turbulence inside of me matched nature's violence. The space in the helicopter squeezed around me, suffocating me even if it was minus twenty degrees outside. I could handle pretty much anything, but the notion of Summer gone from my life scared the shit out of me. I fathomed I could hear the RPG coming at me.

"You must understand," she said. "Alex offered to take me to my sister, who, in my mind, was at the verge of catastrophe. I never intended to take his bribe, but he offered me a lot of money for your notes. Greed offered the perfect screen for me to snoop."

"I get it," I said. "You had to do everything he said."

"Yeah, sure, maybe." Her lips twitched. "Kind of."

"What do you mean?"

"I wrote that damn awful card," she said. "But I added the reason why I was leaving, so you'd know I wasn't just copying Gina's actions."

In my fury, I may have missed Summer's intent.

"And I did copy the board meeting notes as Alex requested," Summer said. "I left them out of order in your drawer so that you knew something was amiss. Although…"

"What?"

"I made a few changes during the process." She smirked. "Have I told you? I'm really good at cut and paste."

I stared. "What?"

"Did you really think I was going to give Alex any advantages over you?" Her eyes cut through me. "No way. Look in your bathroom's trashcan. You are not the only one who can think contingencies. I faked those notes as best I could. And I did a damn good job, if I can say so myself. He got nothing useful from me."

Christ but she was brave. And smart. She'd betrayed me only to protect me. And yet, I was fixated on the one thing that mattered to me.

"But when it was all said and done," I said, "were you really going to leave?"

"Oh, yes," she said. "I was going to get on that plane and fly first class to Miami, fuming all the way and cursing the moment I laid eyes on you."

I'd asked for it. I'd had it coming.

"And then," Summer said, "as soon as I got to Miami, I was going to turn around and board the next plane to Anchorage, economy class, mind you. I was going to hurry back to Alaska, give you a piece of my mind, and ask if I could hang out with you, at least for the winter, that is, if you still wanted me to stick around."

I stared at the woman before me as if she was a mirage. Had she just said what I thought I heard? She wanted to stay in Alaska. With me.

"I love you, Erickson." The radiance in her eyes exceeded the aurora's epic glow. "I love each molecule of your DNA, even if you share it with a complicated group of people. I'm willing to take on the full genetic package, whatever that entails. Mind you, I come in a complicated package too, and I don't really know how much winter Summer can take. So proceed with caution and be prepared for sudden changes. I might have to travel often to get my vitamin D."

Summer loved me. She'd said so. She was willing to put up with me, with my family. She was staying in Alaska, at least for the winter. I smiled, but inside, I whooped with joy. She was staying year-round, she just didn't know it yet.

"Baby?" I kissed the top of her head. "If I have to move to Miami and travel the world chasing after the sun, I swear, you'll never lack for vitamin D."

The music in her laughter made my heart dance.

What was happiness but a promise made to last and a light at the end of the darkness? I hugged Summer close to me. She'd brought my heart out of hibernation and restored me back to life. Life made total sense when she was around.

Summer burrowed into me, settling in for the long wait. She was exhausted. Eventually, her eyes closed, her respiration evened and she fell asleep in my arms, dreaming, I hoped, of our future together. A white layer of snow covered the helicopter's windows, but I caught a glimpse of our reflection in the glass, two bundled figures connected to each other by our embrace. Or by pure stubbornness.

Lucky. That's how I felt. Fortunate to be alive and a little on the cold side. Comfortable, instead of burning inside. Smooth-skinned, cool and healthy.

Some days, life was a cross-eyed bitch. But on a day like today, that fucked-up bitch compensated for all the crap she'd piled up on you and offered you a cup of coffee and an olive branch. It gave you a break, a prize, a reprieve, a chance. It hoisted you from a sinking wreck and deposited you exactly where you wanted to be, at the top of your world, transforming the future into a flight path full of hope.

The reflection in the window shifted to show the image of my parents and Uncle Ben, laughing and playing cards at the lighthouse. The guys drifted into the picture—Shawn, my copilot, Jonesy, my flight engineer, and Danny, he was there as well. My friends took their places at the table and joined my family. The sorrow squeezing my heart eased. It was a slight shift, a barely imperceptible lift of the soul, but it made life tolerable. As the vision in the window faded, I knew

I wouldn't see them again until I joined them in that eternal card game.

I was cool with that.

Meanwhile, it was time to live again. I didn't need the sun to feel the warmth inside. After all, I had Summer in my life. I'd chased her here. I would chase her to the ends of the earth, because some people pursued their dreams while asleep, but others, like me, chased their dreams while wide awake.

* * * * *

Look for TO THE EDGE, the second book in Anna del Mar's erotic AT THE BRINK *series, available now from Carina Press.*

To purchase and read more books by Anna del Mar, please visit Anna's website at www.annadelmar.com.

Available now from Carina Press and Anna del Mar

To learn about kink, she had to learn the ropes.
Yet she never expected to be so compromised she'd need rescuing.
And by him.
The first man she'd ever loved.
The ex-navy SEAL who'd broken her heart.

Read on for a sneak preview of
TO THE EDGE

ONE

My first attempt at submission went from failure to disaster in a whiff. An odd scent teased my nose and rattled my nerves. A prickle of uneasiness crept up my spine. I craned my neck, trying to figure out where the smell was coming from, but I couldn't see much beyond the narrow slits of my sequined velvet mask.

Note to Blog:

Velvet masks may shield, tease and entice, but visibility sucks.

I heard a small sound, a swish maybe? It came from my right somewhere, from the hallway that led to the powder room. I tried twisting my body around in the cage, but I could barely move. My arms were fastened above my head and my ankles were strapped to the bars near the floor. I sniffed the air again. The smell seemed fainter. Maybe it was my imagination, trying to shock some common sense into me and put an end to today's little experiment.

I was alone in the old house. My companion had left some twenty minutes ago, to find himself some coffee in town, he'd said. He'd left me cuffed in the cage so that I could reflect on my irreverent conduct. Right. Good luck with that, buddy. The truth was that he probably needed the caffeine boost in order to tackle a handful like me.

I let out a little groan. Sure, this was crazy, no two ways about it. *Reckless* my mother would say, risky and not exactly consistent with my usually sane behavior. But honestly? I had suppressed my life for others' sake long enough.

But this? A seditious little voice nagged in the back of my mind. I tried to quiet it down, but maybe, just maybe, I'd pushed the edge a little too hard on this one. God, the things I did in the name of freedom.

The tight leather corset dug into my ribs. My arms ached. My legs were tired and my feet were beginning to cramp in the impossibly high heels.

Note to Blog:

Kink garb isn't exactly comfy.

Good God. I was actually going through with this. Me. Clara Luz. Attempting something so far out of my comfort zone, not to mention my family's much-touted moral rectitude. I slumped in my bonds. Was I really so freaking desperate?

A week and a half ago, Annette Collins, the legendary editor of RelevantSex.com, had presented me with a unique proposition. Annette had been my advisor in grad school and as such, the only person who knew about my online adventures. From the beginning, she'd followed sextattle.com, the sex and romance blog I published—anonymously, of course.

It wasn't as if I was particularly versed or gifted in these oh-so-very-fascinating subjects. On the contrary. My relationship IQ measured pretty low on the success scale. But the blog wasn't so much an advice column as it was a forum. Discussion questions came in through an unfiltered inbox, I posted them under different categories, and people talked about them. I was good at research, so I mostly shared facts and links to helpful resources. I followed the old adage: those who can't do, teach. Or, in my case, share online.

Initially, the blog had been an experiment, a grad school project that went unexpectedly viral. But after graduation, the blog transformed into a labor of love, a means to connect with people and the only possible way in which I could pursue my own journey, separate from that of my illustrious mother. These days the blog had a very respectable reach, solid advertising revenues, and an expanding market that had caught Annette's eye. She'd made me an excellent offer to merge my blog with RelevantSex.com.

The catch?

Annette wanted a trial run, a main feature to woo the editorial board and test my range, a fresh, raw take on the topic of sex and submission, a personal account of my first exploration of kink to tantalize her readers.

"It's a fascinating subject," she'd said during our meeting at LeMond's Cafe in Adams Morgan. "Look at the movies. Look at the novels. The public is fascinated by kink, domination and submission. Your readers will be too. An exploration is totally relevant."

"Then why don't you assign someone who's already on staff at RelevantSex.com?" I didn't have any wisdom to share on the topic, zero, zip, nada. "Or better yet, why don't you tackle it?"

"Because I might be biased on the subject." She fastened her glimmering green eyes on my face. "Whereas you, my dear, are sure to bring a fresh perspective to our readers."

Her naughty smile activated my Spidey senses and ignited my blush. I wasn't a prude by any means, but kink? Yep, I'd bring a fresh perspective for sure. As to Annette, any lingering questions I may have had about the extent of her personal kink exposure were fully answered when she plunked down a long, comprehensive list of potential interview sources and references on the table.

Holy crap. I had a mental image of the sober, pearl-decked Annette, dressed in black leather, whip in hand, red curls cascading down her back. I forced my mouth to close.

Annette's project was intriguing but, given my leadership role at the Luz Foundation and my mother's high profile, it was also dangerous to me, personally and professionally. I tried to err on the side of caution. "I might not be the right person for this one."

"Nonsense." She reached over the table and, after tucking a strand of my bangs behind my ear, trailed her fingers down my chin. "You are perfect."

I had to shake off the shock. Had Annette just made a pass at me? No way. My overactive imagination was busy at work, again. Annette was a consummate professional and she'd been a mentor to me for many years. She was just trying to reassure me, something I needed, because I was torn. My brain twirled like a coin in the air, and I had no clue which one of my faces would come up at landing: dutiful Clara or her surly, rebellious twin?

"Come on, Clara." Annette clasped her hands together and grinned. "Say yes. Please?"

Something about the idea of exploring sex's kinky underworld had me shivering inside. I was curious and Annette was right. Her readers would eat it up. My readers would like it too. Most importantly, Annette's proposal offered me an opportunity to reach the one thing I'd spent my entire adult life trying to achieve: freedom. The possibility of doing what I loved on my own terms and the chance to finally cut the ties that bound me to the family trust.

I couldn't say no to freedom. I couldn't say no to Annette or to the sense of excitement growing in me.

I took a deep breath and met Annette's emerald stare. She smirked and gave me an encouraging nod. What the heck. I'd been wavering on the edge of this cliff for a while, but on that hot and humid September day, I jumped.

"I'll do it."

Now, almost a week and a half later, as I teetered on the balls of my feet nearly hanging from the cuffs, the irony wasn't lost to me. To cut the old ties, I'd had to accept some very real bonds. In my search for freedom, I'd stepped into a cage.

I let out a nervous giggle. It echoed in the empty house. Some would think I was exaggerating the scope of my predicament. They didn't know my mother. Senator Margaret Luz had made sure to cut off all my avenues of escape as I grew up. After I finished grad school, nobody in D.C. would give me a job without her express consent. Instead of working for myself as I'd planned, she'd strong-armed me to work for her charity foundation.

As her only offspring, I was more of a prop than a person. Beyond birthing me, she'd designed me; selected the best genetic material she could buy from an impressive catalogue of sperm donors in order to create the perfect daughter. Sure, I owed her my existence, but my chances of meeting her high expectations had been zero from the start.

Of course, she didn't know about my blog. She'd kill me if she did. She'd kill the blog too, and bury it forever. But Annette had gone where no one else had dared and offered me a unique opportunity. If this worked, it would be well worth the effort. I straightened my back. I wasn't a Luz for nothing. I'd make it work.

I tested the cuffs and puffed. Where the hell was Mark Walker? My test-Dom-for-the-day was taking his sweet time getting his damn coffee. I clenched my teeth and groaned. Patience had never been my strong suit. Once I made my decision and committed to the venture, I'd considered the risks and, in true Luz fashion, planned and obsessed over every step.

I wasn't an idiot, so I'd started by vetting Mark Walker thoroughly. Even though he'd come highly recommended by Annette, I'd commissioned a background investigation from one of Washington's premier security firms. Yep, that was me all right, ever the overachiever. Mark passed with flying colors, a model citizen in every way, requirement number one. A little adventure was exciting, but a sadist or a serial killer had no place in my risk assessment matrix.

To protect myself and my name, I'd also had Mark sign RelevantSeX.com's ironclad confidentiality agreement. Then I'd scheduled a preliminary meeting to make sure we were both on the same page. Our deal was kink 101, a limited intro to BDS, no sex or pain. Safety first.

I'd taken equal care when selecting the location for this meeting. The house where we used to summer when I was young was located smack in the middle of Avalon, an island in the Chesapeake Bay. The property was surrounded by a wildlife refuge on all sides. I'd inherited the Victorian beauty from my grandfather, who'd been senator before my mother.

I'd always felt safe here. The house held some of the best memories of my life. It was out of the way, accessible only by ferry, remote, secluded, and most importantly, way outside of my mother's radar, a fact that started to feel a lot like a liability when the odd scent tickled my nostrils again.

This time around, I recognized the smell. Smoke. My heart tripped. Alarm crawled up my spine like a bunch of daddy longlegs. I tugged on the cuffs. They clanged on the bars, but they didn't give. I craned my neck and, peering through the mask's narrow slits, caught a glimpse of white wisps trickling from the hallway into the living room.

Oh, my God. Smoke. A fire? No way. The house hadn't been used in years. Mark and I were the only ones here and we'd done nothing that could possibly start a fire. Right?

Wrong.

I had a memory of Mark Walker as he stepped out of the bathroom holding the lit candle he'd used to introduce me to a little wax-on-ass play earlier today. Lit candle. Matches. Wicker wastebasket.

Holy shit.

My belly turned to ice. The key. Where the heck had Mark put the cuffs' key? In his front shirt pocket, I remembered him teasing me with the act. Crap. I tugged on the cuffs. The cage rattled, my wrists smarted, and yet the cuffs held. Where on earth was Mark Walker when you needed him?

I looked around the room, growing more alarmed by the moment. The wrist cuffs wouldn't budge, but maybe if I freed my feet I could lift my knees and use my weight to bust the chain that connected the cuffs. I kicked off my right shoe, pointed my toes, and contorted my foot, choking down gulps of panic. This was going to take some doing.

A fire. A freaking fire. I railed at a God who amused himself with stuff like this. *Keep your head.*

Use your wits.

Don't panic. It would've been the Luz motto, if we'd had one of those. I ignored the terror squeezing my throat and kept working on the ankle strap. Success. My right foot came free. I started to work on the left strap right away. If I could only do the same with my wrists…

The sound of crackling echoed from the hallway, a low, husky growl. Holy Mary. Maybe I was having a nightmare. I really wanted to pinch myself awake. But there was the small problem of the cuffs. I was not going to die today.

My left foot came free. Hallelujah. I didn't waste any time. I flexed my legs, pulled on the cuffs and, curling my knees into my stomach, added my weight. The chain didn't break. I kept at it, but I needed plan B. I tried screaming for help, but the gag in my mouth muffled my cries and the screech that pierced my ears sounded more like a yowling she-cat.

Note to Blog:

Gags are a pain in the ass.

And who the hell was going to hear me anyway? Avalon's population amounted to 727 souls who lived mostly on the bay, ten miles down the gravel road. The cabin was surrounded by the Luz wildlife refuge, my grandfather's doing. I was in so much trouble.

What would my mother say if they found me out here, burned to a crisp, shackled in a cage? Her embarrassment, not to mention her rage, would probably far exceed her grief. The newspapers. Social media. The scandal. I wiped the image from my mind and concentrated on the cuffs. I wasn't going to burn, wasn't willing to die, not yet, not this way.

A voice caught my attention. A call came from the outside. A call? I squealed back in reply. Within moments, the back doors rattled and then exploded off the hinges. A man broke through, angled forward like a linebacker, tall and broad-shouldered. His run came to an abrupt halt in the middle of the living room. He took in the scene and quickly assessed the situation like a man who was used to danger.

The look of competence in his stare restored my hope for a longer life. Thank you, God! I would've whooped with elation if I could. His eyes widened with surprise when he registered the cage—and probably my attire—but he didn't hesitate as he rushed over.

"Hang on," he said as he unlatched the cage's door. "What the hell is going on?"

I craned my neck to follow his progress, mumbling frantic gibberish through the gag. Something about him was familiar, the wide cheekbones, the straight angle at the jaw, the eyes, black, soulful and deep. My heart jerked to a sudden stop. I did a double take. No way. It couldn't be.

I stole another look at him. My elation turned to shock. Was I losing my mind? I rose on my toes, lifted my face to the heels of my hands, and managed to knuckle my eyes. Maybe I was delusional. Maybe he was a ghost.

Maybe I was suffering from oxygen deprivation, even though the smoke didn't look nearly that bad. I blinked several times to clear my vision. It couldn't be, shouldn't be, and yet, when I looked again, there he was, the same man, the face I remembered so well.

A rush of blood heated my face. No. Oh, no. Never in my wildest dreams had I expected to find him here, now. Of all the people in the universe, he would've been the last I wanted to see me in my current state. How could this be?

His appearance weakened my knees and demolished my fortitude. My rescuer, the one person who'd heard my cries and who could potentially get me out, was also the same man who'd almost destroyed me once. He might not be able to recognize me yet, but I sure recognized him. The last time I'd seen him was right here, in this house, an hour before he broke my heart. It was him. The first man I ever loved.

Noah Blake.

* * * * *

Don't miss
TO THE EDGE by Anna del Mar,
Available November 2016 wherever
Carina Press ebooks are sold

www.CarinaPress.com

Copyright © 2016 by Anna del Mar

ACKNOWLEDGMENTS

MY ACKNOWLEDGEMENT LIST remains a constant, which speaks loads about the amazing folks who've partnered with me. Thanks to Kerri Buckley for her brilliant editing work on *The Stranger*. She made sure the voices in my head matched the voices on the page.

Thanks also to the talented professionals at Carina Press who contributed with their work and enthusiasm to *The Stranger*'s final form, especially Heather Goldberg, Stephanie Doig and Angela James, who runs a top-of-the-line outfit.

As always, my thanks to Nancy Cassidy, who trudges through my manuscripts with such wisdom. Gratitude to my family who support me with their love, and special thanks to my hubby, who puts up with me, even when my mind is thousands of miles away.

Finally, thank you, the reader. We writers are an odd breed. We work long hours to tell our stories to readers we'll seldom get to meet. And yet the reader is always with us, a welcomed companion in a thrilling journey. The mere idea of you enjoying a single word I write, smiling at a line, or lifting an eyebrow at the end of a paragraph fuels and rewards my best efforts. So thanks for coming along in this adventure and thank you especially for giving my novels a chance.

ABOUT THE AUTHOR

AMAZON BEST-SELLING AUTHOR Anna del Mar writes hot, smart romances that soothe the soul, challenge the mind, and satisfy the heart. Her stories focus on strong heroines struggling to find their place in the world and the brave, sexy, kickass, military heroes who'll risk everything to protect the women they love. She is the author of *The Asset*, *At the Brink*, *The Stranger* and *To the Edge* from Carina Press.

A Georgetown University graduate, Anna enjoys traveling, hiking, skiing, and the sea. Writing is her addiction, her drug of choice, and what she wants to do all the time. The extraordinary men and women she met during her years as a Navy wife inspire the fabulous heroes and heroines at the center of her stories. When she stays put—which doesn't happen very often—she lives in Florida with her indulgent husband and two very opinionated cats.

http://www.annadelmar.com/pages/home.html
Anna@annadelmar.com
https://www.facebook.com/AuthorAnnadelMar
https://twitter.com/anna_del_mar

Get 2 Free Books, Plus 2 Free Gifts— just for trying the *Reader Service!*

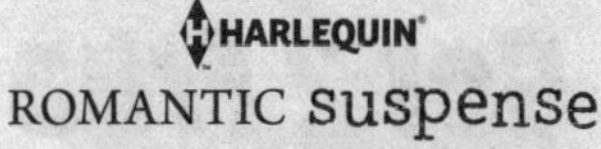

YES! Please send me 2 FREE Harlequin® Romantic Suspense novels and my 2 FREE gifts (gifts are worth about $10 retail). After receiving them, if I don't wish to receive any more books, I can return the shipping statement marked "cancel." If I don't cancel, I will receive 4 brand-new novels every month and be billed just $4.99 per book in the U.S. or $5.74 per book in Canada. That's a savings of at least 12% off the cover price! It's quite a bargain! Shipping and handling is just 50¢ per book in the U.S. and 75¢ per book in Canada.* I understand that accepting the 2 free books and gifts places me under no obligation to buy anything. I can always return a shipment and cancel at any time. Even if I never buy another book, the 2 free books and gifts are mine to keep forever.

240/340 HDN GLP9

Name (PLEASE PRINT)

Address Apt. #

City State/Prov. Zip/Postal Code

Signature (if under 18, a parent or guardian must sign)

Mail to the **Reader Service:**
IN U.S.A.: P.O. Box 1867, Buffalo, NY 14240-1867
IN CANADA: P.O. Box 611, Fort Erie, Ontario L2A 9Z9

Want to try two free books from another line?
Call 1-800-873-8635 or visit www.ReaderService.com.

*Terms and prices subject to change without notice. Prices do not include applicable taxes. Sales tax applicable in N.Y. Canadian residents will be charged applicable taxes. Offer not valid in Quebec. This offer is limited to one order per household. Books received may not be as shown. Not valid for current subscribers to Harlequin Romantic Suspense books. All orders subject to credit approval. Credit or debit balances in a customer's account(s) may be offset by any other outstanding balance owed by or to the customer. Please allow 4 to 6 weeks for delivery. Offer available while quantities last.

Your Privacy—The Reader Service is committed to protecting your privacy. Our Privacy Policy is available online at www.ReaderService.com or upon request from the Reader Service.

We make a portion of our mailing list available to reputable third parties that offer products we believe may interest you. If you prefer that we not exchange your name with third parties, or if you wish to clarify or modify your communication preferences, please visit us at www.ReaderService.com/consumerschoice or write to us at Reader Service Preference Service, P.O. Box 9062, Buffalo, NY 14240-9062. Include your complete name and address.

HRS17R

Get 2 Free Books, Plus 2 Free Gifts— just for trying the Reader Service!

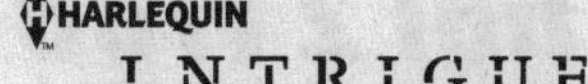

YES! Please send me 2 FREE Harlequin® Intrigue novels and my 2 FREE gifts (gifts are worth about $10 retail). After receiving them, if I don't wish to receive any more books, I can return the shipping statement marked "cancel." If I don't cancel, I will receive 6 brand-new novels every month and be billed just $4.99 each for the regular-print edition or $5.74 each for the larger-print edition in the U.S., or $5.74 each for the regular-print edition or $6.49 each for the larger-print edition in Canada. That's a savings of at least 12% off the cover price! It's quite a bargain! Shipping and handling is just 50¢ per book in the U.S. and 75¢ per book in Canada.* I understand that accepting the 2 free books and gifts places me under no obligation to buy anything. I can always return a shipment and cancel at any time. Even if I never buy another book, the two free books and gifts are mine to keep forever.

Please check one: ☐ Harlequin® Intrigue Regular-Print (182/382 HDN GLP2) ☐ Harlequin® Intrigue Larger-Print (199/399 HDN GLP3)

Name (PLEASE PRINT)

Address Apt. #

City State/Prov. Zip/Postal Code

Signature (if under 18, a parent or guardian must sign)

Mail to the **Reader Service:**

IN U.S.A.: P.O. Box 1867, Buffalo, NY 14240-1867

IN CANADA: P.O. Box 611, Fort Erie, Ontario L2A 9Z9

*Terms and prices subject to change without notice. Prices do not include applicable taxes. Sales tax applicable in N.Y. Canadian residents will be charged applicable taxes. Offer not valid in Quebec. This offer is limited to one order per household. Books received may not be as shown. Not valid for current subscribers to Harlequin Intrigue books. All orders subject to credit approval. Credit or debit balances in a customer's account(s) may be offset by any other outstanding balance owed by or to the customer. Please allow 4 to 6 weeks for delivery. Offer available while quantities last.

Your Privacy—The Reader Service is committed to protecting your privacy. Our Privacy Policy is available online at www.ReaderService.com or upon request from the Reader Service.

We make a portion of our mailing list available to reputable third parties that offer products we believe may interest you. If you prefer that we not exchange your name with third parties, or if you wish to clarify or modify your communication preferences, please visit us at www.ReaderService.com/consumerschoice or write to us at Reader Service Preference Service, P.O. Box 9062, Buffalo, NY 14240-9062. Include your complete name and address.

HI17

Get 2 Free Books, Plus 2 Free Gifts— just for trying the Reader Service!

YES! Please send me 2 FREE LARGER PRINT Harlequin® Romance novels and my 2 FREE gifts (gifts are worth about $10 retail). After receiving them, if I don't wish to receive any more books, I can return the shipping statement marked "cancel." If I don't cancel, I will receive 4 brand-new novels every month and be billed just $5.34 per book in the U.S. or $5.74 per book in Canada. That's a savings of at least 15% off the cover price! It's quite a bargain! Shipping and handling is just 50¢ per book in the U.S. and 75¢ per book in Canada.* I understand that accepting the 2 free books and gifts places me under no obligation to buy anything. I can always return a shipment and cancel at any time. Even if I never buy another book, the two free books and gifts are mine to keep forever.

119/319 HDN GLPW

Name (PLEASE PRINT)

Address Apt. #

City State/Prov. Zip/Postal Code

Signature (if under 18, a parent or guardian must sign)

Mail to the **Reader Service:**

IN U.S.A.: P.O. Box 1867, Buffalo, NY 14240-1867
IN CANADA: P.O. Box 611, Fort Erie, Ontario L2A 9Z9

Want to try two free books from another line?
Call 1-800-873-8635 or visit www.ReaderService.com.

* Terms and prices subject to change without notice. Prices do not include applicable taxes. Sales tax applicable in N.Y. Canadian residents will be charged applicable taxes. Offer not valid in Quebec. This offer is limited to one order per household. Books received may not be as shown. Not valid for current subscribers to Harlequin Romance Larger Print books. All orders subject to credit approval. Credit or debit balances in a customer's account(s) may be offset by any other outstanding balance owed by or to the customer. Please allow 4 to 6 weeks for delivery. Offer available while quantities last.

Your Privacy—The Reader Service is committed to protecting your privacy. Our Privacy Policy is available online at www.ReaderService.com or upon request from the Reader Service.

We make a portion of our mailing list available to reputable third parties that offer products we believe may interest you. If you prefer that we not exchange your name with third parties, or if you wish to clarify or modify your communication preferences, please visit us at www.ReaderService.com/consumerschoice or write to us at Reader Service Preference Service, P.O. Box 9062, Buffalo, NY 14240-9062. Include your complete name and address.

HRLP17R

Get 2 Free Books, Plus 2 Free Gifts - just for trying the Reader Service!

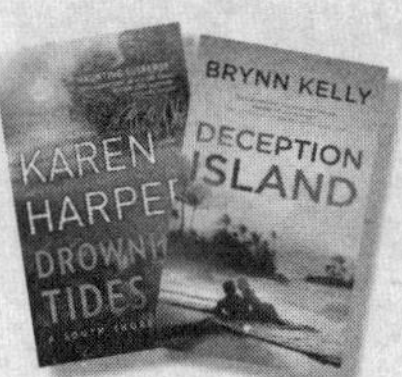

YES! Please send me 2 FREE novels from the Essential Romance or Essential Suspense Collection and my 2 FREE gifts (gifts are worth about $10 retail). After receiving them, if I don't wish to receive any more books, I can return the shipping statement marked "cancel." If I don't cancel, I will receive 4 brand-new novels every month and be billed just $6.74 each in the U.S. or $7.24 each in Canada. That's a savings of at least 16% off the cover price. It's quite a bargain! Shipping and handling is just 50¢ per book in the U.S. and 75¢ per book in Canada.* I understand that accepting the 2 free books and gifts places me under no obligation to buy anything. I can always return a shipment and cancel at any time. Even if I never buy another book, the 2 free books and gifts are mine to keep forever.

Please check one: ☐ Essential Romance 194/394 MDN GLQH ☐ Essential Suspense 191/391 MDN GLQJ

Name (PLEASE PRINT)

Address Apt. #

City State/Prov. Zip/Postal Code

Signature (if under 18, a parent or guardian must sign)

Mail to the **Reader Service:**
IN U.S.A.: P.O. Box 1867, Buffalo, NY 14240-1867
IN CANADA: P.O. Box 611, Fort Erie, Ontario L2A 9Z9

Want to try two free books from another line?
Call 1-800-873-8635 or visit www.ReaderService.com.

*Terms and prices subject to change without notice. Prices do not include applicable taxes. Sales tax applicable in NY. Canadian residents will be charged applicable taxes. Offer not valid in Quebec. This offer is limited to one order per household. Books received may not be as shown. Not valid for current subscribers to the Essential Romance or Essential Suspense Collection. All orders subject to credit approval. Credit or debit balances in a customer's account(s) may be offset by any other outstanding balance owed by or to the customer. Please allow 4 to 6 weeks for delivery. Offer available while quantities last.

Your Privacy—The Reader Service is committed to protecting your privacy. Our Privacy Policy is available online at www.ReaderService.com or upon request from the Reader Service.

We make a portion of our mailing list available to reputable third parties that offer products we believe may interest you. If you prefer that we not exchange your name with third parties, or if you wish to clarify or modify your communication preferences, please visit us at www.ReaderService.com/consumerschoice or write to us at Reader Service Preference Service, P.O. Box 9062, Buffalo, NY 14240-9062. Include your complete name and address.

STRS17

Get 2 Free Books, Plus 2 Free Gifts— just for trying the Reader Service!

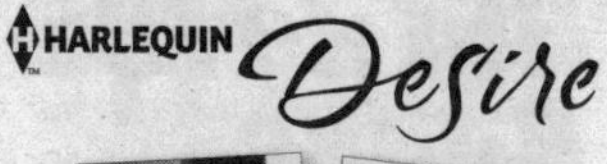

YES! Please send me 2 FREE Harlequin® Desire novels and my 2 FREE gifts (gifts are worth about $10 retail). After receiving them, if I don't wish to receive any more books, I can return the shipping statement marked "cancel." If I don't cancel, I will receive 6 brand-new novels every month and be billed just $4.80 per book in the U.S. or $5.49 per book in Canada. That's a savings of at least 8% off the cover price! It's quite a bargain! Shipping and handling is just 50¢ per book in the U.S. and 75¢ per book in Canada.* I understand that accepting the 2 free books and gifts places me under no obligation to buy anything. I can always return a shipment and cancel at any time. Even if I never buy another book, the 2 free books and gifts are mine to keep forever.

225/326 HDN GLPZ

Name (PLEASE PRINT)

Address Apt. #

City State/Prov. Zip/Postal Code

Signature (if under 18, a parent or guardian must sign)

Mail to the **Reader Service:**

IN U.S.A.: P.O. Box 1867, Buffalo, NY 14240-1867

IN CANADA: P.O. Box 611, Fort Erie, Ontario L2A 9Z9

Want to try two free books from another line?
Call 1-800-873-8635 or visit www.ReaderService.com.

*Terms and prices subject to change without notice. Prices do not include applicable taxes. Sales tax applicable in N.Y. Canadian residents will be charged applicable taxes. Offer not valid in Quebec. This offer is limited to one order per household. Books received may not be as shown. Not valid for current subscribers to Harlequin Desire books. All orders subject to credit approval. Credit or debit balances in a customer's account(s) may be offset by any other outstanding balance owed by or to the customer. Please allow 4 to 6 weeks for delivery. Offer available while quantities last.

Your Privacy—The Reader Service is committed to protecting your privacy. Our Privacy Policy is available online at www.ReaderService.com or upon request from the Reader Service.

We make a portion of our mailing list available to reputable third parties that offer products we believe may interest you. If you prefer that we not exchange your name with third parties, or if you wish to clarify or modify your communication preferences, please visit us at www.ReaderService.com/consumerschoice or write to us at Reader Service Preference Service, P.O. Box 9062, Buffalo, NY 14240-9062. Include your complete name and address.

HD17

Get 2 Free Books, Plus 2 Free Gifts— just for trying the Reader Service!

YES! Please send me 2 FREE Harlequin Presents® novels and my 2 FREE gifts (gifts are worth about $10 retail). After receiving them, if I don't wish to receive any more books, I can return the shipping statement marked "cancel." If I don't cancel, I will receive 6 brand-new novels every month and be billed just $4.55 each for the regular-print edition or $5.55 each for the larger-print edition in the U.S., or $5.49 each for the regular-print edition or $5.99 each for the larger-print edition in Canada. That's a saving of at least 11% off the cover price! It's quite a bargain! Shipping and handling is just 50¢ per book in the U.S. and 75¢ per book in Canada.* I understand that accepting the 2 free books and gifts places me under no obligation to buy anything. I can always return a shipment and cancel at any time. Even if I never buy another book, the 2 free books and gifts are mine to keep forever.

Please check one: ☐ Harlequin Presents® Regular-Print (106/306 HDN GLP6) ☐ Harlequin Presents® Larger-Print (176/376 HDN GLP7)

Name (PLEASE PRINT)

Address Apt. #

City State/Prov. Zip/Postal Code

Signature (if under 18, a parent or guardian must sign)

Mail to the **Reader Service:**

IN U.S.A.: P.O. Box 1867, Buffalo, NY 14240-1867
IN CANADA: P.O. Box 611, Fort Erie, Ontario L2A 9Z9

Want to try two free books from another series? Call 1-800-873-8635 or visit www.ReaderService.com.

* Terms and prices subject to change without notice. Prices do not include applicable taxes. Sales tax applicable in N.Y. Canadian residents will be charged applicable taxes. Offer not valid in Quebec. This offer is limited to one order per household. Books received may not be as shown. Not valid for current subscribers to Harlequin Presents books. All orders subject to credit approval. Credit or debit balances in a customer's account(s) may be offset by any other outstanding balance owed by or to the customer. Please allow 4 to 6 weeks for delivery. Offer available while quantities last.

Your Privacy—The Reader Service is committed to protecting your privacy. Our Privacy Policy is available online at www.ReaderService.com or upon request from the Reader Service.

We make a portion of our mailing list available to reputable third parties that offer products we believe may interest you. If you prefer that we not exchange your name with third parties, or if you wish to clarify or modify your communication preferences, please visit us at www.ReaderService.com/consumerschoice or write to us at Reader Service Preference Service, P.O. Box 9062, Buffalo, NY 14240-9062. Include your complete name and address.

HP17R

Get 2 Free Books,
Plus 2 Free Gifts—
just for trying the Reader Service!

YES! Please send me 2 FREE novels from the Worldwide Library® series and my 2 FREE gifts (gifts are worth about $10 retail). After receiving them, if I don't wish to receive any more books, I can return the shipping statement marked "cancel." If I don't cancel, I will receive 4 brand-new novels every month and be billed just $5.99 per book in the U.S. or $6.74 per book in Canada. That's a savings of at least 25% off the cover price. It's quite a bargain! Shipping and handling is just 50¢ per book in the U.S. and 75¢ per book in Canada.* I understand that accepting the 2 free books and gifts places me under no obligation to buy anything. I can always return a shipment and cancel at any time. Even if I never buy another book, the 2 free books and gifts are mine to keep forever.

414/424 WDN GLQR

Name (PLEASE PRINT)

Address Apt. #

City State/Prov. Zip/Postal Code

Signature (if under 18, a parent or guardian must sign)

Mail to the **Reader Service:**

IN U.S.A.: P.O. Box 1867, Buffalo, NY 14240-1867

IN CANADA: P.O. Box 611, Fort Erie, Ontario L2A 9Z9

Want to try two free books from another line?
Call 1-800-873-8635 or visit www.ReaderService.com.

*Terms and prices subject to change without notice. Prices do not include applicable taxes. Sales tax applicable in NY. Canadian residents will be charged applicable taxes. Offer not valid in Quebec. This offer is limited to one order per household. Books received may not be as shown. Not valid for current subscribers to the Worldwide Library series. All orders subject to credit approval. Credit or debit balances in a customer's account(s) may be offset by any other outstanding balance owed by or to the customer. Please allow 4 to 6 weeks for delivery. Offer available while quantities last.

Your Privacy—The Reader Service is committed to protecting your privacy. Our Privacy Policy is available online at www.ReaderService.com or upon request from the Harlequin Reader Service.

We make a portion of our mailing list available to reputable third parties that offer products we believe may interest you. If you prefer that we not exchange your name with third parties, or if you wish to clarify or modify your communication preferences, please visit us at www.ReaderService.com/consumerschoice or write to us at Reader Service Preference Service, P.O. Box 9062, Buffalo, NY 14269-9062. Include your complete name and address.

WWL17

Get 2 Free Books, Plus 2 Free Gifts—

just for trying the Reader Service!

YES! Please send me 2 FREE LARGER-PRINT Harlequin® Superromance® novels and my 2 FREE gifts (gifts are worth about $10 retail). After receiving them, if I don't wish to receive any more books, I can return the shipping statement marked "cancel." If I don't cancel, I will receive 4 brand-new novels every month and be billed just $6.19 per book in the U.S. or $6.49 per book in Canada. That's a savings of at least 11% off the cover price! It's quite a bargain! Shipping and handling is just 50¢ per book in the U.S. or 75¢ per book in Canada.* I understand that accepting the 2 free books and gifts places me under no obligation to buy anything. I can always return a shipment and cancel at any time. Even if I never buy another book, the 2 free books and gifts are mine to keep forever.

132/332 HDN GLQN

Name (PLEASE PRINT)

Address Apt. #

City State/Prov. Zip/Postal Code

Signature (if under 18, a parent or guardian must sign)

Mail to the **Reader Service:**

IN U.S.A.: P.O. Box 1867, Buffalo, NY 14240-1867

IN CANADA: P.O. Box 611, Fort Erie, Ontario L2A 9Z9

Want to try two free books from another line?
Call 1-800-873-8635 today or visit www.ReaderService.com.

* Terms and prices subject to change without notice. Prices do not include applicable taxes. Sales tax applicable in N.Y. Canadian residents will be charged applicable taxes. Offer not valid in Quebec. This offer is limited to one order per household. Books received may not be as shown. Not valid for current subscribers to Harlequin Superromance Larger-Print books. All orders subject to credit approval. Credit or debit balances in a customer's account(s) may be offset by any other outstanding balance owed by or to the customer. Please allow 4 to 6 weeks for delivery. Offer available while quantities last.

Your Privacy—The Reader Service is committed to protecting your privacy. Our Privacy Policy is available online at www.ReaderService.com or upon request from the Reader Service.

We make a portion of our mailing list available to reputable third parties that offer products we believe may interest you. If you prefer that we not exchange your name with third parties, or if you wish to clarify or modify your communication preferences, please visit us at www.ReaderService.com/consumerschoice or write to us at Reader Service Preference Service, P.O. Box 9062, Buffalo, NY 14240-9062. Include your complete name and address.

HSRLP17